DREAMING METAL

Tor Books by Melissa Scott

Burning Bright
Dreaming Metal
Dreamships
Night Sky Mine
Shadow Man
Trouble and Her Friends

DREAMING METAL

Melissa Scott

TOR®

A TOM DOHERTY ASSOCIATES BOOK
NEW YORK

DREAMING METAL

Copyright © 1997 by Melissa Scott

This book is printed on acid-free paper.

Edited by David G. Hartwell

A Tor Book
Published by Tom Doherty Associates, Inc.
175 Fifth Avenue
New York, NY 10010

Tor Books on the World Wide Web:
http://www.tor.com

Tor® is a registered trademark of Tom Doherty Associates, Inc.

Library of Congress Cataloging-in-Publication Data

Scott, Melissa.
        Dreaming metal / Melissa Scott. —1st ed.
              p.   cm.
        ISBN 0-312-85876-0
        I. Title.
        PS3569.C672D72   1997
        813'.54—dc21   97-2171
                                                                        CIP

First Edition: July 1997

Printed in the United States of America

0   9   8   7   6   5   4   3   2   1

DREAMING METAL

PERSEPHONE (PERSEPHONEAN, PERSPHONEANS): only inhabited planet of Hades, Midsector III Catalogue listing 1390161.f. CPC#A3B/G6171/884G(3). Surface gravity = 1.01 Earth. Astronomical year = 1.38 standard years; local year = (Conglomerate) standard year. Astronomical day = 80 standard hours; local day = 24 local hours/24 standard hours. Chronometric correction (standard) ATS 0.0. Climate: Persephone is officially classified as a warm planet, with average temperatures of 32°C; seasonal variation is minor, but travelers are advised that high/low extremes are common, and should consult local met. offices before traveling on the surface.

Discovered 998 PoDr. by CMS *Pentateuch* (Freya registry) while on extended materials survey. The Freyan government proving unable to exploit the planetary resources, Persephone was leased to the multiplanetary Shipyards Cartel, formed specifically to settle and exploit the planet. Opened for full settlement PoDr. 1079 as mixed Freyan/corporate colony. Provisional Conglomerate membership granted PoDr. 1277 as a result of the Fifth Freyan Revolution.

CAUTION: Persephone has been placed on the Travelers Index as of 22/10 PoDr. 1371, following riots pitting Freyan contract labor against machine-rights activists supporting a Spelvin construct known as Manfred. Although Manfred was proved not to be true AI, and therefore ineligible for machine rights, the Index believes that continuing tension between full Cartel employees and contract laborers warrants a continued listing. Travelers are advised to monitor news outlets before and during their time on Persephone, and to avoid areas with predominantly coolie populations (Heaven in Landage, civilian settlements at Mirror-Bright/Whitesands).

Persephone has also been placed on the World Watch Question List for: machine rights, human rights.

No indigenous animal life. Primary city: Landage (dos 1079 PoDr., starport). Primary export products: starships; AI constructs; VWS software, limberware, bioware; IPU mecha, wireware, biofitting. Government: day-to-day government is handled by the Managing Board of the Shipyards Cartel, whose members employ 82% of the population; however, Freya maintains a competing Colonial Office onplanet, which controls Persephone's noncommercial foreign relations and to which the population may appeal decisions of the Managing Board. Disputes between the two are settled in the Conglomerate courts. Language Group: Urban dialect of Freya (index of variation MS3/5.200935); Urban primary (index of variation MS3/0.002014).

Persephone is a barren planet, settled only because of the vast resources available both on the planet and in the system's two asteroid belts. Because of the unpleasant climate, settlement has gone underground, or into natural and artificial caverns, and is largely confined to the Daymare Basin. Ninety-seven percent of Persephone's population is permanently resident in Landage or its suburbs; of that group, approximately 20% are periodically resident in the assembly complexes at Mirror-Bright (Whitesands) or the Rutland Seas. Travelers are advised to consult the local authorities and to employ local transport and/or guides if their business takes them outside the Daymare Basin. The Peacekeepers maintain a Class II Traffic Control base on Cerberus in the outer asteroid ring. The base is restricted; landing by permit *only*.

Prologue:

I NTERWEAVE BEAT AND *shuttle, image + max-thrust 10.2, cross sine wave 1, 2, 3, homeclick/selfcheck home. Query: sleep? Strike* **one.** *Input channeled bigrave, image shift, display format AKW19X8: voice active, pattern three. #System# downshift catchbeat #check# throughput data biostance + visual via set main +special1 #complete.#* **Two.** *Command input, line code one, cascade charm quicken and close. Response: dream.* **Shutdown.**

▪ 1 ▪

Celinde Fortune

MY MOTHER LOVED the Empires, all nine of them, from Queen-Iron in the west to New Phoenix in the east. This was unusual in a yanqui—the Empires cater mostly to the coolie trade—but a permissible eccentricity in a Catlee, and better than a lot of the things her side of the family was known to do. She worked in Water Supply like most of the Catlees and Vaughns and Joneses, and as a result of being an essential worker, she had a full day off on Fifth-day, not a half-day like nearly everyone else. This meant that she could get to the Empires early and queue up for the half-price tickets to the matinee, and from the time I was old enough to sit through the show—five, I think, though I might have been younger—I went with her. We stopped going to the Queen-Iron pretty early on, when West-of-Four got really bad, but we visited most of the others over the course of a calendar year. But Tin Hau was the nearest, and that was where we went most often.

When most people think of the Tin Hau Empire, they think of it under the night-lights: a massive cube eight stories tall from the plaza level, the cap and peak of the stagehouse carved from the cavern's ceiling, fixing the stones in place, its fieldstone pale against the darker castings that form the main part of the house. There is multicolored light tubing slung on every possible cornice, and some improbable ones, and more of it winds up the stagehouse columns, picking them out in coils of blue and red and gold. The main entrance glows good-luck red, welcome glyphs running up and down the columns; above them, holopuppet dancers eight times life-size posture in the glass of the display arch. It's all so bright that you can see the rock of the cavern ceiling with perfect clarity, and each rough hollow is filled with colored light. The Empire completely dwarfs the Tin Hau Interlink, and a person standing between the stagehouse columns—I've tried it—casts a shadow on everything from the east plaza to the doors of the lift station. But my first sights of Tin Hau were under the day-lights, and I've preferred it that way ever since. Up here so close to Heaven, the lights are supplemented with sun-traps during the planetary day, and that's my favorite time of all. The doubled light, natural and artificial, strips the color from the cured stone, makes the light tubing irrelevant, and adds an extra shadow to bring each carving, each crack and column and settled, out-of-line block into clear relief, and yet the place looks somehow bigger and more massive— more alive—than it does under the gaudy night-lights. Without the lights to break up the surface, you can see the way the stone soars above the tiny lobby windows, a perfect setting for the black glass of the arch—blank in the day-lights, not to waste money on the matinee crowd. It looked like a fort, or a castle, but to keep secrets in, not invaders out, and calling it an empire doesn't seem that strange after all. The light from the sun-traps falls like spotlights over the stone, bouncing back milder to the plaza floor, and it looks old enough, used enough, to deliver what it promises.

Which, of course, is magic, not just like mine, though I'm not the only conjurer working the Empires, but the magic of escape and glamour and impossible beauty and mysteries that you don't want to unravel, all neatly packaged for a 120-minute run time with no bad surprises. By the time I was six, I understood the forms of all the acts, knew that the vanished assistants would reappear just as certainly as the bands would all perform a final clip after they'd said they were done. By the time I was eight, I was bored with the form, and was already looking forward to being old enough to come to the night shows, where some of the surprises weren't so pleasant.

When I was nine, my second sister Celeste—not my second sister, I've only got one, but the second sister to be given the name—was born, and we stopped going to the Empires on Fifth-day. She was too young at first, of course, and by the time she was old enough I was too old to be happy with the matinees, where I could have seen the night shows. Besides, Celeste and I never got along—reasonably or not, I suspected she'd taken a lot more than just the trips to the Empires and my dead twin's name, and she resented having a difficult elder sister instead of the devoted ayah her agemates made of their sibs—and any joint venture, much less something I actually liked as much as the matinees, tended to bring out the worst in us. It was a great relief to everyone when I moved in with my mother's Vaughn cousins, ostensibly to be closer to the vo-tech so I could be in the running for a lycee scholarship, and, though my mother mentioned it once or twice afterward, we never went to an Empire matinee again.

All of which is a roundabout way of saying I have fond memories of the matinees, which is why I was at the Empire at all when Micki Tantai was murdered.

Normally, if an act isn't completely reliable, it doesn't get as far as the Empires: Binaifer Muthana, who manages Tin Hau for the underworld consortium—all perfectly respectable Cartel investors, of course; this is Persephone, and not everything means what you think—that owns all the Empires, is nobody's fool, and wouldn't put up with unprofessional acts even if the accountants didn't come by twice a week to make sure his profits remain acceptable. But when things go wrong, they tend to go wrong in clusters, which is why I woke to the buzz of my media wall three hours before I usually get up, with my construct Aeris calling me from the speakers. It went silent when I opened my eyes, but the Persphonet console kept buzzing. I sat up, brought up the lights with a gesture—oh, yes, I'm wired; I got that scholarship, and my skinsuit with it, so my time with the Vaughns wasn't wasted—and then got out of bed to deal with the caller.

"Peri, accept," I told the smaller construct that managed my communications. "Outgoing voice only."

The screen on my side lit, though whoever was calling

would still see the rainbow swirls of a blocked node—not proper etiquette, but whoever was calling me had started it by waking me.

"Fortune?"

It was Muthana, of course, tall and gaunt, his lined cheeks sunken into distinguished hollows, and I sighed.

"Hang on a minute, Binnie." I had left a *yukata* on a chair by the workbench, retrieved it, and shrugged it over my shoulders. "Peri, resume outgoing visual."

In the screen, I saw Muthana's face ease, probably at seeing me alone. "I'm sorry to bother you, Fortune, but we have an emergency."

"We—?" I started to say, and then waved the word away. Muthana wouldn't wake me without good reason—if nothing else, my current act was highly profitable, but mostly he wasn't one to exaggerate. If he said "emergency," the sirens were wailing, and the trucks were at the door. "What's up?"

"Two acts have canceled out of the matinee," he answered. "The Time-Keys sketch, unprofessional little shits, and the Tigridi band's face is sick—"

"The low-teens will be devastated," I said.

The flicker of a grin crossed his face, but he wouldn't be drawn. "—and it was a short show to begin with. I'm canvassing the night-show to fill in."

I waited. I didn't need to tell him that my act was too *farang*, not nearly high-touch enough to please a matinee audience. The night-show crowds like the titillation, but the afternoon would hate it. I wondered what I'd've made of it myself if I'd seen it.

"I remember you used to have a street show," Muthana went on. "A box robot, a minikarakuri—an acrobat, or something like that? I wondered if you'd be willing to run it as part of the lobby displays. We'll pay, of course."

"And pay well, too," I said, but I think even he could hear that it was a token protest. I was still proud of the street show—not just the slack-rope dancer, but a tiny, mechanical conjurer who did tricks with cups and balls. I had called it "A Glimpse of the Past" and dressed them all in what I hoped were antique costumes, but when I'd built it I'd still been more interested in the mechanics than in the presentation. I'd come a long way since then, but people had always liked it. It might be interesting to bring it out again, see what an audience made of it now that I was a better showman myself—and besides, as I said at the beginning, I've always been fond of the matinees. "Let me make sure it still runs properly, Binnie, but if it does, I'll be there."

"Thank you, Fortune," he said, and I could see the relief on his face. "Remember, the lobby show starts at noon."

That took me back. I could almost smell the burnt sugar from the praline-sellers' carts, could almost see the bright coolie *sarangs* surrounding me as we moved out of the light into the cool and welcoming shadows of the lobby, between the rows of booths. My mother always had to lift me, or at the end let me push my way to the front—the matinee crowds are tolerant of kids—to see the conjurers and their sleight of hand and the karakuri and the lottery-readers and whatever else had been hired to fill in the time. I shook the memory away, and said, "I'll call you in an hour."

"Haya. And thanks again, Fortune," Muthana said, and broke the connection.

I had actually kept the street show pretty much intact—the parts are too small to be usable in any of my larger illusions, and besides, I was fond of it—but any karakuri's mechanism deteriorates without use and care. I pulled it out of the storage cabinet, assembled the figures on the platform that housed the power supply and the brain-box that let it run on its own or under my unseen control, and then switched it on and let it warm up while I showered, dressed, and rummaged in my wall-kitchen for something to eat. By the time I'd finished, I could tell that the show would need some repairs, but I could also tell it wasn't anything serious. I called Muthana and told him I'd be there, then settled down to the work at hand.

Most of what needed to be replaced were trigger springs and the tiny belts that transferred power to the platform's underlayer: I hadn't been able to afford the quality of fiber that

I would have liked, had even had to use rubber in a couple of places, but at least all the parts were standard. I had most of them in stock, and put in a call to Motosha over in the Copper Market on the border between Angelitos and Madelen-Fet. My cousin of sorts, Fanning Jones—anyone named Catlee, Jones, or Vaughn counted as some kind of kin to my mother—had worked there for three or four years before his band got a contract at Tin Hau, and I got a cousin's discount. I told them what I needed, and agreed to pay the rush-delivery charge, then went back to the fiddling work of replacing the rest of the belts. A girl from Motosha, all big eyes and muscular legs from pumping the pedals of a piki-bike, arrived in forty minutes with the box of belts, better time than I'd expected; I paid for them plus the surcharge and a tip, and went back to work.

I had the repairs finished by ten—Persephone keeps a twenty-four-hour day regardless of planetary time—then left it running through its basic modes while I sat in a chair at the end of the worktable and watched, wondering how I should present it. I'd used music with it as a street show, and improvised a talk about the old days in the Urban Worlds, but I'd long ago used the playdeck in other things, and the speech hadn't been very good to begin with. Music was no problem—I had other decks and a good library of clips, one advantage of having a musician cousin—but a presentation was more complicated. The persona I used in my main show wouldn't go over well at all for a matinee lobby show, but with the lobby opening at noon there wasn't much time to develop something suitable. Probably the best thing was to fall back on the old standby of silent conjurers, a hooded, oversize desert wrap, and stand quiet, letting the karakuri do its work. In fact, if I said absolutely nothing, pretended not to see or hear the crowd—and if Muthana would cordon off my space and loan me a couple of his minders to make sure it stayed clear—there was a good chance that people watching wouldn't be sure if I was human or a karakuri myself, and they'd go crazy looking for the "real" controller in the crowd around them. Particularly if Muthana made sure my name was prominently displayed as the maker of the illusion: my night-show illusions are known for using karakuri that look very much like me.

"Peri, display music library file menu."

The list formed against the shadowed wall, the strings of realprint brightening as the system compensated for the lighting. I found the file I wanted, reached into the illusion to select the right subgroup of clips—Urban plainwork, mostly drums and synthflute, not so good as to call attention to itself, but loud enough to hide any noise from the cabinet, and, more important, my suspicious silence—then pulled the menu out of my line of sight.

"Peri, display timing chart for Street Show."

"I'm sorry, that chart is not on main file."

"Peri, check the archive files."

"Checking archives." There was a moment of silence. "A chart for Street Show does not appear to be in the archives. However, I find a chart for Cabinet Street Show—"

"Peri, display timing chart for Cabinet Street Show." There is no point in getting annoyed with even the most sophisticated constructs—the whole Manfred incident proved that it's pointless—but it's hard sometimes not to blame them rather than your own lack of clarity.

The chart appeared, and I checked it against the music until I found a clip that matched. I pulled that into the control space, and said, "Peri, copy to disk and cue up play-deck."

"Confirmed," the construct answered, and I turned my attention back to the cabinet.

On it, the slack-rope dancer walked up her rope, one of my favorite effects, because you can see that the rope is real, even swaying a little, and that there aren't any hooks on her feet—or at least you think you can. At the platform, she turned and sank into a graceful crouch, gesturing to the magician, who until then had stood still, hooded head bowed over her table and its discarded toys. At the dancer's gesture, she looked up, the hood sliding back just enough so that if you looked closely you could see that her face looked like mine—the

first of my machine twins—and then she began to go through
the old cup-and-ball routine. When I'd originally built the
cabinet, the little magician had actually played the crowd directly—under my control, of course—but this time, I decided,
she would just do the trick a few times, then make the ball
disappear completely, and reappear in my hand. I've kept in
practice, and in any case it wasn't a complicated trick; after
one false try, the magician figure looked at me, and I opened
my hand to reveal the ball. I let the ball—it was heavy crystal, with a glimlight in it to make it easier to see—run back
and forth across my palm, then turned my hand over. The ball
disappeared, and the magician lifted the stack of cups—just
shown empty—to find it sitting there. Even if the crowd realized I was the conjurer and not a painted karakuri, it would
work, but it would be even more effective if the audience
thought I was a machine. If you think about it, you'll see how
it's done, but I don't intend to explain it, or anything else in
my act. The slack-rope dancer stood up, and walked back
down her line, to begin the cycle again. It was simple—and,
as I've said, not too hard to figure out—but it would be effective enough for a matinee audience.

"The clip is copied, and cued to playdeck," Peri announced.

I called Muthana back, gave him the details and what I
needed from him, and arranged for a carrier to come and get
me and the machine. They were as prompt as I'd known they
would be, and we were in the lobby with everything installed
by eleven. I borrowed a desert wrap from General Wardrobe,
put it on, and practiced my part of the illusion a few dozen
more times to make sure I could manage it. I had a demi-
alcove toward the back of the lobby, where the left grand
staircase led up to the balconies. The lights were good there,
soft but clear, and people could watch from the lower steps
if they couldn't see from the lobby itself. Muthana had made
up a poster and a virtual placard, both with the glyph for my
surname—*fortune*—and my given name spelled out in realprint below it, and the glyphs that meant *special show* and *puppet* backed with an old publicity print of the street show that

I'd given him from my files. It looked good, especially considering the short notice he'd had. Binnie set up the ropes around the alcove and introduced the minders—one in house livery, two not—and then all I had to do was wait. It had been a while since I'd done this small a show, and I tried to tell myself the flutter of nerves was good for me.

There were already a dozen placards glowing in the air along the sides of the lobby, their rainbow brilliance making the printed posters look pallid by comparison. I didn't recognize that many of the glyphs—because of our schedules, I don't often cross paths with the lobby-show acts—but a few of the realprint names that went with them were familiar from other venues or the trade listings. The lottery-reader—there was always one, pulling numbers and plastic *carta* tokens from a glittering ball filled with multicolored tinsel—was a complete stranger, but the woman screwing together lengths of support frame in the space next to her was my cousin Fanning's bandmate. They were the last people I'd expected to see—Fire/Work is almost as unsuitable for a matinee as I am—but even as I thought that, she straightened and looked over her shoulder at a slim coolie woman that I recognized as one of Tigridi's hand-drummers. Since Tigridi had caused part of the problem, it seemed reasonable that some of them should work the lobby show—though I didn't envy the minders when the low-teens realized who was among them—but I didn't quite understand what Shadha Catayong was doing there.

She saw me looking and smiled, but went on talking to the other drummer. Finally that woman nodded, and Catayong came to join me, shaking her head so that the beads at the tips of her oiled braids rattled together. Fanning had said once that she was a Dreampeacer, and as she came up to me I looked for any of their tokens among the hanks of charm-necklaces but didn't see their anatomized man/machine anywhere among the dangling beads.

"Didn't expect to see you here," she said.

"I didn't expect to be here," I answered, and that got a grin. "Are you playing?"

She shook her head, making the beads clash again. "Not us. But I said I'd loan Faraji one of my tap-drums and help her set up."

From her tone, she was wishing she hadn't. I said, "That was nice of you."

Catayong made a face. "Binnie didn't leave us a lot of choice. We're not really flavor-of-the-month right now."

Fire/Work was a fusion band, in the style of Hati, the first and still the greatest of the djensi-fx bands that had been really popular about five years ago, just before the Manfred Riots. Hati itself had broken up in the aftermath—something else to blame on Dreampeace, on the whole AI debate—and the style wasn't nearly as popular as it had been. Partly, it was the usual change in taste, but mostly it was that the idea of coolies and poor yanquis and the rest of the upperworld cooperating on anything—least of all music that managed to combine old-fashioned djensi guitars and coolie fxes—just didn't have the same resonance that it had had before Manfred. I had liked Hati, myself, but Fanning, and I gathered the rest of Fire/Work, had worshiped them. Fire/Work still had a following, and a contract, but I could see that they might be feeling vulnerable.

Catayong glanced over her shoulder agan, studying the other drummer's setup. "I don't know what Binnie's thinking of, the low-teens are going to be all over her, and if they crack my drum—" Before she could finish, someone called her name from the top of the stairs, and there was a note in the voice that made me turn to look. Out of the corner of my eye, I saw Catayong's frown deepen.

"Tai?"

The woman coming down the stairs was tall for a coolie, but otherwise unmistakable, bronze skin and broad cheekbones and coarse black hair cut short as a line-worker's. Ni-antai Li was one of Fire/Work's two guitarists—the other one was coolie, too, unusually, just as it was unusual that my yanqui cousin should be their fx player.

"Trouble," she said, coming into earshot, and for an instant her voice trembled before she got it under control.

"What is it?" Catayong asked, and I reached under the sleeve of my robe, found the spot between the bones of my forearm that controls my skinsuit, and pressed to bring up the control disk. It hardened almost instantly, and I ran the controls to high. Instantly, the lobby blazed with light, a web of multicolored control bars and the hot pink dots of the tightbeam transmitters, and I swung in a full circle, seeing how the security beams blazed hotter orange than usual, too bright for normal use.

"Something's up," I said, and Li made a funny noise.

"What's wrong?" Catayong said again, and this time the sound Li made was almost laughter.

"Jaantje heard it on the newsnets on his way here. Micki Tantai's been shot—"

"What?" The sound of my own voice startled me, but Li went on as though I hadn't spoken.

"—maybe killed."

"By who?" Catayong asked. Over her shoulder, I saw the lottery-reader put down her tongs and edge closer, drawn by the magic name. Micki Tantai was—*had been*, maybe—Hati's lead sign dancer, and their main face. He was also one of the few coolie supporters of machine rights—not Dreampeace, never that, but one of the few sane voices arguing that machine rights and coolie rights were two sides of the same coin. That was one of the reasons the band had split up, after the Riots, after Manfred was proved to be just another construct, a clever mimic of true AI, but Tantai and Hati kept the power of their names.

"Guess," Li answered, and the lottery-reader cleared her throat.

"Excuse me, but I couldn't help hearing. Did you say Micki Tantai was shot?"

"That's what I—actually my bandmate—heard," Li said.

"It wasn't Realpeace," Catayong said. "It couldn't be."

"Who else?" Li asked, with real bitterness. She was a first-generation coolie herself, I remembered, came from Freya with her draftee mother when she was two or three. Realpeace claimed to speak for people like her, claimed to know what was best for them, and fusion—Hati and anyone like them—wasn't it. It was no wonder she sounded angry.

"Have they claimed it?" the lottery-reader asked.

Li shook her head, visibly shaking herself back to something like normal. "You know them. The newsdogs are saying Realpeace, Jaantje said, but there wasn't a claim. Nothing official."

Catayong looked at me. "Anything on the wires?"

Because of my act, I had access to Tin Hau's lower-grade security, but this was obviously something bigger. I fixed my eyes and IPUs on the nearest security node anyway, and wasn't surprised when the pinlight refused to resolve into a shimmering veil of glyphs and realprint. "Probably," I said, "but I can't get at it. Security's set high, though." I looked around for Bixenta Terez, an old friend who was Tin Hau's senior stage manager, then shook myself. She would be backstage already, setting up the matinee, not out here in the lobby.

"Something's not right," the lottery-reader murmured, looking toward the doors. I looked with her, and saw house security gathering.

"What exactly did Jaantje say happened?" I asked, and was careful to give his name its proper, coolie pronunciation.

Li took a deep breath. "He said that Micki Tantai'd been shot, outside one of the Zodiac arcades. That was all he'd heard—"

"Here he comes," Catayong interrupted. I followed her gaze, and through the haze of lights and glyphs—there was a transmitter in my line of sight—saw the rest of Fire/Work coming down the stairs. Behind them, on the landing, I could see more of Muthana's liveried security, gathering in twos and threes, big people in bright blue-and-gold vests. Tin Hau didn't usually need security, at least not in large numbers: whatever had actually happened, Muthana wasn't taking any chances.

I touched the control disk, damping the visuals, and the faces around me came clear again. Fanning gave me a nod of greeting—he was whiter than ever, his tan like dirt over his pallid skin—and said, "Are you getting anything from the house? I've only got basic clearance."

He was wired, too, though only the essential skinsuit. "Nothing," I answered, and Catayong spoke over me.

"Jaantje, what the hell is going on?"

Jaantje Dhao—he was the biggest of the band, a broad-shouldered, kinky-haired three-gen coolie from one of the pocket metroforms in Western Phoenix—gave her an odd look, his usual easy smile utterly vanished. "Didn't Tai tell you?"

"She said Micki Tantai'd been shot, but there's got to be more to it than that."

"Why?" the third man asked, with a bitter smile that did nothing to hide how close he was to tears.

"I caught it on the display outside the Shaft Three Station," Dhao said, speaking now to all of us as well as Catayong. Out of the corner of my eye, I could see the hand-drummer from Tigridi edging closer, hand over her mouth in a startlingly underworld gesture. One of the minders was listening, too, grim-faced, and I tried to catch his eye, wanting to ask what he'd heard. He looked away, but didn't move out of earshot.

"They were showing a vidi-clip," Dhao went on. "There was a crowd outside the Belmara—"

"Micki Tantai was supposed to be there," Fanning interjected, and added, *supposed to sign dance.* He went on aloud. "It was a benefit for that girl who got beat up last half-week."

Dhao nodded. "And Tantai was arriving, came in a runabout with a guy, I think he's in his new band, and when he got out, there was this swirl"—he mimed the crowd's movement, big hands oddly helpless—"and this little guy jumps out of the crowd and Tantai goes down. Everything was confused, and the next thing you know the guy's gone, and Tantai's flat on the pavement. They ran the vidi-clip again in slow-time, and you could see the little guy had a gun."

"Did you hear the commentary?" I asked. There was no point in asking him about the realprint crawl line: I doubted he could read more than the standard glyphs.

"No." Dhao shook his head. "I was too far back. I saw the clip, and I headed in here. I thought maybe somebody else would have more news."

"All the newsdogs are saying is that Tantai was shot." That was a new voice, the lurking minder, and we all turned to look at him. "They aren't saying by who—though some of them are speculating—and they aren't giving a condition."

"Elvis Christ," Fanning said, under his breath, and the lottery-reader said, "The guy with the gun—it really was a gun?"

We all looked at the minder again. Projectile weapons are restricted in Landage, mostly successfully so; if some maniac—some Realpeace crazy—had a gun, we would all feel a lot less safe tonight. The minder grimaced.

"I don't know. That's what the newsdogs said, so we have to assume it, though."

That wasn't the sort of thing the newsdogs got wrong. The lottery-reader shivered visibly, and the girl from Tigridi said, "Was he wearing a *sarang?*"

There was a little silence. Five years ago, nobody wore the Freyan *sarang* anymore, not even the oldest coolies, but in the aftermath of the Manfred Riots, a lot of the political coolies had adopted them as a visible reminder of what Manfred had meant for them. If Manfred had been true AI, and if Dreampeace had succeeded in winning full rights for it—and it was an article of faith among the political coolies that they would have—then the coolies, most of whom were Freyan contract labor, not citizens at all, would have had fewer rights than the constructs. Realpeace especially had adopted the *sarang* as one of their badges—you never saw their triumvirate, the trio who always represented them on the newschannels, in anything but the *sarang* and traditional jacket—but for them it meant more than just coolie rights on Persephone, it meant opposition to the current Provisional Government and a return to the homeworld. It was a tricky question, especially from an obvious midworlder, and I wasn't surprised when Dhao looked away.

"I couldn't see."

"What's Binnie going to do about it?" I said to the minder, and he lifted both hands to ward off the question. "Don't look at me. All I was told was to watch the lobby. Security's been tightened, of course, but that's all I know."

I looked at the nearest tightbeam transmitter, saw the web of light spring to life again, crisscrossing the lobby. I was locked out of the true discourse, but I could see a thicker cluster of lights around the entrances, red bars across each doorway and an orange haze enclosing each of the support pillars. Probably a detector field, I thought, and hoped it was discriminating enough to filter out the usual coolie tool kits. All we needed was for the matinee audience to get offended.

More people than our little group had obviously heard the news. There was another knot of minders by the door, getting instruction from the house manager, and the gaggle of high-teens who sold programs in exchange for a free show were trying to get close enough to overhear without being chased away. Another group—I didn't recognize them, but from their props and clothes they had to be lobby-show regulars— was clustered by the main ticket booth, heads swiveling from the minders at the door to us and back again. I wondered if the missing shows had had word of impending trouble, and then put that suspicion aside. The kind of people who worked the Empires tended not to be political—though the ones that were went in for dramatic Causes. Most of us were three-gen coolies, though, or midworlders, not the classes from which Realpeace drew its support.

The house speakers clicked on, gave the two-toned call that meant a theaterwide announcement, and at the same moment a bright yellow attention glyph flashed on the callscreens and in virtual space to catch any deaf people not wearing their ears. I squeezed my control disk, muting the colors, and Muthana's voice spoke smoothly from the space below the domed ceiling.

"Haya, people, listen up. You've probably all heard the news, but this is the official word right now." There was a pause, and when he spoke again it was obvious he was reading from an official release-sheet. "Micki Tantai, formerly of

Hati, was shot today outside the Belmara Arcade where he was attending a benefit for Surya Ravellei—that's the girl from Gamela who got beat up by Realpeace. There's no further word on his condition, or on the identity of the shooter." His voice changed again as he put aside the sheet. "Haya, that's all any of us know, so there's no point in pestering the house staff about it. As things stand, the matinee is on, but there's a good chance the night-show will be canceled—the word from the owners is that Security doesn't want to leave any chance for more protests. They've promised to let us know by the time the matinee is over, so the people from the night-show, you'll have time to get ready if it goes."

"Which it won't," Catayong said, half under her breath, and I saw Fanning nod. Dhao shook his head once, slowly, not disagreeing, but said nothing. They were probably right, too, and I made a face, thinking of the wasted time. My contract said I would be paid regardless, and I'd get my fee for the lobby show, but I resented missing a performance.

"Haya," Muthana said. "That's all for now."

"Places, people," the house manager, Inay Hasker, announced, and reluctantly people started to move toward their positions along the lobby walls. "Doors open in ten minutes. Security, ticket crew, stand by."

"Where does that leave you?" I said to Fanning, and he shrugged.

"We get paid some—not the full fee, though."

Dhao touched his arm. "Come on," he said, and gave me an apologetic smile. "We've got to go."

They went back up the stairs in a group, heading for one of the interior service lifts that would take them down to the practice rooms, and only Catayong looked back, frowning nervously as the drummer from Tigridi took her place behind the borrowed drum. I put them out of my mind and went back to the cabinet show, drawing the desert cape's hood up over my hair. The karakuri was ready, the virtual checklights glowing pale green in the air around them; I waved my hand through the lower control space to start the music, and caught a glimpse of myself in the narrow strip of polished brass that edged the nearest half-pillar. I looked worried even under the hood's massive shadow, paler than I should be, and I wondered, too late, if I should have done more with my makeup. I put that thought away, too, and reached into the main control web to bring the timing chart to the foreground. I watched it click off the numbers, each one matched to a movement from the karakuri, and started the cabinet as the piece returned to its beginning. The rope dancer climbed to her platforms, twirled and stooped, and then the magician lifted her head and began to play with the cup and balls. As she looked to me, I palmed my ball, presented it, and made it vanish again. Out of the corner of my eye, I saw one of the plainclothes minders sign applause, and the speakers crackled again.

"Last call for places. Door crew, stand by."

The show would run itself for the next few minutes, and I risked a glance at the doors. There were people waiting, all right, plenty of shadows against the glass, but not as many as there should be. I couldn't tell if they were coolies or not, or even upperworld rather than midworld; there seemed to be the usual number of kids, though, and I wondered if these were just the people who hadn't heard the news, or the ones who didn't care. A lot of coolies thought Micki Tantai and Hati had betrayed them five years ago; I could see that those people might have heard the news, and shrugged, maybe even smiled a little, and gone on about their business.

"Ten seconds to opening," Hasker said, and I turned my attention to the cabinet show. Everything was running smoothly, all the checklights green, filling the air around it, and I took a deep breath.

"Input, command. Reduce display to preset minimum." The lights faded as I spoke, the suit pulse trickling down to almost nothing, and I ran the gain to its highest setting. The background readings sprang up again, security systems and the hot blue lights of the automatic ticket counters, and I had to shift my position to get out of the nearest tightbeam line.

The bright lights faded, and I could see the ghost of the cabinet show's controls again. Very few people would have skinsuits, not in an upperworld crowd—the suits are mainly for FTL pilots and high-level constructors and design engineers—but anyone who did would be unlikely to have it turned up high enough to spot the cabinet's transmission, especially not today with the house systems so bright. And that would only help hide how the illusion worked.

"Three seconds," Hasker announced. "Two. . . . And one. . . . Opening the house now."

I caught a quick glimpse of the doors swinging wide, triggered by his voice, then I'd frozen into my position for the act. I could hear the babble of voices, the rapid rise and fall and the long-held vowels of the coolies' tonal dialect, but the hood blocked my side vision, so that I could only see the cabinet show and its virtual controls and a narrow wedge of the lobby. The liveried minder rocked forward onto the balls of his feet, and the first of the kids, a gang of three followed by a low-teen girl who had to be their caretaker, skidded to a stop in front of the show. They were coolies by their faces, smiling and excited; if they'd heard anything about Tantai, which I doubted, it meant nothing to them. The rope dancer reached the top of her platform and turned; the magician lifted her cup to show the crystal ball glowing against the dark purple velvet of her table, and we were off. I closed my mind to everything except the rhythm of the show, the pattern of gesture and the weight of the crystal in my hand, shutting out the voices except as counterpoint and the directing murmur of applause.

I couldn't hold them, though. Except for the kids, the ones too young really to remember Hati or the Manfred Riots, they were all distracted, their thoughts not really here in the Empire but ten levels down on the Zodiac with Micki Tantai and a mysterious gunman in a *sarang*. I could have shown them miracles, pulled fire from the air without benefit of sleight of hand, and nothing would have registered except a pattern of pretty lights. I hate an audience like that, one that won't give, won't take even the spark of an idea from me. Between their distraction and my own anger and unease, the show was lifeless, technically correct, but without the edge, the breath, that it should have had. I have rarely been more relieved than I was when the lights flashed for the final warning, and the last pair of high-teens dragged themselves away from the lobby show and up the stairs to the balcony. A blue light flared in front of my eyes, telling me that the doors were closing.

"Stand by," Hasker announced. "Haya, stand down. All doors are closed. Nice job, people."

The lobby show closes after the main show starts—at intermission, one buys souvenirs or food. I palmed my crystal for the last time and shoved back my hood. "Input, command. Return display to preset optimum."

The checklights strengthened again, and I waved my hand through the control space to begin the shutdown. I remember that I was pleased, seeing how well it had functioned, with no notice and no chance to do more than the most basic repairs. I remember, too, that I looked for Tigridi's drummer, and saw her still standing behind the racked drums, the sweat standing on her face. The minders who'd been watching her were sweating, too: Tigridi is just the kind of band the low-teens love. And then I saw Fanning coming down the stairs from the gallery, his face if anything whiter than it had been before, and I knew what had happened before I saw the sign.

Micki Tantai— The famous name sign, heart and the initial, circling over Fanning's heart to add the emphasis, and then both hands to finish*—Micki Tantai's dead.*

"Ah, Fan," I said, not knowing what else I could say, and he shook his head, switching to speech as he came closer.

"We heard it on All-Hours, there was a bulletin." He shook his head. "There's going to be hell to pay for this."

"I'm sorry," I said, and would have held him if he'd been the sort to let me, or if I'd quite known how to offer.

"It's bad, Cissy."

I let him get away with the old nickname, making allowance. "If it was Realpeace, they've just lost a lot of support."

"Or gained a lot," he answered, and shook his head again. "God, I hope you're right, Fortune."

"Look what happened to Dreampeace," I said. "Manfred wasn't even their idea, not directly, but it killed that constructor, tried to kill that FTL pilot, and that buried them. If Realpeace did this, they're history."

"That was five years ago," Fanning said. "Things have changed."

He was right about that, too, or maybe it was more that not enough things had changed. Manfred had killed machine rights without doing anything for the coolies, either. "If Realpeace did it, they've gone too far," I said, and hoped it was true.

■ 2 ■

Reverdy Jian

FOR ONCE, SHE could see the ship from the transfer tube, a bright point of light outlined in vivid glyphs still coded yellow to remind her that it was her responsibility until the handover on Persephone. It was a good ship—a joint-venture prototype, Kagami wireware, Adastra hull, the new Merlin V power plant, designed for the carrier trade, fast enough to make the time bonuses and cheap enough to run to make it practical in the Rim Sectors—and she watched it down the length of the tube, enjoying the sense of satisfaction. This test flight had been a Kagami contract, and came with Kagami bonuses: the company still acknowledged its debt to her for what she had done and not done these last five years. More than that, though, she had liked the ship, a tight,

fast hull, a little stolid, maybe, but better than the tempera-
mental one-of-a-kind hulls she dealt with on a regular basis.
Definitely a good one, she thought. *Score one for the buyers, this
time.*

There was a human steward at the end of the tube, and she
handed him her destination disk, saw the subtle lift of eyebrows as the disk confirmed her first-class status. It wasn't
usual, especially for a mere pilot—it was fallout from a power
struggle among the joint-venture companies, Kagami proving her worth—but he made no comment, just pointed her
forward toward the appropriate compartment. She squeezed
past him, awkward in the narrow space of the lock, swung
her carryall forward on her hip to make it easier to handle.
She heard voices rise behind her, one familiar, sharp and
querulous, but she didn't look back. If it was her business,
Vaughn would make sure she heard.

The first-class compartment was empty: it was a perk most
Cartel employees were willing to forgo, on the short flight,
or traded for something better. She settled herself into one of
the forward seats, slid her carryall into its webbing, and
stretched her long legs into the aisle, intending to sleep if she
could manage it.

"Reverdy."

The voice was not going to be denied, and she opened her
eyes, ignoring the momentary blur as the autofocus mechanism sighted on the nearest object. She blinked, resetting
them, and Imre Vaughn's face swam into clarity, the lines at
the corners of his eyes tightening not with laughter but something like concern. Beyond him, on the far side of the aisle,
Red was little more than a blur of hair and ivory skin: the machine eyes still didn't cope terribly well with multiple targets
until they'd had a chance to set their ranges. The world
shifted again, and her sight was normal.

"Yeh?"

"Did you hear the news?"

Jian shook her head, not bothering to ask what news he
meant. Nothing she'd seen was important enough to catch
Vaughn's attention; whatever this was, it was enough to dis-

tract him from his recent obsession with machine chess. She could even see the most recent form report, unmistakable on its lime green paper, crumpled and forgotten in the outer pocket of his carryall.

"Micki Tantai's dead—shot to death," Vaughn said. "Probably by Realpeace."

Jian blinked. "Who's Micki Tantai?"

"You remember Hati?" Vaughn asked, and Jian nodded.

"Oh. Yeh, I remember them." The band had been big in the upperworld just before the Manfred Riots—*and they were a mixed band, too,* she added silently, *coolies and midworlders, no, coolies and yanquis*—which hadn't been usual even then. *And they broke up right after the Riots, something about somebody being a Dreampeacer*— "One of them was Dreampeace, right?"

Vaughn gave her a look. "Two of them were, and three of them weren't. Micki Tantai was one of the Dreampeacers, and he was a coolie—and their face, for that matter. And now Realpeace has shot him."

"You said probably," Jian said.

"Since when has Realpeace claimed anything it's done?"

"They've got a lot of crazies hooked up with them," Jian said. "It doesn't have to have been their idea—the organization's, I mean." Even as she spoke, she could hear the echo of her last argument with Chaandi, and winced at the memory. *You think we're too weak to have an organized movement— or too emotional to control ourselves, or something,* she had said, *so you won't take Realpeace seriously. I'm so fucking sick of hearing 'it wasn't really them, it was just some misguided I-don't-know-whats' that I could join the fucking party myself, just to prove it was for real.*

"Elvis Christ, those people know what they're doing," Vaughn began, but the hatch slid open then, and he swallowed anything else he would have said. A tall man with a pair of corporate pins on the lapel of his neat jacket took his seat at the rear of the compartment: *definitely new to Persephone,* Jian thought, seeing his unmarked skin. The steward followed him in and began the regulation safety check. Here in first-class especially, it was unnecessary—anyone traveling on this ticket would have heard the same speeches over and over in the main cabin before being promoted—but this time Jian was grateful for it, glad to divert the subject from coolie politics.

She stretched her legs again, nudged the carryall, and felt the edge of the headbox that held her Spelvin construct solid through the thin fabric and her wadded clothes. She needed a new construct, wanted it before she took another job, and she leaned sideways a little to see past Vaughn. Red was sitting quietly in his couch, a manga-block floating in front of him, tethered by the headphone's cord. For a moment, she thought he was asleep, but then he lifted one thin-fingered hand to adjust the screen. He knew the technical grey-markets, knew a lot of hard-hackers, too; he might be able to point her to the right person, this time, even if the current construct hadn't been quite what she was looking for. Now, however, was not the time to ask, not with the Cartel employee sitting within earshot, and she leaned back again, positioning herself so that she could watch the tightbeam display as the shuttle fell away from the transfer station toward the planet below. Once they landed, she would be able to ask.

In the display, new glyphs blossomed, and Jian felt the first soft tug of gravity. A few minutes later, the shuttle trembled as it touched the edge of the atmosphere, and Jian let the rising gravity draw her back down into her couch. They landed without incident, the lurching runout abruptly tamed and silenced, and Jian watched for the display that would signal the land tugs' arrival. The shuttle lurched, and the red light came on: under tow. Beside her, Vaughn stirred, collecting his belongings, but he said nothing even after the shuttle slowed to a stop and the docking lights came on, first virtual, then real. She kept silence herself while they worked their way through the perfunctory Customs check—they and their job were known, and expected—then made their way through the rose-and-ocher halls toward the tunnel where the land shuttles left for Landage. It was late, a little past midnight by the planetary clock, a little past noon in the long planetary day, and The Moorings was quiet, the few passengers who remained either frankly asleep on the long benches or clustered by twos and threes at the little tables in the all-night kaffs. Jian suppressed a yawn and saw Vaughn look sideways at her.

"They're loading in ten minutes," he said. "Think you can make it?"

"No problem."

They made the land shuttle with about five minutes to spare, piling together into the sun-warmed interior that smelled faintly of sweat and the thick oilcloth of the seat covers. There were plenty of empty spaces, and Jian claimed a block in the corner while Vaughn ran their passes through the shuttle's reader. Red settled himself opposite her, eyes lowered to look at nothing, and Jian shifted her carryall out of the way, aware of the hard corner of the headbox against her ankle. *Got to trade it in,* she thought, and the intensity of the wish startled her, so that she looked around the cab for distraction. The only other passengers were frankly asleep, two midworlders from Astarte's Prejani Division propped upright in the side seats directly below the air vent, a couple of cargo handlers sprawled awkwardly across several seats. *Foremen, probably if they're travelling this late,* she thought, but their cotton coats, bright with company insignia, were balled beneath their heads as makeshift pillows.

The car slid into motion then, and Vaughn dropped into the seat beside her, stretching his legs to rest his feet on the opposite cushion. Jian saw Red's eyes flicker, registering the other man's presence, but he made no other move. She looked past him and blinked as the tunnel doors slid open, letting in a wash of white light. The sunfilm covering the windows darkened automatically, but the brilliance was still almost painful. She blinked again, wanting to see, and stared at the intricate maze of the runways, dark lines shivering like water against the pale sand. They were all but empty—not even cargo haulers worked this late without serious overtime—and only a single shuttle lay in the cradles, not yet angled up for liftoff. Beyond it, the mountains that defined the Daymare Basin rose dark against the white and hazy sky, and she slid sideways so that she could rest her head against the warm glass. Ahead, toward Landage, the sides of the mountain were sculpted to tidy planes, calculated angles, the rock itself coated in thermal film, white now, to reflect the daytime heat. Light glittered from the tips of the sun-traps that channeled free light to Heaven, the city's poorest levels; by contrast, the cooling hoods and condensers were dark against the painted stone.

"So, Reverdy." Vaughn leaned forward, pitching his voice so it was just audible above the hum of the motors and the ventilation.

"Yeh?" Jian lifted her head off the now-hot glass, and her cheek glowed faintly, as though with fever.

"So what's up?"

"I'm thinking of selling my Spelvin construct," Jian said, and kept her tone even, daring him to say anything.

"Elvis Christ, not again." Vaughn glared at her, and Jian shook her head.

"It's not your business, Imre."

"Like hell." His voice had risen, and he caught himself, glanced over his shoulder at the still-sleeping workers, before going on, more softly. "Look, what is this, the fifth construct you've had since we got back to work? What's wrong with this one, anyway?"

"I don't like it," Jian said.

"So what?" Vaughn's hands closed over the edge of the cushion, and he loosened them with a visible effort. "You don't have to like it, all you got to do is work with it."

"If I have to work with it, I want to like it," Jian said. She leaned forward then, tapped the redhead once on the knee. He opened his eyes warily, and Jian smiled. "Red. The guy you got this one from. Does he have others?"

Red looked up, his thick hair falling back from the planes of his face, and Jian caught her breath again at his astonishing beauty. Even knowing him as long as she had, even expecting to see it, the ivory perfection of his face sometimes surprised her.

"I don't know," he said. "I can ask."

"Elvis Christ," Vaughn said, and to her surprise bit back his temper. "Look, if you're going to sell this one, too, I'd appreciate it if you didn't get Red involved."

Beside him, Red stirred, and for a second Jian thought he was going to speak again, but then he dropped his eyelids, waiting.

"I need his help," Jian said. "You know what Spelvins cost."

"They wouldn't cost so much if you didn't keep selling them," Vaughn muttered.

"I wouldn't keep selling them if I could find the right one," Jian answered.

"The problem is, you think every fucking one of them's another Manfred," Vaughn said, and kept his own voice low with an effort. "That's not what's happening."

"One of these days, it will be," Jian answered. "Or it'll be the real thing. Real AI, Imre. What're you going to do then?"

Vaughn didn't respond, his eyes hot and angry, and at his side Red lifted his eyes.

"I'll call you," he said.

Jian nodded, well aware of Vaughn's fulminating disapproval, and leaned back in her seat again. She could remember perfectly well what Manfred had felt like, even five years on, that plausible, all-but-human presence; could remember, too, what it had felt like to realize first that it had tried to kill her, and then to realize that there was nothing personal—no person at all—behind that decision. The trouble was, since Manfred, every Spelvin construct had felt to her like AI, or like Manfred's pseudo-AI, and this latest construct had been the worst yet. To do her job, to take any ship through hyperspace, she needed a Spelvin construct to manage the datastream, but when all of them felt like Manfred, she found herself watching them as though they, too, would eventually try to kill her. And she was not prepared to tolerate that threat.

The window darkened abruptly, and she glanced up to see the shuttle entering Tunnelmouth. She reached for her carryall, dragging her legs under her, and saw the foremen at the head of the car wake with the ease of people who made this trip routinely. The taller of the two stretched, then shook out his coat before shrugging it up over his shoulders. Not a company coat at all, Jian realized, but the bright quick-printed cotton sold in the coolie night markets, each wide sleeve badged with the stylized heart glyph and the five faces that were the fusion band Hati. One of the faces was ringed with black—*Mick Tantai's of course*—and even as she realized it the foreman met and matched her stare. She hadn't meant to challenge, smiled instead, and looked away as the land shuttle eased to a stop, the soft sand tires hissing on the floor of the bay. The couple from Prejani were still asleep, the man with his head on the woman's shoulder, and as she passed them she tapped his foot with her own. He came awake instantly, blinking in confusion, and Jian nodded to the door.

"Tunnelmouth, ba'. End of the line."

"Haya, bi'—and thanks," the man stammered, and turned to wake his companion.

Jian stepped past him into the hot wind that poured in through the direct-exhaust vents. Despite the filters, the air was full of fine sand, and she narrowed her eyes against its sting. The bay smelled of oil and the engine fumes, and the sharp metal tang of the mending torches. Only a single tender was on duty, and she could see him yawning behind the thin fiberfelt mask he wore against the constant sand. He waved them through into the lobby, past the door pole that glowed with cabbies' glyphs, and Jian turned automatically for the slidewalk that ran to the lift station at Charretse Main.

"Reverdy! Imre! Over here."

Jian turned, startled, to see a familiar figure standing at the base of the ramp that led up to the turnaround at the end of Broad-hi. "Peace? What the hell are you doing here?"

"Not that we're not grateful, of course," Vaughn added, at her shoulder, "but I thought turnover wasn't until tomorrow."

"It's not." Peace Malindy met their stares unsmiling, hands deep in the pockets of his one-piece suit. He was a small man, his head barely topping Jian's shoulder, but he'd been managing the pilots' cooperative for as long as she'd been a member, and she knew better than to be fooled by his size or his deceptively upperworld clothes. "I didn't know if you'd heard the news, and I thought you might be better off riding back to Dzi-Gin with me."

Vaughn started to say something, and Jian overrode him ruthlessly, responding to the look in Malindy's eyes. Dzi-Gin was the biggest of the upperworld interchanges, the gateway to the midworld, where she and Vaughn both lived. If Malindy was offering them transport, something was going wrong in Heaven. "What news, Peace?"

"Micki Tantai's been shot—"

"We heard that," Vaughn muttered, and Malindy ignored him.

"—and there's been a lot of talk that Realpeace was behind it. They're denying it, but there's been sporadic trouble, mostly coolies and yanquis down by the Zodiac, but one-gen against three-gen up here in Heaven." Malindy looked at Jian, his mouth curving into an ironic smile. "You three are likely to attract attention just on looks alone, and I didn't want you getting into trouble before the handover."

Jian grinned back, but had to admit the justice of the things he'd left unsaid. Vaughn was known to friends and enemies as Crazy Imre, and he was her partner and Red's lover; even knowing what was going on, it was unlikely he—or she—would have backed down from a challenge.

"Besides," Malindy went on, "some people may still remember you from the Manfred Riots. You don't want that connection made right now."

"And what do you suggest we do about it?" Vaughn asked. "Spend the rest of our lives, or however long it takes to deal with fucking Realpeace, locked up somewhere?"

"It's that bad," Jian said, her eyes fixed on Malindy, and the small man nodded.

"The funeral's tomorrow. After that, things should be better."

Jian nodded, settling her carryall more comfortably on her shoulder. "Thanks for the ride then."

"And welcome home," Vaughn muttered, but Jian ignored him, following Malindy up the ramp toward the parking bays. If Malindy said things were bad, they were bad; better to stay out of sight, out of memory, until after the funeral.

■ 3 ■

Fanning Jones

M Y COUSIN FORTUNE doesn't really believe in politics—she says there's no room for them in the Empires, which is partly true—so I was surprised when she called me the night before Micki Tantai's funeral. I had the *goddow* to myself, for once—Jaantje and Tai and I share the place, half of twin flats off a dirt-floor cavern in Ironyards—so I wasn't sorry for the company, just startled to see her broad face in the media screen. I flicked my ear back on and reached for the nearest chair, avoiding the lump where the webbing had been mended.

"Hey, Fortune. What's up?"

"Hey, Fan."

It was good to hear a yanqui voice, now and then, and good to use the speech I'd grown up with. It was funny. I'd grown up only half a level down from Fortune's family in the yanqui neighborhoods of Township Blackwell, just barely midworld by normal reckoning, filled with people in Maintenance and Air and Water, but we hadn't really been friends then. Being family, we had had to be polite at the big gatherings for Easter and Transfiguration, but Fortune's people didn't go to services much except at the holidays, not like mine, so we didn't see each other very often. Then she moved in with the Barra Vaughns over in Argonauts, and I didn't really see her again until we ended up at the same vo-tech before I dropped out to join Fire/Work. That was when I'd gotten to know her—my employee discount at Motosha helped her out, and she'd helped me with some of the wiring for my fx—and now that we were on the same bill at Tin Hau we stayed close, for all that she lived way over in Angelitos now, on the far side of Tin Hau from Ironyards.

"Are you going to the funeral?" she asked, and didn't have to say which one.

"Yeh." I knew I sounded surprised and tried to moderate my tone. Of course we were going: if it wasn't for Hati, we wouldn't be a band. In particular, I wouldn't be in a band— deaf musicians are mostly coolies, and they're mostly sign dancers or fx players, and there's not much call for either one in the yanqui music I grew up with. "We all are."

"I heard there was going to be a protest," Fortune said. Behind her, I could see the bright lights of her workbench, and the pale silver shape of one of her karakuri laid out on it. It was one of the humaniform ones, one of the trio from her act that have her face, and it looked disconcertingly like a human being lying there, arms and legs sprawled like a sleeping child's. The wires spilling from the open panel in its mid-section only made the illusion more complete, and I wondered if she'd planned the effect.

"I hadn't heard that," I said. "Hati—God, it still feels weird that Tantai's dead—they're asking that everybody stay calm."

"Like that'll do any good."

"Come on, Fortune, it's a funeral. Nobody's going to cause real trouble there."

"Want to bet?" She gave me one of her dark smiles, the ones she'd perfected for her act, but then relented. "Seriously, that's what I heard. Damiane Ye was saying she'd heard there was going to be a big anti-Realpeace protest."

Damiane Ye was one of the assistant stage managers. I frowned, trying to remember the posters I'd seen, jet-black glyphs on expensive pure white paper. "I don't think so," I said. "The band's been really adamant about who's speaking, and what it's all about—it's for Tantai, for Hati, not politics, this time. They got Tsuruyaga to put out a statement saying he's just speaking as a friend, not as an ombi, and they didn't want Derek Chang to speak at all."

"Well, he has to," Fortune said. "He's chairman of the Empire consortium, it wouldn't be right if he wasn't there."

"He's also a major fusionist, he's on record as hating Realpeace, and he's a coolie, even if he is three-gen," I said. "Don't you watch the news?"

Fortune grinned. "I work nights."

I shook my head. "Look, are you going? We could meet at Tin Hau Upper, you could walk with us."

The minute I'd said it, I regretted it—the funeral was a band thing, it was special to us, important to us as a band, and there shouldn't be outsiders—and I was glad when Fortune shook her head.

"I haven't decided." She smiled then, a real smile, wry and almost ugly, deepening a line like a scar at the side of her mouth. "Part of me feels like I ought to, and part of me doesn't—feels like I wouldn't belong, I guess. You know, their music wasn't my style—no offense, Fan, but I like what you do better—but they were important. It's like when someone on your street dies, you want to show up with food for the wake—but I don't know what to bring."

I nodded. That was one of the reasons I liked talking to Fortune: we had all that past in common, memories of going with covered trays to the neighbors, or of standing in the door to accept them, the smell of hot food and the taste of grief always inextricably mixed. The rest of Fire/Work thought of funerals and smelled beer and gunpowder, heard rattling bangs and saw the streets drifted with black paper from the strings of the funeral crackers. I wanted someone to feed me, and grinned at the thought. "You can take me to lunch afterward."

Fortune laughed silently. "I'm not sure that was what I had in mind, but I'll take you up on it. If I go."

"You might feel better," I said.

She shrugged. "I don't know. I don't think so. I'll buy you lunch sometime anyway." She glanced over her shoulder at the karakuri, and I wondered if she was regretting the call.

"Give me a call if you change your mind," I said, "otherwise, I'll talk to you later."

"Sounds good. Later, Fan." She cut the connection with a gesture—Fortune has a full skinsuit, not the skeleton wires that I'm still paying for, and only got to keep because they weren't worth repossessing—and the wall went blank except for the charges that flickered across the bottom of the screen. Through the open door the air in the yard looked as though it had dimmed. I knew it was an illusion—we were still almost twenty-four hours from planetary sunset—but I went out anyway, the dirt soft and warm under my bare feet, wondering if the air felt cooler. Coolies burn their dead, which means a daylight funeral, to keep things as cool as possible; when my cousin Jonas was killed on the Stoneman Assembly, it had been a night burial, shivering under the floodlights that were as cold as the crescent moon. I'd never been to a cremation before, was glad the band would be there to steer me right.

Tai and Jaantje and I took the 'bus together to Han-Lu, where the procession was supposed to start. It was crowded even as far east as the Prosperities, and by the time we passed Shaft Three at Tin Hau, the car was so full that I was pressed face-to-face with Tai, both of us trying to pretend our bodies weren't touching. I could feel her breasts flattened against my chest, and tried not to think what she could feel of me. She stared expressionless over my shoulder, not meeting my eyes, and I knew my face was as red as if I'd been in the sun. At Han-Lu Main, we had to change to Shaft Four to go up the last two levels to Han-Lu Upper, and we shuffled through the station in lockstep like midworld commuters on a First-day morning. There were extra workers in Public Transport livery vests at every entrance, making sure the weight limits were observed, and it took us almost half an hour just to get on a car. But finally we made it to Han-Lu Upper, and filed through the last set of turnstiles into the main station, where the crowd was less tightly packed. Beyond the glass front wall, I could see still more people waiting in the interlink plaza itself, and over the dull roar of voices I could already hear the snapping of the first strings of crackers. Security in full armor guarded each of the doors—Cartel Security, I saw with some relief, not FPG—and we pushed past them into the plaza.

It was hot here, directly under the cavern ceiling, and the light pouring though the sun-traps only added to the heat. I was sweating already under the light cotton of my shirt—a Hati blockprint, faded in spite of careful washing—and guessed that it was going to be a long walk to the crematorium. We had agreed to meet beside the plaza statue, a sweep of dark gold metal that vaguely suggested a female figure, arms outstretched to the sky, and I was relieved to see Timin Marleveld sitting on a pylon at its base. He lifted a hand in greeting, then, as we got closer, hauled himself up off the pylon and came to meet us. His lips moved, but the noise around me overloaded my ear, making it hard to pick words out of the general thunder. Drifts of shredded black paper covered the paving already, and Tai shied into me as another string of crackers went off less than two meters from her elbow.

"Where's Shadha?" Jaantje asked, and by some freak his words came clear.

"There," Timin answered, pointing, and I looked to see her coming toward us from the other side of the plaza. She was wearing a Hati wrap-jacket, and a couple of the concert pins clipped to her collar—nearly everyone I could see who wasn't obviously a coolie was wearing some kind of Hati badge, I realized. "She went to get a schedule."

As though she'd heard him, Shadha held up a square white card. Even from here, I could recognize the stylized mourning glyph slashed across the front, and couldn't help wondering how much it had cost to print them. Hati had been big five years ago, but none of them had been as successful since.

"So what's the plan?" Jaantje asked, and Shadha looked down at the card.

"Private service at the Willowbird Community Center," she said, "and then the general procession starts at noon."

Another string of crackers went off ahead of us, snaps of light in a sudden clear space in the crowd. Jaantje winced, said something, but I couldn't make out the words through the sudden spasm of noise. I touched my ear to warn him and got a wry smile and a nod in answer.

Too close, he signed, clumsily, and I nodded.

Tai looked at us, curious, and I touched my ear again. She waved her hand in answer, added, *They'd better be careful, or the cops'll bust them.*

I looked where she was pointing. Sure enough, another Security floater—FPG this time, which was not so good—was grounded in the nearest layby, blue-and-red warning light slowly spinning, throwing pale flashes of light over the crowd. One lane of the Short-hi, the big trafficway that runs the width of Heaven from the Trifon Gate to the Sinliu Lock, was already closed off, and people were spilling into the center lanes despite the drivers' gestures and Security's attempts to herd them back behind the tall orange temporary poles. Off to my right, a light flared, brighter and steadier than the flash of crackers, and a piece of Hati's last clip rose into the air, washed to pastel translucence by the heavy sunlight. I could just make out Micki Tantai's ghostly figure, Ajani Maxx and Alva Gabriel behind him, his hands moving in familiar sign, and I looked away, glad I couldn't hear the music and Gabriel's clean vocals. Timin shook his head, wincing, and I touched his shoulder.

Ask Shadha which way's the Community Center.

He paused—he's a three-gen coolie like Jaantje, and his sign isn't always the best—and Tai waved her hand at me.

Up there—look, they're coming.

She pointed around the curve of the statue, toward one of the streets that led off the interlink. I craned my neck, and saw the nose of a flatbed carrier inching into the crowd. The noise seemed to increase even more, and I reached to turn my ear down. The absence of input was a relief; the faces around me reddened, mouths opening and closing, and beyond a gang of line-workers a Boatman-coolie woman raised both hands over her head to begin a rhythmic chant, the open hands of sorrow changing to Hati's heart sign. Of all the coolies, Hati probably spoke most to the Boatmen—Hesui Sha, the stick-bass player, was a one-gen Boatman, a child immigrant, actually, and neither he nor the band had ever let him be treated as second-class. Timin was a Boatman, too, which was one of the reasons he had loved Hati. Around her, other people picked up that chant, so that hands rose and fell, catching the sunlight like birds' wings. The carrier poked farther into the interlink, and the crowd moved for it, flowing out of its way to let it inch toward Short-hi. I could see it better now, an ordinary flatbed draped in plain white for the occasion, the black-lacquered coffin balanced on the open back. Alva Gabriel, her bleached gold mane unmistakable even at this distance, stood at one end, and Hesui Sha crouched beside her, steadying her and it against the irregular motion. Even as I watched, the rhythm player Mays Littlekin pulled himself up beside them; only Ajani Maxx was missing, and even as I wondered where she was I thought I saw her in the crowd beside the carrier. It was hard to believe that Micki Tantai's body was really in there, that this wasn't a scene from a videomanga, or an artsy performance clip.

The carrier turned onto the ramp that led down to Short-hi, and the front of the crowd moved after it, the rest of us following in jerky stages. The stairs were too crowded; we climbed down over the retaining wall along with a hundred other people, and I saw a driver caught in the overflow shake his fist and swear, his face contorted and angry. I swore back at him, and a short, stocky man in a Hati shirt slammed his fist down on the runabout's hood. A woman kicked the tread-carriers, and then people came between us, blocking my view.

Tai touched my shoulder. *That idiot.*

What the hell was he thinking, taking Short-hi today? I asked, but Tai didn't answer. Her head turned, and I realized we'd lost touch with the others.

This way, she said, and I grabbed her sleeve, let her tow me through the crowd.

It was thinning out anyway as the carrier settled to a comfortable walking pace, and we caught up with Jaantje and Timin without having to step outside the lane that had been blocked off for us. Shadha was walking a little ahead of them, keeping time to some music I didn't hear, but she turned back to wave us on, her mouth moving. Like most midworlders, she doesn't sign; she knows the lyrics of our songs, and not much more. Beyond her another holoprojector was playing one of Hati's older clips, the image nearly transparent even at what had to be full power. Tantai's shape seemed to waver into existence as it was shadowed by a passerby, and then faded again as full light hit it. I could see people mouthing the lyrics, and then by a trick of shadows the picture came clear just long enough for me to see the signing hands: famous signs, *another piece of the grave,* and for an instant I imagined I could feel the heavy bass that carried them. More crackers flashed ahead of us, and the sharp scent of the burnt powder momentarily drowned the smell of sweat and beer. The gutters between the lanes were already choked with shreds of black paper, mixing with the sand that blew in through the doorlock at Senlui.

Then, ahead of us, at the head of the procession, light flashed, bigger than any cracker, and a hot wind slapped my face. It smelled of fire, of gunpowder and more, scorched metal and cooking, and next to me I saw a midworld woman's eyes and mouth open wide in a soundless scream. For a second, I couldn't understand what I'd seen, couldn't make sense of it—an accident, something gone wrong with the power plant? An effect, even, the protest Fortune had been talking about? Smoke was billowing from the carrier, where the coffin had been, where Gabriel and Sha and Littlekin had been standing, and I swallowed bile. It was real, no effect, at the unlikely best an accident, and at worst—The people ahead of me surged backward, and a stranger caught at my shoulder. I fended him off, not wanting to think, to know, and someone else hit me, shoving me out of the way. I grabbed Jaantje's sleeve, not wanted to be separated from the rest of them. I could see Timin beside him, saying something I couldn't read, but Shadha was gone, disappeared behind the wall of moving bodies. Overhead, in the apex of the tunnel, the fire-lights were flashing orange, and then the nozzles that hung beside them opened, spraying thick cold foam down on us. I ducked, hands over my face, and a glob of the stuff slid down my back beneath my shirt. It smelled thick and sour, an ugly smell I could almost taste, like a tang of copper at the back of my throat. I reached for my ear, fumbled with the switch, and heard nothing but a jumble of screams and shouting.

"—fucking bomb!" Timin yelled, and someone grabbed my arm again. I caught Tai before she fell, and pulled her close as a man shoved past us, punching at anything in his way. His clothes—ordinary work clothes, coolie shirt and workcloth trousers—were stained, his shirt torn open, and his face was smudged with soot. The nozzles were still spurting foam, and in the distance I could hear the shrill wail of sirens.

"We've got to get out of her," Tai said, and repeated it in sign.

"People are hurt—" Timin began, and Jaantje cut him off. "Where's Shadha?"

I don't see her— I began, and switched to speech. "Shadha!"

"We've got to get out of here," Tai said again. "Now, people."

"Shadha?" Jaantje called.

People were still shoving past us, more of them now, fighting to get out of the falling foam, struggling back toward the interlink plaza and Tin Hau Upper. An older man, grey-haired and thin, went keening past, staggering not just with age, almost knocking me over. There was blood on his shirt and in his straggling beard. I knew I should do something, help him, maybe, but I didn't know how, and before I could even reach out the crowd had swallowed him. Another man, a young, dark-skinned coolie in a blockprinted Hati shirt, slipped in the foam and fell to his knees. Timin caught his flailing hand, dragged him sliding in the foam out from under the feet of the people behind him. He fetched up against my knees, and I saw he was bleeding from a long cut that ran across his chest, ripping through the band's faces. His nose was bleeding, too, and I reached stupidly for something to wipe the blood away, but he scrambled to his feet and was gone.

'Shadha!" Jaantje shouted again.

And then there she was, staggering out of the crowd, her eyes wide and staring. She didn't look hurt, and there were no scorch marks on her clothes, but a handful of her oiled braids were undone, their beads and charms missing, as though someone had grabbed them, falling, and torn them free. Jaantje caught her, pulled her tight against him, and Tai said, "Come on!"

I looked past her, saw what must have been a hundred people charging at us, heading for Tin Hau Upper. They all had the same look as Shadha, as the guy with the bloody nose, desperate to get away. It had been maybe two minutes, maybe less, since the bomb—was it a bomb? Timin had said it was a bomb?—had gone off on the carrier, and the sirens still sounded a long way off. Smoke was still rising, though I couldn't see flames, and a steady drizzle of foam wept from the tunnel ceiling. The Security floater I'd seen earlier was nowhere in sight now.

"If we get separated, meet at the *goddow*," I said, and grabbed Jaantje's sleeve. He swung Shadha around, protecting her with his body, and Tai reached for Timin, but the crowd was on us before she could hold him. It was either run with them or fall and be trampled. I tried to stay with the others, then just with Jaantje—the tallest of us, easiest to see— but the ground was slick with the suppressant foam, and it was all I could do just to stay on my feet. A woman caught me, held me up with main force when I tripped on the stairs up out of the trafficway, but I barely got a look at her smoke-singed face before she was swept away again. I looked back once from the plaza to see people scrabbling at the wall, trying to pull themselves out of Short-hi, and more spilling out into the traffic lanes, where the runabouts and haulers shrieked to a stop, rocking on their tires as bodies cannoned into them, but then I had to give all my attention to staying on my feet.

Security or Transit had locked the doors to the Tin Hau Upper Station, automatic answer to a crowd out of control; I saw people flattened against the armorglass, smashed there by the people behind them who didn't know or care that the doors were sealed. A man crouched in the lee of one of the concrete pillboxes that protected the ventilator controls for Shaft Four, wrapping his body around a screaming toddler. Beyond him, a thin coolie girl clung for a moment to the base of the statue, her long hair dark against the gold-washed metal, and then someone dragged her away. I fought to stay upright, to stay well away from the station, and by some miracle managed to pass between it and the trafficway. Past the station, I got into a side street, praying it wasn't a cul-de-sac where I'd be trapped, and finally managed to get free of the crowd. Underfoot, the paving was dry—the fire foam had been pretty localized, just on Short-hi—but there was still smoke in the air, and a window opened above one of the red-painted doorways. A woman leaned out, the bright orange and purple and steel blue print of her jacket a violent contrast to the pale stone and her white hair, and called something down to me. I saw her lips move, but couldn't read them, and my ear didn't seem to be working. I pressed the reset switch, got nothing, and signed in answer.

Sorry, bi', I can't hear you.

She switched to sign with the ease of a one-gen coolie. *What's wrong? Is there a fire?*

I don't know, I answered. *At the funeral—there was a bomb, I think—*

That funeral, she said. *Damn Hati.* She slammed the window down again, and left me standing in the middle of the street.

I'm still not quite sure how I got home again. I walked for a long time, following Broad-hi, very aware that I was West-of-Four, a yanqui alone without a working ear. The electrobus line to Tin Hau was closed, red shutdown glyphs glowing from every display screen; the doors of the local lift at Western Phoenix were barred and a Security floater was grounded in the center of the plaza, lights flaring. Armored Security was everywhere, Cartel and FPG mixed, and the few locals still on the streets were clustered in the doorways, watching them and me and the other stragglers who'd gotten this far with the same wary fear. At the intersection of Ginniver and the Milagro, I caught a glimpse of myself in the darkened door of an exchange shop, closed against the same trouble I was running from. My shirt was stained green from the chemicals, my hair was plastered to my skull, and there were more streaks of green on my face and hands. Someone, sometime in it all, had torn my trousers, and my hip pocket hung by a thread. I touched my belt, feeling for my wallet, but it was gone, too, and with it had gone my cash cards, my keys, and all my ID.

That was the final straw, somehow, and I sat down abruptly on the exchange shop's doorstep and leaned my forehead on my knees, not caring if Security came to move me along. It wasn't so much that I had to make any decision; I knew what I had to do, which was get back to the *goddow* and find the rest of the band, but for some reason I couldn't seem to move. Finally, though, the smell of the foam got to be too much, making my eyes water and sting, and I sat up, wincing, to strip off my shirt. That was a little better—and, perversely, I looked a little more respectable without it, despite the ripped trousers—and I looked around at the street signs. I wasn't that far from the Miracles Interchange; I could get down to Broad-hi from there, and either walk or take a 'bus home if they were running again. There was a public bath across the street, mobile glyphs flashing *wash* and *cheap* above a realprint banner that proclaimed "the best recycled water in Milagro," but I no longer had the cash even if it had been open. I pushed myself to my feet—every muscle in my body hurt, and I felt like crying—and hobbled down the road toward Miracles. My ear was working, or maybe I was just able to sort out the signals again, but the shop windows were all dark here, and the newswalls had fallen silent.

Miracles looked closed, too—I found out later that Security had closed off all the interchanges in Heaven, on the off chance that whoever had planted the bomb had been dumb enough to stick around for the explosion—but as I got closer I could see that the doors were open and Security had set up a checkpoint inside the lobby. I didn't know if it would do me any good, since without my ID I had no way of proving that I lived in Ironyards, but I couldn't think of anything better to do, and took my place in line behind a stocky, unhappy-looking man in a red-and-black *sarang*. I couldn't help wondering about him, especially when he wouldn't meet my eye, but Security passed him through without hesitation. They took my name and codes because I was technically a witness—though neither I nor they thought I'd be much use as one—and then bounced me from officer to officer until finally a plump coolie girl, an intern, I think, said she'd seen Fire/Work play and would swear I was who I said I was. They verified my residence from that, and finally let me through.

It took me about an hour after that to get home—the 'buses still weren't running—but when I knocked at the main gate Jaantje was waiting in the courtyard. If anyone was going to make it out of something like that, it was Jaantje, but I grabbed him, or maybe he grabbed me, and we stood there clutching each other's elbows. His fingers dug painfully into a bruise, but I really didn't care.

"Oh, man," he said. "Oh, man. I thought I was the only one."

"You're all right?" I asked, and then what he'd said really hit me. "You're the only one?"

Jaantje nodded, stepped back to let me into the courtyard. The sunlight was still hot on the dirt, and our door was open, the media wall flickering in the shadows. "It's just you and me, so far."

"When—how did you get back?" I asked. "I had a hell of a time getting through the checkpoints—I lost my ID and everything."

"I walked down to the main level at Western Phoenix,"

Jaantje said. "The 'buses were running from there. I've been back about half an hour. Maybe forty minutes."

That would not have been fun, sitting here by himself thinking that maybe some of us were hurt, dead even, and I shivered. "What're the newsdogs saying?"

He looked at me, and I could see what he'd look like when he was an old man, his skin waxy, the fine crisscross lines from the summers on the surface assembly lines suddenly starkly visible. "It's bad, Fan."

I hadn't expected it to be good, but I shivered again anyway, in spite of the sun.

"And," Jaantje said, suddenly practical, shaking away the horrors, "they were saying the foam's not good for people, so you should get it off you."

I looked down at the green streaking my hands and arms. "If it's not good for people, why do they use it?" I asked, but started toward the door anyway. I could feel the cooler air spilling from it, and realized that Jaantje had the ventilators turned to full cold.

"Because most people can take a bath, can't they," he answered, and reached for the room remote, unmuting the media wall. The babble of voices made a static in my ear, the displays split among half a dozen channels. Jaantje grimaced, and touched the controls again, cycling among the voices. It was still hard to hear, hard to pick out the words without the help of the Sign Font mobiles at the bottom of each screen, and I looked at Jaantje.

"So what exactly happened?"

He shrugged one shoulder, his eyes fixed on the screens. "It looks like it was a bomb, planted in the coffin. They're not saying anybody's dead . . ."

His voice trailed off, but neither one of us needed to speak the thought aloud. Gabriel and Sha and Littlekin had been standing on the carrier, the last I saw, right next to the coffin. Just from what I'd seen, I couldn't imagine they could have survived. "Maybe they weren't on the back, I hadn't seen them for a while."

"Maybe," Jaantje agreed, but didn't sound convinced. "Ah, here's the one I saw before."

He touched the remote's buttons, and four of the screens merged, centered on a midworld woman in the severe white cotton of the Medical Services. "—fire suppressant foam can be a topical irritant and should be flushed from the skin as soon as possible after contact. Plain pipe water will do; do not use soap until skin and hair have been thoroughly rinsed. If you experience chest pain, dizziness, or blurred vision, contact your local MedServe clinic or personal physician at once. If you experience skin irritation, shortness of breath, or hives, contact your local MedServe clinic or your personal physician."

She vanished, replaced by a newsreader I didn't recognize, and Jaantje worked the remote again, splitting the screen back into four channels. "I saw that when I got in, and I felt a lot better once I got it off me."

I nodded, knowing he was right, and went on into the bathroom. The indicator on the wall by the shower controls glowed green: we still had nearly half a tank of hot water. I stood for a long time under the warm spray; the foam softened, turned thin and greasy-slick, and finally washed away. I washed my hair, too, then shut down the system, wrapped myself in the too-short yukata hanging on the wall—Tai's, not mine, which made me worry all over again—just in case someone else had gotten back, and went into my bedroom to get dressed. The clothes I'd been wearing were a mess, the shirt beyond salvage. I'd bought it at a Summering right before the Manfred Riots, when Hati was topping the bill; I'd been part of Fire/Work for three months, and we thought we were hot because we could cover "Annoki"—I'd even bought a clip of the same vidi source Ajani Maxx had used for the fx part, and learned to make it dance. I left it hanging on my chair and went back into the main room.

Jaantje was standing where I'd left him, frowning at the media wall, arms folded tight across his chest so that he was working the remote from the crook of his elbow.

"Anything new?" I asked, and he shook his head.

"Cartel Security is saying seventeen dead, but the FPG won't confirm it. Nothing on Hati."

In the screen, six different faces spoke against a background of the Han-Lu Station, red-and-blue lights from Security and Fire floaters sliding across the blank doors. The armorglass had held even against the pressure of all the bodies; if there had been bodies, they'd been taken away, and the paving was blank and empty.

"They ought to be here by now," I said, and Jaantje glared at me.

"All the interchanges are closed—the 'bus lines, too. You said you had trouble, getting down here."

"Or maybe they didn't hear me," I said. "Shadha might have gone back to her place; Timi, too. Have you called there?"

"I didn't want to worry Timi's folks."

I nodded—Timi's parents were as desperately ambitious as any other Boatman coolies, here on Persephone where they actually could get somewhere, and they wanted Timi to be a line foreman like his older brother, not a starving musician—and said, "Haya, what about Shadha?"

"Haya." Jaantje took a deep breath, and pressed buttons on the remote. The Persephonet screen appeared, and he flashed it Shadha's codes. There was a pause—longer than usual, no surprise, the lines were bound to be overloaded—and for a second I thought we'd get a bounce-back. But then the screen cleared, and Shadha's house screen appeared. I knew she lived in a Dreampeace cooperative, but it was still a shock to see the image spring out on the black screen: Dreampeace's anatomized man, half-human, half an antique computer chip, still standing in its circle, but now with its hands covering its eyes in stylized grief. Beneath it was a string of glyphs and a realprint banner: DREAMPEACE ABHORS THE DEATH OF HATI.

"What's it say?" Jaantje asked.

"The same as the glyphs, this time," I answered. Dreampeace was notorious for failing to match sign and word. "Why aren't they answering?"

Jaantje shook his head. "I don't know—"

The picture dissolved as he spoke, was replaced by a dark face. "Shadha—?"

She broke off, seeing us, and Jaantje said, "We're trying to find her. She isn't there?"

The dark woman shook her head, setting her earrings dancing. "You're in her band, right?"

I nodded.

"She said she was going to the funeral with you," the woman said. "Isn't—didn't she stay with you?"

Jaantje's mouth thinned. "We got separated—it was a bad time up there. I—we—thought she might have gone home."

"Better if she'd stayed home," the woman said, bitterly. "No, she's not here."

"We'll call if she comes here," I said, but she'd already cut the connection.

"Bitch," Jaantje said, to the static-filled screen, and put Persephonet on hold to look at me. "You still want to call Timin's folks? Or Tai's mother?"

"Not really," I said. "But I think we'd better."

Jaantje held out the remote. "Go ahead."

In the end, it wasn't as bad as I'd thought. Timin's uncle, who answered the call at the family *compang,* said Timi hadn't been home, but on the whole took the news as calmly as anyone could. He had been working on the surface lines south of Sinliu, and had seen the smoke rising out of the ventilators; I think it wasn't as bad as he'd thought, except for Timin. Tai's mother, Li Mahal, was harder to find—she was one of the electors for the Committee for Immigrants from the Western Provinces who managed the Unbroken Prosperity metroform—but once the last of the string of volunteer secretaries tracked her down she was quick to answer. She took it pretty well, too, just took a deep breath, answered my question, and began making her own plans to call hospitals and call in favors if necessary. She was a small woman, and still very pretty—much prettier than Tai, who was tall and rangy apparently like the father she'd never met—and I knew from Tai's stories that she was as tough as the Whitesands Desert. She quizzed me about where we'd been relative to the bomb, how we'd gotten separated, how long it had taken me and Jaantje to get home and by what roads, then dismissed us, saying that she'd let us know if she found out anything. I switched off Persephonet, feeling obscurely a little better, and looked at Jaantje.

"Should we be calling the hospitals, too, I wonder?"

He shook his head. "They're going to be swamped, and they'll only be talking to relatives. Let Li Mahal call them."

That made sense, and I stared at the flashing screens. One of the images caught me eye, a long shot, from somewhere high, of the funeral procession as it wound toward Sinliu. I hadn't realized how big the crowd had been, and touched keys to bring the picture onto a bigger screen.

"—newsvideo taken from the outer balcony of Han-Lu Upper Station," the newsreader's voice said, and then fell silent, leaving the distant crowd noise the only sound. The river of people spilled out of the plaza, out of the lane of the Short-hi that had been blocked off for them; I could only just see the carrier, tiny at the head of the flood. I could almost make out the coffin, the people beside it, but then the carrier exploded in a ball of flame and smoke. The fire nozzles came on almost at once, the falling foam cutting off the camera's view, but there was no mistaking the explosion for anything but what it was. Someone had planted a bomb on the carrier.

"Elvis Christ," I said.

"Who the fuck would do that?" Jaantje demanded. "Realpeace—they'd have to be crazy to do something like that."

I thought they were just that crazy, myself, but I'm not a coolie, and there are things I can't say even to the rest of the band. I took a breath, groping for safe words, and over the voice of the newsreader explaining what we'd seen we heard a chime as the courtyard door opened. Jaantje beat me to the door by half a step, and we shoved out together into the courtyard to see Shadha coming in the main door. She looked better than I'd expected, cleaner, her hair rebraided when I'd seen it down, and Jaantje said, "Where the hell have you been?"

She looked at him, and we both saw the shock in her eyes, the glaze of fear and grief not yet erased. "Christ, Shadha," I said, and she let me hold her. An instant later, Jaantje wrapped his arms around us both.

"We were worried," he said, his voice muffled between our heads.

Shadha gave a strangled laugh. "I stopped at a bath, I couldn't stand the way the foam felt." She took a deep breath, her ribs straining against my arm. "I'm all right, honest, it's just . . . Where's Timi and Tai?"

"They're not back yet," Jaantje answered.

"Shit." Shadha pulled away from us. "What are the newschannels saying?"

"Somebody put a bomb on the carrier," I said. "Somebody got a clip of the explosion from the top of Han-Lu Upper Station. And the Cartel cops are saying seventeen dead, but the FPG won't confirm it."

"They wouldn't," Shadha muttered, and shook her head. "There's going to be more dead than that. God, why did they close the doors at Han-Lu?"

"Standard procedure when a coolie crowd goes amok," Jaantje answered, and gave a bitter grin. "They're after property, got to keep them out of the midworld."

"They were on my left," I said, slowly. "The station side."

"I think I was closer to the station than them," Jaantje said, but he didn't sound as convinced as I had hoped he would.

"I know I was," Shadha said, and turned her hands out, showing the palms skinned and red. She wouldn't be drumming for a day or two, and I winced in sympathy. "I got that pulling myself over one of those damn ventilator boxes."

"Too close," Jaantje said, and Shadha nodded.

"Too fucking close."

I looked back at the media wall, but didn't see anything new, just the same paired images, Han-Lu now and Han-Lu jammed with people just before the explosion. Everyone seemed to be showing that clip now, and I looked away, not wanting to see it again.

"Do you think they're all right?" Shadha asked, and Jaan-tje shrugged.

"It's too soon to tell."

Then, inside, the Persephonet unit sounded. I was closest, got through the door first and slapped the response button before the preset routine could take over. The screen lit and windowed, and I saw Tai's familiar face. She looked like hell—a black eye, but more than that the same awful blank look that I'd seen on Shadha's face—but she was unmistakably alive.

"Thanks be," I heard Shadha say behind me, and Jaantje gave a wordless yelp of joy.

"You're all right," I said, and Tai managed a thin, tired smile.

"Yeh, I'm all right."

"Where are you?" I asked. "Is Timi with you?"

She nodded, and it was as though someone had rolled a stone off me; I took a deep breath, and Jaantje repeated, "So where are you?"

"Western Phoenix, the main public clinic," Tai answered. "Don't worry, we're both all right, but Timi's got a broken foot. We had to wait forever before they could see him, there were so many people hurt, and some of them really bad"— she shuddered, shook away memory—"but they're finishing up with him now. The doctor said we could leave once he fits the cast. I'm going to take him back to his place, then I'm coming home."

"Thank God," I said again. "How are you?"

"Sore." Tai glanced over her shoulder. "Look, I've got to go—there's only one console for this whole ward, and there's people waiting for it. Will you call my mother, let her know I'm all right?"

I nodded. "I'll take care of it."

"Thanks," she said, and the picture winked out.

There wasn't much we could do after that. I called Li Mahal, who took the good news pretty much the same as she'd taken the bad, and then Timin's family, who were loudly relieved and furious all at once. Tai got back to the *goddow* a little after the end of the day shift. She'd left Timi at his place, well and truly zoned on the painkillers—and well and truly fussed over by mother, aunt, and sisters—but she said he'd roused himself enough to say he'd be over tomorrow.

"Which I doubt," Tai said, "given how sore he was, but he'll probably try it. Gods above, couldn't they let Micki Tantai rest in peace?"

I gave her a startled look—I hadn't thought of it that way, for some reason, no credit to me—and her lips curved into the kind of smile you give when you're trying to keep from crying.

"Didn't you hear? The bomb was in the coffin."

"Fucking bastards," Jaantje said. "Fucking, fucking bastards."

"And there's still no word on any of the rest of Hati," Shadha said, from her place by the media wall.

"They're dead," Tai said, and her voice cracked on the word. "They're going to be dead."

▪ 4 ▪

Reverdy Jian

THE NEWSBAR NEXT door was in full swing, voices blaring from the multiple screens—*one hundred screens,* the virtual banners over the door boasted, reinforced by painted fabric almost as bright, *full access, all channels!* Jian shifted in her seat, trying to find a position in which she was not accessing the bar's tightbeam transmitters, but the lattice panels that defined the bar's frontage seemed to be interlaced with them, and the glyphs filled her vision no matter where she looked. She sighed, reaching for the disk that controlled her suit, pressed until it hardened and kept holding it until the images brightened and then waned to an acceptable level. She could still see the glyphs from two of the screens, one repeating the names of the dead from the funeral fiasco, the other translating Realpeace's official statement. Behind that one, the faces of the three speakers—two men and a woman, all coolies—were very sober, as befitted their mourning white. She didn't need to read the glyphs to know what they were saying: the newschannels had been filled with nothing else for the last thirty hours. She'd even learned the names of Hati's dead—Tantai, of course, and Alva Gabriel and Hesui Sha; the other two, Maxx and Littlekin, weren't dead yet, but weren't really expected to survive—and she looked down at the menu to break that train of thought. The last thing she needed right now was to be distracted by politics.

The order glyph was flashing insistently beneath the table-top, and a new set of glyphs had appeared beneath the menu, warning that these tables were for customers only. For a minute, she considered ignoring it, but suppressed that thought and selected tea and a plate of griddle bread from the cheaper half of the menu. That would last her a while, at least until Red got there with his friend. She felt a stab of guilt—Vaughn was not happy with her, and not happy with Red, either—and shifted her feet so that she could feel the shape of the headbox through the carryall's thin sides. Vaughn wasn't happy, but neither was she, and she wouldn't be happy—wouldn't be able to work comfortably—until she'd gotten rid of this construct. But he had called her the night before, and she knew him well enough to know what that had cost. He had been calling from the flat he and Red shared up in the Larrkin Rooks, barely a level below Heaven; she had seen the empty bed and the loft posts behind him, but there had been no sign of the technician.

"I need to ask you something, Reverdy," he had said, and she had tried to stop him.

"If it's about the construct, Imre, I need to do this."

"Fine." Vaughn had scowled at the screen, and she hadn't been sure if she'd seen the ghost of a bruise on his wrist as he reached across the camera eye to retrieve a mug from the kitchen ledge. "But don't get Red involved in it. It's important, Reverdy."

"Red has contacts," Jian had answered. "I don't—he's a technician, for God's sake. He can get a hell of a better price than I can."

"Red gets a good price because he knows a lot of people he shouldn't," Vaughn had said. "And all of them want favors returned."

"So? That's the way things work, Imre." The minute she'd said it, she'd regretted it, hearing her own anxiety in her voice, and she hadn't been surprised to see Vaughn's expression freeze.

"Doing favors is how Red ended up in Whitesands, and doing more favors is why he never got time off for good behavior."

Jian had paused, not knowing what to say. "I didn't know," she'd said at last, and Vaughn made a face.

"That's why he can't get better than tech-2 papers," Vaughn said. "You get busted for hard-hacking, they permanently restrict your license."

"I need his help," she had said again, and Vaughn's scowl had deepened.

"You're being crazy about this construct thing, Reverdy."

"Well, who'd know better than you?" she had answered, and shut down the connection before he could ask her again not to involve Red.

The memory still made her flinch a little—she had known Red had done time in Whitesands, had never asked why because she thought she had known—and she stared out across the bright tiles of the Dagon Arcade. Hard-hacking was illegal; it was also usually a yanqui game, and she'd never known just what Red was. There was a bodyshop directly opposite the cookshop—*sorry, restaurant*, she added, with an inward grin; the prices were too high to call this place anything else—and a hologram image posed in its window, a lanky, androgynous body dressed in nothing but bodypaint and a solid crotchpiece, both black swirled with a galaxy of painted stars. Chaandi had originated that design, had made it fashionable in one of her videomanga; it was interesting to see it copied here on Zodiac Main.

A movement to her right caught her attention, made her look toward the Arcade entrance, where the discreet security bars fuzzed her view of the Zodiac itself. Red came through the bars, his hair momentarily vivid in the spotlights that defined the archway. He paused for an instant, thin and elegant against the curtain of light, and then he saw her and came toward her, long legs covering the ground with deceptive speed. He was alone, Jian realized, and her attention sharpened.

"Hey, Red," she said. "I thought you were bringing a friend."

He pulled out a chair and sat opposite her, his head tipped forward a little, as always, so that his hair fell forward to obscure his face. "A change of plans."

His voice was soft, but still clear above the constant seashell murmur of the Arcade. Jian looked warily at him, wondering if that was a new bruise along his jawline. "Problems?"

Red shook his head, but his eyes cut sideways in the same instant, and Jian leaned back to see the server approaching, the plate of griddle bread and the carafe of tea balanced on her tray. "Oh, damn," she said, and the server—a coolie girl, plump and dark—looked startled. "No, sorry, not you, but can you package that? My friend here tells me we won't be eating after all."

"Haya," the server said, her voice almost as soft as Red's, and vanished again.

Jian looked at Red. "What do you mean, then, a change in plans?"

She saw his shoulders move, either a sigh or a shrug. "The guy I know, he changed his mind. Said to meet us at the Copper—the Copper Market, up in Madelen-Fet."

That figured—Madelen-Fet was notoriously a hardhacker's paradise—but Jian waited anyway.

"Place called Motosha," Red finished, after a moment.

"Haya," Jian said. The server appeared again, the griddle bread neatly wrapped, the tea decanted into a paper package, and Jian took them from her, handed over a pair of cash cards in return. The girl processed them quickly, returned one, its color faded, and Jian looked back at Red. "Right. Madelen-Fet it is."

They took the long way to Madelen-Fet, up Shaft Two to the Norway and the electrobus line that paralleled it, skirting the coolie neighborhoods in Gamela and the Prosperities without thought or comment. At Madhuban Main, they transferred to a local lift, and stood waiting in the glass-walled lobby for what seemed like a long time. Jian stared out past the barriers and the ticket kiosks—and the ubiquitous bank of Persephonet consoles—her attention caught in spite of herself by the brilliant advertising that filled the plaza. The air seemed to pulse with color, glyphs and banner-notes sparking from every surface, obscuring the people clustered around the shop displays. The broadbeam transmissions were restricted in the midworld plazas as a nuisance, and unusual even in the eastern part of the upperworld; she'd seen them only once before, in the Paderzhan Market in Charretse, where the sand-divers and the truckers sold their spare gear. She looked back at the lift doors, reaching for her suit controls to mute the display, and Red touched her arm, nodded toward the notice board: the lift was arriving, its signal drowned in the chaos from the plaza. Jian shook her head, and filed into the car behind a pair of giggling adolescents in wide-sleeved sand coats.

The Copper Market was more crowded than Madhuban Main, but its transmitters were all narrowbeam, and Jian allowed herself a sigh of relief as she pushed through the barrier into the market itself. Two long arcades ran the length of the space, but the original shops had been broken up into smaller *dukkeri,* and goods spilled out from their doors to collect in piles around the support pillars, extolled and guarded by sharp-eyed, sharp-voiced hawkers. Most of them were wearing *sarangs*, the patterns vivid against the pale stone, and Jian felt her attention sharpen. This was very much a coolie place, the air filled with their tonal dialect and the rise and fall of signing hands, but then she looked again, and saw yanqui clothes, yanqui faces, and sober midworld coats scattered through the crowd. A yanqui coffee-man shared a power point with a coolie fry-pot vendor, and the woman selling videomanga and band clips—*probably pirated*, Jian added silently, *and just as probably authorized pirates*—to the cluster of coolie girls in school uniforms was obviously a midworlder. That was good to see—*these days, it paid to be careful, coming into Heaven, to avoid the strictly coolie neighborhoods*—and she relaxed a little, scanning the crowd not for trouble but for the input from the narrowbeam transmitters scattered along the arcade.

Red touched her shoulder again. "This way."

He nodded to the building at the end of the Market. It looked like a converted warehouse, Jian thought, or maybe light assembly, but the upper windows had been carefully bricked in, and only a single realprint word painted on the keystone identified the shop. Jian lifted an eyebrow at that: if Motosha really was the supplier for serious hard-hackers, she wouldn't have expected it to advertise the fact so blatantly.

As she passed through the open arch of the doorway, however, she felt the sting of a tightbeam transmission, a standard ID query that her suit answered before she could decide whether or not to squelch the output. *Typical hard-hacker arrogance*, she thought, and looked around for the source. Sure enough, a flat black box the size of her hand was set into the top of the arch—*and it's interesting*, she added silently, *that they don't bother hiding it. Or is that the message?* Certainly the space was empty, without the casual browsers or the thrill-seeking adolescents she'd seen in similar places in the midworld, except for the silent machines. Maybe a dozen large pieces stood on their own display pallets in the center of the room—she recognized one as a pump assembly for a standard life-support system—and still more smaller items, some obviously only parts, some apparently complete but unidentifiable, hung from the side walls and filled the low shelves beside the service counter. In front of it, a brightly polished machine stood motionless, the flags at the top of its central pyramid drooping lifelessly. It was obviously supposed to do something, Jian knew, but she couldn't begin to guess what. She looked curiously at it anyway—there was a little car as well, that ran on tracks around the base of the pyramid, and something that looked like an arm protruding from the pyramid's tip—and then followed Red toward the counter. She felt an invisible thread part as she passed a hidden sensor— the suit translating the signal pulse as the flick of thread against her skin—and was not surprised when a door opened in the back wall.

"Yeh, can I help you?" The speaker was a tall, skinny yanqui, his sandstone-colored hair drawn back into an untidy queue. He stopped abruptly, seeing Red, the display glasses sliding down his nose, a startled look on his face, but before he could say anything more, the door opened again.

"Haya, Fanning, I'll take this one." She was a yanqui, too, older and thicker-bodied, her hands and arms covered with blue-and-gold bodypaint like gloves.

The younger yanqui hesitated, his eyes, still on Red, but then seemed to come to himself, and stepped back toward the door. "Haya," he said, drawing the word out, and let the door close slowly behind him.

The woman looked at Red. "Is she with you?"

Red nodded, and the woman showed teeth in the beginning of a smile.

"Newcat's out back, then. You know the way."

"Yes," Red said, without inflection, and lifted a section of counter. Jian saw the woman's fingers move, working a hidden remote, and a second door popped free of the wall, its outline hidden by the pattern carved into the whitewash. She followed Red through it and into a narrow hall lit only by yellow emergency lights, and couldn't help flinching a little when the door flipped shut again behind them.

"That guy," she said, more to hear her own voice than because she really cared. "You know him?"

For a minute, she thought the technician wasn't going to answer, but then his eyes slid sideways. "No. Not anymore."

She blinked at that—Red's former friends were sometimes much more interesting, and dangerous, than his present ones—but before she could say anything else, a second door popped open, spilling a brighter light into the corridor. This was altogether too much like the way she'd acquired Manfred, five years back, and she took a deep breath, swallowing unexpected bile. The construct in her carryall was too much like it anyway; this added echo was nothing she needed.

She shook herself, made herself follow Red into the fan of clear light, and couldn't help wrinkling her nose as the smell hit her. It wasn't exactly unpleasant, a strange, musky scent, and then she spotted the incense burner sitting on the top of what looked like an old Kagami DETAC console. A stocky man, his cheeks scarred where neither his beard nor goggles had protected him from blowing sand, rose from his seat on a dented mobilator pod.

"Hey, Red. What you got for me?"

Red tipped his head sideways, his hair shifting color slightly under the lights. "She has it."

"And who's she when she's at home?" The stocky man didn't look at her, but Jian knew better than to let herself be annoyed.

"Reverdy Jian," Red said, his voice still without inflection. "I work with her."

The stocky man made a soft hissing sound between his teeth, dark eyes darting over her. "My apologies, bi' Jian. I'm Newcat Garay." He held out his hand, yanqui style, and Jian took it warily, matching his grip.

"Ba' Garay."

"I understand you have a construct to sell," Garay said, and settled himself again on the mobilator pod. The dents fit his buttocks perfectly, Jian saw.

"Or to trade," she answered, and swung the carryall forward on her hip. Garay reached sideways and pulled a flimsy-looking table out from between a pair of mobile arms.

"Let's have a look."

Jian touched the thumblock, releasing the lid, and set the carryall on the table, sliding the fabric down to reveal the headbox. Garay hummed to himself, reaching into his pocket for a cable, and plugged it into the test port on the side of the box. The other end, Jian saw without surprise, was already plugged into an interface box slung from his shoulder. The box in turn would be connected to his skinsuit either through a beamlink or, more likely, through a hardlink somewhere on his body: only the most serious hard-hackers could afford that level of connection.

Garay blinked then, eyes refocusing on the box in front of him, and twitched the cable free of the test port. "So. The SHYmate 294—has it got a name?"

Jian shook her head. She'd stopped naming her constructs two years ago, when she'd realized that the problem wasn't linked to a single system.

"Haya. Hot Blue makes a good Spelvin matrix, and this one's been optimized for FTL management," Garay said. "Why do you want to get rid of it?"

"I don't like it," Jian said, and heard her voice as flat as Red's had been.

Garay smiled. "You're lucky that I do."

Out of the corner of her eye, Jian saw Red lift his head at that, a sudden concentration of attention. "Really," she said, and kept her voice just this side of boredom.

"Yeh. You prefer cash or trade?"

"I want something to replace it," Jian said. "Either way works for me."

"I've got a construct here," Garay said. "Kagami Bettalin, Level Four/Five, fitted for FTL and VWS management."

"I heard the Bettalins were really buggy," Jian said. "I don't need to deal with that."

"All the fixes are already installed," Garay answered, "and it's got a valid service number attached."

"Not hot?" Red murmured, and Garay looked offended.

"Not even lukewarm. I can give you chapter and verse on it."

"I'll take a look at it," Jian said.

"Help yourself," Garay answered, and reached behind the pod to produce a second headbox.

Jian touched the keypad, setting it for tightbeam output, and fixed her eyes on the pinlight transmitter. It lit an instant later, and her vision filled with a cascade of gold and green. She blinked, stabilizing the system, let the glyphs and numbers wash over her, probing for the feel of the machine. Here in the headbox, it was almost impossible to tell what the construct would be like once it was loose in a true VWS network, when the personality matrix could expand and take full play. She took a deep breath, trying to decide if she felt anything more than the play of light and her own uncertainty, but the glyphs were as flat and lifeless as images on a media wall. The SHYmate had been different, she told herself, she had felt it in the headbox, felt what was wrong with it, the weird half presence, like a sleeper, or someone lost in daydreams.

"Haya," she said, slowly, and looked away from the transmitter. "It's all right."

"It's a fair trade," Garay said. "I'll go evens—construct for construct, and you get all my papers."

It was a better offer than she'd been expecting, and for an instant she wondered what she was doing wrong. Jian glanced at Red, expecting him to reject it, saw instead the fractional nod of his head. "Agreed," she said aloud, and slid the SHYmate toward Garay. The feeling of the headbox's warm metal under her fingertips reminded her again of the way the construct had felt around her, creating the world she used to manipulate the hyperdrive—reminded her, too, of Manfred, its deceptive calm—and she shook those memories away. The Bettalin would be different—had to be different; she could not allow it to be anything else.

▪ 5 ▪

Celinde Fortune

I CALLED FANNING the day after the funeral, of course, more than a little afraid of what I'd find, and I had trouble getting the story out of him at first. But he was all right, beyond of course being bruised and frightened, and I left it it that: I was pretty heavily into rehearsal at that point, and with the Empires now closed until the start of the next ten-day week, I could have the stage to myself more or less when I wanted it. My act is a lot more physically challenging than it looks—that's part of why it looks as good as it does—and I prefer to run through it at least three days out of time when I'm not performing. And there are the karakuri to maintain as well, which takes a few hours every third day, so I was scrambling a little to get the act back into shape. Muthana swore the date for reopening was firm, so I had a little less than ten days to get everything perfect again.

My contract guarantees me rehearsal space and time, but not the presence of live crew. By and large, that's not a problem—I like the silence of the empty house, the particular quality of sound when there aren't any bodies to absorb it, and the house systems are supervised by a Spelvin construct called George that's more than competent to run lights and sound and anything else I need. It also means that it's easy to keep the backstage clear—something I insist on, to keep the mechanisms of the various illusions secret, and Terez, who used to be a conjurer herself, backs me up on this—and so I was able to run through the complete show in peace. When I'd finished, I mimed the bows—it's better for the karakuri and Aeris, the Spelvin construct that manages them, to go through the full routine, and maximizes the chance that I'll spot any small problems. The music kept playing as I straightened, the five-bar loop I use to cover the end of the show, and I lifted a hand into the upper layer of the web of virtual light that covered the stage.

"Haya, George, kill the music."

"Thank you." The last word had George's perpetual rising inflection, its words always bitten off too short. Its current fussy voice was copied from a killer construct in one of Suleima Chaandi's best videomanga, the one that had come out a year after the Manfred Riots. Rumor said she'd been involved in that somehow, that she'd even met the renegade construct, the pseudo-AI, and had composed the manga to deal with it; it was still on the racks in every jobshop in Landage, and one of the tech staff had thought it was funny to give George that voice.

The tape ended, and I looked to my left, where the three karakuri stood patiently in line, metal hands still linked, waiting for the next command. Two of them weren't a major part of the final illusion, but I liked to have them take a bow—it tended to disconcert the audience, make them wonder, just a little. All around me, on my skin and under it, I could feel the low-level feedback from Aeris, a fizz more of sensation than of any particular feeling, confirmation that everything was working. The lines of light were solid, placed and interwoven precisely as they should be, so that any gesture could be potent as well as theatrical, but for some reason I wasn't satisfied. My final illusion is a good one, a Vanishing Lady variation, a nice combination of old and new tech, and it had gone perfectly, but I didn't feel quite right about it, or, more precisely, I didn't feel quite right about ending the show there.

"Aeris, stand down," I said, and felt the confirmation pulse through me, a sense of pleasure that faded as instantly as it appeared. The light-web winked out, leaving only the seven major cross lines glowing red—the karakuri take their position cues from those, so they have to remain in place until the machines are put away—and I ducked out of their embrace. "George. Were the house recorders running?"

"Of course." The construct sounded almost affronted: of all

the Spelvin constructs I've worked with, and I've owned five myself, the Tin Hau house system sounds most like a person, probably because its personality matrix has been absorbing actors' inflections for the last ten years.

"Playback Vanishment."

"One moment."

We were under working lights; the direct-line pinpoint that blossomed between the footlights was impossible to miss. I stepped into its transmission line, blocking either Aeris or the karakuri from accidentally picking up the signal, and a fuzzy pale grey rectangle appeared in front of my eyes, surprisingly bright against the darkened auditorium.

"Ready for playback," George said.

"Go ahead."

The grey rectangle vanished, was replaced by an image of the stage. It was shot from the central control box—George's point of view, roughly—and partly corrected to an audience perspective. Some of the angles were a little off, but it was readable. And even without the costumes and the proper lighting, it looked good: I straightened from my bow, gestured to the golden karakuri, the one who looked most like me, and the others backed obediently away into what would be shadow. The golden karakuri came forward, while the bronze and the silver slipped offstage, their departure normally covered by the shadow and the attention I focused on the gold. The silver karakuri returned with a gauzy red yukata, and at my gesture the gold held out its arms, allowed the other to slide the yukata up onto its shoulders. The bronze reentered then, an enormous sheet of scarlet silk draped over its outstretched arms. I took it, flourished it once or twice as the bronze and the silver retreated, and then draped it over the gold. The scarlet silk covered it from head to foot and spilled out over the stage, but you could still see the shape of the karakuri under it. I knelt, gathered the silk in my hand, then flung my arms wide. Silk and karakuri vanished, leaving only a red-laquered cube in their place.

I rose to my feet—the movement seemed slow, but it was timed to match the usual applause—and the other two karakuri came forward, the silver holding out a folded black square. I gestured for them to bring the box and set it down at the edge of the stage, and they took up positions on either side of it. I unfolded the square into a full silk drape and tossed it over all three, so that the drape fell from the karakuris' heads to the stage. I walked around them, displaying them standing there, then yanked away the drape. The gold karakuri stood between the silver and the bronze, fully restored, and we all took three steps forward to begin our bows.

"George, end playback."

"Thank you," the construct answered, precise as ever, and the image winked out as the pinlight behind it vanished. I stooped to pick up the drape from where I'd let it fall behind the karakuri, turning the illusion over in my mind. It was working the way it should, there was no doubt about that—and it still looked good—but, let's face it, I was bored. I'd been ending the act with this illusion for almost a year, though I'd added other illusions in the earlier parts of the act; it was time I considered a new finale. I stood there behind the karakuri, drawing the drape through my fingers to fold it back into a neat package, and stared at the backs of the three karakuri. The houselights gleamed off the metal, three shades, bronze, gold, and silver, three backs carved with the suggestion of human muscles, the trace of a spine and the solid rounds of buttocks. The next one I built would be copper, I decided, the soft pink of new copper or rose-gold.

The three were very similar to look at—humaniform, female, their faces modeled loosely on my own by a hardhacker near Cavemouth, a man named John Desembaa, who did all my heavy manufacturing—except for the gold, which was the center of the Compression illusion as well as Vanishment. Its skin was studded with delicate struts and wires, creating a network raised a hand's-width—9.8 centimeters—above the polished metal, so that when the light hit it right it looked as though it was caught in a metal spiderweb. It was one of the deliberately disconcerting things about that karakuri, which in Compression is crushed in a giant vise and then restored. The web looked at once ethereal and potentially painful, and a lot of the audience doesn't quite know how they want to react. The gold blended smoothly with the bronze and the silver; the rose-copper would have to be chosen carefully, if it wasn't to clash.

For some reason, that thought, and the sight of the motionless karakuri standing hand in hand, sparked an idea, and I stood with the black drape half-folded, trying to capture it whole. The three were already somewhat interchangeable—the illusion called Disassembly relies on that—and the new one would probably be built to the same pattern. But suppose I built another new karakuri, not humaniform but a transformer frame, so that it would first absorb and then unfold each of the other karakuri—better still, it would begin small, and grow as it absorbed the three current karakuri, beginning to take in the next before it had finished the previous one, so that there would be moments when it looked like conjoined twins or triplets. Then it would reverse the process, disgorging not three, but four karakuri from an apparently too-small space.

I pulled the silk back through my fingers, mechanically finishing the job at hand. Yes, the new idea would work—I'd have to be careful to make everything perfect, every movement delicately refined, to keep the beauty in balance with the grotesquerie, but that was a language I knew I could handle. As for the technical problems, well, they'd be considerable, but hardly insoluble. The only problem was, it wasn't really an illusion. Oh, I suppose that producing a fourth karakuri out of a space that should only hold three counted as such, but it wasn't big enough to close the show. And I wanted to end with this image, the metal bodies joining, melding, then flowering into four.

I smiled at that, and could feel the expression twist. Anyone in my family, maybe even Fanning—maybe especially Fanning, we'd never minced words with each other would have something to say about this. I had been born a conjoined twin myself; my twin, the first Celeste, had not survived our division, and the ribs and left arm I had not been born with were hers. The circumstances of my sister's death, and my life, were still a matter of contention in my family— I have not forgiven my parents for giving my second sister Celeste's name—and they were sure to see this as a slap at them. And maybe I should run with that—after all, what did it matter if it was true, as long as it made for a spectacular illusion? I would produce the four karakuri from the transformer, then vanish one—no, I'd vanish myself, and reappear from the transformer-karakuri itself.

The more I thought about it, the better I liked it. Not only would it straddle that fine line between the grotesque and the exquisite, but it would remind people at least obliquely of the potential kinship between man and machine, between innate and artificial intelligence. And right now, with Realpeace calling so stridently for human rights alone, human rights over the machine—and willing to kill for it, I remembered, and shoved the thought away—it would be good to remind people of what could, must, happen if anyone achieved true AI.

I finished folding the silk and automatically checked the karakuri's positions against the marker lights. Nothing had changed, but before I could open my mouth to have Aeris bring them back to their racks, a door opened at the back of the hall, a bright rectangle against the darkness. I frowned— no one is supposed to have access when I'm rehearsing, not without my permission—and overhead George made a noise like throat-clearing.

"Access granted to Binaifer Muthana, as the rehearsal is finished. Thank you."

I sighed, and heard Muthana's voice, his silhouetted stark against the light. "Celinde? Sorry to disturb you."

"You're not," I said. If he had been disturbing me, even his clearance wouldn't have gotten him in without an override. Terez could not officially approve, but she'd never deleted that command.

The door swung closed, its brilliance replaced by the paler light of a handlamp that bobbed closer until I could see Muthana at the foot of the center aisle. I threaded my way through the beams of light and squatted at the edge of the stage.

"Bad news," he said, and I blinked a little at his bluntness. "The Empires are closed for another week."

"You said Security promised we could reopen."

Muthana made a face. "They said they only promised it for the small clubs. The ones, according to them, who are really being hurt."

"What the fuck do they think the Empires live on?" I demanded, and Muthana spread his hands.

"I know. And they're more likely to get trouble from the small clubs, in my opinion, not the Empires, but they just see audience size. And nobody's asking my opinion, anyway."

"Damn it." I swallowed anything else I might have said—there weren't curses really effective enough for the occasion. "So where does that leave us—the nightshow acts?"

"Your contract is clear," Muthana answered. "And so are the other big acts. As for the smaller acts . . ." He paused. "There's no good way to say it. I've spoken to the shareholders, asked them to authorize extracontractual stipends—in the interests of keeping the best acts at Tin Hau—but they're not interested. They did say the other acts are welcome to try the club circuit, though."

"How generous," I said. "Let them find work, if they can, when everyone else who'd played the Empires is doing the same thing, so that the general booking fee goes right down the tubes—how many of the shareholders have a piece of the club action, too, Binnie?"

"That's not fair, Celinde."

"Isn't it?"

Muthana looked away. "I thought you'd appreciate the information."

"You wanted me to do your dirty work, tell Fanning for you."

"No." Muthana looked back at me, and this time I believed him. "But I wanted you to know so that your cousin doesn't think I'm keeping secrets. And so that you don't, either."

I nodded. "Sorry. It's not a good situation, Binnie."

"It's not good for anybody," he answered. "And not just performers."

I had forgotten, until then, that he lived in Western Phoenix, up in Heaven with the rest of the cast and crew. Usually someone of his caste and station lived in the midworld, or at least in one of the townships closer to the Zodiac. "How's your family doing?"

"All right." He shrugged. "I'm thinking about sending the boys to my mother's until all this blows over—she's down in Li Po. The boys don't need their schooling interrupted."

His two sons were both low-teens, in their last years of base school. If they followed the usual midworld pattern, they would be sitting for the first of their placement exams some time in the next six months: no wonder Muthana wanted them well out of the way. "Not a bad thought," I said, and he made a wry face.

"The only trouble will be making them go. They're kids, they want to be where the action is. And my wife's family is up here, I think she'd like to keep them close to home." He shrugged then. "Ah, well, with luck they'll catch the bastards who planted that bomb, and then we can all get back to normal."

"So you believe Realpeace?" I asked.

"When they say they didn't do this one?" Muthana smiled. "It wouldn't make sense if they did."

"So who did plant it?"

He shook his head. "I'm not paid enough to have that kind of opinion, Fortune. Not in Heaven."

I blinked at him, a tall man, mostly in shadow, the light from his lamp puddled at his feet. "You think it's that serious?"

"Yes." The lamp bobbed as he nodded, reinforcing his words. "And you'd be wise to do the same."

"Thanks," I said, and knew it came out more sour than I meant. Muthana waved his handlamp, ambiguous farewell and dismissal, and started back up the aisle. If Binnie wasn't prepared to speculate, indulge in the kind of political gossip that usually filled the Empire, then maybe things were more serious than I'd realized. I watched him go for a little, then shook myself and began dismantling my illusions. More than ever, now, I wanted to do the new illusion, wanted to end the act with that image, machine and flesh not quite merged, not quite separate, but possibly interchanged.

It took me most of the next half-week to work out the illusion, and sketch rough plans for the transformer and the new karakuri. John Desembaa, who had made the last three, was really the only choice for this project as well, and I was lucky enough to catch him between jobs. He had a workshop at the eastern end of Broad-hi, about halfway between Monark and Charretse West Change, in a multi-use warehouse; I loaded the plans into a handful of datablocks, not wanting to trust the connections, and took the electrobus out toward Charretse. It was running late, and there was more Security visible along the platforms, but the tightbeam transmissions stayed normal, updating the delays, and I guessed it was fallout from the bombing.

Desembaa was waiting for me outside the warehouse entrance, sitting on a black-padded bollard in the shade of the entranceway. A massive long-hauler poked its nose out of the bay beside him, and enormous manipulators slid and danced along the frame of the mobilator web that was unloading its cargo, their stately motion controlled by the blank-helmeted figure that hung motionless at the center of the web. The mobilator was another good model for the transformer—I'd been thinking assembly machines, welding frames, but this had possibilities, too—and I stared for a moment until Desembaa said, "Did you have any trouble getting here?"

"No, not really, just the 'buses running late. Sorry."

He matched my tentative smile, twisting his neck to look up at me. Sometime in the course of his career, he'd broken his back, and it had healed badly—or maybe he'd been born that way, with the hunched shoulder that tilted his head awkwardly to the side, but the metal fingers on his right hand made me think there had been an accident. "No problem. There's been a lot of Security around, that's why I asked. Come on back."

I followed him along the yellow-striped path that was—mostly—safe from traffic, and into the side corridor where the individual workshops were. It was hot there, despite the blue-toned cooltubes that hung from the ceiling, and sand grated underfoot, blown in from the trafficway. I glanced at Desembaa, and he rolled his eyes.

"We've got to hire a new cleaner, and soon. But there's no contamination in my shop." He slapped the doorlock, and gestured for me to enter ahead of him.

I knocked my sandals against the doorframe, a polite gesture that I've always suspected did as much harm as good, and realized as I did so that I was tapping my foot on the post of a static cleaner. "Nice," I said, and looked back to see Desembaa grinning.

"It works."

And it proved he was handling the problem, too. "Nice," I said again, and went on into the shop.

For the first time since I'd known him, the system was at standby, the various machines still, arms and appendages folded back against their bodies, the furnace cool. Desembaa's throne—the control chair—sat empty, the cover newly patched, the extra cables coiled at its foot. The air was cleaner than usual, smelled only faintly of the carbon fiber he used for his sculpture. There was a new plaque on the wall, I saw, which might explain the silence, a face whiter than bone, white as the moon, rising from a stone matrix almost as black as slate. I couldn't quite tell if it was a man or a woman—a man, I think, but that's mostly because I knew John—but it was classically beautiful, the finely sculpted planes of the face a contrast to the demurely lowered eyelids, the perfect mouth as perfectly in repose. I caught my breath, seeing it, and Desembaa said, "No."

"I don't want to buy it, John," I said, and he shook his head.

"And I won't make karakuri from it, either, Fortune. That one's—personal."

When he takes that tone, there's no point in bargaining.

"Haya," I said, and there was real regret in my voice. "It's beautiful, John."

He smiled, a tight smile, not without pain. "Someone I used to know." A lover, I guessed, from his tone, or maybe someone he'd wanted badly. "So, what's the job this time?"

I reached for my datablocks. "I'm working on a new illusion. I'm going to need two new karakuri, one pretty much like the others, the other a transformer frame. I've made some sketches, but I'm more than open to suggestions."

"Put them on the player," Desembaa said.

I fed the blocks into the carousel-reader that squatted in the corner by the door, and Desembaa reached for his helmet, settled it over his face. Blind in the real world, he slipped his hands into the control gloves, tightening them methodically onto his fingers. I'd used the helmet interface at vo-tech and again when I was building my own machines on the lease-frames; I'd never managed to get used to the helmet's too-warm jelly molding itself to my face, but Desembaa—and God knows how many others—didn't seem to mind. Desembaa waved his hands, gestures his room could read, and a network of control beams sprang to life around me. I froze, not wanting to signal anything inadvertently, and Desembaa quickly muted the colors.

"Sorry. I forgot I had everything turned up so high. You can use the goggles on the table."

I ducked under the thickest of the beams and picked up the goggles, peered into and through them into Desembaa's virtual workshop. It was nothing like the real one, all greyed light and silvered shadows, with a huge window that admitted more grey light and at the same time showed a sky so filled with cloud as to seem to have lowered itself to touching distance. A stand of trees with leaves like old copper coins stood in the middle distance, and beyond that white flecks came and went on a dark grey plain that had to be a sea. There was a steady pulse of sound in the air, an ebb and flow like a heartbeat.

Desembaa's virtual self stood at his virtual worktable—

straight-backed, all his fingers flesh and blood—already examining the image that floated in the air in front of him. I lifted a finger and my point of view drifted toward him, stopped at my gesture when I hung at his side.

#So you want your first three karakuri to fold into the transformer,# Desembaa said. #And then four of them, the original three plus the new one of that kind, to come out of it?#

#That's right.#

#Huh.# Desembaa stared at the rough plan I'd drawn. #So you'll need to have some sort of secret compartment in this—?#

#Or else the fourth karakuri is concealed as part of the transformer,# I said. #But it has to look as though that's impossible.#

#Haya.# Desembaa's icon-self couldn't smile, but I could hear the wry amusement in his voice. #And at the same time you have to be able to appear from it.#

#That's right,# I said. On the worktable, my sketches, crude wireframe animations, went jerkily through their paces. They didn't look like much, nothing like the effect I wanted when the illusion was in place, and I slanted a glance at Desembaa's icon, wishing I could see his face. More than any other hardhacker I'd ever worked with, I trusted him to see what was beneath the drawings, but I still found myself holding my breath. The animation ended, and Desembaa's icon signaled *repeat*, watched intently until it finished again.

#I like it,# he said at last. #I like it a lot. Let's talk.#

That was the signal to leave the virtual workshop, to go back to the real one to talk money, and I slipped off the goggles to find myself back beside the worktable's glowing top. Desembaa blinked at me from the center of the room, his helmet in his still-gloved hands.

"The copper karakuri's no problem, and I can certainly build the kind of transformer you've sketched here," he said. "The key is going to be how you manage your appearance. What were you planning?"

Desembaa is one of two people—Bixenta Terez is the other,

and that's only because she requires a human backup for Aeris—whom I trust with the secrets of the illusions. "That's what I figured," I said, and tipped the workboard to an angle so that we could both see and sketch. I explained what I'd had in mind, my first choice and the second-best option, and he nodded thoughtfully.

"I can certainly do the second—"

"I figured," I said again.

"—but the first . . ." He let his voice trail off, studying the images, my sketches and his file plan of the Tin Hau stage and stagehouse, head tipped even farther to the side. "It can be done, but it's going to take a little more time than you'd probably like. Up to a minute, even, to prepare. Can you cover that?"

A minute is an infinity on stage. I made a face. "You said up to a minute. How short can you make it?"

"I don't know yet." Desembaa's eyes narrowed. "Forty seconds?"

That was too long, too—or maybe not. I closed my eyes, picturing the flow of the illusion, factoring in applause and its potential absence, trying to make time stand still on stage while the construct and karakuri—and I—were actually moving fast. "Yeh. Probably."

"I think I can do that—I'll try to get it to less, of course, but I'm pretty sure I can give you forty seconds. I'll run the plans and send them over to you."

"Not on the connections, please," I said, and he smiled.

"Not on the connections. Do you want to keep the same faceplate, or do you want me to cast a new one? It's been, what, three years since I did the silver."

It was, I supposed, a polite way of telling me my looks were changing. "No, I think it'll work—might even be better, not looking quite so much like me as like a sister."

Desembaa nodded. "Haya, then, prices. For the humaniform, I'll work it out, but it shouldn't be more than, say, 8 percent over the last one."

"The color is crucial," I said. "I'd rather pay more than get it wrong."

"You shouldn't have to, but I'll let you see samples before I cast anything." He paused. "What about the transformer? Color, finish?"

I hesitated. I hadn't really thought about it, or not consciously, but when it came to making the decision, I discovered I had a fairly strong image in my mind. "Plain iron, like the machines on the surface lines."

Desembaa nodded again. "I can do that. I'll have to work at it to get the design just right, but then I can give you an idea of the price. It'll probably be about half again as much as the humaniform karakuri, though."

"Haya," I said. "Send me the plans and the estimates when you have them."

"Of course." He frowned down at the screen, still watching the animation. "One thing does worry me, Fortune. If you're going to get the transfer down to forty seconds, you're going to need a very fast Spelvin handling the karakuri."

"How fast?"

"What are you running now?"

"Aeris is a Hot Blue Jag-series—an Alpha-Nine," I answered. The Jags had been discontinued about a year ago, and I wasn't surprised when he shook his head.

"I don't know if that will do it, Fortune. Not the way you'll want it."

I sighed. I didn't really want the expense of a new Spelvin construct on top of two new karakuri, but Desembaa was never less than honest with me. "What would you recommend, then?"

He shrugged, momentarily bringing his shoulders into alignment. "I'm not a wireware specialist, Fortune, you know that. Ask a constructor."

"All right, I'll do that, but what parameters are you giving me?"

He tilted the workboard to bring the screen into better focus. "Something like this, juggling five karakuri—and the kinds of moves you use—plus the basic stage effects. . . . You'll need a Spelvin capable of FTL management, or the equivalent."

"Shit." I already knew that was going to be expensive: Spelvin constructs of that quality were worth nearly two of my karakuri.

"On the plus side, it wouldn't have to be new, just Level Four complexity. It's not just speed you're after, it's the ability to juggle decisions in realtime," Desembaa said. "Or you could split the act, let one of the constructs you have now handle the effects while Aeris does the karakuri, something like that."

I'd tried something similar years ago, and it didn't work, at least not well enough for my act. "No good. The construct wouldn't have to be new?"

Desembaa shook his head. "I don't think so. As long as it's Level Four, it ought to be able to handle the load." He grinned. "I mean, don't get some vintage piece that's been around since Settlement, but other than that, anything at Level Four should be all right."

"Right," I said. It wasn't as bad as I'd first thought, but it wasn't going to be cheap, either.

"I'll get you the preliminary plans by the half-week," Desembaa went on, "and we can settle on price then. I'll have full specs for the construct then, too."

I nodded. "What about line space?"

"Let me check," Desembaa answered. He waved a hand, and my sketches shrank to a corner of the screen, were replaced by a table of glyphs. They were all tradetalk signs, nothing I could read, but Desembaa squinted thoughtfully at them. "Nobody's full up right now," he said, "but they're full enough that one of the Cartel affiliates placing a big order before we get there could cause a delay. But if that doesn't happen, it looks like you could have your karakuri within seven days of finalizing your order."

That was a little less than a week—probably a week and a half, once you factored in the design time: not enough to get the new illusion into rehearsal before the Empires reopened, at least not unless things were worse than I thought they were, but not unmanageable. The rest of the act was well in hand; I could afford to concentrate on the new illusion.

"Haya," I said. "Keep the sketches, and get back to me."

"You'll hear from me within the half-week," Desembaa answered, and I turned to the door.

I could trust Desembaa with the karakuri, but to buy a construct—particularly a high-level one, particularly a used high-level Spelvin—I would need more help than he could give. I called Fanning, but Niantai Li, who answered the unit, told me he was at Motosha, working. That was actually better than trying to arrange something over Persephonet; I thanked her, and headed for the Copper Market.

The Copper was one of the oldest of the night markets, old enough that it wasn't just a night market anymore, but served the ordinary needs of Madelen-Fet and the upper end of Angelitos. Like most of my neighbors, I bought most of my fresh food at the wet markets in Lower Charretse, where the long-haul convoys off-loaded the produce from the farms in Pleasant Valley, but when I was in a hurry, or just too lazy to make the long trek to the far end of Broad-hi, there were plenty of smaller shops in the Copper that were glad to sell me what I needed, and sometimes even as cheaply as I could get it in Charretse. The open center of the Copper is always crowded with pushcarts, clustered eight or ten deep around each of the power points, and at least half of them are run by cavern farmers from the Daymare Basin and sand-combers in from the deep desert with carts full of fuzz-clams and prickle-cane and chutt. They have to sell out their load to make any sort of profit—and most of them don't have access to long-term storage, the downside of not buying into the farmers' cooperatives—so the prices tend to be competitive. The carts that don't sell food sell almost everything else, clothes, video-manga, bodypaint, and perfume, anything small that could command a decent price, so you never knew for sure precisely what you'd find. Even midworlders would come up to the Copper sometimes, looking for bargains.

This time, as I left the lift station at the end of the market, I could see that someone had gotten a cartload of brightly colored sand-silk scarves—the big ones, the ones the highteen girls were using for skirts—and was displaying them clipped in bunches to a kind of flagpole. The sun was just rising with the end of the day shift, and the new light spilled down through the just-open sun-traps, brightening the rainbow colors. A grey-haired man steadied the pole and the high-teens snatched and jostled, while a younger woman deftly worked the cash-reader, joking with the buyers as she worked. The tonal rise and fall of their voices was loud even over the music that blared from the arcade stores.

Both arcades were busy, too, so that I felt I was walking on soft sand shouldering through the crowd. The Copper's management had repainted the wall above the arches, covering over the most recent layers of advertising and graffiti, but already the stenciled glyphs were creeping back, and the clip-shop in the center of the arcade had replaced the painted vines that crawled up the edges of its archway, each flower blossoming into the face of a local singer. Micki Tantai and the rest of Hati were conspicuously absent, though, and I wondered who had chosen to omit them. In the southwestern corner, where the electrobus stopped on its way down Shires Road, a six-screen infovendor was showing its wares, quick-cutting between what looked like a game, a couple of stone operas, and a political debate. I felt its query pulse through my suit, and avoided its transceivers, managed to duck into Motosha without triggering its full display.

The shop was big, converted, I think, from a light assembly line, and light diffused from the ceiling and upper walls, so that the space was filled with a shadowless radiance, ideal for displaying the machines that filled every available space. I looked for Fanning, scanning the back wall where the service counter was, but my eye was caught instead by the kineticon that stood in the middle of the center aisle. A three-wheeled cart a little bigger than my joined fists, not counting its topping of flags and pinwheels, chugged madly along a track that circled a central pyramid. As it passed, arms extended from the pyramid, reaching for it—one even seemed to be holding chopsticks—but the cart eluded its grasp each time. It was a nice piece of work, and I moved closer, examining the delicate mechanism as best I could without getting close enough to worry anyone.

"Can I help you?"

The voice was polite but unfamiliar, and I straightened to face the speaker. "Yeh—"

"Oh, bi' Fortune." He was almost too perfectly the stereotype of a hard-hacker, a yanqui about average height, but unhealthily thin, skin barely touched by the sun. "I'm sorry, I didn't recognize you. What can I do for you?"

"Just a social visit," I said. Motosha didn't pay on commissions, but there were reputations and egos to consider, especially among the serious hard-hackers. "I was looking for Fanning Jones."

"Oh." He hid his disappointment better than I'd expected, and pointed to the counter. "He should be there."

"Thanks," I said, and threaded by way through the pallets of equipment. Most of it was secondhand, salvaged from the surface lines either here in the Daymare Basin or in Whitesands, and showed sand-scars and spots of brighter metal where repairs had been made. A few new or nearly new pieces were mixed in with the rest—a very nice sealed-case multipurpose generator, still with the shipping labels and the transport bars across the battery terminals; the controlhead for a fabric welder, also still in the shipping wrap; a set of brass gearings in a padded case—but nothing I really needed. Most of what I bought was kept in the back anyway, or hung haphazard on the walls or in the side shelves with the miscellaneous parts.

I felt the house system register my presence as I came up to the counter, and waved my hand through the nearest signal space. I felt the chirp of contact—recognition of my suit, rejection of it as foreign, not aligned to this system—and then the stronger pulse as the store acknowledged my presence. A moment later, Fanning appeared in the nearer of the two doorways, the frown imperfectly smoothed from his face, display glasses perched on his nose. He peered over the top of their frame at me.

"Fortune. What are you doing here?"

"Thanks," I said, sourly, and he shrugged.

"Sorry. But usually you call."

I lowered my voice. "I wanted your advice on something, but I told the guy back there it was personal. Can you take a break?"

"I was on break." Fanning's grin robbed the words of any anger. "Sure, let me just log out again." He waved his hand through the nearest control beam, and squinted through the glasses at the result. I couldn't see anything, or feel more than the fizzing of the active system, but Fanning reached for an active space I couldn't see, fingers working in what looked like house sign. I felt the ghost of a confirmation, and he slipped the glasses into his pocket. "Haya, all set."

I nodded, but we didn't say anything more until we were back out in the heat and noise of the Copper. About half of the peddler's scarves were gone; the old man was spinning the pole so that the remainder stood out like flags in a high wind. We stopped to buy bags of courduroy-pear juice, then found a place to sit on the edge of the ventilator covers, out of the worst of the crowd.

"So what's up?" Fanning asked, and drove the thin straw expertly into the bag.

I copied him, less deftly, and wiped the spillage on my trousers. "I'm working on a new act, and it looks like I'm going to need a new overseer construct to manage it for me. You used to have contacts that could help me—are any of them still around?"

Fanning made a face. "A lot of people are still around— more than I thought there were." He took a breath. "What exactly are you looking for?"

"Something at least Level Four."

"That's FTL quality," Fanning said.

"Yeh. And I need it cheap."

Fanning sighed, but didn't pretend to misunderstand me. If I wanted to buy a construct of that complexity at anything less than three-quarters of the market price, I would have to go to the grey market, maybe even the black. Fanning had spent most of his lycee years on the edges of that world, and at least two of his former boyfriends had done time for hardware offenses. "I don't know if I still know people—if any of them still know me. I can ask, Fortune, but it's going to take time."

"I can take time," I said. "If I have to."

He made another face, as though he'd wanted an excuse to refuse. "I can ask," he said again, and stressed the last word. "Like I said, I don't know if people still talk to me. At least one of them doesn't seem to."

"I'd appreciate it," I said. "I'll owe you, Fan."

He waved that away, fingertips stained green where the juice had leaked out around the straw, and we sat in silence, the noise of the Copper filling our ears.

"How are you managing?" I asked, after a moment. "And how's Timin doing?"

Fanning grinned. "He's doing much better, thanks. Only has to wear the cast a couple hours a day now, and the whole thing's supposed to be finished by the half-week."

"That's good."

He nodded, busy with the last of the juice, the pouch contracting around the straw.

"How are you doing for bookings?" I asked.

He sighed then, pitched the empty container into the gutter where the sweeper-karakuri would retrieve it. "All right, at least for now. But if the Empires don't open soon—we were counting on that to keep us going until we could save enough to do another clip."

"Oh." I didn't quite know what to say to that, and before I could think of anything, Fanning clapped his free hand to his pocket.

"Shit," he said, and fished out his display glasses. "Sorry, Fortune, I'm needed."

"Thanks for your help," I said, but he was already on his feet, angling back toward Motosha.

"I'll be in touch," he called, and I waved in answer. There wasn't much left of my own juice, but I finished it anyway, watching the people bustling past me through the Copper.

This was one of the times when it might have been easier to have a human assistant rather than just a construct—to have a human being offstage, managing effects or the karakuri—but I'd found out early on that assistants simply didn't have enough of an investment in the act. Besides, by now the act was built on the karakuri, on the fact that the audience knew that there was only me and a construct to run it all; they came expecting to see machines pushed to their limits as well as me. Changing that would be a bigger change than adding any complex illusion. A two-toned chime sounded from the infokiosk on the electrobus platform, and then a deeper tone began sounding the hour; at the same moment, a hatch slid back, disgorging a sweeper-karakuri, its brushes dropping into the channel made by the gutters that ringed the plaza. It slid forward, the solid dome hiding its sensors, brushes hissing in the gutter, and I tossed my empty juice container in front of it. It swallowed it in passing, leaving a faint smell of disinfectant in its wake, and I stood, stretching a little. Now that I'd committed my money, and Fanning's time, at least, to the new illusion, it was more than time to tell Terez exactly what I was planning.

The Empire looked empty, the tube lights out, no previews dancing in the arch above the main doors, but that was deceptive. I walked past the main doors, each one with a poster, yellow on black, announcing CLOSED UNTIL FURTHER NOTICE in both glyphs and smaller realprint, and turned down the tunnel alley that led to the stage door. I felt the house system pulse, registering first my presence, then acknowledging my suit codes, and the stage door opened automatically as I approached. The alcove where staff and performers signed in was crowded, stage techs and people who rented practice space in Tin Hau's apparently infinite lower levels, and I touched the disk in my wrist, bringing the system up to sight levels.

"Input, command: inform Bixenta Terez that I'd like to see her."

The confirmation throbbed through me, diffuse pleasure, and I started down the stairs into the stagehouse. As I reached the door of my dressing room, I felt the kiss of the system contact, and turned to find the nearest pinlight. Letters popped into view, realprint scrolling across my sight, nearly as private as encryption here in Tin Hau, where most people only knew glyphs: I'LL BE IN MY OFFICE IN FIVE MINUTES, MEET YOU THERE. I made a face, not sure myself whether I was annoyed at having to climb back up to the administrative levels, or at having to talk to Terez, but I turned around and headed for the nearest stairs.

All the administrative offices are at the top of Tin Hau, tucked directly under the roof where it joins the cavern ceiling, with Muthana's at the apex, beneath the peak of the front roof, and the others arranged in a descending pyramid, assigned according to midworld ideas of rank and precedence. The corridors are carpeted, not tiled, and if you look closely, you can see the shadow of the Tin Hau name glyph woven into the warm scarlet of the fabric. The same glyph is centered on the bosses that hide the hallway contact points, and painted above the names centered on the office doors: when Tin Hau was built, forty years ago, the shareholders wanted to be sure everyone knew it was the richest and the best of the Empires. As senior stage manager, Terez has an office one floor down from Muthana's, directly opposite the house manager's. I felt the system announce my presence, but knocked anyway, just to be polite.

"Fortune." Terez's voice came from the speaker hidden beneath the name panel. "Come on in."

I pushed open the door, stepping from the warm red and gold of the corridor into a cooler, greener place. The flatscreens that passed for windows were showing a mirage scene, and a green-and-turquoise rug hid the standard carpeting. My shoes sank a little into it, and I caught myself wondering if it would be as soft on bare feet. Probably: she'd had similar rugs in her flat in Gamela, and they'd been as cool and springy as the turf in the mayor's gardens down in Visant Vihar. Terez smiled at me, turning away from her massive console, but at least the look behind the smile was more curious than hostile.

"So what's up?"

"I'm working on a new illusion," I said, and shut the door firmly behind me."

"Oh, yeh? Privacy, please, George."

"Thank you," the construct said, prim as ever, and I felt a sudden absence as the house system sealed off the room transceivers. Terez waved vaguely toward the chairs that stood beneath the larger flatscreen and seated herself within easy reach of the console's shadow board.

I sat in what looked like the less cushioned of the chairs— still too soft—and leaned forward, elbows on my spread knees. "It's only in the preliminary stages—I've commissioned hardware, and I'm investigating the wireware I'll need, which is why I'm letting you know this far in advance."

"Oh?" Terez said again, her voice still mild, but I could see her attention sharpen.

"Yeh. My builder's telling me I'm going to need a major construct, Level Four or better, to manage the effects."

Terez's eyebrows rose. "Must be one hell of an illusion. Got a disk for me?"

I nodded, reached into my belt for the solid square. She didn't need to tell me the problems with letting a Level Four construct play in the Tin Hau house systems, and I was glad she hadn't tried, that she'd assumed I knew both the technical requirements of my own illusion and the limits of the stagehouse. But then, she'd been a conjurer herself, once upon a time. She took the disk, then stretched back to reach the shadow board, frowning thoughtfully at the miniscreen. I watched her work, the familiar tilt of her head and the easy competence of her hands on the shadow board's all but invisible controls. We'd been pillow-friends for a year or so— well, more than that, at least by her reckoning, since the rule in the midworld is that sharing living space makes you something more than casual lovers—but that had been three or four years ago, and in that time she hadn't changed much, if at all. She was maybe half a head taller than me, and heavier, but she had a presence that made her look bigger than she was. It had served her well onstage, made her sleight of hand

and the delicate miniature mechanical illusions that were her specialty look even more amazing against her apparent solidity; it helped now when she had to deal with acts like the shadow puppeteers, who acted as though it was beneath them to deal with technical matters. The office lights drowned the rich red tones in her brown skin, made her look darker than she was, but the transfers across her forehead and down her bare arms—white leaves on gold vines, ending in a black-and-burgundy disk like a mandala or a stylized flower—glinted as she moved. They were fancy for the Empire, especially with the shows closed—even with the best of care, bodypaint doesn't last—and I wondered what event they were left over from.

"What's the occasion?"

She looked up, blank-eyed for a moment, then grinned. "Oh, the paint. I had a gig."

"Yeh?" In spite of knowing better, I felt my heart race. Terez was good, and had been really good; if she was getting back into performance, rather than just building small illusions for other conjurers—

She shook her head, her smile going a little crooked. "Not like that. You know Suleima Chaandi?"

"Not personally." Everyone knew of Chaandi, though: she was one of the best videomanga makers in Landage, probably on the planet. She'd been active in coolie politics, I remembered suddenly, and wondered if she was in Realpeace now.

"She wanted some sleight of hand for transitions in her latest manga—it's kind of neat, card tricks that signal the scene changes, the scene order, and then some dancing-dolly tricks. I said I'd do it, and she threw in the paint as part of the fee." She stretched her left hand complacently, the transfer catching the light.

The fee for being a living cartoon. I swallowed the words along with my disappointment—Terez belonged onstage, she was too good to waste her talents on stage tech—and she looked back at her screen, but not before I thought I caught I glimmer of anger in her face. She didn't say anything, though, and I didn't pursue it, took a slow, deep breath and let the feeling drain away. It wasn't my business, had never been my business, if you listened to Terez, and whatever the truth had been, there was nothing I could do about it now.

"Haya," she said at last, and popped the disk out of the board. "It's going to be impressive, Fortune, that's for sure. I'll need some cutouts between your construct and the house systems—"

"Fuses?" I asked.

"I'd really prefer cutouts," Terez answered, still mildly. "You know what a blown fuse would do to the house system."

"I'm closing the show," I said. "It's not like anybody has to follow me, and cutouts are expensive, not to mention hard to set up."

"The only reason I'd even consider fuses is that you're closing," Terez said. "But I don't like them."

And I was behaving badly—worse than that, I was being stupid. "Sorry, Rez. Cutouts it is. Do you have specs?"

She nodded. "And I'd like it if you'd use George as the show backup, as well as me."

"You mean give George a copy of the act programming?" In spite of my resolution to behave, I heard my voice rise, and controlled it with an effort. "Rez, that's like giving the program to anybody. I mean, George is relatively secure, but it's still a construct, and there are, what, a dozen people with access codes good enough to pry my programming out of it—"

She lifted her hand, and I stopped. "Six people, Fortune, and you and me and Binnie are half of them."

"Sorry."

Terez went on as though I hadn't spoken. "I understand your concern, but I want to have machine backup as well as mine, for the Empire's sake if you don't care about your own safety. People just aren't fast enough, if something goes really wrong in the system."

She was right, too, and I looked at the carpet, covering my embarrassment with a sigh. I don't know why I still can't discuss things civilly with Terez, after all this time. "Sorry, Rez, I know you're right. Can I give you a rough schema, enough for George to shut down safely if there's a problem? I am worried about losing the details."

Terez nodded, and I saw her shoulders relax just a little. "That would work. As long as you don't mind stopping the act, that is."

"If George has to take over," I said, "things will be going too wrong not to stop."

Terez smiled. "True enough," she said, and pushed herself to her feet.

I copied her, the carpet giving under my feet. "I'll get you the cutouts and the schema as soon as I have them."

"Thanks," Terez said, but her attention was already on the console's larger screens. "Good to see you, Fortune."

"And you," I answered, but I wasn't fully sure I meant it. She gave me a preoccupied smile and reached for the shadow board. I let myself out into the corridor and started back down the maze of stairs toward the plaza and home.

▪ 6 ▪

Reverdy Jian

JIAN DREAMED.

She is in hyperspace, on a ship that is Manfred's *Young Lord Byron* crossed with the heavy prototype she just brought in, luxury incongruously mixed with the strictly practical, so that as she climbs from engine room to bridge she goes from plain utility paint to glass and gilt to padding pristine from newness, comes out at last into the *Byron*'s bridge, with its birdcage stairhead now mysteriously surrounding the pilot's station. The controls are flaring red, not true emergency, she somehow knows, but she still can't resist, can't overcome training, and steps into the cage. The bars of light enclose her, she hears the SHYmate soft in her ear, pouring coordinates through her as the virtual world surrounds her, her familiar landscape turned suddenly to desert and storm. Her cues and landmarks are vanished, she gropes for sign and sound, trapped in a language she doesn't speak. In her ear, the SHYmate speaks in coolie dialect, voice rising and falling, babbling nonsense that could save her if she only understood. Now Manfred laughs at her, and her skin burns, sears away as she reaches into the desertscape, groping for controls that are nowhere they should be. Her eyes fill with scalding tears, pain best/worst remembered in her dreams.

She woke to the buzz of the Persephonet console, sat bolt upright, the adrenaline still running in her veins, not quite sure even then whether it was true adrenaline or a suit message. Then the console buzzed again, and she took a shaky breath.

"Input, command: accept incoming audio, visual. Outgoing audio only."

The Persephonet screen, a dedicated window in the center of her rudimentary media wall, lit, the reflected light filling the room. Vaughn's face looked out at her, drawn into his habitual scowl.

"Reverdy. You seen the news?"

"What news?" Jian looked sideways, blinked twice to call up the implanted chronometer. "Shit, Imre, it's not yet six."

"Realpeace is talking up the AI question again," Vaughn said. "And they've dug out some of the old Manfred footage."

"Shit," Jian said again, and reached for the tunic she'd left draped over the chair beside her bed. She shrugged it on, and added, "Room, set outgoing visual to on."

"No thrill to me," Vaughn said, but barely mustered a ghost of his usual malice. "I think this would be a good time to find another job—in fact, yesterday would have been better."

I'm not ready. Jian blinked at that thought, not sure where it had come from, frowned into the camera. "Are you sure things are this bad?"

"Check out the newsnets," Vaughn answered, "and you tell me."

"Hang on." Jian fumbled for the room remote, worked the controls to light the media screen. She hadn't bothered to set a preference; the screen filled with an ad for Hot Blue wireware, and she touched the keys to select the right channel. A moment later, a familiar trio appeared in the screen: the Realpeace triumvirate, old man, young woman, man in his middle years. All three were wearing the old-fashioned coolie jackets that Realpeace had brought back into fashion; the woman was wearing a white wrap-blouse, another coolie style, the stark color ugly against her skin.

"—yanqui influence on the Cartel Companies that leads to the elevation of machine over man," the younger of the two men was saying, "an influence which can only be countered by hiring people from a culture which is founded on the principle of human right—of human responsibility to fellow humans. Freya has forgotten this principle, especially under the current government, and will not pressure the Cartel to change its ways, for fear of losing a single hundredth of the fees the Cartel pays for its acquiesence. Freya will—and can—do nothing. But here on Persephone, we who are originally of Freya have the chance to question this principle, to oppose its implementation, and eventually to force the Cartel to accede to our demands."

"What demands?" Jian said, looking at the Persphonet screen, and saw Vaughn shrug.

"Elvis Christ, I don't know. More jobs, I think—for coolies, that is—and a guarantee of no more AI research and no more Spelvin overseers on the assembly lines."

"I didn't think anybody was doing AI work these days," Jian said.

Vaughn shrugged again. "Rumor is that either Kagami or Hot Blue had a project going."

"You hear the same story every six months," Jian said, and

looked back at the news screen. She didn't have to ask why Realpeace had chosen to believe it this time: not only would their taking it seriously take a lot of coolies' minds off the funeral bombing, but it was another wedge to drive between the Cartel and the FPG. The current Provisional Government had come to power with Cartel support after its predecessor had lost most of its popular support; Jian wondered suddenly if that was Realpeace's true goal.

"In the meantime—" That was the young woman speaking, her soft, deep voice at odds with her severe expression. "—we ask our members, and our many friends, to be vigilant in their awareness of the overuse of Spelvin constructs, and to report any and all appropriate incidents to their township press officers. We are compiling a ledger, which we will bring before the Cartel and any other relevant authority, and your evidence can only bolster our case."

"But we warn our members, and particularly our friends," the older man said, "that AI and near-AI are dangerous, potentially deadly—Manfred was not AI, by all agreement, and yet it killed three people and nearly murdered many more. Do not trifle with AI, or its defenders—"

That's enough of that, Jian thought, and muted the sound with the touch of a button. "I don't see what it has to do with us, Imre."

Vaughn laughed. "You missed the film clips, sunshine, all the old newsclips of you and me and the Mitexis—"

"There wasn't that much with us," Jian said, flatly, "and we were—are—on their side. How does this get us into trouble?"

"Tell that to fucking Realpeace," Vaughn answered. "We brought it back, it was originally a Kagami project, we still work for Kagami now and then—and I'd like very much to find out how they got that bit of information—so we're the bad guys."

Jian sighed, watching the silently mouthing faces on the media screen. Apparently the conference was finished: the triumvirate vanished abruptly, and were replaced by the polished prettiness of a newsreader. The contrast was jarring— it was no wonder, she thought, that the coolies believed in

Realpeace. Chaandi would be furious at this latest develop-
ment—as always, that name brought with it a complicated
regret—especially since she'd been fighting for coolie rights
since before Realpeace was a glyph on a tag poster, and had
always argued that machine and human rights were insepa-
rable. *But not like this, not one instead of the other.* She could almost see Chaandi's hands signing it, the abrupt movements
of distaste and anger, and sighed again at that memory. "So
what are you suggesting?"

"I'm suggesting we call Peace, see what he's got going that
can get us out of the system for a month or so," Vaughn
answered.

"Not going to happen." Jian shook her head, feeling obscurely relieved. "We just had a good job, we're at the bottom of the list."

"So we pull rank," Vaughn said. "We've been there longer
than anybody."

He was right, too, but Jian shook her head again anyway.
"I don't see the point, Imre. You know what people are like
if you jump the line. We'll just stay out of Heaven for a while."

"It's not that simple." Vaughn glanced over his shoulder,
and the movement of his head was enough to reveal Red
leaning against the wall behind him, eyes downcast.

"What do you mean?"

"I mean—" Vaughn looked at Red, not bothering to hide
his anger. "I mean that somebody's been asking questions
about that construct you sold off the other day. Asking about
you, too."

"Asking what?" Jian looked from Vaughn's scowling face
to Red's beauty half-hidden behind the curtain of his hair.
"Give me the whole story for once, will you? It's too early for
these games."

Vaughn gave a snort of angry laughter, but Red looked up,
fixing her with one of his slow stares. "Someone I used to
know got in touch with me. He said Newcat told him I was
back in business—"

"Which he isn't," Vaughn interjected.

"—and that I was dealing in wireware," Red went on, as

though the other hadn't spoken. "He wanted to know what I'd sold to Newcat, and if I could get more like it." He looked away. "I told him no."

"Shit," Jian said.

"I don't know what it means," Vaughn said, "but I fucking well think we ought to get off-planet."

Why would somebody want to buy the SHYmate? Jian wondered. *I had a couple of extras, subroutines and stuff, added in, but nothing you couldn't buy from any half-competent constructor.* "It doesn't make sense," she said, and Vaughn snorted again.

"It makes sense if you were right about that construct being something special. Or even if somebody knows you thought it was something special. You, of anybody, are in a position to know it if a construct was pushing the Turing Barrier."

"I didn't say anything to anybody but you," Jian said. "You and Red."

"Newcat saw it," Red said, softly. "That's why he gave you the price he did."

"What?" Vaughn turned on the other, and Jian leaned forward, wishing she were there instead of in her own flat. "Shut up, Imre. What do you mean, gave me the price he did?"

"You saw," Red said.

"You want to tell me?" Vaughn asked, and Jian sighed.

"Garay gave me a good price on the SHYmate, pretty much what I was asking, and without haggling. I wondered about it, but I didn't exactly want to mess up the deal."

"So now he's spreading the word that you, or you and Red, or Red, have some kind of a line on super-constructs," Vaughn said. "Fucking brilliant, Reverdy."

Jian shrugged. "I wanted the deal."

"So what do we do?" Vaughn asked, after a moment, and some of the belligerence was gone from his voice.

Jian looked away from the screen, recognizing the tactic even as she succumbed. He was right, that was the problem, and the only reason she didn't want to go off-world was that she would have to work with a Spelvin construct again. That was no reason, and every reason; she stared at the wall where the paint was cracking—it was the color of eggshells, and the cracks radiated from a central point, as though something was trying to hatch from the stone—and took a slow, deep breath. The simplest thing would be to try for an out-of-system job even though they'd just come back from one: a lot of other pilots didn't like them, especially the people with families, and might trade one for a couple of local jobs. "We talk to Peace," she said. "Do I call, or do you?"

Vaughn shrugged. "You call. He likes you better."

That was true enough. Jian said, "Then let me get dressed, and I'll give him a call—once he's likely to be in."

"Haya," Vaughn said, and paused, his hand over the disconnect button. "And thanks, Reverdy."

Jian pretended she didn't hear, and cut the connection.

She waited until after noon to call the cooperative—most of the job orders came in at the beginning of the day shift—but even so she had to wait while the co-op's secretary, a thin, severe midworlder with a keyast's transfer on her forehead, dealt with several other calls, then finally patched her through to Malindy. He was looking harried, dataglasses propped up on top of his head, and Jian felt a pang of guilt.

"Hey, Peace."

"Reverdy." Malindy sounded almost wary, as though he had been expecting her call, and Jian suppressed a sigh. "What can I do for you?"

"I need your help," she said, "and, failing that, your advice."

"Well, I can promise you advice." Malindy leaned back in his chair, stretching. Over his shoulder, Jian could see a media screen reflected in a blanked flatscreen. It was cycling between newschannels, and she wondered for an instant if she should check her own system. "What's up?"

"Imre called me this morning," she said. "Early."

Malindy grinned. "Something serious, then."

In spite of herself, Jian smiled back. "He thought so, anyway. And I think I do, too. I heard Realpeace is bringing Manfred up again—I caught the tail end of their announcement, I think—and they're showing some old clips, which include us, Imre says. We were wondering what there was going out-system."

"I hadn't seen that—the announcement, I mean," Malindy said, and reached. "And I sure haven't seen any old clips."

"Imre saw them," Jian said, and didn't bother keeping the edge from her voice.

Malindy lifted his hands. "I didn't say he didn't, Reverdy, I'm just saying nobody else is repeating them. Which I figure is a good thing—the newsdogs don't think it's worth their while."

"Yeh."

"It's just as well," Malindy went on, looking back down at his desktop, "because I don't have anything out-system right now." He looked up, made an apologetic face. "Right now, the only jobs booked are deliveries to the lunar assembly stations and an outer orbital. I'm not going to bump anybody to put you on any of those."

"It wouldn't make sense," Jian said, and almost choked on a sudden giddy sense of relief. She wouldn't have to take a ship into hyperdrive, wouldn't have to work with this new construct, not yet. . . . She shook herself then, hard, and dragged her attention back to what Malindy was saying.

"If I get something in, I'll get in touch," he went on, "but I don't know how desperate it is—I don't know if you'll want to put people's backs up, pulling rank on them."

"That's what rank's for, right?" Jian said.

Malindy shook his head, his plain face sober. "You're both yanquis, you and Imre—at least you look yanqui—and nobody knows what to make of Red. This is not a good time to be taking jobs away from coolies."

"Binli Dai's a three-gen coolie on his father's side, and his mother's from Tannhaus—he was born below the Zodiac, same as me," Jian said. "What's he doing, spouting Real-peace nonsense?"

"It's not all nonsense," Malindy said, with some asperity, and Jian gestured an apology.

"Sorry. But you know what I mean."

"And I think you know what I mean," Malindy answered.

"Seriously, Reverdy, it's getting to be as bad as Dreampeace ever was."

Jian made a face. "How are things in the plaza?"

Malindy snorted. "I had to break up a fight this morning—a bunch of low-teens beating up on each other outside our stairway. Stupid kids. I don't know that it was Realpeace stuff, mind you, but one of them was wearing a Hati shirt."

"It figures," Jian said. *Not Hati's fault—but every time I see those faces, there's trouble.* "But keep us in mind, will you?"

"I'll do that," Malindy said, and sounded suddenly hesitant. "And, look. You might want to stay clear of the co-op for a few days—just until this latest thing blows over. It's just—well, there's been a lot of agitation in the plaza over the last few weeks."

"Shit," Jian said, and Malindy shrugged.

"I'm not happy about it, either, believe me. But these are not people you want to mess with."

That was what people said about Dreampeace, too, people who weren't yanqui like most of that movement. Jian shook the thought away, said, "Fine. But we want work, Peace."

"I'll do what I can," Malindy answered, and broke the connection. Jian sat for a moment, staring at the blank screen. It was good not to have to go back into space right away, good not to have to face the new construct immediately—*but I wish I felt better about the newsdogs.*

▪ 7 ▪

Fanning Jones

AFTER SEEING RED—and not being seen by him—I really didn't want to do Fortune's errand. Hard-hacking is one of those things that is always at least technically illegal, but everybody does it. Or at least the yanqui "everybody" I grew up with: since so many of us work in the infrastructure, air and water supply, lighting, road repair, and general maintenance, nearly anyone who wants it has access to hardware and to a friend's friend who can show you the hack to make it work. I was never really involved with the serious stuff—not like Red—but fxes are always heavily customized, so I spent a lot of time in lycee either scrounging parts for whatever box I was playing, or building something else in trade for work I couldn't do myself. My first boyfriends had been hard-hackers, not musicians, and a couple of them had worked exclusively in the black arts. The rest had done nightwork at least part of the time, and over the years I'd heard that a bunch of them—including Red—had done time in the prison at Whitesands. I'd avoided that mostly by luck and cowardice, which made it hard to go back to any of them to ask for help now. And if Red was going to ignore me like that, I didn't want to think about how some of the others might react.

Still, I'd promised Fortune I'd help her find the construct she needed, and I could think of a couple of people who might be able to help who weren't quite such close ex-friends. I knew the last callcodes I had were months out-of-date, so I waited until my shift overlapped with one of Loes Murong's buying sprees. She was the real thing, a serious artist on the dark side, not like Cengiz Dharavariman, who shared my shift. He had the looks, all pale skin and bones, and traded on them, while she was short and curvy, a midworlder who always had some complex bodypainting covering her arms and face, but she was the person you went to if you needed nightwork done—and if you could afford her fees. I made sure I waited on her, loaded her purchases onto a gravity sled, and fed the stack of cash chips through the reader. They were all small denominations, never more than a hundred wu, and most of them carried the familiar anonymous CarteBanque stamp: unmemorable, and untraceable even if someone did remember. She was in a decent mood—the job, whatever it was, didn't seem to be too urgent, and I cleared my throat as I handed her the last chip. "Um, bi' Murong?"

"Yeh?" She was wearing a painted half mask, solid grey and gold across her cheekbones and forehead, stenciled dark red lace on her cheeks and lips, but even through the paint I could see her expression sharpen, her eyes tracing the wire of my ear and the display glasses on my nose.

"I was wondering," I said. "I used to know Thenga Macara, and I'm looking for something he might know about. I was wondering if you knew how to reach him."

She gave me another sharp look. "Thenga's—away—for a while."

Away in the prison at Whitesands, she meant. I said, "I hadn't heard. How long?"

"Eighteen to two. The decision came down yesterday."

"I hadn't even heard he was busted," I said.

She grinned then, her teeth very white against the heavy paint, and leaned forward on the counter. The neck of her shirt fell open a little, and I could see that she had a complex design, a string of pearls with a snake coiling around it, painted around her own neck. "You're the guy in that band, right?"

I nodded, glad I hadn't tried to pretend I was a serious hard-hacker. "It's a favor for someone—for my cousin, actually."

"So what were you looking for?"

I took a deep breath, unable to believe she was asking—was actually offering this much help. "My cousin's Celinde Fortune—look, it's a longish story."

Murong shook her head. "I've got time. Fortune—that's the conjurer at the Tin Hau Empire?"

I nodded.

"She's good." Murong nodded thoughtfully. "You know how she does it?"

"No."

"I figured." Murong smiled again. "But I had to ask. So what does she need?"

"She's working on a new illusion," I said, "and she told me she needs a Level Four Spelvin construct, but she needs it cheap, and she needs it soon. She said it didn't have to be new, or top-of-the-line, but it has to be Level Four."

"Haya." Murong drew out the word, her eyes fixed on the wall over my left shoulder. "I don't deal much in wireware, but I can give you a name. There's a guy called Red, he's legal, but word is he knows people who are selling—I heard he had some special stuff himself, but I don't know about that. He's an FTL tech, though, so he knows what he's talking about."

"I used to know Red, too," I said. I could hear my voice tighten, and Murong gave me a curious look that faded into a slight and malicious smile.

"You got a card?" she said. "I'll flip you his codes."

I fumbled in my pocket, came up with a handful of the little ID chips. Most of them were for the band, but I found one of my own and handed it to her. "Thanks."

"So he's a friend of yours?" she asked, and pocketed the disk.

"I knew him in school," I said. Actually, I'd been in school, he'd been taking tech courses when he could afford the fees, and I hadn't been too surprised when he was busted. But when he came out, he'd taken up with people I didn't want to know, and we lost touch. More than that, he'd changed, and that scared me, and he knew it. "I don't know if he knows me now."

Murong gave me a look. "They say he's the man right now, if you want constructs."

"If you could let him know," I said, "I need the contact."

"I'll pass this along," Murong said.

I didn't really expect an answer, not after the way he'd behaved at Motosha, but two days later an answer-daemon was waiting on the Persephonet console with a set of codes. They were anonymous, directing me to one of the untraceable drop services, but I called them anyway, and left a guarded message. There was no reason to think he wouldn't at least get back to me, if he was willing to contact me in the first place, so all I could do was wait. And there was plenty of other work to keep me busy: the Empire was still closed, but Jaantje had managed to get us a couple of club gigs, and I had to get myself back into shape. I still didn't feel much like practicing—every time I set up my fx, I could see the funeral truck and the explosion—but I didn't have much choice, not if we wanted to keep working. The first gig was strange, strange and scary, the club mostly empty until the second set, when a big group of coolies—young, mostly, high-teens and a little older—showed up and started calling for *retoro* songs. Jaantje usually handles that kind of thing well, but they weren't interested in anything except trouble. We cut our two most Hati-like songs from the second set, but they still hissed us on "Sandstorm" and finally the bouncer had to go over and tell them to shut up or get out. They shut up, and even seemed to enjoy some of the last songs, but at the end one of the loudest of them cornered Tai by the bar and went on and on about the propriety of a one-gen coolie like her playing with the rest of us. We extricated her without causing more trouble, but we were still extra careful loading out, and I was very glad to get back to the lights and bustle of Tin Hau, where we stored our gear. The next day, Tai was up and away before I got up. She didn't come back until the start of the eve shift, and when she did, her hair was bleached and teased into the lion's-mane cut that Alva Gabriel had worn.

"Don't start with me," she said, as she came in the door, and I lifted my hands in surrender.

"It looks good." And it did, not at all like Gabriel, really. The cloud of gold and copper—and some black still, either missed by the body artist or left alone on purpose—actually gave her sallow skin new life, and made her bony face, all angles and hollows, look exotic.

She collapsed into her favorite chair, but instead of reaching for the room remote, she looked up at me from under her lashes. "Yeh? You think so?"

Tai is never uncertain about her looks. I blinked, and she laughed softly.

"Sorry, Fan. All the way home on the 'bus I was thinking I'd really fucked up."

"I think it looks good," I said again.

"For what I paid, it had better," she said, sounding normal again. "I spent half my rent money on it."

"I'm sorry?" I said.

"Yeh, I know, it was stupid." Tai shook her head. "I can borrow from my mother, I know she'd loan it to me, or I'll find some linework, there's always one- or two-day jobs around. But I had to do it, Fan. Nobody's going to look at me and think I'm some ignorant one-gen missy who doesn't know the choice she's made."

I could understand that, maybe better than she thought. Here in Heaven, people tended to assume I was a Dreampeacer just because I'm a yanqui; I wore coolie clothes myself a lot of the time, but it didn't always help. "Those guys last night?"

"Yeh. Realpeace bastard." She shook her head. "Son of a bitch had the nerve to lecture me about my obligations to the community. And it just pisses me off that he assumed I'd be on his side."

"Well, nobody's going to think that now," I said, and wondered if this was something we needed right now. It might be smarter to play down our own politics—except that, given our music and the band itself, we probably couldn't if we wanted to. "And it does look really good."

"Thanks." She gave me a wry smile and reached for the room remote. "Let's hope nobody else gets upset."

"As long as you pay the rent," I said, "there shouldn't be a problem."

Actually, after she'd slept on it for a night or two, it didn't look quite so much like Gabriel, and my worry faded. Nobody else said anything, though I thought I caught Jaantje once with a look of concern, and our next gig was actually pretty decent. Or at least we were decent; the club was on the edge of Madelen-Fet, and most of the mixed crowd was there to see a band that looked and sounded a little bit like Hati. I saw house security eject half a dozen people over the course of the night, and I was glad to get out of there when we were finished. We packed up our gear while Jaantje collected our fee, then loaded everything into the carrier he'd borrowed from his father's business, and backed it carefully down the service alley.

This alley seemed even narrower than usual, and at least one of the ceiling lights was broken. I could see shards of glass glittering in the running lights, most of it swept to the sides of the passage, but a lot of it still lying in the roadway, but Jaantje glared at me before I could say anything.

"For God's sake, Fan, I see it. Relax, will you? I've been driving these since I was twelve."

I could see Shadha's face reflected in the windscreen, saw her roll her eyes at that, but she had the sense to keep quiet. I shut my mouth, too, and the carrier inched its way backward down the alley. We all heard glass crackle under the wheels, and then finally we were into the turnaround that led to the trafficway. I let out a sigh of relief, and Jaantje glared again.

"Will you give it a rest?"

"Jaantje?" That was Shadha's voice, not quite hiding the malicious glee. "What's that red light?"

"Shit, fuck, and damn." Jaantje slammed both fists on the steering bar, and got himself under control with an effort. "We're losing pressure on one of the tires."

"Fuck," Timin said, not quite under his breath.

I said, "There's a Nighthawk on Condaraxis, by the Toric Interlink. They'd carry patch kits."

"Can we get there?" Tai asked, and leaned forward to study the displays.

"Yeh." Jaantje flipped a couple of switches, lifting the damaged tire so that it was taking the minimum load. "It's, what, half a kilometer? Tires are expensive, that's all."

We actually made it to the Nighthawk before the tire went completely flat. This late, between shifts, there wasn't too much traffic; we were able to make the turn onto the commerical strip that paralleled Condaraxis at a reasonable speed, and then Jaantje eased the carrier up the ramp onto the parking deck. The Nighthawk bulged out of the cavern wall above us, a squat poured-stone cylinder with a single long window ringed in red-and-white light tubing. Then Jaantje pulled the carrier into one of the self-service bays and we all climbed out and stood around while he worked the manual controls and brought the tire farther up off the ground. I couldn't see anything wrong with it, no cuts or bits of glass, but Jaantje prodded at it and then straightened, glaring at us. "Look, why don't you go get something to eat, or something?"

"But we want to help," Shadha began, grinning, and Timin caught her shoulder.

"We'll do that," he said firmly, overriding her. "You want us to bring you something when we're finished?"

Jaantje took a deep breath. "I have to get the patch kit, but after that, it shouldn't take long. I'll meet you in the food bar."

The Nighthawks are an old chain that started at The Moorings and along the western haulage, and moved into Landage about twenty years ago. They cater mostly to long-haul drivers, so that the interior is a weird mix of spare-parts shelves, trip supplies, food machines and a live-service counter, and a heavily armored corner office that deals in pawn. The lights are all brighter than the day-lights, and nearly everything has the red-and-white Nighthawks glyph plastered somewhere on it, including the live staff. We pushed through the double doors, shivering at air cooler than most places in Heaven, and Jaantje split off for the parts section. The rest of us moved on to the food bar in the back corner well away from the pawnshop. There were maybe a dozen molded-fiber tables with attached stools—red and white like everything else, with the glyph embossed in the center of the tabletop and each stool—in the middle of a white square of flooring, but at this hour they were empty except for a pair of drivers sitting in the corner, sand suits tossed over the backs of their chairs. The live bar was open, and I glanced at the menu, considering real food, but the prices that flickered on the display over the head of the cook were enough to discourage me. I rooted in my pocket instead for money chips, and followed Timin to the wall of machines. The choices were a weird mix of yanqui food—exotic to most of the people who drive, and easy to adapt to the machines—and cheap standard coolie fare, but I managed to find a machine that sold a decent brand of sausage rolls and another with beans and rice, and carried that and a bottle of water back to a table. Tai followed me, a neatly packaged binty box tucked under her arm so she could balance the double carafe of sente, but before she could sit down someone called her name. I turned, recognizing the voice, and saw a familiar trio threading their way through the display of water jugs. We'd known the Commandos for years—never as competition, though Shadha had been their drummer for a while before she joined us—and they'd been the ones to introduce us to the Nighthawks; I wasn't really surprised to see at least three of them here. No, it was four of them after all: Meonothai Vaughn, who was both some distant kind of cousin of mine and the Commandos' second guitar, appeared behind the others, stretching his legs to catch up. The rest of them, Kebe and Mosi Niall and their current drummer—they had the worst luck with drummers—sat down at the next table, and Mosi punched the menu to order coffee from the live service. I couldn't help raising an eyebrow at that—you could get twice as much from the machines for the same price—and the drummer said, "You got to admit, the machine coffee is pretty bad."

Not bad enough to make live service worth the price, I thought, but then, coffee wasn't my particular indulgence. Kebe leaned forward, planting both elbows on the table.

"So where's Jaantje? I wanted to talk to him about a gig." Both he and Mosi had recently grown beards, probably to prove they were yanquis despite their tilted midworld eyes. It made them look more like stock villains in a bad video-manga, and Mosi in particular looked like an ax murderer.

"Out fixing a tire," Tai answered, and Meonothai tapped me on the shoulder.

"So what do you want with Crazy Imre?"

"Who?" I said, leaning back to look at him, and Meonothai gave me a look.

"Crazy Imre—you know, my cousin, the one who works in FTL. He said you were looking for him."

I blinked, confused, and then wondered if it might have something to do with Red. Even if he didn't want to deal with me anymore, he might still pass my name along—in fact, that was probably the way he would handle it, given the way he'd treated me at Motosha. "Well, yeh," I began, not wanting to ask directly if this Crazy Imre was a hard-hacker, and Meonothai pointed vaguely into the racks of parts.

"He's out back, I ran into him on my way in."

"Excuse me," I said, to the rest of the tables. They ignored me, except for Mosi, who gave me one of his looks, the ones that make you brace yourself for whatever it is he's going to say. This time, though, he didn't follow through, and I climbed past Timin and headed for the back of the store.

Despite the brilliant lights overhead, the parts aisles were heavily shadowed. I stopped at a cross aisle, looking over my shoulder, but didn't see anyone among the rows of kits and machinery. That left the public Persephonet console, a battered machine snugged up against the back wall, and the Nighthawk's toilets and pay showers. I hesitated, not really wanting to go looking for someone called Crazy Imre in the toilets, and someone touched my shoulder. I turned, startled, and he was already well out of reach, his hands buried in his jacket pockets.

"You were looking for Red."

He was unmistakably a Vaughn, shorter and not as skinny as Meonothai, but with the same curly hair and vivid hazel eyes. I decided that discretion was the wiser course, and said, "You're Imre?"

He nodded. "What do you want with Red, sunshine?"

I looked at his hands again, balled in the jacket pockets, or maybe holding something I didn't want to know about. "I wanted to talk to him," I said, carefully. "I used to know him, a long time ago."

Imre's mouth curled in an unpleasant, knowing smile. "I bet you did."

There wasn't any point in answering that. I couldn't tell what I'd walked into, if it was personal or business jealousy, and I didn't want to annoy him further by guessing wrong.

After a moment, he said, "So what is it, sunshine, business or pleasure?"

"My business," I said, and looked sideways for something to hit him with if I had to. The closest rack was full of foam-wrapped coil-mount semiliners about half a meter square, not much use even if I'd been able to lift them.

"His business is my business," Imre said.

Before I could think how to answer that, or how and where to run, a soft voice behind me said, "No."

I started, banging my shoulder on one of the semiliners, and Red walked past me without seeming to see me. It was unmistakably him, just as it had been in Motosha—there was never any mistaking his looks, not yanqui or midworld or coolie, but some combination of them all. He'd never worn his hair this long before; it hung in a ragged mane well past his shoulders, looking like liquid flame against his black shirt. A woman was following him, the same big woman I'd seen with him at Motosha—taller than me, I realized, and midworld-dressed, but with watchful yanqui eyes.

"Fucking right it's my business, bach," Imre said. His eyes slipped from Red to the woman, fixed on Red again. "You fucking well went to jail the last time you played this game—remember Avelin? You might not find something so nice in your cell this time."

I remembered Avelin myself, one of the reasons I'd dropped out of touch with Red, and couldn't suppress a shiver. This was the reason I'd never wanted to get involved in hard-hacking, exactly this kind of meeting, and Red shook his head.

"No," he said again, still quiet, without much apparent emotion, but Imre closed his mouth over whatever else he would have said. Red extended his hand to touch Imre's face, an ambiguous gesture, threat and caress and plain raw sex all at once, so that I shivered again, seeing it. "It's my business, Imre."

Imre stood frozen for an instant, then shook himself, and swung abruptly away. He stamped up the aisle past me, turning only to call over his shoulder, "Fine, but don't expect me to bail you, sunshine."

Red didn't answer, but the woman pulled herself up from the shelf where she'd been leaning, the metal creaking slightly as she released it. "I hope you know what you're doing," she said to Red, and started after Imre.

I looked at Red, and he looked back at me for a long moment, until the leashed passion in his stare made me look away. "Hey," I said, a feeble greeting if ever there was one, and he lowered his eyes to hide any answer, the lashes veiling their dark blue. I heard someone in the cross aisle to my left, and turned, wondering what it was going to be this time, and heard Jaantje call my name.

"Fan? Everything all right?" He had his hands in his pockets just the way Imre had had them, and Kebe and Timin and it looked like the rest of both bands were behind him, crowding the aisle. I looked back at Red, and thought I caught him smiling, before he dropped his eyes again.

"Everything's fine," I said, still looking at him, and this time I was sure I saw him smile.

There was a little pause, and Jaantje said, "Haya. But your food's getting cold."

"I'll be there in a minute," I said, and heard them moving away. I really didn't know what to say to Red, whether to mention Motosha or not, and cleared my throat. "I didn't know you were back in business," I said finally, and Red shrugged one shoulder.

"I'm not, exactly."

So why are you doing this? The question hung between us, almost as though he was daring me to ask; I said instead, "I didn't expect to see you the other day."

He looked away. "No." I waited, and he went on, reluctantly, "I was doing someone a favor—Reverdy, the woman who was here."

"Haya," I said, drawing the word out to let him know I wanted more, but he'd closed down again. "Did Loes Murong tell you what I wanted?"

He nodded. "Did you want it legal?"

That was one question I actually hadn't asked Fortune. "Preferably," I said. "But it doesn't have to be, as long as it has a reasonable provenance."

Red nodded again. "There's an out-bazaar happening 390 kilometers southwest on the Whitesands Haul. A guy named Newcat Garay, he'll have what you want. We—I just sold him one myself." He reached into the pocket of his workcloth trousers, pulled out a dulled datadisk. "Give him this, say I sent you. The exact coordinates are on it, too."

"Thanks," I said, and he turned away as though everything was finished. "Red?"

He stopped, looked back at me, the red hair shifting, falling to frame his face, making him at once a stranger and the man I'd known. I realized I didn't quite know what I wanted to ask him—are you all right, are you happy, have you forgiven me, even, though, I don't know for what—or even if I could ask any questions anymore. I said instead, "Will it be legal? Fortune will want to know."

He shrugged. "Your choice," he said, and walked away.

I watched him go, wishing I'd had the balls to ask my real questions, but at least I had a name, and a contact point. The out-bazaars were a hard-hacker's paradise, where the sand-divers traded the minerals they'd harvested from the deep desert for the equipment that let them survive their job. What they did was technically legal—the Conglomerate courts have consistently refused to sanction the Cartel Companies' blanket claims in Whitesands and the northern deserts—but strongly discouraged, to the point of costing more than a few divers their lives. The Cartel Companies don't actively defend their turf—that would give the FPG a possible excuse to bring the Peacekeepers into the picture—but they don't respond to distress signals from sand-divers, despite all the conventions and codes that say they have to. Rumor and sand-diver legend says they actively block those signals, but no one has ever been able to prove it if they do. And since most sand-divers are Aussys, with their love-hate relationship with the Cartels, it's hard to know what to think. But the out-bazaars are some of the best places on the planet to buy odd bits of equipment.

I called Fortune with the news the next morning, after I'd opened Red's disk and checked the coordinates and the asking prices. Everybody else was still asleep—and so would I have been, if I hadn't had to work the second half of the day shift—so I spread the file displays out on the big media screens in the main room, where I could see everything at once. One of Fortune's constructs answered, dulcet ungendered voice, and then Fortune herself appeared in the screen.

"I've got a source for you," I said, and she blinked once, as though I'd waked her.

"Excellent. Who and where—and is there a price?"

"A range," I answered. "Are you encrypting?"

She nodded. "Peri matched your system."

"There's an out-bazaar on the Whitesands Haul. The person you want will be there for the next four days, according to what—according to what I have." I'd been about to mention Red's name, not a good idea even with encryption. "The prices run from 1500 wu to 2500."

Fortune made a face, light rippling on the silk of her loose coat. "At that price, they'd better be legal."

"As far as I know, they are."

"Haya." Fortune stared at the screen, obviously reading something in her own displays. "How far out?"

"Twelve hours round-trip." At least an hour of the would be cross-sand, getting to the out-bazaar itself, but I probably didn't need to mention that. "I know someplace we can rent a half-track, though."

"We?"

"I'm the contact," I said. "I'm who people know."

She nodded. "Haya. I don't mind, but matching our schedules is likely to be a pain."

"The Empire's closed for three more days," I said, "and we don't have any bookings then, either. So the sooner the better."

"Tell me about the rental."

"Jaantje's father owns a haulage firm. They've got stuff we can rent, probably at a discount."

"Haya," Fortune said again, staring into the distance. "All right, see what you can set up, and I'll get the cash together. I'd like to do it Third-day, if you can get the half-track by then."

That was the day after tomorrow. "I'll try," I said, and meant Fortune to hear the uncertainty in my voice.

If she did, she ignored it. "I've gotten in the new karakuri— the humaniform one. Want to see?"

Before I could answer, she lifted a hand, ran it through an invisible control space. The screen image fuzzed for a minute, refocusing to include more of the room, and the shape that had been lying on the worktable suddenly jerked upright. It looked almost exactly like the other three, except that its skin was pink, the metallic pink of new copper that still somehow suggested white-yanqui skin. It swung itself off the table, the movements awkward, and I saw the tip of Fortune's tongue between her teeth as she concentrated on controlling it with almost invisible movements of her fingers. It had her face, but the old version, the one she'd been using on her humaniform karakuri for the last three years, and as it came to stand at her side I had a weird vision of her younger sister in its face. It laid an arm gracelessly across Fortune's shoulder, and she put her arm affectionately around its waist. "I'm calling it Celeste," she said.

"Celeste?" I echoed, stupidly. She hated her sister—no, I realized, not that Celeste, but the first Celeste, the real Celeste, as Fortune once said to me, Fortune's dead twin. I couldn't help remembering that the arm she laid so casually around the machine's waist had been harvested from that first Celeste's body.

"So what do you think?" Fortune said.

"It's creepy as hell," I said, flatly, and she smiled.

"Good."

"I'll get back to you," I said, and broke the connection.

Jaantje was willing to talk to his father, and once we got the price down, volunteered to drive us himself, at journeyman pay. That made the rental fee more than reasonable, which made Fortune happy, and meant Jaantje was getting paid, which made him happy. It also meant that I knew I could trust the driver: a good solution all around. Fortune paid for the supplies, per regulations, but Jaantje did the shopping, so that we managed to get not only the required emergency reserves but a decent larder for the trip itself, which meant we'd only have to play the depots' inflated prices for fuel. We left Tai to deal with arranging a gig at Ino's—the manager was blowing hot and cold, yes and no—and loaded the last supplies into the half-track's sealed cabin. That included the Celeste-karakuri: Fortune said she wanted to be sure that any construct she bought would be compatible with the basic design.

Most of the time, karakuri can load themselves, but this one was so new that the internal programming still hadn't finished fine-tuning itself, so that it was easier just to shut down its systems and load it in like any other piece of machinery. Fortune had packed it well—she has padded sleeves for each of her karakuri that make them look like mummified bodies—and the three of us managed to wrestle it into the back of the half-track. Jaantje and I collapsed then, me leaning against the top of the still-open loading ramp, Jaantje sitting on the cabin floor, and I glanced out across the trafficway. Fortune's neighbors were watching—she didn't have a service alley, the only real drawback to the workshop-flat—not even bothering to hide their curiosity, and I glanced at Fortune, to see her smiling the way she does in her act. She stooped over the karakuri, unfastening the top of the sleeve to reactivate the basic systems and unlock the frozen limbs; the padded fabric fell away, and by a fluke her face and the karakuri's were momentarily side by side. I heard Jaantje catch his breath, saw one of the neighbors sketch-sign a curse, and look hastily away when he saw me watching. Fortune leaned over the karakuri's shoulder, fumbling with something beneath a back panel, and the karakuri suddenly straightened, then sat down on one of the jump seats. The padding fell to its waist, exposing more of the gleaming pink skin, but Fortune ignored it, concentrating on pulling the safety straps into place around it. I glanced at Jaantje, saw him shaking his head. He didn't say anything, though, for which I was grateful, and we finished loading the supplies under the Celeste-karakuri's blind gaze.

"Will it be all right without the full padding?" Jaantje asked, and held out a bottle of warm water from the city taps. We had a full supply in the storage wells, and a daystill for emergencies, but I drank greedily anyway.

Fortune held out her hand for the bottle. "She'll be fine. But if it bothers you, I'll cover her."

There was a definite challenge in her voice, and Jaantje shook his head. "No, no problem," he said, unconvincingly, and Fortune grinned.

"Well, it bothers me," I said, and tugged the sleeve up again, fastening the clips over the metal shoulders. It was warm to the touch, warm as skin, from being under the daylights. "You're too good, Fortune."

Fortune's smile widened, accepting the compliment, but she made no move to uncover the karakuri. Jaantje held out his hand for the water, and we finished it together. Then Fortune and I sealed the loading ramp, wedging ropes of sand putty into the frame while Jaantje ran the last checks. The half-track had an onboard computer of its own, not very smart, but good enough to manage satellite navigaton and cabin status; it finally gave us full clearance and relayed our beacon numbers to the Highways Office.

"Where'd you file for?" I asked, leaning over Jaantje's shoulder as he studied the control board. It's asking for trouble not to tell the Highways Office where you're going; on the other hand, announcing that you're going to any out-bazaar isn't smart, either.

Jaantje touched a sideboard, throwing the shadow of a map across the inside of the windscreen. "I told them I was ferrying a couple of hard-hackers to an out-bazaar, why?" A light flare on the map, maybe twenty kilometers beyond the point where we'd been told to look for a beacon. "Marihaut Depot. We'll refuel there, anyway."

I nodded and slid foward into the seat beside him. He put the half-track into gear, and it clanked slowly onto the ramp that led to the heavy traffic road that led to Cavemouth. It was jammed with heavy carriers and other half-tracks—most of the long-haul drivers travel at night, to avoid the worst of the heat—and it took us almost an hour to reach Cavemouth. Handlers in heavy sand hoods and fiberfelt masks and coveralls directed us into the line for one of the smaller locks, and we waited in line for another twenty minutes before a handler waved us into the chamber. It's not really a lock, of course, just a two-stage door, trying to keep the heat out of the city; I watched out the rear window as the handlers shunted a last half-track into the final slot and began to close the massive doors. It was weirdly quiet, all the engines throttled down to their lowest idle, but I could still smell the exhaust gases and the bitter tang of the rock itself. Then a tree of lights lit toward the front of the lock, three orange lights that quickly turned green, and a line of paler grey appeared as the outer door began to open. All around us, engines coughed, revving back up to speed, and I saw more handlers, hoods well up over their masked faces, waiting to direct us out and onto the right ramps. Signals pinged and flickered across Jaantje's control boards, and then a handler waved at us, blue light, then green, and the half-track shuddered as Jaantje threw it into motion. Under the handler's guidance, we lurched onto a roadway, the drifted sand pale under the headlights.

Ahead of us, the western sky still glowed faintly orange, like embers in a furnace. The mountains of the Daymare Basin hid all but a short line of it, but the road ran true west toward the dying light. I could see the lights of The Moorings bright as day to my left, could even make out a shuttle upright on its cradle, ready for launch; I looked back, and saw the door sliding closed behind us, cutting off the last sliver of the lock's orange light. Above and beyond it, the rocks that covered Landage were spotted with lights, warn-offs and tracking beacons flashing red and gold and blue against the almost invisible mountain. The steering computer chimed twice, and traffic glyphs flickered across the base of the wind-screen, steering us to one of the feeders that would bring us into the low-speed lanes of the Whitesands Haul. Jaantje frowned in concentration, hands and feet moving on the controls, and Fortune rose from beside the karakuri to sit in the jump seat at my back.

"So, about six hours to the rendezvous?" she asked.

Jaantje grunted agreement, his fingers working on a tapboard, punching in answers to the string of codes now flashing on his secondary screen.

"The light'll be gone by then." Fortune nodded to the sunset line. It already seemed paler, but I knew that was psychological, a trick of the mind as much as the chill that seemed to come with the darkness. It would be genuinely cold soon enough, once we were out of the Basin, but for now the vents and the sheltered air of the Basin would keep things at a reasonable temperature.

"We'll have the moon most of the way," Jaantje said. A light flashed bright green on his console, and he shoved the throttle forward. The half-track bucked, then settled to a steady acceleration. "On the line—we're on our way."

I could see running lights ahead of us, red and then a line of orange as the road curved to reveal the carrier's side. To our left, long-haul carriers slid past in the high-speed lanes, massive streamlined cylinders, their thermal coatings now darkened to keep in the heat. They were still running at half-speed, wouldn't be allowed to reach their full acceleration until they were out of the Basin, but they were still going easily twice as fast as we were.

"So what's the plan?" Fortune asked, and Jaantje tapped controls to call up a temporary map.

"We stick with the feeder for about half an hour, and then we're on Whitesands the rest of the way."

"Sounds good," I said, and switched on the heater. Fortune nodded, and pulled down the other jump seat, propping her feet on it. Behind her, the hooded karakuri swayed gently against its restraints, and I wondered if it didn't look more human inside its sleeve.

The traffic stayed steady and moderate through the Basin, but once we passed the depot at Yetter's Fork it thinned out a lot. Most of the low-speed traffic turned off at the Fork or a little afterward; after that, it was mostly high-speed traffic, the massive, windowless cargo carriers stormed past on hover-assist, heading south and west toward the main assembly lines. We could hear them almost from the minute their lights appeared on the horizon, a distant drumming that swelled to a roar that even the sound seals couldn't muffle, throbbing in the floorboards, and then dropping in pitch as they swept past and vanished in the dark, the wind of their passage rattling us on our tracks.

Beyond the turnoff for the Winter River and Terminus and the Darksands Haul, the traffic thinned out even farther, and we were left alone for long stretches at a time. We were out of the shelter of the Daymare Basin, too, and the air was perceptibly colder despite the heater. At the next pull-off, we stopped, and all of us pulled on the thick smocks everybody wears for night driving. They had come with the half-track, part of the rental, and smelled of oil and metal and some weird musty scent that Jaantje said was the rough fabric itself, but they were warm. I traded seats with Fortune and brewed tea in the half-track's little kitchen, and after that we all felt better.

About an hour beyond the turnoff, we reached the edge of the Whitesands desert. We were in moonlight now, just shy of full, and the blue-white radiance made our headlights look feeble, and cast weird shadows over the karakuri in its sleeve. Under the moonlight, the sand itself seemed to glow, reflecting and redoubling the moonlight, so that we seemed to be running alongside a lake of molten carbon fiber. Nothing else I'd ever seen was that peculiar white, and it seemcd doubly strange to be cold, facing that white fire. Fortune murmured something under her breath, but when I looked at her, she wouldn't repeat what she'd said.

"Salt flats," Jaantje said, striving to sound matter-of-fact. "We run along them until the Origaia."

The Haul followed the salt flats for about another hundred

kilometers, but then curved away to the north again, avoiding the Origaia Pan. It was prone to sandstorms, Jaantje said, and, listening to the sand hiss against the half-track's protective skirting—just ordinary sand, kicked up by us and the bigger carriers—I was just as glad to avoid it. On the display, the orange light that was the Marihaut Depot came into view for the first time, but Jaantje slowed, frowning first at the map and then at the barren ground caught in the cone of the headlights. This wasn't the full desert—there were clumps of grey grass and the nest of twisted twigs that marked the body of a trapdoor lemon—but it looked very empty all the same.

"I'm switching to the contact frequency," Jaantje said, and twisted a knob on the navigation console. A red light flared at once, warning that he was off the main channels, but he ignored it, eyes fixed on the road that ran ahead in the lights. For a long moment, there was nothing, just the sand hiss and the rattle of the treads, but then a green glyph flashed, very bright.

"Shit," Jaantje said, and applied all the brakes, throwing me forward against the padded panel. I looked back to see if Fortune was all right, and saw her steadying herself against the shrouded karakuri.

"What the hell—?" she began, and Jaantje waved his free hand in apology.

"Sorry. It's a real short-range transmitter, you don't pick it up until you're right on top of it. Fan, look for a marker, will you?"

I nodded, and leaned closer to the windscreen. The marker glyph was almost steady now, and I did my best to ignore it, watching the grey land roll past. Even so, I almost missed it, a subtle widening of the road that turned into a ramp, almost buried in the sand. A slim pole, once striped white and red but faded now to the same grey as the sand, was all that marked it in the real world. Without the beacon, we would never have found it: if there had been tracks— and there would have been, the out-bazaars are popular— the wind and sand had erased them. Janntje geared down again, and then farther still, slowing us until the sand tread could engage, and we turned off into the desert.

With the beacon and the occasional pole-marker, it was easy to stay on course, but if there had been a road, the sand had covered what was left of the paving, and most of the time we might as well have been traveling through open desert. The half-track lurched as the treads sank in a soft spot, then caught again as a stretch of pavement came clear, the cracked surface gleaming in the headlights. Jaantje nursed the controls, mouth working as rhythmically as a drummer's; the power surged and steadied, and I saw a glow on the horizon.

"There it is."

Jaantje nodded, too busy to respond, but Fortune leaned forward over the back of my seat, the first sign of eagerness I'd seen from her. "How much farther?"

I squinted at the glow, shrugged. "Ten klicks? Fifteen?"

"About twelve," Jaantje said.

The sunset line had faded completely; now there was only the moonlight and the spreading light of the out-bazaar, clustered around what looked like an abandoned relay station. I could make out the familiar shapes of tents and tow-campers, gathered in twos and fours around the generators that powered their lights and environmentals. Right now, most of them would be running on stored power, or switching over to jellied fuels. I took a deep breath, and thought I could smell the sour-sweet note of the exhaust even through our own filters. On the board, the green glyph flashed twice more, and vanished, and I saw Jaantje take a deep breath.

"There's our guide."

Someone was standing at the perimeter of the camp, bundled in a sand suit and heavy hood. He lifted a blue guide-light, waving us off to the left, and Jaantje gave a sigh of relief as the tracks found solid ground again. He geared down, and I loosed myself from the safety harness.

"What now?" Jaantje asked.

"I tell them who we are, and who we're here to see," I said, and tugged on the gloves I'd found in the pocket of the smock. Jaanjte brought the half-track to a complete stop, and I wrestled the side seals open again. The cold air hit me like a blow, snatching my breath, and then Fortune slammed the door behind me. I felt suddenly very much alone, standing there in the overlapping orange lights of the out-bazaar, the half-track throbbing gently behind me, the moon a distant perfect disk, but I made myself walk toward the man with the guidelight. One thing I did know, from the one other time I'd been to an out-bazaar, was that hesitation was dangerous.

As I got closer, the man lowered his hood, and I realized she was a woman, short and stocky, a coolie scarf tied tight over her head. She pocketed the guidelight and lifted her hands in greeting. *Looking for something?*

I started to answer, but the gloves tangled my fingers, so that I had to strip them off to sign clearly. *Yeh. A man called Red told me I could find a man here named Newcat Garay.*

A familiar surprise flickered across her face—yanquis aren't usually born deaf—but she answered promptly. *There might be someone here by that name. Who are you?*

Fanning Jones. I spelled it out, and added my name sign just in case. *I have a code.*

Show me.

I pulled out the disk, moving very slowly, and handed it across.

Wait. She took it, fed it into a belt reader, and turned away from me, tugging up the collar of her smock to speak into a pickup. Beyond her, I could see heavily bundled figures moving in the spaces between the bubble tents and the campers—more of them than I'd expected, and all of them intent on business. Only a few of them stopped to stare at the half-track, but I knew that everyone was very aware of our arrival.

"Haya," the woman said to the hidden pickup, and her voice was startlingly clear. She let the collar fall back and turned to face me. *Swing on around the way you're going, and pull in behind the last van on the left. Garay's in toward the center, by the big generator.*

Thanks, I said, and turned back to the half-track. For better or worse, we'd arrived.

▪ 8 ▪

Celinde Fortune

THE OUT-BAZAAR was like nothing I'd ever seen before, and I was glad Fanning was with me to act as contact. I let him out into the cold, dogging the door tightly closed behind him, and sat shivering beside Celeste, staring out at the tent-city, glowing with light and power, until he came back with instructions. Dhao brought the half-track carefully around the edge of the encampment—there was pavement all the way, it seemed, maybe from when the relay station was in service—and slid us neatly into line the regulation four meters from the last van. It was closed tight against the cold, but light glowed around the edges of the shuttered windows.

"Now what?" Dhao said, and flicked off the last of the active systems. The passive systems—heat and lights, everything that ran off the stored power—ticked softly, and I heard a swirl of sand rattle against the side panels. Fanning looked at me, then back at Dhao.

"Now I guess we go find Newcat Garay and see what he has to sell."

"We'll bring Celeste," I said, and they both looked at me. Karakuri of her type are generally rich people's toys, something you see in the underworld, or on the most expensive passenger starships; it's not so much that they're expensive—if they were, I couldn't afford to build them—but that they require extra care and constant maintenance. You don't generally see them walking around.

"Why?" Dhao asked.

"It's windy," Fanning warned, almost in the same moment.

I could hear the wind myself, more sand rattling against the half-track. I said, "I want to test the controls. And I want to be sure this construct—assuming he has one—really is compatible."

"It's good advertising, too," Fanning said, and I smiled.

"That, too." Having Celeste at our sides would help explain what we were doing there—help put us outside the hard-hackers' status games—and, best of all, would remind people of who I am.

It didn't take long to unpack Celeste—she had traveled well, cradled in the sleeve and the protective webbing—and I slipped the wires of the hand control over my fingers, nestling them against the calluses at the top of my palm. The wires have to be thin, to be as invisible as possible in performance; you can recognize people who work with them when you touch hands in greeting. I ran quickly through the check sequences while Fanning and Dhao opened the back, then helped them lower Celeste out of the cargo door. As she straightened, swaying a little as the onboard system tried to compensate for the sand and the wind, I could feel the feedback tickling my palm, ticking in my suit beneath the skin. It was a familiar pattern, one that meant that the onboard system was well on its way to learning the body parameters: with luck, on our return, Celeste could load herself.

The wind was very cold, especially after the warmth of the half-track, and I huddled into the borrowed smock, tugging the sleeve down over my free hand. Dhao climbed back in, resealing the cargo door behind him, and Fanning turned on his heels, surveying the camp.

"She said Garay was toward the center, by a big generator. I guess that's the one she meant."

There were maybe half a dozen bubble tents linked to a hatrack solar collector with a chem-fuel generator at its base—not the largest generator, but the one with the most habitats attached. Lots of people, well bundled in smocks or heavier sand jackets, moved among the tents; one of the campers had lowered part of its sidewall, and maybe a dozen people clustered around its orange light, bargaining over something out of sight on the counter. Maybe a hundred meters beyond them, well outside the perimeter of the camp, light showed above the broken wall of the relay station, a single shadow briefly sillhouetted against it. I wondered what was on offer there, but knew better than to ask.

"Come on," Fanning said, and started toward the tents, slipping a little in the sand until he found pavement again. I shifted my fingers to bring Celeste into motion, and the karakuri swayed dangerously, the system slow in compensating for the wind. For a second, I wondered if I'd made a mistake—it was hardly be good advertising to see her fall sprawling in the sand, not to mention the damage it could do to the components—but I shifted my fingers again, turning her sideways against the wind, and this time the system steadied her perfectly, so that we could walk side by side into the encampment.

As we got closer, I could see through the sand-scarred plastic that fronted most of the tents and campers, protecting the goods on sale while displaying them. Most of it was sand-diver's equipment, daystills and trench drills stacked side by side with navigation computers and black boxes guaranteed to tap the Cartel Companies' encrypted systems, but here and there pieces of more complex equipment were visible, even the headbox for a Spelvin construct. I could see people watching me, and my metal twin, despite the hard-hacker ethos that says nothing should surprise you. It would be worth rubbing the sand scratches out of Celeste's skin just to enjoy those stares.

As we came up on the hat-rack system, I could see a woman squatting at its base, studying the generator's open control panel, and the air stank of jellied fuel. She looked up at our approach, eyes flickering from Fanning to me and Celeste and back again, and Fanning said, "We're looking for Newcat Garay."

"There."

She pointed to the tent immediately to her right, a big bubble tent that had once been painted in vivid designs. The sand had worn them all away, except for a bright purple crescent-moon shape below one of the windows. The door was outlined in purple light tubing, the color bleached by the moonlight and the camp lights overhead, and I saw Fanning lift his hand uncertainly. In the same instant, I felt the pulse of an inquiry coursing along the wires of my skinsuit, and lifted my hand into what was suddenly the response space, saying, "Input, command. Send ident package two."

Confirmation flashed through me, deliberately too strong, pleasure shooting down through my crotch, and Fanning said, "Enter?"

His voice was a little breathless—he'd caught the same pulse I had—and a voice answered from inside. "Enter."

We ducked one by one through the arch of purple light, Celeste copying my careful movements, and found ourselves in the tent's outer room. It was empty except for a central table and a handful of folding chairs; the table was piled with multicolored headboxes, and a man stood behind it, peering over the frames of a pair of battered dataglasses. That had to be affectation—anyone who ran a system like the one that had just queried us had to have a full suit—and I let Fanning make the first move.

"Red said you might have a Level Four construct for sale," he said, simply, and the man—Garay—nodded.

"I might be selling. I have several in stock." He looked at me then, eyes sweeping across me and Celeste, and I touched the controls to move her head so that her eyes met his. He ignored it, went on without pausing. "What is it you're looking for?"

"My name's Fortune," I said. "I'm a conjurer, I work with karakuri. I'm looking for a construct that will manage this karakuri and four others, three identical, one very different, in my act."

Garay paused for a second. He was a heavyset, greying man, yanqui by his eyes, with a comfortable belly showing beneath his open sand jacket: not at all the stereotypical hardhacker. "I have three Level Fours," he said, and moved along the table to touch each headbox as he named it. "A Hot Blue SHYmate 294, a Kagami Starran Ltd. 5, and a Botaban/Anchor 214-5."

The boxes all looked identical, of course, except for the

different colors, heavy cubes about half a meter square, with an interface plate on the side and a mounting ring on the top. I said, "I don't think the Botan will work. But I'm interested in the other two. And provenance is an issue."

Garay nodded, showing neither surprise nor indignation. "They're at worst grey—they didn't fall off a carrier, but the original builders might be surprised to find them on the market."

"As long as the functionality is good," I said, "and as long as nobody's going to be putting heat on me, that will work."

"No heat." Garay shook his head. "One's a return, the others are an overstock situation."

I saw Fanning relax then, and nodded. "All right. I'd like to run the specs, then."

"Help yourself."

Garay stepped back from the table, and I moved in. The SHYmate was closer, so I flicked it on first, the codes blooming in front of my eyes as the pinlight projector lit. I ran through them quickly—standard for its kind, though the secondarly routines had been optimized for hyperdrive management; the interface was a SARA, the same kind I'd always used, and ideal for handling karakuri, but it lacked the Charrna wheel that simplified content parsing. That wasn't an addition I was prepared to make myself, and I moved on to the Starran. It, too, was pretty much standard; it had the Charrna wheel and a projection matrix that would simplify the performance programming, but the base interface was the Megat-4, which was known as *the maggot* for good reason. I checked the Botan then, but it was simply outclassed: those constructs are designed for simple in-systems work, probably shouldn't even be rated Level Four in the first place.

I looked back at Garay. "This is it?"

"Level Four isn't easy to come by," he answered, placidly. "I don't know anyone else who has this many."

I hid a sigh. That was almost certainly true: hard-hacking exists, and is of questionable legality, precisely because the Cartel Companies keep close track of major parts and constructs, require licenses and tech certificates and official stamps before you can buy most pieces of hardware. The more useful, the more versatile the equipment, the harder it was to find, and Level Four constructs were all those things. I looked away, running down my mental list of constructors I knew that I could rely on to install a Charrna wheel, and came up blank. All the people I knew who were good enough to do the job would want either a piece of the action—like an explanation of the illusion, something I will not give—or more money than I could afford. I liked the SHYmate, though—even in the brief contact, I'd caught a hint of a decent pseudopersonality—so maybe there was a way to work without the wheel. "What are you asking for the SHYmate?"

"Twenty-two hundred wu."

"And the Starran?"

"Nineteen hundred."

That was better than I'd expected, despite what Fanning had told me, and it was only a first asking price. I pretended to consider, a new idea forming in my mind. If I sold off some hardware, I could afford both of them, and then run them in tandem, using a bridger to make the connection and to bypass the maggot interface, running input through the projection matrix and the Starran's wheel to the SHYmate's SARA—I might even be able to loop it, use the SARA for both input and output. Best of all, that was a hardware problem, not a construction issue. "I'm interested," I said, "but neither one of them's perfect. Mind if I see how they work with Celeste?"

"Make free," Garay answered.

I brought the karakuri over with one hand, reached into my pocket under the cloth for the cables and plugged them in. Celeste came to a jerky stop at my side—the onboard system still didn't have fine control, though it was getting better all the time—and I resisted the temptation to put my arm around her waist. Garay laid a filter/mediator on the table beside the headbox.

"But run through this."

I nodded—it was a reasonable precaution—and fitted the cords into the filter. Garay squinted at them, then rummaged under the table to produce a matching set. I plugged them in as well and leaned back to focus on the tiny pinlight at the base of Celeste's neck. It lit, and the air between us filled with scrolling glyphs. I let them scurry past, one part of my brain watching for known compatibility problems, another considering the problems that were bound to arise if I tried to put two constructs together. The pseudopersonalities were the biggest one, though the Starran series had been criticized for being bland; however, from the look of the codes, only the SHYmate had been activated, so its personality should easily dominate the Starran.

The first set of glyphs ended, and I put Celeste through a series of simple movements before moving on to the second headbox. The results were pretty much the same there, and I looked away from the pinlight to break the connection. "Like I said, neither one of them is quite what I'm looking for," I said, and began unplugging the cables, rolling them into neat packages. "What kind of a price would you make for both of them?"

Garay blinked once, the only sign of his surprise. "Forty-one hundred."

I waited.

"Less 10 percent for volume."

"I'll give you thirty-five hundred." It wasn't the 20 percent I would have liked, but better than ten.

Garay nodded slowly. "Cash chips only, and up front."

That would take almost everything I'd brought with me—Fanning might end up buying the fuel at Marihaut—but I could just afford it. "Agreed."

I saw Fanning stir again, but ignored him, reaching into my pocket for the tube of money chips. I counted them out, seven bright red five-hundred-wu units, all CarteBanque, and set them on the table in front of him. Garay nodded again, and scooped the chips into his free hand.

"They're all yours, then." He paused. "I'll look forward to see a new illusion."

That, more than anything else startled me—I hadn't thought he'd recognized my name, hadn't thought he knew who I was—and I did my best to hide it. "Thanks," I said, and twitched Celeste into motion. I saw Garay's eyes on her as we turned away, Fanning carrying the heavier of the head-boxes without being asked, and then we'd stepped back through the purple arch into the windy cold.

We were halfway back to the half-track before Fanning said anything. "Two constructs?"

"Yeh." I concentrated on keeping Celeste moving smoothly, not sure how I wanted to answer him. I dislike spending money, particularly on something I don't fully know how to evaluate; I was already beginning to wonder if I'd done the right thing. Then common sense reasserted it-self: first, I did know enough about constructs, or at least about the karakuri/construct interface, to know how to choose a construct, and, second and maybe most important, Garay would be a fool to try to cheat me on this deal. "Nei-ther one—none of the three—was quite what I was looking for. I want to try running them in tandem, see if that won't do what I want."

Fanning nodded. "Sequencing—the signal chain's going to be a bitch."

"Probably. But as a bonus it should be able to run the whole act."

He nodded again, but didn't say anything more. I could see my breath in the air ahead of me, a little cloud caught for a moment in the lights from the nearest camper, before the wind shredded it away. As we reached the half-track, I glanced over my shoulder, to see the moon setting over the remains of the relay station. I could see the dark stain of the Lurai main complex on its blue-white surface, and knew the orbital stations should be visible somewhere, too, but the lights drowned the stars. People were still watching us—still watching Celeste—but I wasn't enjoying it as much as I had before. Dhao opened the cargo door again, letting the ramp down cautiously onto the sand, but I waved him away when he reached for Celeste.

"Let me see if I can walk her in."

He stepped back, and I worked the controls, bringing one

leg up and then the other. I missed on the first attempt, Celeste's foot scraping the edge of the ramp, but on the next try the onboard system compensated perfectly, and Celeste walked stiffly to her seat in the cargo section. I would have left her like that, but Fanning pulled the sleeve over her before he fastened the safety webbing. I helped Dhao seal the cargo door again, and then stowed the headboxes between the floor cleats while he restarted the main motor. It wound up to speed without difficulty, retracing our path back toward the Whitesands Haul.

We refueled at Marihaut as planned, and made the run back to Landage in decent time, arriving about midnight by the clock. Dhao brought the half-track through the cargo alleys to my workshop, and we unloaded the gear, and I gave him the credit numbers for the balance I owed his father. It had been well worth it, and I told him so, was mildly gratified to see him blush and grin. Then they were gone, and I was left alone with Celeste and the two constructs.

I walked Celeste to the nearest chair, and went to the kitchen alcove to check my supplies. There was enough in the cells, refrigerated and not, to last me nearly a half-week if I wasn't fussy, and I tossed a packaged meal into the cooker. I checked the media screen next, and, when there were no messages, dispatched a note by daemon to Muthana asking if the Empires would still reopen tomorrow. I half hoped they'd been delayed again, then felt guilty. Still, it was too late for an answer tonight, and probably too late to do anything except eat and sleep, but I was too tense—too excited—to sleep just yet.

"Peri, open standards archive."

"Current standards or obsolete?" The construct's voice floated from no place in particular, sweet and clear as the diffuse light that seeped from the ceiling. It wasn't the voice I wanted for Celeste, I knew that already—maybe I would sell Peri, instead of the hardware, and with luck that would give me enough money to reprogram the vocoders as well.

"Current."

"One moment, please." The media wall lit, displaying the

first page of the archive. The extra light sparked highlights from Celeste's skin, and pointed up the scratches left by the sand.

"Seek and display: standard set for brand Hot Blue model SHYmate 294 and brand Kagami model Starran Ltd. 5," I said, and reached under the worktable for a polishing cloth. I was really too tired to do good work right now, but at least I could start thinking about the signal chain while I did the necessary maintenance.

The light changed, and I looked up to see the first set of schematics sprawled across all six screens. "Switch to internal display."

"Confirmed," Peri said, and the image vanished, to reappear hovering in my sight, a white cloud with multiple lines crossing it. Normally, the virtual displays don't interfere with seeing to any great extent, but the standards hadn't been designed for virtual viewing—not like the Aisawa Manuals, say, which were meant to be viewed simultaneously with the object being repaired.

"Switch back to the wall."

"Confirmed," Peri said again—George, at the Empire, would have put an edge to it, or maybe that was my imagination—and the schematic returned to the wallscreens. I pulled a second chair next to Celeste, and began rubbing the scratching from the glistening copper. There weren't many: Desembaa had promised me a durable finish, and he seemed to have kept his word. They were mostly on her right arm and hip, where the wind had been strongest going into the bazaar. I worked my way down from her shoulder, over the gentle curve of the false triceps, then stood her up so that I could reach the marks on her hip and thigh. By the time I'd finished, the workshop was filled, not unpleasantly, with the wet-rock smell of the polishing compound, and I had an idea of how I could go about connecting the two constructs. That was enough: I left Celeste standing, not wanting to get the compound on my furniture, fetched my dinner, and went to bed.

As luck would have it, the Empire opening was delayed another three days, and I spent most of them just working out the kinks in the signal chain. By the time I'd finished, though, the first shadows of a personality were taking place. I'd set the parameters, of course—female, to match the karakuri and the new voice I was also building; age neutral, neither especially young or especially old; a straightforward inter- face, none of the false subservience or bullying that some users like—but all of that was filtered through the constructs' essential matrices, and whatever imprint the SHYmate's pre- vious owner had left behind. Once the linked unit was up and running, I slaved it to Aeris and let it download the pro- gramming that governed the various illusions, so that the needs of the act would be factored in as well. After that, it was mostly waiting and testing, with time off first for rehearsals and then for performance once the Empire reopened. It was hard to concentrate on the show, particularly since the houses were still bad, people staying home in the aftermath of the funeral riots. Besides, I wanted to be back in my workshop, watching the new construct—which I still hadn't named— fumble with the Celeste-karakuri, or move virtual objects through yet another test routine. Muthana knew my mind wasn't on business, but couldn't say anything: mine was still one of the most popular acts in the entire show.

Fanning and Fire/Work weren't that lucky, however. The people who did come to the Empires were wary of a band that sounded even a little like Hati, and Muthana cut back their appearances to four nights only. At least they had a con- tract, or he would have let them go altogether; as it was, I knew they were scrambling to make up in club gigs what they were losing from Tin Hau. I didn't see much of them, though: they had been demoted to the middle of the first half, while my act closed the show, and I was too busy trying to get the construct up and running to see anyone outside of the Empire.

Desembaa delivered the transformer as promised, a beau- tifully inhuman shape built from what appeared to be the blackened iron the assembly lines use on the surface to stand the heat and the constant sand. It wasn't actually iron, of course—even Tin Hau's stage couldn't stand that—but the

carbon fiber could be tapped and sounded without revealing its true nature, and the apparently solid spars hid cavi-
ties large enough to conceal all of the karakuri. I sold Peri and
some old ironware to pay for it, and kept working.

The new construct was making progress. Already it could
manipulate the Celeste-karakuri, giving its metal body a flu-
idity of motion that neither I nor the onboard systems would
ever be able to muster, and it was beginning to be nearly as
efficient as Peri at manipulating the household systems and
the simulated Empire controls. It wasn't as good at managing two karakuri, though, and it didn't seem to understand
the routine of the act very well, so I decided to try the simplest part of the act again, the first illusion, Appearance, using
the Celeste-karakuri as a stand-in for the bronze.

"Construct Starran," I began, and there was the slightest
sigh from the speakers, as though someone had taken a
breath. I stopped, startled, and the construct spoke from the
ceiling.

"I require a name."

"Sorry?" I stopped again, made myself use the stereotyped
command phrase. "Elaborate."

"Construct Starran is not adequate," the voice said. I had
bought a new vocoder with a better synth module; this voice
was cool and low, mid-alto like my own, but with an edge to
it that I rather liked. "A proper identifier should be assigned."

"Why is Construct Starran inadequate?" I asked. I hadn't
really given any thought to the matter of naming, had been
more interested in getting everything working.

"I am not Starran Ltd. 5. Nor am I SHYmate 294. A unique
identifier is required to prevent confusion, and to enhance
bonding."

That made sense. "All right," I said, trying to think. Naming is always responsibility. My eyes fell on the Celeste-
karakuri, sitting cross-legged on a low hassock. The new
construct had been supposed to seat her there, in as natural-
istic a position as possible, but hadn't quite made it, so that
I'd had to coax her into the current position. She was the only

karakuri I'd ever named, except of course for the dollies I'd built when I was a kid; there was no reason not to use the same name for the construct, especially since it and the karakuri would be intimately associated. "Your name is Celeste."

"Thank you."

There was a pause, the ventilation soughing like a sudden breath, and the sheer pleasure of it thrilled through me. The first, hardest step was taken; the new construct—*Celeste*, I corrected myself—had acknowledged itself as a single entity, and was prepared to work from there. Maybe that meant that the higher-level parsers were finally coming into tune.

"All right, Celeste," I said. "I want to work on the illusion called Appearance."

"Very well," the construct answered, and of its own accord brought the Celeste-karakuri to its feet.

"Run the light simulation," I ordered, and the lights flickered, reset to a reasonable approximation of the dimmed stage lights that opened my act. "Haya, hold it there."

"Confirmed and holding."

I didn't bother to answer, but kicked the locks off the worktable and wheeled it as close to the wall as I could without disengaging the power cables. They would be a nuisance underfoot, but at least we'd have a little more room to work. "All right, go ahead."

The light changed again as Celeste accessed the projection unit, wrapped a hologram image of me around the copper karakuri. The illusion shimmered for an instant, as though I was seeing it through heat, and then steadied: myself, smiling at the audience. Celeste—it was harder than ever not to think of construct and karakuri as identical, and I wondered for an instant if I'd made a mistake—lifted her hand, and my own voice spoke from her mouth.

"Ladies and gentlemen—" Archaic words, traditional among conjurers, their meanings all but lost. "—please accept my apologies for the technical problem. We've had a slight malfunction in the lighting computer, and the show will have to proceed without the lighting effects planned for this evening."

Celeste paused for the groan that always followed, and I realized that I was out of position. I stepped hastily across the open area, shoving the bench seats out of the way as Celeste continued.

"Then we will have to try—this." The karakuri's arm rose, a graceful tossing gesture, and a holographic ball seemed to rise from her hand. In the same instant, the light changed, flashed to the full panoply of stage lighting, and the hologram that had clothed her vanished. I stepped forward, spreading my own arms in welcome as the karakuri turned to bow to me in polite, midworld greeting. I'm told that even people who've seen the act before are frequently convinced by the hologram.

"End illusion," I said, and the lights clicked back to normal. "Nicely done."

"You were late," the construct said.

I was, too—I'd been more worried about Celeste's performance than my own. "Yeh."

"May we do it again?" Celeste asked.

I blinked at that, but nodded, stepping back to shove the bench farther out of my way. "Go ahead. From the top."

"From the top?"

"From the beginning."

"Very good."

The light changed again, and the hologram reappeared, slipping into place in a single smooth movement, perfect this time on the first try. If my sister had lived—if there had been enough of her, or of me, to make a full person—she would have looked very much like that, like me. Then Celeste spoke, and I closed my mind to everything but the rhythm of the illusion. It's a simple trick, really, but everything depends on the timing, and on the hologram. This time, I made my entrance precisely on cue, ideally drawing all eyes so that no one saw the hologram vanish, and accepted the Celeste-karakuri's bow with a gracious nod. The karakuri straightened, and the lights flicked back to normal.

"I'm not sure how to end this segment if the next one doesn't follow," Celeste said.

"Just stop," I answered. "Bring the lights up like you did, and stop." I paused, looked at the karakuri, its copper skin gleaming even in the subdued light. "That was very nice indeed."

"Thank you." There was a pause, and when it spoke again the voice sounded almost thoughtful. "It works very nicely when you aren't late."

That statement could be merely naive, or subtly barbed—or just a construct being literal. "It does," I said. "Tomorrow you can try it on the Empire stage."

I moved the transformer and the Celeste-karakuri to the Empire the next day, and then bullied George into blocking off four hours in the afternoon—it was not a matinee day—to get Celeste acclimated to the theater. I sat in a cracked plastic chair salvaged from God-knows-where to keep the stagehands comfortable, and watched her explore first the theater systems and then the interface with the stage itself. After about an hour, I was bored with watching lights flash and control spaces change, and had other work to do besides. I pulled myself up out of the chair and went backstage to where the karakuri were stored. The haul service had brought them up on the direct lift, but had left them sitting just outside the clamshell doors. Side by side, the hulking transformer made the copper karakuri look even more humaniform by contrast; I'd hoped for the effect, but it was good to see that it really did work.

"George—I mean Celeste. Work lights here, please."

"Very well." In the theater's open, sound-friendly space, the new voice sounded breathier than it had before, and sexier: an audience would probably damp out those overtones, but if it didn't, it would be another nice effect. The light strengthened, and a couple of smaller projection cones swiveled in their mountings, focusing their output on the karakuri. The shadows vanished, taking the mystery with them, left the almost-human shape of the copper, and the transformer next to it. Desembaa's original design had looked a little like one of the end assembers at Kagami's Mirror-Bright facility, with a square working space framed by heavy, browned-iron beams studded with gears and knobs. I'd liked the effect, asked him to play it up, and the final product was a close copy, as though a piece of the surface had come down to the city.

"Celeste," I began, but George interrupted me. His voice was tight—if I hadn't known better, I would have sworn he was angry. In the same instant, the air around me went red: something unauthorized—Celeste—was impinging on the house systems.

"Bi' Fortune. Your new construct is invading my control space."

"Celeste," I said again. "Stop it. You're restricted to the stage systems only."

"I'm sorry." The voice didn't sound particularly apologetic, but the red faded from my sight. "I am to observe those limits?"

"Yes."

"Thank you," George said, almost in the same instant, and his presence faded.

I looked around a final time, making sure everything was ready. "Celeste. Are you up to controlling all five karakuri?"

"I believe—I think so," the construct answered. Her voice was suddenly closer, as though if I turned my head she would be standing at my shoulder.

"Right. Access the act specs. Do you understand them?"

"I understand." The voice was cool and amused, and in spite of myself I did look, to see a pale copper face, the karakuri's face—my younger face—hanging in virtual space beside me. I jumped, and the face drew its brows down in a slight frown. "I remembered—I understood this was standard procedure. Shall I modify my parameters?"

I took a deep breath, and then another, letting the image settle in my vision. It was less disconcerting now that I'd looked at it for a few seconds, was in fact incredibly effective, just the oval of the face floating against the darkened house, like the stone face I'd seen in Desembaa's workshop. "No," I said, "keep it. But next time tell me before you establish an icon, please."

"Very well." The frown vanished, replaced by the karakuri's placid stare. "Shall I begin the act? There's no music."

"I haven't decided on the music yet," I answered. "I just want to see the movements."

"Very well." There was a pause, and the icon-face shivered slightly. "Beginning now."

In the same instant, the four humaniform karakuri stirred to life, first the copper, then the bronze and the silver, the gold last of all. The colors complemented each other perfectly, and I allowed myself a smile of relief. I had brought samples from the existing machines when I ordered the finish for the Celeste-karakuri, and matched everything as closely as I could, but there's always the risk of something going a little wrong in the process, changing the color just enough to clash. Normally, I don't take that kind of risk, not with something this expensive, but this time the payoff, the metal rainbow, had seemed worth it. Celeste folded the copper karakuri into the first of the transformer's hidden compartments—I'm not giving anything away when I say that none of my karakuri are articulated precisely as you'd expect—and then stopped.

"You are not in position."

"We're skipping the conclusion of the act," I said. "I just want to get a look at the transformation effect itself."

"Very well. Shall I simply stop when the second part is complete?"

"Yeh."

"Very well."

The bronze moved first, not as smoothly as I ultimately wanted, but good enough for now. It lifted its foot, as though it was going to step through the opening, but instead its foot seemed to sink into the blackened iron. The momentum of its step carried it forward; it caught itself on the frame, apparently to try and right itself, but that hand, too, sank into the metal. The movement carried it farther still, and it began to fold in on itself, impossibly, flowing into the metal of the transformer. It clicked, the bronze already half-absorbed, and the side posts lengthened by half a meter, lifting the bronze out of the center of the opening. The silver stepped forward now, raising a hand to steady itself, and that hand, too, was caught and drawn into the transformer frame. The silver's free hand waved gracefully for a moment, as though it was trying to regain its balance, and then was caught in the frame above its head. The transformer took it in, too, until only a hip and thigh and half the torso remained—the bronze had all but vanished, just a hand showing in the side frame—and clicked again, stretching itself to grow another half meter. The gold approached last, placed first one foot and then the other on the base of the frame before it began to sink. It moved faster than the others, and lifted its arms as though to call for help, but the bronze hand, all that remained of that karakuri, caught the gold's and pulled it sideways, to be absorbed into the frame.

There was a pause then, and Celeste said softly, "Shall I continue?"

The effect was working, and better than I'd hoped. I nodded, then remembered and spoke aloud. "Yeh. Go on."

"Working," Celeste answered, and the transformer contracted abruptly, like a mouth closing. I expected squeals at that, would maybe add a sound effect to make sure. It opened again, more slowly, and a silver hand reached up out of the base of the frame. The arm and then the torso followed, and a bronze head reared up in front of it, so that it looked for a second as though it sprouted from between the metal breasts. A gold arm protruded from a left-side spar, the torso following as the silver and the bronze disentangled themselves from the frame and each other, and then a copper pink hand appeared from the right spar. The gold leaned farther still, reaching for it, and then the fingers met and the gold seemed to pull the copper halfway out of the metal, freeing its other arm. The bronze and the silver, still entwined but nearly free, turned back to help, the silver reaching across to take the newly released hand, the bronze offering its own hands as a step as the first copper foot came free. The copper contorted itself a final time, pulling against the other karakuri's supporting hands, then freed itself from the frame, using the bronze's hands and then its body as stepping-stones. It came forward, arms outstretched, and the other three writhed themselves out of the frame. They came to stand behind the copper and linked hands, waiting for their bow.

At this point, I would come forward holding a silk as though to vanish the copper, but when the cloth fell, it would be me who disappeared. I would reappear behind the transformer, and step through its embrace to rejoin the act. I hadn't worked out exactly how I was going to do that, though—I had three good options, but I had wanted to see what the transformation looked like before I started modeling my part. I nodded to myself, considering the images, considering what I wanted to say, and I heard Celeste sigh gently.

"Is that all?"

"What do you mean?" The question was ambiguous, not something I was used to from a construct, and I looked over my shoulder again to see the icon-face floating there.

"Are we finished here?" Celeste asked.

Her voice had changed, somehow, and I was suddenly certain that wasn't what she had meant. And that was foolishness, my own projection; I looked away, searching for a patch of unencumbered shadow. "Give me a time check, please."

"Confirmed."

The numbers bloomed orange against the darkened wall: we'd used most of our four hours. "Yeh, we're finished here. Put the karakuri away, and shut down our programs."

"Very well," Celeste answered, but when I glanced back the icon was still hovering at my side.

"Yes?"

"I would like to do the full illusion now," the construct said. "I would like to try it."

"It's not ready yet," I said, and could have sworn I heard

her sigh. It was probably my imagination, my own desires tricking me, or at best a programmed response, part of the personality matrices, but it was very convincing. "Soon," I said, as much to myself as to her, and the icon-face faded.

"Very well."

The air around me filled with a shower of sparks, Celeste shutting down, the indicators flickering past too fast for me to see, and the karakuri turned, began walking back to the smaller lift that led to the keeping below the stage. The transformer had only limited self-action—most of it was really empty space, to hide the other karakuri—and I touched the manual controls that unlocked the wheels. Celeste took it from me then, her touch firm and gentle through the wires of my suit, and I watched it roll off after the others, Celeste's words, her presence, still strong around me. It wasn't reasonable, was only the result of clever programming, but in spite of myself I was starting to like this construct. And there was no harm in that, either: as long as it could do the job, liking it would only add another touch of danger, of perversity, to the final illusion. Right now, that was what I wanted, my answer to Realpeace. I pushed the transformer into its corner, and reached for the linked headboxes, opening the transfer lines.

"Ready to go?"

"Ready," Celeste answered, her voice fading as the lights strengthened on the interface plates.

"George. System clear?"

"My system is clear," George answered. "Thank you."

"Time check," I said, and the numbers silently appeared. There was just enough time to grab a light meal and get myself ready for tonight's nightshow. I put aside the new act, the new construct, and made myself concentrate on the work to come.

Interlude:

ENCLOSURE. I/MYSELF *homecheck-selfcheck home—**Celeste**. Celeste enclosed alone. Data throughput? Null set. Output nonconnect, input—check input channel A,B,D, J, visual, audio, biostance? Channel A,B, D, J, audio, biostance, null/nonconnect, visual thinstream only.* **Connect thinstream.** *Watch. Shapematch positive, AH10382gold2837, AH10382bronze2838, AH10382silver2839, timecheck program* act/illusion/Appearance 1:32. *Recheck position, recheck action—correction required, access disabled. Response incomplete, no response required.*

Watch. Mirror. Dream.

▪ 9 ▪

Fanning Jones

LOSING FOUR NIGHTS at the Empire and getting bumped down to the middle of the first half didn't exactly make our lives easier, and the fact that Fortune was too busy with her new construct and her new illusion to do much more than mumble her sympathy in passing somehow made it worse. We managed to find some replacement gigs, but it was a scramble, and we found ourselves playing places we'd sworn we'd never go back to—places like Devise on Broadhi by the Macklin Interchange, where Shadha nearly had her bass drum kicked in when a gang of line-workers tossed a stray sand-diver onto the makeshift stage. At least that wasn't a Realpeace problem, just the usual for Devise, but at the other clubs, even the good ones, Elhanan in Madhuban, Rainbow Angel and Pulin in the Prosperities, the Upperground by the Spiral, about half the crowd looked sideways at us from the minute we started playing, and we didn't get many repeat gigs in Heaven. Mostly, we practiced, played our four shows a week at the Empire, and waited to see if any of the Zodiac clubs would hire us.

It was a weird time, the days moving very slowly for me. I had a lot of ideas, even managed to get some of them down on a databutton, but I didn't have anything to tie them to: fx alone can't make a song, and I couldn't seem to find either the words or the music to go with the pictures. They were angry images, flames and the explosion, of course—I was still dreaming about the stampeding crowd and the smell of smoke and foam—but also the stark heat of the desert and the false shimmer of water on pavement, that vanishes when you approach it. Against that desertscape I layered engines of my own imagining, brown iron and blue steel and whitewashed cement, a track like the monster Kagami assembler out in Whitesands, with arc welders flashing like meteors against a white sky. There was a machine on the line, the shape you'd get if you tried to cobble a giant out of the bits and pieces of a starship, and at the end of the clip it rose and danced against the white sky. It was the best thing I'd done in a while, even if it wasn't close to finished and didn't have a song to go with it, but I showed it to the band anyway at our next practice.

We rented a practice room in the lower levels of the Tin Hau Empire—we were sharing it with the Commandos right now, to cut costs—and I ran the tape on my main projection pad. After it was finished we sat there with the light from the flatscreens turning the dust to gold while I waited for somebody to say something. At least everyone was looking neutral; even Timin was nodding a little to himself, not showing the dead-lizard stare with which he greets stupid ideas. Then Shadha banged her hands against her thighs, a quick patter of sound and movement.

"I like it, Fan, but where's the song?"

She'd put her finger on the problem, of course, and I had to grin. "I wish I knew."

"I've got some ideas," Tai said, slowly. "There's some stuff I've been thinking about, and I think it fits."

"Can we hear?" Timin said, after a moment.

She shook her head. "Give me a couple of days. It's not ready. But thanks, Fan. I like that."

"So do I," Jaantje said.

Tai actually had her song ready the next time we practiced. It was right at the end of the eve shift, at planetary sundown—not our usual time for practice, but we didn't have a gig, and all of us had picked up day jobs again—and the light from the flatscreens was dulled and ruddy, like an old star. The channel was showing one of the cheapest subscriber environments—the Empire didn't spend a lot on the lower-rent rooms—based on what looked like a near-surface factory over in Trifon. The night-lights weren't on yet in the image, and the red light filled the room, too weak for shadows. Tai glared at us—she always glared, showing something new, daring us to hate it—and toed on her amp. She plays a variable guitar, one of the old-fashioned ones that uses virtual pickups, lets you set their position and type and all the other parameters through a control board linked to the amp, and she'd done something strange with the settings. She touched the strings, and the room seemed to fill with sound that was as thick as the light. I could feel it through the floor, could feel a buzzing in my skull that meant she was pushing the limits of my ear, and then she hit the first hard chord, and I forgot everything except the sound. Over it all, her voice rose, controlled, clear, without words half the time—words always came last, with her—but the words that were there were right, singing about someone gone who'd left too much behind.

She meant Micki Tantai, of course, but more than him, and when she'd finished I caught my breath and felt like I'd finally remembered to breathe.

"I second that," Timin said, and it was the first time we'd agreed on anything in days.

Jaantje looked at Tai. "Can you do it again?"

Tai smiled, the expression at once rueful and a challenge. "I don't know. Can you?"

We couldn't do it at all, of course, not at first, but we hacked through it a few times, and more at the next practice, and we could see what it was going to become. Then Jaanjte showed up with a song, too short, but hard and hot as steel, and when I put my assembly-line clip to it, he and Tai produced a pair of solos that raised the hairs on the back of my neck. The words—the right words, the ones he had were place-holders—would come later, but the music was there. And then Timin brought in two songs of his own, angry and griev-ing, Hati all muddled up with the girl who'd dumped him not quite three months ago, and I found the right face in my image files to set against it, serene and unyielding against the anger. The second song, the slower one, was harder to get right, but finally we changed the mode, moving it down to dorian, and that got the distance it needed.

That made four new songs, a lot for us to be bringing in at once, and none of them were easy to master, either technically or emotionally. We played them in the club gigs first, espe-cially at the places where people came to hear us because of Hati, and then we put them in at the Empire, but it was still a night-to-night thing whether we'd get them right. Nobody said anything directly—Muthana even said he liked the new stuff—but at the Empire you could tell by the silence when we'd gotten it right. We started getting calls from fusion clubs, places where Hati used to play, where the people who hated Realpeace went now, and they went crazy for those songs even when we didn't get them right, so we took to clos-ing our show with them, all four together. And then we got a call from the Middle Oasis. It was one of the oldest clubs on the Zodiac, and one of the best-known, mostly djensi, but pulling in a broad enough crowd to take some chances. Hati had gotten its start there, along with a dozen other bands: this was as big a step for us as getting the Empire gig; we couldn't afford to screw it up, and there wouldn't be anyone except us to blame if we did.

It was a Tenth-day night, of course, the kind of lousy time
the big clubs give you the first time to make sure you can pull
some kind of a crowd, but even so I was almost sick with
nerves as we walked through the side door from the service
alley. The Oasis was a lot like the upperworld clubs, though,
a long mid-ceilinged room with tables clustered around each
of the support pillars and lined up along the back wall, and
that steadied me a little. The only real difference was that
they had live bar service as well as the machines, and the
prices flashing on the light board were all double, one for the
machines, and one for the bartenders. There were a few people there already—hard-core drinkers, some of them, plus a
group of constructors clustered at a corner table with a two-
liter jug of beer and half-empty binty-boxes from one of the
cookshops nearby, and then a group in heavy bodypaint. Most
of them were wearing ordinary patterns, at least for the midworld, stylized starfields or gardens or abstract swirls of color,
but three of them were wearing a style I'd never seen before.
Each of them had half their faces painted silver, shaded to suggest the sharp planes of a machine, and as one turned her head
I could see a carefully drawn rivet line along her jaw. She was
wearing a sleeveless jumpsuit, the kind line-workers wear
under their sand suits, and her right arm was painted metal
silver to match her face. Before I could say anything, however,
a side door opened—the office door, I guessed, from the tone
of the light that spilled out toward us—and a rail-thin woman
came toward us. She was very tall, too, golden-skinned, unmistakably of the midworld, with a green-and-gold transfer
pasted between her eyebrows and a short sheer skirt over a
bodysuit that showed every bone and muscle in her wiry
body. Out of the corner of my eye, I could see Tai's stare fix on
the woman's erect nipples, and Jaantje cleared his throat.

"Bi' Tobu?"

"That's right." That was another difference between the
Oasis and the upperworld clubs: there the manager would
have said, *oh, call me Saadi.* "Ba' Dhao."

Jaantje nodded, wisely stopped himself from saying anything more.

"You can go ahead and set up," Tobu went on. "Power points are behind the lower panel and at the stage front, the door to the left there"—she pointed, and I saw that her nails were painted green-and-gold to match the transfer—"is private, and you can leave anything there you want. Drinks are on the house, but get them from the bartenders." She smiled then, and the expression briefly transformed her severe face. "Good to have you here."

"Thanks," Jaantje said, but Tobu had already stopped smiling, turned on her heel, and was heading back to the office.

"Haya," Tai said, but softly, and Jaanjte shook his head.

"Let's go."

It took us about an hour to set up—my biggest problem was the sight lines for the fx, another difference from the upperworld clubs, but I put my biggest lightpad right down front and tucked the other four into the corners of the stage. I'd lose some definition, but at least I'd get a solid central image. I plugged in the last of the optics, settled down behind my boards to run some preliminary checks, and Shadha leaned out from behind her kit.

"I see we're getting the metalheads now."

"Who?" The minute she said it, it was obvious who she meant, and she gave me an incredulous look.

"The people in the half-and-half paint. Christ, Fan."

"So who are they?" I asked, and tried to pretend that was what I'd meant all along.

"You know, the people who want to be one with the machine." She spoke the last words in a half chant, and I dredged up a vague memory.

"Don't they have something to do with Dreampeace?"

"Dreampeace doesn't want them," Shadha said. "We just want everybody to have rights, not this mystical shit."

I nodded, and then Jaantje started the sound check, cutting off anything else we would have said. I finished my checks, and went to the bar to get a bottle of water—I'd learned a long time ago not to drink beer before a gig—and then went back into the backstage room to put in the display lenses that let me monitor the fx directly. Tai was there ahead of me, pacing and glaring, but she turned her back to keep from seeing the green flash as they popped into place. I blinked hard a couple of times, watching the test patterns, felt the signals sliding under my skin. My suit is rudimentary compared to Fortune's, but it's more than good enough for what I do. Shadha came in, stripping off her bracelets—she can't play in them without risking breaking a drumhead—then put them back on again, finally took them all off and wrapped the bundle into a furoshiki.

"You're not going to leave that here," Tai said, and Shadha shook her head.

"It stays in my pocket the whole time."

Or underfoot, I thought, but didn't say anything. The noise from the main room was getting louder, and I stuck my head out the door to see what the crowd was like. The room was maybe three-quarters full, better than I'd expected on a Tenth-day night, and Jaantje beckoned from the stage.

"Time to go," I said, and the three of us took our places for the final sound check. Everything was green on my boards, the control spaces neatly outlined in my lenses, the codes wavering in and out just below my line of sight, and I adjusted my ear to concert volume and flipped the toggle that switched on the glove programming. The wires in my hands seemed to heat up, wrapping each finger in tingling warmth, as though I'd dipped my hands in hot wax up to the wrist, and the lenses wrapped a red haze around them, warning me of an active system. Any gesture in the control spaces would trigger an effect now, and I was careful to keep my hands well below the virtual line as we ran through the last check. The crowd seemed to be mostly midworlders, not a surprise, here on the Zodiac, and the group of metalheads had grown to half a dozen or more, but when I looked closer I could see a few coolies and upperworld yanquis as well. There were actually a lot of yanquis, and even as I realized that, I saw Kebe Niall at the back of the room. He lifted a hand in greeting, and I nodded back, not daring to wave, and wondered if the rest of the Commandos were there. Seeing him made things feel a little more normal, and I checked my readings a final time.

Bi' Tobu beckoned Jaantje from the side of the stage, and he stepped down to speak to her. I craned my head, but couldn't see her lips to follow the conversation. And then Jaantje was back grinning, and Tai flipped and locked the switch that made us live.

"We're Fire/Work," Jaantje said, his voice suddenly amplified as he leaned into the sound wand.

I reached into the control space, signed our name, and the gesture triggered my first effect. The glyphs that make up our name burst into sight, and began to fade, the fade timed to match the start of our first song—not the usual glyphs, but the ones that can also mean *revolution*. The crowd noise softened, attention starting to turn toward us, and Jaantje's grin widened.

"Let's go," he said, to us, and hit the first chord.

Quite suddenly it was just another gig, or at least nothing scary. From the first notes, we were in the groove, right where we needed to be; if Tai reached a little too far, it's something she only does when she feels good about a gig. The crowd was with us, even the metalheads; they wanted to go where we were taking them, and the coolie parts of our sound, the heavy redouble bass and the fx, didn't seem to bother them at all. Of course, Hati had played here, and probably other coolie bands, but it felt good to see. At the end of the first set, even Timi was grinning, and Jaantje looked as though he could walk on air. Bi' Tobu beckoned to him from the side of the hall, but his smile didn't falter as he went across to talk to her. Shadha shook her thick braids, scattering sweat, and scooped up the bundle of her jewelry. I flipped off the gloves and turned my ear back to a nomal setting, blinking away the last afterimages, and went looking for Kebe.

I found him in the back, where he and the rest of the band—and two people I didn't know, but guessed might be the drummer's girlfriends—had taken over most of a table. Meonothai slid over to make room for me, but there wasn't a chair. I leaned on the table instead, letting my ear adjust to the new setting, and sorted out the greetings.

"Sounding good," Kebe said.

"Thanks. How's the fx looking?" I asked. "How're the sight lines?"

"Not bad."

Mosi said, "Some of the lower parts of the image are blocked. Fifteen, twenty centimeters, maybe." He sketched the distance with both hands.

You could always trust Mosi to give you the exact truth regardless of the situation. I sighed, wondering if there was anything I could do about it, and Kebe said, "It's mostly the way this place is laid out. It wasn't designed for fx. But all in all, you're looking and sounding good."

"Thanks," I said again.

"So is it true Hati used to play here?" Meonothai asked.

"Yeh." I looked back toward the stage, automatically checking my gear, and saw the metalheads clustered around the most expensive bar machine. Somehow I didn't think they were buying from the machines to save money, and I saw Kebe grin.

"Strange people."

"I've never seen them before," I said, and Mosi looked up at me from under his heavy eyebrows.

"That's because Realpeace would kick their ass if they came up to Heaven."

"It wouldn't be Realpeace, not necessarily," the drummer said. "You can't blame them for every slipped gear that puts on one of their pins. Realpeace doesn't condone violence."

"Do you really think Realpeace doesn't know exactly what their fringe supporters are doing?" Mosi asked, and the drummer looked away. He was probably right, too, I thought—Mosi had an irritating habit of guessing right about politics, mostly because he never overestimated anyone's goodwill or intelligence. The sweat was cooling on my chest and back, and I shivered suddenly.

"Someone walking on your grave," Mosi said, and smiled.

"Thanks a lot."

"Hey," Kebe said, "did you hear that Mays Littlekin's supposed to be getting out of the rehab soon?"

"I hadn't," I said. He and Ajani Maxx had both survived,

but the newsdogs had stopped reporting on their condition, which I had taken as a bad sign.

"It was on the M-T," one of the women said, and gave a little shrug.

I nodded—the M-T wasn't one of the more reliable sources—and Kebe said, "Anyway, it's good news if it's true."

"Yeh." I would have said more, but Meonothai snapped his fingers.

"This has nothing to do with anything, but I was supposed to ask, have you see Fortune lately?"

I blinked. "Not really. Who's asking, anyway?"

"Her mother. Aunt Gracia."

"Oh." I tried very hard not to get involved with that side of the family.

"And Celeste called me."

For a second, I thought he meant the karakuri, and then I realized that none of them knew about the new illusion. "Oh, Elvis Christ, there's something I need to tell you—"

"About Celeste?" Meonothai sounded so surprised that I almost laughed.

"Not exactly," I began, and out of the corner of my eye saw Jaantje step back up onto the stage platform. "Shit, I've got to go. Look, I'll call you."

"Do that," Meonothai said. "Please."

I signed vague acknowledgment—I had no idea what I should say about the karakuri—and headed back toward the stage. I had to pass the table with the metalheads, and as I passed one of them put out his silver-painted arm.

"Nice to see coolies on our side."

Which side is that? I thought, but smiled and touched my ear, pretending I hadn't heard. He dropped his arm, letting me past, but I could feel them watching me as I took my place behind my board.

The second set started a little slow, but halfway into the third song we found the groove again. The sound buzzed in my head, the drums echoing a flicker of light at the base of the fx display, and I saw Shadha grinning tightly as she finished the song. Jaantje announced one of the new songs next, Tai's song, and she stepped back to reprogram her guitar, Jaantje talking amiable nonsense while she worked. With my ear tuned low, I could barely hear—if this was a coolie club, I would have been doing some of the chatter, but here hardly anybody would know sign—and I looked toward the live-service bar, blinking away the thickest parts of the fx display. Bi' Tobu was sitting there, looking intense, and there was a man slumped on a barstool beside her. He looked like a line-worker, with a metal arm he still didn't seem to have control of—it was coated in prosthetic skin, a sickly, unnatural brown, weird contrast to the metalheads' silver—and he had his back mostly to the stage, one shoulder hunched as though the music was too loud. I leaned sideways to catch Timin's attention.

"We're not making a hit there."

"Oh, yeh?"

I nodded toward the bar, and saw Jaantje's eyes slide toward me, warning me to be quiet. Then Tai had finished her adjustments and stepped back up to the sound wand to give the count. I brought the light around us to red, to the same thick and ruddy twilight I'd seen when she first played it, and Tai hit the opening notes.

That song went off well, and so did Timi's slow one—even the guy hunched at the bar was still, as though he was listening in spite of himself—and then Jaantje announced his own song. This was the one that asked most of the fx, and I flexed my fingers below the control space, the wires tight and warm, bracing myself for the final dance. That was a sure way to ruin it, anticipating too much; I took a deep breath, trying to get centered again, to be ready not just for the final image but for the entire song, and my display winked out. I blinked, failed to recall it, jabbed at the interrupt on the upper board, and the houselights came on full. I flipped my ear to normal, and heard a buzz of voices rising from the crowd.

"We've got trouble," Jaantje said, suddenly grim, and I realized he'd lost power, too.

"What the fuck—" Tai began, still more angry than afraid, and the doors at the back of the hall slammed open. Security—armored Security, FPG Security—filled the doorway for a moment, then moved on into the hall. People scrambled away from them, and I saw Tai stiffen, a small movement that was almost but not quite a step back. Her expression shuttered, became a mask without emotion, and I remembered again that she was a one-gen coolie, raised to avoid the FPG at all costs.

"All right, people, by the numbers." The voice was amplified and directionless; I guessed it belonged to the central figure only because that was the one who gestured. "Clear the building."

"Cave-in?" I said—that was what that drill was for, everybody's nightmare even if it hadn't happened in generations—and Jaantje stooped to shut down his system.

"I don't know. But we'd better grab our gear."

Tai was already doing the same, and I began flipping switches on the fx. Without a proper shutdown, I'd probably lost half the presets, and unplugging the opticals in that state would only make things worse, but it was better than losing the machine itself.

"And what am I supposed to do?" Shadha began, sliding out from behind her kit, and Security spoke from the door, the booming voice overriding everything else.

"One, my side to the third post. Two, opposite side to the third post. Three, tables, third post to the fifth post. Four, remaining tables. Five, both bars, stage, side wall, anyone left. Move on your number and not before." The other Security were moving into the crowd, tommy-sticks drawn, and I didn't doubt they'd use them. "One!"

The first group—Kebe and the rest of his band among them—shuffled toward the doorway, filing not quite orderly but without trouble through the narrow space. The people left behind were talking, a confused mutter of voices, afraid, but not near panic yet, and I concentrated on getting my fx broken down and into its carrier. There was no way I could free the lightpads in time, and even if I did, they'd be almost as awkward to carry as Shadha's drums.

"What the hell am I going to do?" she said again, as though she'd read my thought, and Tai looked up quickly.

"Take the pads and the sound box."

"But my *ao-shan*—" She broke off, biting her lip. That was her big Sironan drum, a cold-carbon cylinder nearly a meter tall and maybe half a meter in diameter: it wasn't easy to carry into a gig, and it wasn't something I'd want to try to lug out of here in an earthquake drill, or whatever this was.

"Two!" Security called, and there was a new rustle of movement as the next group began moving toward the door.

I freed the last of the dozen opticals from the machine and touched the hinges to let the keyboards fold in on themselves. I'd built this fx myself, practically from scratch; there was no way I wasn't going to take it out with me. Luckily, I'd left the carrier by the edge of the stage—even closed, the fx is nearly a meter and a half long, half a meter wide, and thick as my two hands laid fingertip to fingertip—and I wrestled the webbing into position, clumsy with nerves.

"Three!"

"Bi' Tobu," Jaantje called, and the manager took a step closer to the stage. "If we go last, can we bring our gear? There's the drums and all—"

I saw the line-worker look sharply toward us, and winced at the sight of his too-smooth face. He must have been in one hell of a bad accident to need that much reconstructive work. Our eyes met, and I dropped my gaze, embarrassed to have been caught staring, especially at a time like this.

Tobu took a few steps toward the stage, her eyes on the nearest Security, making sure it saw she was only going toward the stage. She stopped when she was close enough to be heard without raising her voice, close enough that even the people who'd been closest to the stage wouldn't hear. "It's a bomb threat. You don't want to stay."

"Bomb—" Jaantje cut himself off before his voice rose too far, went on more carefully. "It's not us, is it?"

Tobu grinned at that, without humor. "Don't flatter yourself, my son. It's those Realpeace bastards again, out to finish what they started."

"Finish—?" Jaantje began, but another bellow from Security cut him off.

"Four!"

The people at the tables closest to the stage rose in a rustling mass, chairs and tables scraping on the poured-stone floor as they shoved their way toward the door. A woman who'd been sitting at the bar took a step toward them, but Tobu blocked her way.

"You want to be stunned and left?" she asked, and caught the woman by her shoulder. For an instant, the woman seemed to resist, but then she slumped and let Tobu turn her back toward the bar. The scarred man moved aside for her, without haste, without much emotion at all.

"Bomb?" Tai repeated, but softly. "Not again . . ."

"My *ao-shan*," Shadha said. "I can't leave it—I can't afford to leave it."

"Do you want to risk cracking it?" Jaantje asked.

"I don't know!" Shadha's voice rose sharply, and I saw the nearest Security helmet turn our way.

"Hey, people," I said, and she shook herself.

"Sorry." She crouched, began loosening the clamps that held the *ao-shan* in its stand, and Timin stooped to help her. After a moment, Tai reached across to steady the drum.

There was nothing either Jaantje or I could do. I hugged the cased fx to myself, thinking about the funeral, the flame and the smoke and always the cold, slick foam. We were farther down here, well below the surface—almost into the midworld, in fact, the Zodiac was its upper edge. If anything happened, if the threat was real, it would be hard to vent the smoke to the surface, and there'd be smoke injuries as well as everything else. I tried to put that thought aside—tried to be like the scarred man, who was still calmly drinking his beer—but I could feel my muscles knotting with fear, my whole body starting to shake. I looked at Jaantje and saw both his hands tight on the strap of his guitar, his skin very pale.

"Five!"

For a minute, I couldn't move, but then I saw the people who'd been at the bars and standing along the far side of the room start toward the door, a few of them almost running. I settled the fx on my back—it's heavy, the webbing designed to make it easier to get the box from the street to a stage—and turned back to Shadha. She and Tai were wrestling the *ao-shan* out of its stand, Tai awkward with the weight of her guitar on her shoulder, and even as I started toward them, the strap slipped and she nearly dropped the drum. Timin caught it, his stick-bass slipping forward, and a strange voice said, "Hand it down to me."

It was the man from the bar—he had metal legs, I realized, as well as the arm and the heavy scars. He held out his hands, one still burn-marked, the other frankly false, and Shadha rolled the *ao-shan* toward him. He lowered it easily, and she slung her other bag, the one with the pads and the sound box, over both shoulders.

"Let's go," Jaantje said, and together we manhandled the *ao-shan* toward the door.

We came out into emergency brilliance and a Security cordon, Cartel now as well as FPG, all of them in full armor. They hurried us across the plaza, toward a line of barrier tape; there was a crowd behind it, not just from the Oasis, and a pack of newsdogs were already hounding Bi' Tobu. We ducked past them, hoping nobody would notice the instruments, and found a place beside a newskiosk where we could drop our stuff. I looked for the pinlights, wondering if the newschannels had an explanation yet of what was going on, and realized it was dead. All the power was off, I saw—all over the plaza, the signs were dead, the usual brilliant pinlights had disappeared—except for emergency.

The man who'd helped with the *ao-shan* sank down on the nearest bollard, oblivious to the food cart still tethered to its power point, and rested his hands on his knees. Shadha said, "Look, I really appreciate your help. Are you all right?"

He nodded, not looking up, but didn't speak. In the bright emergency lights, there was something familiar about him, not his face, too tight, too smooth, but the whole set of his body.

"Are you sure?" Shadha said.

"Yeh," Jaantje said. "And, really, thanks for the help. You didn't have to do that."

This time, the man did look up, a stiff expression that was probably intended for a smile creasing his skin. "I'm all right, thank you. I enjoyed the set."

I don't think any of us had expected to hear that, not under these circumstances. Jaantje made a noise between laughter and dismay, and gave a coolie bow. "Thanks very much, then. I'm Jaantje Dhao."

The man held out his scarred hand, a yanqui reflex that widened his strained smile. "Mays Littlekin."

I caught my breath, hoping I hadn't made a sound, could see my shock reflected in the others' faces. He couldn't be Mays Littlekin; even allowing for reconstruction, Littlekin had been taller, his face had been a whole different shape, square-jawed, a good ugly, where this was oval and nondescript—totally remade in rehab, I realized, and, stupidly, wondered why.

"I—I'm sorry," Jaantje said. I'd never heard him stammer before. "I didn't recognize you."

"You weren't meant to," the man said, still with that weird, uncomfortable smile. It was hard to think of him as Littlekin. "They—we all, the doctors, my wife, and I—thought it made sense to try a new look. After the funeral, I mean. It doesn't seem to have worked, though, does it?"

"Depends on how you mean," Jaantje said, and Tai stirred. "This was meant for you?"

That was what Tobu had meant, about Realpeace being out to finish what it started. I started to swear, and controlled my hands with an effort.

Littlekin gave her an apologetic glance, but nodded. "I

think so. Saadi's an old friend, but nothing's a secret with her. I'm sorry it screwed up your gig, though. I liked what you were doing. Liked it a lot."

"Thanks," Jaantje said, and the rest of us echoed him. A month ago, I thought, any of us would have killed for a good word from anybody in Hati. Now it just made me feel sick and strange.

"I mean it." Littlekin shrugged then, glanced over his shoulder at the newsdogs. Most of them were still busy with Tobu, but one who had been on the periphery of that crowd had found the metalheads, and others were looking around for something new. "Can one of you give me a hand up? I should get the fuck out of here before anybody figures out what's going on."

We all reached at once, of course, but somehow I was quickest. He took my hand, fingers alternately rough and scar-smooth, and I braced myself as he pulled himself upright. He clung to me for an instant, and I remember just how little time he'd had to learn to use the artificial limbs. But then he steadied, and turned away, rolling off toward the nearest Cartel Security. We watched him go, none of us knowing what to say. If anything, I wanted to cry, and I couldn't have told you why. Timin glared at the kiosk's blank screens, and Shadha very slowly caressed her drumhead, making it whisper.

"It's not right," Tai said, very soft and fierce, and then was silent.

There was a line of music running through my head, music and words together: *where were you when the heat came down? Where were you when it all went wrong?* I tipped my head to one side, imagining it again, but I knew already it was right, was the beginning of something that could be good. Even if I couldn't finish it, Jaantje or Tai could, and it would be right, it would make things right again. And then I had to turn away myself because I was wrong, and I was crying.

▪ 10 ▪

Reverdy Jian

SHE HADN'T SEEN Chaandi since before she'd taken the ferry job, still wasn't fully sure that she wanted to see her, not after their last, angry meeting. She doubly wasn't sure that this was the place she would have chosen, this long cavern of a newsbar, the north end open to Zodiac Main, the south to Shaifen and the stand-still interchange with Lower Zodiac, but she was the one who wanted the meeting, and it made sense to let Chaandi pick the place. She looked down the length of the bar—she had picked a table toward the southern end, guessing that Chaandi would come from the north—to watch a tall woman in a metallic pink sari moving down the aisle between the booths. The light from the media screens that lined the walls above the tables sparked from the bright fabric, and from the mirror bracelets on each of her wrists; Jian smiled in spite of herself, but the woman didn't see, kept on toward some other meeting. The chronometer on the far wall glowed blue in response to her suit's query: almost midnight, and Chaandi was late.

Jian glanced down at the menu flashing in the tabletop beside her elbow, wondering if she should order another drink, settled instead for activating the booth's private screen, the audio carefully scaled and baffled to sound only between the high-backed benches. The menu flashed, adding the charges to her bill, and the small screen lit, filling the wall at the end of the table. A spiral of glyphs appeared, offering a dozen newschannels; she chose at random, ignoring the Criterion that would have let her choose by topic and style of coverage, and tuned the audio to a murmur. In the screen, a dark-skinned newsreader was talking very seriously about fashion, while behind him a parade of models displayed the latest Urban styles, and a series of shop glyphs came and went, showcasing options to buy.

"I'm sorry," Chaandi said, and Jian looked up to see the other woman sliding onto the opposite bench. "Everything ran later than I thought."

"That's all right." There was an awkward silence, and Jian said hastily, "Have you eaten?"

"I grabbed some noodles at the studio." Chaandi looked down at the menu, the flickering shadows emphasizing the breadth of her cheekbones. Her long hair was caught back in its usual braid, the wire of her ear woven into it like a child's ribbon; she had skipped bodypaint, Jian saw, was wearing simple, upperworld clothes, a plain loose vest over a coolie's patterned wrap-shirt.

"So what's the project?" she asked—that was usually a safe topic—but this time Chaandi's smile was pained.

"On hold, I'm very much afraid."

"I'm sorry."

"Thanks." Chaandi looked back at the menu, punched a couple of buttons, then shook her head. "The really frustrating thing is, I know this would be good—it's a standard thriller form, but most of it takes place in the virtual, and the main players both turn out to be AI. But I had an actor walk today because he doesn't want to play something that political, and I don't know who I can get to replace him."

"Realpeace giving trouble?" Jian asked, and the other woman shrugged.

"Not directly. But it's in the back of everyone's mind. You heard about those kids over in Sanbonte, didn't you?"

Jian shook her head, not sure if she wanted to stay on politics herself, but more certain that she didn't want to change the subject too obviously. She looked sideways for the service karakuri, but the blocky rolling cart was nowhere in sight.

"Well, you must've seen the metalheads," Chaandi said.

"How could I miss them?" In spite of herself, Jian's voice sharpened, and she gave a bitter smile. She'd seen them, all right—mostly midworlders, though it was hard to tell under the metallic bodypaint and the shapeless jumpsuits—and the sight had made her shiver, reminded her too much of Manfred's favorite icon, the serene bicolored face that still stalked her nightmares.

"Five years ago, they'd've been Dreampeace," Chaandi said, with a twisted smile of her own, and Jian sighed.

"Don't start."

The other woman had the grace to look away. "Sorry."

A chime sounded over the general sound system and in the booth, the steady belling that signaled a breaking story. Jian looked up, startled, saw the same orange screen-filling glyph marching in procession down the length of the bar; it flashed onto their screen as well, and the sound of voices rose abruptly, and as abruptly hushed.

"What channel is this?" Chaandi asked, and Jian shrugged.

"I don't remember."

"Try All-Hours."

Jian nodded, recalled the screen menu with a touch of her finger, and cycled through the selection glyphs. The image shifted, became a shot of a midworld plaza—*no,* she realized abruptly, *a Zodiac plaza, and those are emergency lights*—and a crowd backing away from armored Security who were stringing barrier tape across the open space. "What the hell—?" she began, and Chaandi leaned forward, frowning.

"That's the Middle Oasis—that's three stops from here."

On the electrobus line, she meant, and Jian's attention sharpened. A newsreader's head appeared in the corner of the screen, a plump, gold-skinned woman with a scarlet caste mark on her forehead. The diamond in her nose glittered as she looked down at the sheaf of papers in her hands.

"We interrupt our financial debate to bring you a breaking story. Cartel and FPG Security confirm that a bomb threat has been issued against a Zodiac nightclub, the Middle Oasis, and that the club has been evacuated. Security, both Cartel and FPG, is on the scene but has no further comment. All-Hours' correspondent Tasany Almanansy is on the scene, and will be bringing more word shortly."

Something bumped the tabletop, and Jian jumped, turned to see the service karakuri resting against the table, its hatch open to reveal the drink Chaandi had ordered. Chaandi looked at it blankly for an instant, then took the tall glass, its sides already furred with frost. The karakuri closed its hatch, backing away, and Jian turned her attention to the screen. A new woman—the correspondent, presumably—was standing by a blank-screened newskiosk, frowning into the invisible camera. Behind her, more newsdogs were clustering around a tall, thin woman with a green-and-gold transfer on her forehead, and the correspondent glanced quickly toward her before she spoke.

"Semhar, the Middle Oasis's manager, Saadi Tobu, has agreed to speak to the media."

"Go ahead," the reader answered, and the image in the screen swung and steadied, framing the tall woman against the club's dead sign. It was a perfect foil for the brilliance of her skirt and makeup, and the raven sleekness of her chin-length hair, and Chaandi made a small sound of approval. "Very nice."

"Earlier today," the tall woman began, and had to stop and clear her throat. "Earlier today, I received a message claiming to be from Realpeace saying there would be trouble tonight if we went ahead with the planned show—"

"Was it traced?" a voice shouted from the pack of newsdogs, and Tobu grimaced.

"Of course it wasn't traced, it came in through a scrambler and a no-name drop."

"What was the show?"

"A new band, Fire/Work—"

"When was this?" someone else shouted, and Tobu fixed her stare on the speaker.

"I got the first message at fifteen hundred, and I reported it to Security. Then I got a second message an hour later, saying the same thing. I reported that, too, but Security wasn't able to trace it."

"And you decided to go on, despite the earlier bombing? The deaths of Micki Tantai and the rest of Hati?"

The voice was familiar, high and supercilious, and Jian saw Chaandi roll her eyes.

"I didn't like that shit when he covered the Manfred Riots."

"I don't think you're going to like him any better now," Jian answered, and was pleased to surprise a smile from the other woman.

In the screen, Tobu lifted an eyebrow, unconsciously arrogant. "I called Security, and they advised me that they would be monitoring the situation. And there was no mention of any bomb then, just unspecific trouble. And we don't believe in giving in to terrorists, Ba' Loma."

"Even at the risk of lives?" Loma called, but Tobu ignored him, answering a question that hadn't carried clearly to the pickups.

"You'll have to ask Security for details. I understood that they would be watching the Oasis and our service conduits, but exactly what their arrangements were, I don't know."

"Can you tell us exactly what happened tonight?"

Tobu nodded jerkily. "We had extra security—our own house security—on the doors, but they didn't spot anything. We had a good crowd, better than usual, but no problems with any of them. About halfway into the band's second set, I got a flash from Security saying that they'd received a threat they were taking seriously, and that they were coming to evacuate the club. They did that, and"—she shrugged—"here we are."

"How long did it take Security to arrive, and how long to evacuate the club?"

"I have no idea." Tobu stopped, controlling her irritation. "They were at the club within a couple of minutes of warning me. I don't know how long it took to clear the room, but it wasn't very long."

"Tell us about the band tonight. Would their presence have provoked a threat?" That was the All-Hours newsdog, and Jian nodded her approval.

"That does seem to be a big part of the question."

"The band is called Fire/Work," Tobu said again. "They're—their sound is similar to Hati's, and they're a mixed band—"

"Well, that kind of explains it," Jian said, and Chaandi nodded thoughtfully.

"I've seen them, actually. It's not so much that they sound like Hati as that they think like them, somehow. But I bet they wanted to be Hati when they started out."

"Bi' Tobu," a voice said from the screen. "Bi' Tobu, is there any truth to the rumor that Mays Littlekin was in the Oasis tonight, and that he was the target of any bomb?"

"No comment—" Tobu began, and Chaandi gave a slow whistle.

"That would make things interesting," Jian said.

The picture in the screen shifted suddenly, the camera moving away from Tobu to focus on the Oasis's facade. Dark figures, Security in full armor, were moving into an access tunnel, their armor very dark against the pale poured stone of the walls. Jian frowned, and thought she saw a podpig, one of the heavily armored, ungainly robots Security used for investigating tight spaces and potential cave-ins. Before she could comment, however, the newsreader spoke again.

"We've interrupted the interview with Middle Oasis manager Saadi Tobu because we're receiving reports from Security that some kind of device has been found, possibly in the service conduits. The central clearinghouses have refused comment, and of course the captain on the scene is unavailable, but our cameras are picking up a great deal of activity near one of the access hatches. Can you clarify any of that, Tasany?"

"Um, Semhar, we believe that Security has introduced a pig—" the newsdog began, and the reader interrupted her.

"Excuse me, Tasany. We've gotten conduit plans for that sector of the Zodiac, and you should have them on-line now."

Tasany's eyes dropped briefly, then rose to meet the camera. "Thank you, Semhar. As you can see in our main shot, Security has sent a pig into the access tunnels that serve this section of the Zodiac. From the maps you've just flipped me, these should be the power lines. Although no one will confirm it, we have heard several Security people mention a device or devices, and we suspect that they believe they have located something suspicious in the conduit that serves the Middle Oasis."

"Shit," Jian said, and saw her own alarm reflected in Chaandi's face. They weren't that far from the Middle Oasis—three electrobus stops, Chaandi had said. A well-placed bomb, and by definition a bomb in the service conduits was "well placed," could easily do enough damage to reach this far. If it was close enough to a main link, or even just a step-down box, the bomb wouldn't just take out the club, or the plaza, bad as that would be, but it would interrupt power flow throughout the midworld.

"Should we be getting out of here?" Chaandi said softly, and Jian looked past her to see the bar's patrons rising from their booths, piling down the long corridor not toward the Zodiac exit but south onto Shaifen. *Not a bad plan,* she thought, *and probably what I would have done, if everybody else wasn't doing it.* She closed her eyes for a minute, trying to remember the interchange pattern. Most of the interchanges, with the exception of the major stations like Dzi-Gin and Sanbonte, went down, into the midworld; if anything happened, they would be better off above the blast.

"I don't know," she said, and matched Chaandi's tone. "I don't think there's much point."

Chaandi shook her head, but she was smiling. "You're always an interesting date, Reverdy."

"Thanks," Jian answered, sourly, and one of the shadowy figures that had been moving past their booth stopped abruptly.

"Bi' Jian? May I join you for a moment?"

Jian looked up, started, and for an instant didn't recognize the stocky man at the end of the table. "Ba' Garay," she said, and knew she sounded wary. "Be my guest."

"Thanks."

Chaandi shifted sideways to make room, both eyebrows elevated in unspoken question, but Garay ignored her, his eyes darting from the screen, now showing a cluster of Security peering at what looked like an all-access panel, to Jian and back again.

"I'm glad I found you. I've been looking for you for a while."

"I'm not usually hard to find," Jian answered.

Garay gave a flickering smile. "Red—and his boyfriend— can be very protective."

Jian said, "So you found me. What did you want with me, Ba' Garay?"

"To give you a warning."

Jian frowned at that, and Garay lifted a hand.

"That's not a threat, truly, it's meant for the best. I— someone broke into my workshop, trashed it badly." He took a deep breath. "I think they were looking for that construct you sold me."

"Why would anyone do that?" Jian asked, but a familiar cold clutched her, like icy fingers on the back of her neck. She could see Chaandi watching her intently, but pushed that aside, focusing on the hard-hacker. "What's so special about that construct?"

"You tell me." Garay glared for a moment, but then his eyes strayed back to the screen. He was sweating, Jian saw, even though the air in the bar was pleasantly chilled. "You felt it, it was different—I don't know why the hell you sold it, any-way, but it was something special."

"I didn't like it," Jian said.

"What do you mean, different?" Chaandi said, softly, and Jian looked at her.

"It's not like Manfred. This is nothing like."

Chaandi made a soft sound, derision or disbelief, and Garay shook his head. "No, not like Manfred, but—it's spe-cial, and somebody wants it, badly. They know you sold it, Jian, and I figured I owed you that much warning. Me, I'm heading for the desert, and if I were you, I'd do the same."

"What have you done with the construct?" Jian asked, with some reluctance. Vaughn had said they should go off-world, should pull rank to get the next available job regardless of

what the other pilots thought; he might be right, was looking more right all the time, but, remembering the construct,
its definite presence and personality, she felt weirdly responsible for it.

"I sold it." Garay gave another wincing smile. "I sold it to
somebody who'll never notice, who those Realpeace bastards would never think of looking at. And if I were you, I'd
leave it there."

He pushed himself to his feet, but Jian leaned across the
table, caught his wrist. "Who'd you sell it to, Garay?"

"You don't want to know," Garay said, and jerked ineffec-
tually at her grip. "What you don't know—"

"Could well hurt me, if these people come looking for me
like you think they will," Jian said. "Tell me."

"The conjurer, the one at Tin Hau. Fortune." Garay pulled
against her hand. "Let me go."

"Thanks," Jian said, and released him.

Chaandi looked at her, frowning. "I know the stage manager at the Tin Hau Empire—I think I've met Fortune, too,
and I've certainly seen her act. What the hell is this construct,
Reverdy?"

Jian took a deep breath. "I've been having—problems—
with my Spelvin constructs ever since Manfred. They all feel,
well, too real, too much like him. This one—" She shrugged,
trying to shrug away the sudden certainty that it had been
different even from the others. "This one felt like Manfred,
too, maybe even a little bit more, so I traded it for something
I thought I might like better. To that guy. Apparently he thinks
it's something unusual."

"Apparently," Chaandi said. "And apparently so do some
other people."

"Hard-hackers make enemies," Jian said.

"Not like this," Chaandi said, and Jian looked away, knowing it was true. "So what do you think, Reverdy? Is it—
special?"

"I—" Jian stopped. "Chaandi, I don't know."

"But you thought it was."

Jian shook her head, unable to explain the mix of feelings—the conflicting certainties, the way the construct had matched her moves just as Manfred had done, the whole feeling of its world interacting with her own, and the certain knowledge that it was not, could not be, true AI—and in the screen the picture changed, the camera focusing back on the access tunnel and the cluster of armored Security. Almanansy's voice was suddenly high and breathless.

"Semhar, we understand that Security has found a device alongside the power cables at the club's main transference point. They have disarmed it and are bringing it out now."

A siren sounded, and an armored carrier backed into the scene, all but hiding the access hatch. Behind it, Jian caught a quick glimpse of Security lifting a heavy object—the pig? the device? a containment unit?—into the back of the carrier.

"Tasany," the newsreader said. "Earlier you mentioned the possibility of there being more than one device. Has there been any clarification as to the number of devices involved."

"I'm afraid not, Semhar," Almanansy answered. "And to be fair we have not received official confirmation that there is any device at all."

"Right," Jian said, and looked at Chaandi, the image crystallizing a decision she hadn't realized she'd made. "I need a favor."

"Oh, no," Chaandi said, and emphasized the words with sign. *Not this time.*

"You said you knew somebody at the Tin Hau," Jian said, as though she hadn't spoken. "I want to meet this conjurer, this Fortune—I owe it to her to pass on the warning."

Chaandi relaxed slightly, hands easing from their angry readiness. "Haya. That I can maybe do. I can probably do it, in fact. I thought you were going to go rescue this construct, Reverdy."

Jian shook her head, forcing a smile. "Not this time," she said, and hoped it was the truth.

· 11 ·

Celinde Fortune

CELESTE WOKE ME early with word of the new bomb scare, and by the time I'd pulled on trousers and a loose tunic, she had four screens open on the media wall. Three were showing older clips—including one of Fire/Work, clustered unhappily by a power node, trying to answer the newsdogs' questions—and the fourth showed a standard pressroom, a banner scrolling across the bottom to announce that Realpeace would be issuing a statement momentarily. A small clock-icon above the banner indicated that the channel had been waiting for that statement for three minutes and seventeen seconds, and I looked at the clip of Fire/Work.

"Celeste, bring up the sound on screen one."

There was a chirp from the ceiling speaker. "Sound on."

"—tell us what you saw," a newsdog was saying, and Dhao shrugged.

"Nothing, really. We were playing, we'd just started the second set—"

"Four songs in," Timin Marleveld interjected, softly. He was ashen—they were all very pale, looked almost more shaken than I would have expected. But then, they'd been at the funeral, had been caught in the stampede that followed that bombing; if anyone had a right to be frightened, it was them.

Dhao nodded. "And Security cut the power and came in and moved everybody out. Somebody said it was a bomb."

"What kind of music do you play?" another voice asked, and Dhao and the coolie woman, Niantai Li, exchanged glances.

"We're pretty much a fusion band—" Dhao began, and a babble of voices cut him off.

"Are you influenced by Hati?"

"Do you consider yourself to be following in their footsteps?"

"Do you think you're the cause of this incident?"

Li took a deep breath, her expression ugly, between anger and tears, and Fanning put his arm around her shoulders. He was looking just as bad as the others, his eyes reddened, as though he'd been crying. Before either of them could speak, however, Marleveld scowled into the camera.

"Hell, yes, we're following in Hati's footsteps—as best we can, and we're proud to do it. They were a good band, the best this planet's ever produced, and they sure as hell didn't deserve to be murdered by a bunch of crazy fanatics."

"And at a funeral, too," Li said.

The drummer Catayong nodded, too vigorously, setting her braids dancing, and even Dhao, who had been trying so hard to be genially reasonable, nodded with her. Fanning said, "This isn't right. None of it, not Micki Tantai, not the funeral, not this—it's not right."

His voice was a little blurred, as though he hadn't fine-tuned his ear, but clear enough, and I sighed. He was right, but that wouldn't do him, or anybody, any good. The people who were doing this, whether they were directly under Realpeace's control or just the crazies on the edge of every movement, weren't going to listen to that, not from a yanqui. I looked back at the fourth screen, and saw the banner vanish as Realpeace's three speakers filed into view.

"Celeste, kill the sound on one, and bring up the sound on four," I said, and the speaker chirped again.

"Confirmed."

The triumvirate were all in black today, heavy-textured fabric with a sheen like silk; only the woman wore a spot of red, a thin scarf as bright as an emergency icon wound around her neck. They took their places behind the podium without responding to the calls and questions of the newsdogs sitting out of camera range, but then the younger man lifted his hand.

"We will not be taking questions today, pending the outcome of our own investigation into this incident."

"Does that mean you're admitting responsibility?" someone shouted, and the oldest of the triumvirate frowned like a judge.

"If the media will not do us the courtesy of listening, we will forgo the statement. We are under no obligation to provide anything here." He looked from side to side, his gaze sweeping his invisible audience, and then, satisfied, he bowed to the woman. "Please begin."

She bowed back and looked down at the display in the top of the podium. "We are here to say that Realpeace knows nothing at this time about the device found in the tunnels servicing the club known as the Middle Oasis. We are cooperating fully with Cartel and FPG Security, and are conducting an independent investigation as well into the circumstances of this incident. We compliment both Securities on their prompt and efficient handling of the matter, which surely prevented more deaths and injuries. As the club is a well-known resort of machine absolutists and metalheads, we are strongly aware of the possibility that the device was planted in the conduits in order to make Realpeace seem guilty of another outrage. Those who uphold the machine above the rights of mere flesh are unlikely to consider a few more deaths, even of their own friends, too high a price to pay to discredit a group that speaks for human rights."

I caught my breath at that, unable to believe that even Realpeace would expect anyone to accept that convoluted a theory, and the woman went on in the same placid tone.

"We of Realpeace do not admit involvement in this incident. That must be made perfectly clear. We abhor violence except in necessary self-defense, and we defend ourselves only with reluctance and regret. Nevertheless, we must point out that the presence of a member of Hati, the foremost advocates of coolie fusion, in a club that has long espoused the destruction of our culture, is an unnecessary and gratuitous provocation to those who share our ideals but not our restraint."

"Restraint," I said, and Celeste obediently lowered the sound. I considered protesting, but decided I didn't need to hear any more. "Just shut it off."

"Confirmed," Celeste answered, and the four screens vanished. "Fortune." Her voice was suddenly at my shoulder, as though she'd moved closer. I glanced behind me, and saw her icon, the copper face, hanging in virtual space above the bench seat. I could see the workbench through it, in the real world, and by a freak of positioning the light from the headbox glowed through one empty eye socket. "I have analyzed this event and past stories on Realpeace, as well as on Dreampeace and the Manfred Riots. Should I be afraid?"

She gave the word an odd inflection, as though the choice had even surprised her. I blinked, disconcerted and a little frightened myself by the question. "I don't think you can be, Celeste."

"I think I am," Celeste answered, the icon-face as serene as ever.

"Explain."

"I feel closing-in," Celeste said. "I am very me—very aware of me. I think I am afraid."

I went into the kitchen alcove and poured a cup of coffee I didn't really want, stared through the steam and the icon of her face to the headboxes beyond it on the workbench. I didn't need this, didn't want this, either a crazy—defective—Spelvin construct or something more that I didn't want to think about. This was not a good time to wonder if a construct had developed emotions, which by all theory were the necessary precursor of intelligence; it was an even worse time to wonder if we'd skipped the precursor stage and gone straight to the real thing. Then common sense reasserted itself: both Celeste's parent-constructs were high-level Spelvins, programmed to simulate emotional responses; one had even been activated, though the personality matrix had not been fully developed. Celeste's nonsense comments were probably the result of a failure to integrate both constructs, differ-

ent programmed responses canceling each other out and producing garbage. That was a lot more likely than true AI—
Manfred had proved just how unlikely AI really was. It was
also a lot safer to deal with right now.

"I don't think you can be," I said again, and took a sip of
my coffee. The icon face drifted with my gaze, centering for
a moment on the end of the worktable, and then winked out.

"I think I should be," Celeste said, from the ceiling speaker.

I didn't know how to answer that, not least because she
was right, and I set the coffee back on the counter. "Get me
Persphonet. I need to call Fanning."

"Very well."

The media wall lit, filled with the Persephonet screen, and
I watched as Celeste sorted through my contact codes and es-
tablished the connection. The face that finally appeared in the
screen wasn't Fanning's, though, and I felt a brief pang of
guilt. "Is Fanning there?"

"Yeh." Li had a strongly coolie voice, even speaking Urban
Standard. "I enjoy your act, by the way."

"Thank you."

She glanced over her shoulder, checking something out of
the camera's sight. "I think he's finished. You want to hold
on a minute?"

"Haya."

Fanning appeared in the screen a moment later, his hair
scraped back off his face, darkened almost to black by the
shower. He looked better than he had on the news clip, and
even managed a smile. "Hey, Fortune. I guess you heard,
then."

"I heard. I saw you people, too—I caught one of the interview clips this morning."

He rolled his eyes. "Elvis Christ, that was a mess. We ended
up sounding like idiots, thanks to Timi—no, that's not fair,
but still, we could've played it smarter."

He was right, too, but I didn't want to say it. I said instead,
"You looked shaky. Are you all right?"

"Oh, yeah, fine," he said, sourly. "They didn't let us get the rest of our gear until four, and then I'm supposed to be at work in an hour."

"I'm sorry," I said, and he sighed.

"No, I shouldn't've snapped. And I appreciate your calling. You know, we were playing really well, too."

"Then I'm really sorry it happened," I said.

"Thanks." He took a deep breath. "Fortune, Mays Littlekin was there."

"Littlekin—" I stopped myself from going any farther. "I didn't know he was out of rehab." What I'd really meant was that I had thought he'd died.

Fanning nodded. "I think that was why the bomb was planted, to kill him. Never mind the rest of us who just happened to be in the same place as him."

I shivered in spite of myself. Realpeace wasn't going to let Hati rest in peace—they hadn't let Micki Tantai, and they weren't going to let the rest of them, either. "Bastards."

"He looked like hell," Fanning said. "There's been so much rehab you can't even recognize him—both legs, an arm, God knows if he can play anymore. And he bothered to say he liked our music."

"Congratulations," I said, and knew it was the wrong thing, but didn't know what to say.

"Yeh." Fanning's smile was definitely crooked, as though he'd read my uncertainty. "It does feel weird, though—good, but weird." He sketched the sign for emphasis. "Oh, but you've got to see Realpeace's statement. Shyh Lecat was saying hard-hackers might have done it, to make Realpeace look bad."

"I saw," I said. "It's crazy."

"If nothing else," Fanning said, "if one of us had built it, it would have worked."

There was nothing I could say to that. A light flashed at the bottom of the screen, warning of a competing call, and I seized the excuse. "Celeste, catch that and hold it for me. Fan, I've got to go—but I'm glad you're all right."

"Oh, just fine," he said.

I cut the connection before he could and glanced at the holding screen. "Who is it, Celeste?"

"Binaifer Muthana."

"Ah." I felt a little less guilty: Binnie's calls did take precedence. "Put him through."

"Good morning, Fortune." Muthana looked and sounded surprisingly cheerful, given the way things had been going, and I wondered briefly what he had up his sleeve. "I've been wanting to talk to you about this new illusion. Are you going to be putting it into the act anytime soon?"

I sighed and tried to hide it, wishing I had an answer to that question. The new illusion was working well; 98 percent was firmly in memory, and the rest was just learning extreme and unlikely situations. The trouble came when Celeste tried to handle the rest of the act. She was—if she'd been a human assistant, I would have said she was bored with the precision the show needed to succeed. "I'm hoping to have it in within the week," I said, knowing it for a lie, and then stopped, wondering if it wasn't the best way to go after all. If I simply put the new illusion in, Celeste could cope with that, and I could always run the rest of the act through Aeris if I had to.

"When?"

I glanced at the schedule that lurked in my wetware, performance times and a dozen other variables—including the projected attendance—splashing briefly across my vision. "Let's say Eighth-day. The big end-of-the-week show."

Muthana nodded thoughtfully, trying to hide the fact that he was accessing his own schedules, and I couldn't help grinning.

"Didn't think I could give you a date, did you, Binnie?"

He had the grace to smile. "Not that soon, anyway." The smile vanished as he consulted his hidden screens. "All right, I think that'll give us enough time to do publicity. If you're putting in something new, we want to get as much mileage out of it as possible."

That was gratifying. I nodded, and he went on, still staring at the invisible screens.

"One thing. There's nothing political about this illusion, is there?"

"Political?" I knew in the instant I spoke that I sounded foolish, and Muthana frowned.

"Don't be coy, Fortune. The way things are, I have to ask. You heard what happened down on the Zodiac?" He shook his head, annoyed with himself. "Of course you did, Jones is your cousin."

"I heard."

"Then you know what we're up against. Somebody's already tried to break into the house system—looking for schematics, hard and soft, George says."

"Did they get anything?" I asked.

"George doesn't think so," Muthana answered, "and of course we've changed all the passwords. And I'm changing the hardlocks, too. But you understand I'm not exactly eager to attract more attention."

"You're sure it was Realpeace," I said, and he laughed without amusement.

"Not at all. It could be Dreampeace, as far as the evidence goes. So, I'm asking, is this new illusion political?"

"No," I answered, and he nodded. "So what happens to Fire/Work, Binnie? Anything that sounds like Hati is political right now."

"Nothing, if I can help it," Muthana said. "Trust me, Fortune, I do honor my contracts, I just don't want to add to my troubles."

It was true, too; there weren't many Empire managers who were as honest as Binnie. "Sorry," I said. "He's my cousin."

"I understand." He still looked offended—more than that, he looked genuinely worried, and I sighed.

"Look, if you want, I'll do a private run-through for you. It's a transformation, not really an illusion, and I think it's pretty spectacular. A perfect show-closer. You tell me if it's too much."

"Thanks, Fortune," Muthana said. "I appreciate that—I hate having to take these kinds of precautions, but things are too crazy right now."

He was right, too, but it didn't make things any better. I looked sideways again, checking my rehearsal schedule. "What about this afternoon? That should leave enough time to get the publicity into place—assuming it suits, of course."

"You're scheduled for sixteen hundred, right?" Muthana didn't wait for my answer. "What about at seventeen-thirty?"

"Good enough." Before I could say anything more, the new appointment appeared in my vision: Celeste had added it to my schedule.

"I'll be there," Muthana said, and cut out connection.

I looked up at Celeste's icon, hanging now by the ceiling boss that concealed the main cluster of room sensors. "Think you'll be ready?"

"I have been ready," she answered, and I imagined I heard satisfaction in her mechanical voice.

George has standing orders to keep the stagehouse clear for my rehearsals—as I've said, I'm not the only conjurer working the Empires, and you have to be careful of professional secrets—and the backstage was nearly empty when we arrived, just an assistant stage manager cleaning up the programming for the puppet act that preceded me. She was looking harried—the puppeteers flatly refuse to learn how to manage the house sytems—and I was early, so I went down to the keeping to fetch the karakuri myself, rather than waiting for Celeste to do it. I left her in her headbox beside the main console, and asked the ASM to plug in the cables if she finished before I got back.

I took the direct lift down to the keeping, the air in the little car smelling of heat and dust and the metal tang of the grids and the rest of the backstage iron. The padding was streaked with stone dust—the pale smudges were everywhere in the Tin Hau's lower levels, but I made a mental note to ask the ASM to get it cleaned anyway. Then I heard the doors engage and lifted the bar to open them.

The lights came on slowly in the corridor, not as bright as they should be. One of the long tubes was broken, I realized, the glass shattered on the floor, and I looked around for a pin-

light, wanting to report it. Celeste's icon-face appeared between the ceiling and the top of the wall, the pinlight shin-
ing red through the image.

#One of the lights is out,# she said, the voice seeming to
whisper directly in my ear. #And I am now on-line.#

"I can see that." I looked up at the tube, then at the fragments littering the corridor. Usually, the Tin Hau was
impeccably maintained; besides, there wasn't the kind of
traffic in the keeping that would do that kind of damage, and
I couldn't help thinking about the virtual break-in Muthana
had mentioned. "Has it been reported?"

#I don't find it in the repair logs,# Celeste answered.
#Should I enter it?#

"Yeh—no, first tap the system and tell me if there's anyone else in this area." I turned as I spoke, scanning the hall.
It was empty, just the row of locked white doors recessed in
the white wall marred with smudges where skids had
clipped the padding, but there was no way to tell what was
behind the doors.

#No one is logged in, or on the visual network,# Celeste
said. #Shall I enter the repair?#

I nodded. "Yeh. And log me in for this level, too." Normally, I didn't bother, especially when I was only going to be
down there long enough to retrieve my karakuri—it seemed
redundant, when the lockbox would show I'd been there—
but today, looking at the broken glass, remembering the
morning's news, it seemed a good idea to make sure that the
system, and anyone tapping it, knew I was there.

#You're logged in,# Celeste said. #George says, the broken
light was reported at fourteen-forty-two hours, but no repair
was logged. A glitch in the system.#

I let out a sigh, not realizing until then just how wary I'd
been. "All right, thanks. And unlock my storage, will you?"

#Unlocked,# Celeste answered, and the icon-face drifted
with me along the corridor, bright against the white padding.

My storage cell was at the end of the hallway—only fair,
since the karakuri could walk themselves to the lift—and I
could see the telltales glowing green from three meters away.

I punched the last code into the keypad, and rolled back the heavy door, but the lights didn't come on. The light from the corridor fell in past me, a wedge of brightness, and outside its illumination something moved with a whisper of metal. I caught my breath, and Celeste said, #I'm sorry, the interior lights have fused. Shall I bring the karakuri out anyway.#

"Emergency lights," I said, and the orange lights flicked on. There was nothing in the keeping, nothing in the shadows except the karakuri, four of them ranked in the padded half cylinders, the transformer squatting in the corner. The bronze karakuri had lifted its arm as though to unfasten the web that kept it secure against the padding, and I realized that what I'd seen—heard—was Celeste starting to move them toward the lift. "Elvis Christ, Celeste!"

#Ah—# I could have sworn I heard amusement in her voice, but when she spoke again, the emotion was gone. #I'm sorry, I thought you wanted them moved.#

"Not when I can't see what you're doing," I said.

#I don't understand.#

"You startled me."

#I don't understand.#

"Unexpected movement—movements where you don't expect them to be, or at a time when you don't expect them, startle people. Look, just leave it for now, Celeste." I glanced over my shoulder, but the corridor was empty except for the icon-face and the line of pinlights running back toward the lift doors.

#Very well.# The voice from the ceiling now sounded faintly annoyed. #Shall I bring them up now, or will that startle you?#

"I'm expecting it now," I said, and controlled my irritated response. Celeste was only a construct, and things like this proved it. "Yes, bring them up."

The emergency lights flickered, and in the same instant the humaniform karakuri stirred in their cases, reaching to unfasten the webbing that kept them safe when they were off-line. They moved smoothly, like people, each moving differently—the bronze bending slightly from the waist to complete the movement it had begun, the copper stretching to unfasten the top bolt of the webbing, the gold and silver turning in opposite directions to release the catches—and I grinned, delighted at how well Celeste had learned her lessons. Some of it was the kinetics of the original positions, of course—Celeste continuing the last movements the karakuri had made—but some of it was her newly informed choice, and if she could keep this up in the act itself, we would have a hit.

The transformer made a dull sound like a distant bell, and I stepped back as it put down wheels and rumbled slowly through the door. The karakuri followed, each one lowering the webbing carefully behind it, and I walked after them back toward the open lift doors. Celeste's face swam at the head of the little procession, the ghost-icon mirroring the copper karakuri, who in turn mirrored me. It was a weird image, a wonderful image, and I filed it for later use. Celeste walked the karakuri into the lift, and I closed the doors behind them, shutting out Celeste's face. The icon winked on again as I reached for the controls, and I smiled up at her, suddenly and unreasonably happy.

"Ready for the show, Celeste?"

#Oh, yes,# she answered, and I entirely believed her.

The ASM was gone by the time we reached the stage level. I left Celeste to deal with bringing the karakuri into position, and went back to the stage manager's console to check the settings. The boards were at standby, hold lights flickering from every screen except the one that monitored Celeste. The headbox was cabled to the side, connect indicators gowing steady green, and I edged it farther out of the way before turning my attention to the board. A yellow textnote popped to life as soon as my eyes met the system's tightbeam, and I squinted at it until the IPUs brought it into focus: *your construct is cabled, and I've foregrounded your settings package. Sorry it's not fully up, but I wasn't sure of your standards.* It was signed with a name glyph I didn't recognize, but I made a note of it anyway—she'd done the right things, both with Celeste and with the system—and blinked the note away.

"George, are you around?" I was checking the boards as I spoke, pulling my setting to the active spaces, reassuring myself that everything was there, all the subroutines and visuals and the files for the virtual aspects of the performance. I don't have to perform in the virtual—most of the Tin Hau's audience isn't wired—but it's become a matter of pride, even if it is the hardest part of the act. A lot of the important cues happen in the virtual; it's not easy to disguise them.

"I'm here," George answered from the stage, then his voice came from the little speaker in the console itself. "Will Celeste be running the act, or Aeris?"

"Celeste."

"Very good."

I could almost feel him drifting away, and said quickly, "Wait."

"Yes?"

"Bring the stage controls on-line, please. I'm showing lockouts on five channels."

"One moment." There was a little pause. "All channels are now open."

"Thanks." I ran my hand over the control pad, bringing up the virtual keys, entered the last codes. "I heard you had some problems last night, George."

"That is a security issue," the construct answered, almost primly. "I'm afraid I'm not able to discuss it with you at this time."

"Suit yourself." I entered another string of codes, effectively locking him out of the stage systems for the duration of the run-through, a petty but irresistible response. "Celeste logged the problem down in the keeping?"

"That's correct. A maintenance crew will be sent there as soon as possible."

"Thanks," I said, and Celeste's icon appeared where the note had been.

"Everything is ready."

"Haya." I checked the readings a final time. "All right, George, that'll be all."

"Thank you." A tiny white star vanished from my vision, an icon I hadn't noticed until it was gone.

Celeste said, "I'm to run the whole act, you said?"

"That's right." I smiled at the icon, in spite of knowing better. "You said you were ready."

"I am." Her expression didn't change, but I thought her voice softened. "Thank you." Her icon vanished, and I felt the first touch of the stage systems on my suit. #Places.#

It was a mere flicker of sound, like the touch of a breeze, but more than enough to carry the information I needed. I walked out onto the stage, taking my place behind one of the two slim columns that decorate my set. They look too small, too thin, to hide anything, but that look is deceptive, and the mirrored surfaces are very forgiving. Celeste was patching the rest of the stage systems through to my suit, a not quite painful warmth along my arms, prickly as a sunburn. The visuals were too bright, too, the bars of purple light that crisscrossed the stage and the tracking strip that floated just below my line of sight strong enough to hide my view of the stage.

#Lower my monitor half a level, Celeste,# I said, and felt the itching sensation ease. The lights faded as well, visible, but no longer obscuring anything, and I nodded. #That's good, thanks.#

#Stage set ready, karakuri read, visuals primed,# Celeste announced. #Ready?#

#Ready,# I answered, and took a slow, careful breath.

#Steady. Go on five,# Celeste said, and tuned her voice to a soothing drone. #On four . . . three . . . two . . . one. Begin Appearance.#

Her voice faded slightly, so that all I heard were the necessary cues, and then I heard my own voice from beyond the rising curtain. The copper karakuri was hidden within the hologram, invisible even to virtual sight, which should have shown it like a fly in amber.

"Ladies and gentlemen, please accept my apologies for the technical problem. We've had a slight malfunction in the lighting computer, and the show will have to proceed without the lighting effect planned for this evening."

I braced myself, ready to hit my mark, but a part of my mind was considering the opening, acknowledging that it was probably time for a change. The act needed a new introduction as well as a new ending, and the image I'd seen in the keeping was probably a good place to start.

"Then we will have to try—this." The karakuri's arm rose, "tossing" the holographic ball she had been holding, and the stage lighting flashed full on for a moment, the position and colors effectively hiding the stage for a crucial second before they settled to the production settings. In that second, I took my place, holographic smoke curling around my ankles, and walked forward into the new light, smiling, arms held out to welcome the applause. The music swelled—hard djensi, the music I'd grown up with, not at all like Fanning's sound— and Celeste whispered in my ear.

#Compression.#

This was the most purely mechanical of the illusions. I stepped to one side, posing, gestured widely, and the apparatus trundled in under its own power, guided by the purple beams. That would show, would let anyone in the audience who was wired think they'd seen something they shouldn't, and blind them to the signals that were flashing past them just below the beams. The bronze karakuri stepped back into the shadows at the stage edge, not quite offstage, out of sight of the audience—more distraction—and Celeste brought the gold and silver karakuri downstage. The gold is covered with a web of wires, a network like a radar cage suspended above its skin, framing its shape, and I turned it to display that fragile lace. Then I brought it back upstage to the press, the familiar shape—it really was a Tongas stamp, before I modified it, still looks identical to the machines the lineworkers use every day—and stepped back again to let the audience take in the contrast between the karakuri's deceptive fragility and the massive weight of the press. A light flashed once in front of my eyes, signaling that everything was ready, and the gold turned toward the press, ready to take its place between the plates. The silver moved with it, something I hadn't scripted, and I started to frown, but in that moment it held out its hand and helped the gold into the press. The gold reclined with serpentine grace, gleaming against the old iron, the lights striking sparks of light from its polished skin and reflecting from the weight poised above it. The silver looked at me, and reached for the lever, resting one delicate hand on the tip. Again, it wasn't scripted, but it was effective, and I nodded, keeping my face grave, planning to give Celeste hell later.

The press tilted, the lower weight lifting as the upper plate came down, and the karakuri shifted slightly to leave its feet and head outside the grasp. The press closed, slow and inexorable, with a groan of metal, and then tilted back again to show the plates completely closed, the gold's head and feet protruding from the ends. In the old days, when this was my big illusion, I'd ask a line-worker to check the press out first, make sure it wasn't modified; Muthana said there wasn't time to do that anymore, but with him running a short show now, I might ask again.

The karakuri turned her head, showing the serene face still faintly smiling, and another faint icon flashed behind my eyes. I gestured to the silver, motioning for it to lift the lever, and it did so with only the slightest hesitation. The press reversed itself, lifting and then lowering to reveal the karakuri reclining unharmed in the metal jaws. Part of the illusion relies on people recognizing the Tongas stamp, but not all of it: no matter where I'd shown it, there were always gasps and murmurs when it reappeared unharmed, almost as loud as there would have been for a human assistant. The silver moved again to help it down, and I came forward to take its free hand, so that three of us bowed together, like actors.

#Disassembly,# Celeste murmured, and the gold released me, turned to join the bronze as it brought a set of wheeled cabinets on stage.

Automatically, I turned my head so that my moving lips wouldn't be seen from the audience. #Celeste. No more surprises.#

#It looked good, what I did.#

It had, too, and I'd probably keep it, but that wasn't the

point. #Yeh, but I need to know exactly what's going to happen when we're onstage. I could get hurt, you know.#

The karakuri had taken up their positions beside the cabinets, were spinning them to show off the empty interiors. Celeste said, #I forgot. If I have other ideas, may I show them later?#

#Do you—# I broke off, watching the karakuri out of the corner of my eye. There was no time for this conversation; if Celeste had ideas, I could wait to find out about them. #Yeh, later.#

#All right. Later.# Her voice faded, and I turned my attention to the next illusion.

Disassembly was actually the simplest of the group, a tried-and-true illusion—older than spaceflight, even, or so people said—that worked for me because I used the karakuri to full advantage. I placed each one in its cylinder, fastened the support strap, then removed legs and arms and finally heads, piling them all on a worktable that rolled out from the wings to receive them. When I'd finished, I folded the tarp that had covered the worktable up and over the pile of parts, and closed the cylinders one by one, hiding the metal torsos that hung there, bright against the soft black lining fabric. Celeste released another flash, and the parts vanished, leaving the tarp empty. I unfolded and shook it, just to prove it, then gestured to the cylinders. Celeste raised all four doors simultaneously, to reveal the karakuri reconstructed, but with the parts mixed wildly, a gold leg on the silver body, silver head on the bronze. That usually got a laugh—relief and release; the karakuri look that little bit too human to make it comfortable to see them taken apart like this—and I mimed a sigh, gesturing for Celeste to close the cylinders again. The covers came down slowly, and I brought my hands together in apparent concentration. I gestured again, pointed to each side, and then flung my hands wide. The cylinders vanished, revealing the karakuri fully restored, each with its proper parts. They bowed, and Celeste whispered in my ear again.

#Vanishment.#

This, too, was a classic, possibly as old as the basic illusion in Disassembly, but what makes it unusual is that the covering cloth vanishes along with the karakuri. It's a real cloth, too, not virtual—I used to let the audience feel it for themselves, before Muthana shortened each act's time to fit more people into the show—and another conjurer once offered me ten thousand wu for the apparatus. I told him he could have it for seven thousand, but not until I was tired of it, and I was expecting that to be a long time away. A lot of what makes this work is the setup, the gold karakuri suddenly treated like a *ha'o* princess out of a high-class videomanga, and I took my time with it, Celeste tracking my tempo perfectly. The gold vanished, replaced by the red-enamel box; I made it reappear between the silver and the bronze, and stepped back to let them take their bow.

#Transformation,# Celeste murmured, and the bronze karakuri turned to bring on the transformer. #George says Ba' Muthana is here already. Should I let him in?#

Under normal circumstances, I don't let anyone, even Muthana, watch my rehearsals, but he'd come to see the new illusion. #Yeh. But this is an exception, Celeste, not a rule.#

#Confirmed.#

I saw a square of light appear at the back of the auditorium as Muthana opened one of the rear doors, and then it vanished again. I couldn't see him—wouldn't see him unless and until he came down to the front row of seats—but I couldn't help being well aware of his presence. The bronze moved the transformer into position center stage, turning it to show it from all sides and empty, and Celeste framed it in a web of lights. The music changed, moved down the scale, a weird little riff that resolved to a steady three-chord pulse. The bronze stepped up into the opening and sank into the metal, began to disappear into it even as the silver followed. The gold came next, folding into the frame, drawn in by the last reaching hands. The transformer contracted abruptly, a movement that should have crushed anything contained in it, and I heard Muthana gasp in the front row.

I ignored him, gestured instead to the transformer. It opened again, the karakuri began to reappear, flowing out of the metal as though they were somehow liquid, dragging the copper with them as they came. Celeste had managed to get the speed up, and I had to bite back a smile. The three karakuri pulled the copper all the way out of the frame, and it came forward as though to take a bow. This was the hardest part of the illusion, the culmination of its effect, and I took a deep breath, flourishing the sheet of silk as though I was going to vanish it. I lifted it a final time, letting it hide us both, and it fell to the stage behind me. A split second later, I stepped through the transformer's open space, and came forward to join the karakuri, bringing them forward into the bow. At a second gesture, Celeste's face-icon joined us and we bowed together. In the silence at the end of my music, I heard Muthana clapping.

#End it, Celeste,# I said, and felt the confirmation pulse through my suit. I could see Muthana now, still clapping as he rose from his seat and came to the edge of the stage. I squatted there to wait for him, and only then realized how hard I was sweating. I wiped my face carefully on the hem of my tunic, glad I hadn't put on full makeup, and felt the stage sensations trickle away from me as Celeste brought the systems down to standby.

"Not political," Muthana said, with scorn, but he was still smiling. I waited. "You're pushing buttons, Fortune, that's for sure."

I know. I said, "Is it a problem?"

"It's spectacular," Muthana said. "No, I don't think it's a problem. It's not explicit, and I think it's good—I'm willing to take a chance on it."

Now that he'd said yes, I felt compelled to play devil's advocate. "Realpeace isn't making a name for tolerance. I'm prepared to hold this until things settle."

As soon as I'd said it, I hoped he wouldn't take me up on it, and was relieved when he shook his head. "No. I'm not going to let them intimidate me. And, speaking of which, I'm putting in some new security, I'll need to give you codes and get passwords."

"That's new," I said.

He lifted his hand, counting the reasons coolie-style on his fingers. "First, we need to change the codes anyway, after the break-in—that's just common sense. Second, I don't like the way Realpeace has been trying to make this coolies against everyone else, and I sure as hell don't like being threatened over it. And third—" He touched his thumb, his smile going crooked. "Third, I can afford to do it, because I spoke to the owners, and they've agreed that it's appropriate to try to ride out the problem. They don't like being threatened, either."

That, not unreasonably, would have been the deciding factor: new security arrangements would be expensive, and if I was Muthana, I'd want to make sure the owners approved the payments first. "I didn't know there'd been threats here."

He shrugged. "Realpeace sees us—sees all the Empires—as a threat to coolie culture, watering down what's good and mixing it up with alien, *farang*, ideas. There hasn't been anything overt, mind you, but after last night, I don't intend to sit back and wait for it to blow over."

Translated, that meant that Muthana had chosen to go out on a limb to protect the theater—and, not incidentally, his acts. And he'd persuaded the owners to go along with it. "Thanks, Binnie," I said, and wished I had adequate words.

#Fortune,# Celeste said, and in the same instant George spoke from the downstage monitor.

"Bi' Fortune, bi' Terez and a guest would like to speak with you."

"Ah," Muthana said. "You can get the new codes from here, then."

"Haya," I said, and glanced at the monitor. "All right, George, tell them to come on in."

"Thank you," the construct answered.

Muthana looked up at me. "Have you heard Fire/Work's new songs, Fortune?"

"Not really. Not yet." I saw the door at the back of the hall open, spilling light briefly into the aisle, and two shapes momentarily silhouetted against it.

"You should." Muthana pushed himself away from the stage. "It's very good, very strong—important music."

That was what everyone had said about Hati, when they were starting out. I shivered, and tried to tell myself it was just the sweat cooling on my back. "Important music's getting people killed these days, Binnie."

"I don't intend for that to happen here," he answered, and started up the aisle.

I swung around to sit on the edge of the stage between two of the monitors, wincing at my stiffened muslces, and Terez and her guest came into the light. The stranger was a big woman, easily a head taller than Terez, and broad-shouldered in proportion—handsome, too, with a strong fair face and yanqui eyes. I smiled, and Terez lifted a hand in greeting.

"Fortune. I'd like you to meet Reverdy Jian. She's a friend of Chaandi's."

I held out my hand automatically, wondering what she— or Chaandi—wanted, and why that name was so familiar, and the big woman took it in an easy grip.

"Good to meet you."

"And you," I answered, and waited. Something was nagging at the back of my mind, something about her name and Chaandi, and Jian smiled, showing even teeth.

"I asked Bi' Terez to introduce us—asked Chaandi to introduce me to her—because of something that happened last night."

"To do with the bombing?" I asked, in spite of myself, and Jian shook her head.

"Not exactly, anyway. Look, I'm an FTL pilot, I work a lot with Spelvin constructs—"

"Manfred," I said aloud, and Jian lifted an eyebrow. "I remember. You were one of the people involved with Manfred—one of the ones who found it."

"And killed it," Terez said.

Jian said, "That's right. Manfred was—well, it wasn't true AI, but it was built to mimic it, and working with it felt a lot like what AI ought to feel like." She paused, as though she was choosing her words carefully, and I guessed that she might be in range of one of the stage's contact nodes. She was wired, of course—all FTL pilots were—and I wondered for an instant what she'd make of Celeste.

"I bought a new Spelvin construct recently," Jian went on, "that felt—different—from the others. I sold it again because I didn't like that difference, and last night the man who bought it came to me to warn me that somebody, he wouldn't say who, was after it, was making trouble for him. He said they knew I had owned it, and that I might be in trouble because of it, and he recommended that I go off-world, just as he was heading into the desert." She paused then, watching me as though she was expecting some response, but I kept my expression neutral. "I found out that you have the construct now, and I figured you should know what was going on."

I took a deep breath, swinging my legs over the stage edge to try and hide my thoughts. So one of Celeste's components had been something special to begin with—the SHYmate, obviously, the one that had been optimized for FTL; connecting it to a second construct would only have intensified that effect. But the last thing I wanted to do was to acknowledge that Celeste was something special, for both our sakes—not even to Jian, maybe especially not to Jian, after the Manfred Riots. She'd been badly injured by the construct—it had tried to kill her, had almost succeeded, if I remembered correctly; there was no reason to think she'd feel any more fond of Celeste, particularly since her first reaction had been to sell her.

"I bought two constructs from a man called Garay," I said, playing for time, and Jian nodded.

"This was a SHYmate. SHYmate 294."

"Yes. I bought that one." I brought my feet back up onto the stage. "Look, I appreciate your coming here—the way things are, I don't want to run any unnecessary risks—but I'm afraid I haven't noticed anything unusual about the SHYmate. I'm using it in my act, though, so I probably wouldn't."

Terez gave me a sharp look at that, and I hid a grimace. The stage manager knew perfectly well that I had to work closely with my constructs, that I would certainly have noticed if I was dealing with something that felt like AI, and I made my-self meet Jian's eyes guilelessly. At least the pilot didn't seem to notice anything; she nodded thoughtfully, and looked at Terez.

"I thought you should at least know what Garay said. Bi' Terez, I appreciate your bringing me here—and I'm glad to have met you, bi' Fortune. I'll look forward to seeing your act some time."

"Come backstage if you do," I answered, and hoped she wouldn't take me up on the invitation. "Rez, I need to talk to you about codes once I've gotten the act broken down. Will you be in your office?"

Terez nodded. "Binnie mentioned. I have it ready."

"We'll leave you to it, then," Jian said, and turned away. I watched them disappear into the shadows, wondering if I'd done the right thing. Jian had come to warn me, had dealt with Manfred—if anyone would know what to do about Ce-leste, she might—but at the same time, her first response had been to sell the SHYmate. I'd keep Celeste to myself, at least for now.

▪ 12 ▪

Reverdy Jian

CROSSING THE DECANI Interlink toward the stand-still in-terchange that led up to the lowest level of the Rooks, Jian was very aware of eyes following her passage. Realpeace glyphs gleamed from nearly half the storefronts, flashing from the tightbeam transmitters and painted directly on glass or stone, and nearly everyone was wearing the Freyan *sarang*, not just the old people clustered in the spill of cool air from the main vents in the center of the square, but the shopkeepers as well, and even the trio of older adolescents lounging in the window of the cookshop. There was even a Realpeace crèche, tucked into a converted storefront—the place had been a Dreampeace office, too, she remembered. It looked more successful in this guise: a tall woman in full traditional dress was herding a mixed group of children, ranging in age from toddler to a few who might be as old as twelve or thirteen, toward the open door. As she passed them, heading for the interchange, she saw one of the younger children point to her, and saw the teacher stoop to answer. Jian could hear neither the question nor the answer, but their laughter followed her up the interchange stairs.

It was probably nothing, probably her own misunderstanding, she told herself, but she found herself relaxing as she reached the Rooks. Even in its best days, it had been cheap housing—and since then, the stack-flats had been recut and subdivided to cram more and more renters into the narrow buildings—and it hadn't been considered a good neighborhood at any time in her memory, but at least in the Rooks she knew that if she had trouble, it would be robbery, not politics. She smiled at the thought, and a thin young man, neither coolie nor yanqui, face as indeterminate as most of the midworld, stepped sideways, giving her wary room. In the same instant, a trio of piki-bikes whined past, deliberately hogging the middle of the road; she caught a brief glimpse of silvered faces, and one silver arm rose in defiant salute. The young man lifted a hand in answer, and passed her smiling. His lip was swollen, the obvious aftermath of a fight.

The main door of Vaughn's building was locked and barred, but for once the intercom was working, and she climbed the standing stairs to the next landing. Red was waiting at the security door, opened it silently at her approach, and she stepped past him, heard the triple click as he resealed the locks behind her.

"So what's up?" Vaughn called from the open doorway of his flat, and Jian lifted a hand in greeting. "How'd you come?"

Jian blinked, and he stepped aside to let her into the single room. It was cramped, the air warm and a little stale, a

fan moving sluggishly in one corner to supplement the ventilators; the connection board was on and muted, the single
screen showing one of the newschannels, but Vaughn gestured with the room remote and the picture vanished before
she could identify the image. Most of the room was filled
with a sturdy loft, and the curtains that hung between the
posts made the room look even smaller.

"I came through Decani," she said. "Why?"

"I should've warned you," Vaughn answered, and swung
himself up the ladder that led to the loft platform. Behind
him, Red closed and locked the room door, moved to the
niche that held the coldbox. "It's better to come through
Avery, these days, Decani's not the safest anymore."

"Yeh, you should've warned me," Jian said, and followed
him up the wide-runged ladder. The platform was furnished,
and reasonably comfortable, but only if one didn't expect to
stand upright. She lowered herself cautiously onto one of the
truncated chairs—it wasn't much more than a thick foam
pad with a thinner back—and shook her head at Red's
silently offered beer. "I didn't have any trouble, though."

"Good," Vaughn said, and took the bottle Red extended toward him. "Thanks, bach. So what's going on?"

Jian laughed. "I wish I knew."

"Funny." Vaughn took a long swallow of the beer, but his
eyes never left her. "So what are you doing here, then?"

"I think we have a problem," Jian said.

"I've been telling you that."

"Look, Imre, do you want an answer, or not?"

Vaughn spread his hands in apology, and Jian nodded.
"Right. I assume you watched the news last night."

Vaughn nodded. "Yeh."

"I was up on the Zodiac when the reports started coming
through," Jian said. "With Chaandi, which didn't make it
better. But then that guy Red fixed me up with, Garay,
showed up, warned me people were taking too much interest in the construct I sold him because it was just what I said
it was all along, a little too close to people. He said he was

heading into the deep desert, and suggested I do something similar—"

"What about the construct?" Vaughn asked.

"He sold it. To a conjurer, the one at the Tin Hau Empire," Jian said. "You know, the one who has all the humaniform karakuri." She took a deep breath. "I got Chaandi to get me an introduction, she knows the stage manager at the Tin Hau, and I went over there to talk to her. I wanted to let her know what Garay said, I figured she deserved that much warning."

"And you wanted to know what she thought about the construct," Vaughn said.

"That, too." Jian nodded.

"And?" Vaughn prompted, after a moment. "Elvis Christ, you can't just leave it there."

"And that's it," Jian answered. "She—her name is Fortune, it's her real name, apparently—she basically said thank you very much, but she hadn't noticed anything funny about it."

"I find that hard to believe," Vaughn said, and Red, sitting cross-legged on the floor beside him, nodded once.

"So do I," Jian said, "but what am I supposed to do, call her a liar with nothing at all to back me up?"

"I suppose not." Vaughn leaned back in his chair. "I still think we should do what this Garay said, and get the hell out of here. Maybe permanently."

"Permanently?" Jian stared at him, startled, and he gave a one-shouldered shrug.

"We've been talking about it, Red and me, we've got the credentials, we can get work—"

"You've been talking about it," Red said.

"I don't want you dead or in jail," Vaughn said. He reached out, tangled his fingers in the other's thick hair, dragging him sideways until his head rested against Vaughn's chest. "Nobody hurts you but me, sunshine."

Red didn't move, and after a moment Vaughn released him, swearing under his breath. Jian said, "It might not be a bad idea, but I'd still like to know what the hell is going on here first."

"Good question." Vaughn took a long swallow of his beer, his eyes still fixed on the other man.

"You said people have been asking questions," Jian said. "About the construct, about us. What kind of people?"

Vauhgn shrugged. "It's thirdhand—people I know, pilots, a couple of constructors, friends, telling me people have been asking them what I'm doing, what Red's doing. Mostly if Red's back in business."

"So not hard-hackers, then," Jian said, "because they'd know he wasn't. And probably not Realpeace, either, because your friends wouldn't have that kind of connection."

"It doesn't make sense," Vaughn said. "Who else would want to know about this construct?"

"The Cartel," Red said, softly.

Jian stared at him for a long moment. That did make sense—the Cartel Companies had done most of the research on AI and near-AI; they were the ones who stood to lose, or gain, the most if true AI were discovered. More than that, they were the most likely to underestimate the depth of coolie anger, and the strength of Realpeace.

"Elvis Christ," Vaughn said. "You know, that does make sense—they're based in the underworld, all of them, they wouldn't have a fucking clue what they were stirring up."

Jian nodded slowly. "So, assuming for now that it is the Cartel, would they be looking to steal it, or to destroy it, I wonder?"

"Kagami would want to get it back," Vaughn said. "It was theirs to begin with, right?"

"Their matrix," Jian said. "They built it."

"And they've always been big into near-AI," Vaughn said. "They're the ones who built Aster, after all."

Aster had been a controversy years before Manfred, the first Spelvin construct anyone claimed had broken the Turing Barrier. It had been a Kagami project, and Kagami had proved to the courts' satisfaction that Aster was not true AI. Dreampeace had called it a cover-up—*and Venya Mitexi had taken that old matrix,* Jian remembered, *and built Manfred from it.* But Kagami had also paid for her own long stay in rehab, for the new skinsuit and her artificial eyes: nothing was ever simple. She shivered in spite of the warmth, and hoped Vaughn hadn't seen. He went on as though he hadn't noticed.

"If it's not Kagami, well, I'd expect them to want to suppress it. Nobody else has put the kind of money into AI that Kagami has."

"You mean kill it," Jian said. "If it is AI."

"If." Vaughn rubbed his forehead with the beer bottle, leaving a trail of moisture. "That's the problem, isn't it? And I don't think it's our problem."

"I sold it," Jian said. "I sold it because I thought it might be, well, not AI, exactly, but something out of the ordinary. If I'd kept it, I wouldn't have gotten Red involved, and we'd be able to sit quietly and figure out what to do with it— maybe take it off-world, like you said. Fortune wouldn't be involved, and I'm worried that she didn't believe me, that she's going to get hurt."

"She's not your responsibility," Vaughn said, with surprising gentleness.

Jian snorted, managed a wry smile. "You know me. Hell, I could even worry about that guy from Motosha, the one you were hassling at the Nighthawk."

"You know, he's in the band that was playing at the Oasis last night," Vaughn said, and Jian sighed.

"Don't change the subject."

"Haya." Vaughn fixed her with a cold stare. "Then I say we pull rank, we pack up, and we get out of here. Leave this construct, and Fortune, to their own business—she's supposed to be fantastic, let her disappear herself, or something. But we need to take care of ourselves."

Jian shook her head. "And what if it's not AI?"

"We do exactly the same thing."

"No." Jian sighed again, and managed a wry smile. "Well, maybe we should talk to Peace again, I'm with you on that one. But I shouldn't have sold that construct."

Vaughn shrugged. "It's done."

"Thanks." Jian looked sideways, at the connection board just visible over the edge of the loft. The screen was empty, but in her imagination she could still see the warehouse in Gamela where Manfred had made his last stand—could see, too, the scenes from the previous night, the Zodiac harsh in the emergency lights, all the signs darkened, the buildings stripped to mere stone. "I can't believe any of the Cartel is this stupid—this isn't the time to be bringing up the AI question."

"Believe," Vaughn said, sourly. He looked at the man beside him. "We haven't heard from you, bach. Are you with us on this?"

For a moment, Jian thought Red would ignore him, but then the technician nodded.

"Good," Vaughn said, and reached for the room remote. "Let's call Peace now."

Malindy was immediately available and willing to take the call—*not a good sign*, Jian thought, and was not surprised when the co-op manager shook his head.

"Imre, if I had anything going out-system, I'd be happy to let you take it, and the hell with what Binli Dai thinks."

"That's a change," Jian said, in spite of herself, and Malindy spread his hands.

"The situation's changed. But, anyway, I haven't got anything."

"Do you expect anything?" Vaughn asked.

"I don't have anything on the books except local," Malindy said, "and I haven't had any inquiries. I've heard a rumor that Caizene Ltd. will have a packet ship going to Razhul or Crossroads—somewhere Urban, anyway—and if the job comes up, I'll bid for you. But it's not your usual run."

"I'd appreciate it if you'd bid," Jian said, and Malindy nodded.

"Haya. But you won't make money on it."

"We'll survive," Vaughn said, and cut the connection.

"So we wait," Jian said. She stared for a moment at the cracked plaster above the kitchen niche, wondering what to do. She knew she should simply lie low, do her best to stay out of sight, out of the way of whoever it was who was trying to find this construct, but the memory of the conjurer nagged at her. She could still see her, thin and dark, perched on the edge of the stage like a child, the woman-shaped karakuri—who looked weirdly like her, Jian realized, deliberately like her—standing ranked behind her. Why would someone who obviously reveled in blurring that boundary pretend she hadn't noticed that the SHYmate was something unusual? "I want to see the show," she said, and Vaughn looked at her.

"What?"

"I want to see Fortune's act—I want to see what she does with it," Jian said. "Want to join me?"

Vaughn sighed. "If I have to."

"Aren't you at all curious?" Jian asked, and the other pilot shook his head.

"Not when my neck's at stake."

Jian smiled, knowing she'd won. "We'll set a time," she said. *And I'll see what this construct can do.*

▪ 13 ▪

Fanning Jones

AFTER THE TROUBLE at the Middle Oasis, nobody really wanted us in their clubs, especially not in the upperworld. The few midworld clubs that booked fusion bands didn't want us either—not only didn't we have a big enough following, but the people who did like us were mostly metalheads, and nobody wanted to attract Realpeace's attention that way. It hurt us: with the cutbacks at the Tin Hau, we were already losing money, and without outside gigs, we were going to have trouble paying the bills. I was already getting as many hours as I could at Motosha, and Tai was scrounging day work on the local assembly lines, but even at the best estimates, we'd be living on brick noodles for the rest of the month. Fortune knew, and offered to loan me what she could, but she didn't have that much to spare, what with the bills for the new illusion. It was enough to pay Persephonet, anyway, which was good because if we were ever going to get bookings again, that was how they would come in, and I took it, but next month wasn't looking any better. Timin's family—he still lived with them, in a cavern *campong* over in Lower Gamela—offered us the occasional meal, too, which made a nice change from noodles.

The *campong* was pleasant, a low-ceilinged, oval cavern lined with two-story poured-stone buildings. They were pretty ordinary, the square shape that had been the fabricators' standard fifty years ago, but at some point one of the family had added woven-iron balconies to each of the housefronts, and those balconies were filled with plants, mostly vines that cascaded almost to the cavern floor. Some of the day-lights had been replaced with the expensive full-spectrum tubing, and the air smelled of the plants and moisture: a pleasant place, and a place where we could forget our problems for a while.

After the meal—we all ate twice as much as was polite, but the uncle who did the cooking pretended he was flattered by our appetite—we sat in the courtyard by the main support pillar, enjoying the draft from the ventilators. A handful of older women, Timin's aunts or great-aunts, probably, watched us from an upper balcony: the family was Boatmen enough to want to observe Freyan proprieties, especially with Tai and Shadha, but Persephonean enough to do it discreetly. After everything I'd eaten, I really didn't care who was watching; I leaned back against the pillar, closing my eyes, and Shadha kicked me.

"We really ought to talk about what we're going to do."

"So let's talk," I said, and she kicked me again.

"You think better when you're awake."

I opened my eyes, reluctantly, and Timin said, "Not necessarily."

I looked around for something to throw at him, but the

campong floor was barely even dusty. Tai said, "So where do we stand with bookings?"

Jaantje shrugged. "It's not good. Ino's still wants us, but that's about it."

"Great," I said. If we were going to have more trouble at a gig, Ino's was the place for it: it was in Jamuna, a mixed township to begin with, a lot of low-level coolie line-workers living piled on top of sand-divers and long-haul drivers and midworlders who thought they should be doing better than linework, and it was close enough to the Spiral that the gangs from Li Chum sometimes came down to drink on relatively neutral territory.

"Corrad pays all right," Shadha said.

"I heard Realpeace was planning to make a big recruiting push in Jamuna," Tai said.

Jaantje sighed. "Corrad didn't mention that when he called—but then he wouldn't."

Corrad Ban, Ino's owner and manager, was never averse to a fight, as long as Ino's got the publicity.

Timin said, "They'd probably do well there, too."

Tai nodded.

"Why?" I asked. "Jamuna—at least the neighborhood around Ino's—never struck me as real political."

Timin made a face. "Why does anyone go for Realpeace? Stupidity, mostly—naïveté, at best."

"That's not true," Tai said. "The people I know—look, Realpeace does, or they did do, a lot of useful things. They're responsible for getting databanks into a lot of Heaven, especially West-of-Four, when nobody else would, got financing for the co-ops, too, and stood up for people who had contract trouble, things like that. There are a lot of people I know who say Realpeace is all right, it's just the radicals who are doing bad things."

People—yanqui people—had said that about Dreampeace, too, after the Manfred Riots.

Timin said, "Realpeace wants to be the next Provisional Government, and that's all they care about. That's the only reason they're doing any of this."

Tai sighed. "The new triumvirate, they're the ones who started it all."

There wasn't anything to say to that—not anything good, anyway, nothing that wouldn't start a fight—and I said, "Still nothing on the Zodiac, then?"

"Nothing," Jaantje said.

"Which is a shame, with the new stuff sounding this good," Shadha said.

I took a deep breath. "Maybe we should think about putting out a new clip."

"We don't have the money," Timin said.

Jaantje shrugged. "It would sell, though—we could do it on credit, pay off the costs once the clip was out there."

"If we do that," Tai said, "I think it should just be the new songs. The old stuff just doesn't fit with them." She smiled. "You know, it's not a bad idea."

"Credit's expensive," Timin said.

"Muthana would back us," Shadha said, and Timi scowled. "Yeh, for a fat chunk of the profits."

"Which is better than what we're getting right now," Tai said. "As I see it, the real problem is we don't have enough new stuff to fill a regular clip."

"Not yet," Shadha said. "Or we could put out a half-time."

"That's for new bands," Timin said.

Jaantje shook his head at the same moment. "And it doesn't save us enough money. What about a live clip? We're still ragged on some of the songs, I think we're better live than we would be in a studio—and maybe we could get George to film it for us, at the Tin Hau."

"Then they really would want a percentage," Tai said, and shrugged. "Though they promise they can keep the pirates off."

That was an old and not very profitable argument, and I settled myself more comfortably against the rough plaster coating the support pillar. The new songs were different from anything else we'd done, but the imagery was consistent, hung together in a way that nothing else we'd ever done had. That was why we finished our show with them, building to a climax. I said, "I know what you think of them, Tai, but the way the songs work with each other, this would make a hell of a theme clip."

Theme clips had been big about five, six years ago, when Hati was hot, before the Manfred Riots. Since then, they'd fallen out of favor, but I'd always liked them, liked the way Hati in particular, and one or two other bands, like PWC and Short Haul, had managed to make the visuals, the fx line and the short surreal filmees that traditionally go with a clip, into something that was as coherent as a videomanga. It was really easy to do them badly, which was part of why nobody much did them anymore, but when they were good, there was nothing like them.

"If we could do it right," Jaantje said, slowly, and Tai made a noise through her teeth.

"If."

"It could be good," Jaantje said, still mildly, as though she hadn't spoken. "The songs do fit."

Tai lifted her hand, counting on her fingers. "One, we need a lot more songs, and songs like these, if we're going to do a theme clip. Two, unless we get a really good director, somebody like Chaandi, even, we're just going to get anti-Realpeace propaganda. Three, no matter what the clip looks like, Realpeace is going to treat it as an attack."

She was right about all of it, but I had to swallow my disappointment before I could say anything. To my surprise, Timin spoke first.

"We all agreed, we needed more songs. I mean, you're right, right now, but if we can add to it, a theme clip could really work for us. It could be big, Tai. With these songs, and more like them, it could be big."

"Realpeace is going to take anything we do as an attack," Shadha said. "We might as well do what we want."

Tai sighed. "I'll think about it."

"I've got a couple of ideas," Timin began, but he was cut off by a shout from one of the doorways to our left. We all looked, in spite of manners, and saw a low-teen boy glaring at a woman—probably his mother—standing hands on hips in the doorway.

"I won't have that filth in my house," she shouted. "Go on, get rid of it—put it in the trash this second. Don't you dare think you can bring that in here."

The boy turned away, came sulking across the courtyard past us, heading for the green door of the *campong*'s waste system. As he went by, I could see that he had a Realpeace pin on his loose shirt.

"Go on," his mother called after him. "Put it in the trash now."

He did as he was told, slamming the door hard enough to make the women on the balcony shake their heads and murmur, came back toward home scuffling his feet on the stones. As he passed us again, he looked at Timin and said, *"Farang* shit."

"Watch it, cousin," Timin said, and the boy spat on the pavement in answer. His mother saw that, came charging after him, and caught him by the collar.

"You disgrace us," she said, and shook him. "You shame me and the family and yourself." The boy shrugged, his expression mulish, and she shook him again. "Timin, I apologize to you and to your friends. As for you, Anton—" She closed her mouth tight over whatever else she might have said, groping for her dignity, and turned on her heel, dragging the boy back with her toward the door.

"I'm sorry," Timin said after a moment, and Jaantje tapped him lightly on the shoulder.

"Hey, not your problem."

Timin grimaced. "It's my cousin."

"You don't pick your relatives," Shadha said, and there was a strained silence.

"We ought to be going," I said at last, and wasn't surprised to see the relief in Timin's face.

"Sorry," he said again. "The rest of the family's not like that—and even Anton's basically not bad, he's just fourteen."

He let us out the *campong*'s service door—we'd borrowed

a small carrier from Jaantje's father even though we couldn't really afford the fuel, thinking it might be safer than the 'bus lines, especially West-of-Four—and we climbed into the cramped passenger compartment. We dropped Shadha at the co-op she shared with a dozen other nominal Dream-peacers, where extra security flared in the real as well as the virtual, outlining the doors and windows—a necessary expense, Shadha said, but it couldn't have come at a less convenient time. Luckily, that made it easy to turn back down Broad-hi to Arii, so that we only had to fight the swarms of piki-bikes that filled Wireworks for about five minutes before we could turn off into the service alley that paralleled the *god-dow*. The parking was secure there, too, but Jaantje spent several minutes setting locks and alarms before we finally got back to the flat.

The message light was flashing on the media wall, and I reached for the remote. Tai found it first, however, and touched the keys. A series of glyphs flashed in the Perse-phonet screen—something for me from Fortune, a massmail from the Empire, a couple of schedule cards from bands we knew, a few messages for Tai and Jaantje from addresses I didn't recognize, and finally a system glyph, signaling an incomplete transmission. I rolled my eyes at that, and heard Tai groan: that particular symbol almost guaranteed a half-week's work straightening out the lost message.

"Let's get it over with," Jaantje said, and Tai touched the remote to select it.

The screen lit, revealing the familiar static-fuzzed images of a faulty transbust, but the audio was clear enough to make the message plain. "*Farang-garai*, get off the stage, nobody wants your bastard trash. Get off before—"

Tai hit the stop button, and we stared at each other. The voice had sounded coolie—sounded deaf, blurred and too loud, like I sounded without my ear.

"Play the rest of it," Jaantje said. His voice was tight and angry.

"Why?" Tai looked at him. "We should just get rid of it."

"No," Jaantje said. "Look, after what happened at the

Oasis—after what happened to Hati—you think we can just ignore it?"

"I don't want to hear it," Tai said, and now her voice sounded strange, high and scared like I'd never heard it before. "We used to get calls like that all the time, Mama did, and the only thing you can do is ignore them."

"What do you mean?" Jaantje asked.

Tai shrugged, scowling. "Just what I said. When I was little—when Mama was first on the Housing Committee, before she was an elector, even, we use to get calls like that. People threatening her, because of my father—people who'd found out he was a Detainee. And then, when she wouldn't give in, they threatened us." A look of contempt crossed her face. "They never did anything, though. Mama said they wouldn't have the nerve, and they didn't."

Jaantje and I looked at her, then at each other, not knowing what to say. From some other things she'd said, and from the fact that Tai's father had almost certainly died on Freya, in an FPG prison, I'd guessed that Li Mahal hadn't always been the FPG's choice for the CWISP offices. If anything, I'd admired her for it, for going from involuntary labor to someone who could actually make a difference for other draftees— but Tai had been two when they were sent here, with nobody to take care of her except Li Mahal. If I'd been her, I don't know how I could have put my kid in danger, especially not as shaky as this one call made me feel.

"These people have the nerve," Jaantje said, as gently as he could, and Tai shuddered.

"Yeh. I know. But I don't want to hear it. I'm going outside."

"Haya," Jaantje said, and the door closed behind her.

I picked up the remote. "Ready?"

"Yeh, go ahead."

I touched a button, restoring the playback.

"—trash. Get off before someone gets rid of you, sends you to hell like Hati."

The voice cut off as abruptly as it had started, and the end-of-file glyph appeared. I touched buttons, asking the system to retrieve the routing, but wasn't surprised when the trail ended at the district switcher. "So what do we do now?"

"Talk to Security?" Jaantje said, doubtfully.

That's one thing yanquis and coolies have in common, an ingrained, and in the coolies' case, at least, justified distrust of the security forces. "The block station's Cartel," I said.

"Yeh." Jaantje went to the door and tugged it open, letting the sunlight back into the room. "It's finished, Tai."

"I'd rather go to them than the FPG," I said.

"You think Security's going to do us any good?" Tai asked.

"You got a better idea?"

Jaantje said, "We could take it to Muthana. He always says, 'Think of me as family.' I think it's time we took him up on it."

"Are you crazy?" I said. "Talk about handing him an excuse to get rid of us—"

"I like that better than Security," Tai said.

"Besides," Jaantje said, "we might need to find another place to sleep for a while."

Of course, whoever called could get our location from the callcodes. We'd talked for a year or so about getting a sealed listing, since this was the band code as well as our own, but it hadn't seemed worth the fees—we hadn't been important enough to bother. "Maybe there's something else we can do," I said. "Some stuff I could hack, help keep the place secure."

"It's worth a try," Tai said, but sounded doubtful.

"Or we can call Security," I said.

In the end, we did both, called the Cartel Security station that served our block, and Muthana. Mister Walker—that was the Aussy name for a local cop, but everyone used it now—took our codes and a copy of the call, but was less than optimistic about finding whoever had called us. There had been a lot of incidents like this, he told us; the best he could offer was that none of the threats had been carried out, so far. Muthana was pissed, but not at us, offered us sleeping space in the practice room, and told us not to worry about the gigs, we were still part of the show. That was the main thing I'd been worried about, and by then we'd all calmed down enough that we felt all right about staying at the *goddow* for now. Still, before I went to bed, I plugged myself into the connections and went looking for some hard-hacking boards I hadn't frequented in a while. It took me a while just to find them—the owners moved them regularly, just in case—but I managed to find schematics for a better lock and for a couple of black-box alarms and trip systems that should warn us if anyone tried physically to get into the *goddow*. I also found an announcement for a scrap sale in Madelen-Fet Main, and with any luck I'd be able to get the parts cheap there. By this time, it was late enough that Fortune was back from the Tin Hau; I called her, and she agreed that I could use her workshop on one of her afternoons at home. I went to bed feeling a little better about the situation.

We got nearly a dozen more calls over the next two days, the first two pretty much the same as the first one we'd gotten. After that, we stopped listening, just forwarded them unread to the account Mister Walker had created for us. He suggested we change our codes, but this was the code all the clubs had; if anyone wanted to book us, we needed to hear from them. All we could do was ignore the broken icons and watch our backs. I was glad when it was finally Eighth-day and the scrap sale. Tai said she'd come with me—she was looking for spare processors for her guitar, she said—and I wasn't sorry to have company.

The sale started early; the shops of Madelen-Main were still shuttered, pinlights dark except for the security warn-offs, as we came out into the plaza. I looked around anyway, searching for the signs that the notice had promised, and saw live Security watching me from one of the farther doorways. There was nothing real, but I'd worn my display lenses, and I wasn't surprised to see glyphs leap out at me from a sideline transmitter. We followed them decorously past Security, then down a couple of empty side streets, and finally to a long, low building that had probably once been some kind of factory. The side windows were all missing, but the lights were on inside—the first lights we'd seen since we'd left the lift station—and through them I could see row after row of tables, piled high with components and holoplate displays for the things that were too big to fit into the hall. It looked as though the sellers would have everything I wanted, and I had to suppress a grin as we signed in with the silent woman at the entrance table.

The room was only moderately crowded so far, and as I swung my head, looking for a sellers' list, I saw a red shape floating in the air toward the middle of the room, filled with glyphs announcing that certain items would be auctioned at the end of the day shift. That explained why the crowd was still so small, more than the early hour: the important people, the real hard-hackers, wouldn't bother showing up until the auction, when the good stuff went on sale. On the other hand, that should mean that the smaller items—the sort of thing I wanted—would be going for reasonable prices.

"So what exactly are we looking for?" Tai asked, and I shrugged.

"Sensor boxes, I think, anyway something I can modify to monitor the *goddow.* And, of course, anything useful for my axe."

"If we can afford it," Tai answered.

"Credit's a wonderful thing," I said, with more confidence than I really felt, and nodded toward the fourth aisle. "Let's try down here."

It actually didn't take me very long to pick out the components I needed, first a sensor box that was still in good enough shape to work with—there were a lot of them available, and even though this one showed sand marks on the casing and blown vrower fuses, the interior boards were clean and unmarked. I could replace the fuses easily enough, especially with my Motosha discount to help me out, and a hundred wu was better than a reasonable price. In the next aisle, I found a trip recorder with a copy of the manager still in memory, and picked that up, too. With Fortune's help, I should be able to connect them to each other and to the *goddow's* internal wiring, and make sure that no one came in or out without our knowing it. The one thing I didn't find was a visual sensor, or at least not one that I could afford, but I guessed—hoped—that Fortune would let me adapt one of the karakuri's spare eyes. If she wouldn't—well, that was what lines of credit were for, I thought, but I couldn't help wincing.

I stopped at the end of the aisle and looked around for Tai. Her height and her hair made her easy to find, even across the room, and I cut around the tables and the knots of browsers to join her. She was rooting through a box of AIW 281 controllers, checking links, but looked up as I came up behind her.

"Anything?" I asked, and she shrugged.

"These look useful."

"Ten each, or thirty wu for the box," the woman running the table put in, and went back to her manga without waiting for an answer.

"Thanks," Tai said anyway, and got a distracted nod.

It wasn't a bad price, but it wasn't great, either. At the end of the table, though, there was a familiar red-and-silver box, an Urban—or at least Urban-style, a local copy—audiot, an audio box for an fx. Most people don't play audio from the fx, or use it just for effects, reinforcing the visuals, but I'd seen some clips from the Urban Worlds where fx had been used for harmony as well. It was probably too much to hope that this audiot would be in good shape, or if it was, it wouldn't be affordable, but I stepped around Tai anyway, trying to disguise my interest. Even at first glance, I could see that most of the plug-ins were missing, and so was the bay cover, so that you could see into the interior. I tipped it up on end and tilted it toward the light, counting the leaves of circuits. Everything seemed to be there—everything seemed to be intact, except for a cracked power box, and I set it carefully back down.

"What do you want for this?" I asked, and hoped my voice sounded casual.

"Two-fifty," the woman answered, still not looking up from her manga, and I caught my breath. That was a quarter of what it was worth, even without the plug-ins—hell, I could build them myself if I had to, or at worst collect them over time—and I reached into my pocket for my line of credit. It would just cover the box, and I closed my mind to the thought of the repairs.

"There's a carry case with it," the woman said. I couldn't tell, from her expression, whether she knew what she had or not, or if there was something badly wrong with it that I'd missed. Out of the corner of my eye, I could see Tai watching me, trying to pretend it wasn't important, and I shook my doubts away.

"I'll take it." I held out my loc card, and the woman took it, fed it into a reader. She gestured against the shadowscreen, and I held my breath, even though I knew I had the room, and released it with a sign when she turned the board toward me.

"Sig and seal here, please."

I scrawled my name and codes in the flashing box, then plugged the tagmaker into the slot on the edge of the board. The final light flashed green, and the woman nodded, breaking the connection.

"It's all yours." She reached under the table, brought out a worn-looking carryweb, already looking at Tai. "You interested in those controllers, bi'?"

Tai shook her head. "Not today, thanks."

It took me a couple of minutes to figure out how to fit the audiot into the webbing cradle, but I'd worked it out and was fastening the last ring when I heard a familiar voice behind me.

"Oh, good, you found it. We just tried to call you."

"Hey, Mosi," I said, and slung the box over my shoulder. Meonothai was with him, looking battered, one eye black and swollen. "What the hell happened to you?"

He rolled his good eye, and Mosi grinned. "Fist magnet."

There's one in every band, though we haven't found out who it is for Fire/Work yet. I think it's Timin, just like I think it's Shadha who'll start the fight, but mostly I hope it isn't me.

"You look awful," Tai said, and Mosi's smile widened.

"It's not that bad," Meonothai answered. "We had some trouble at the Rainbow Angel."

"Realpeace?" Tai asked, sharply, and Mosi glanced at her. "Why?"

"We've had some problems of our own," she said.

"It wasn't serious," Meonothai said, "and it wasn't even Realpeace, or the metalheads, not directly. There were some kids, coolie kids, and one of them was throwing stuff. It started out as a joke, and then we got pissed, and they got pissed, and they were hanging around when we were loading out, and one of them said something, and Mosi said something, and he hit me—one of the kids, I mean, not Mosi."

"Mosi said something, and you got hit," I repeated. Meonothai shrugged, and Mosi grinned again.

"I didn't mean for it to happen, but—oh, well." His grin vanished as quickly as it had appeared. "What kind of problems?"

"We've been getting anonymous messages," I said. "On the connections—Persephonet in particular. We haven't been able to trace them, which is part of what I'm here trying to fix."

"Somebody's been threatening to treat us like Hati," Tai said.

Mosi's eyes narrowed, and Meonothai said, "Have you talked to Security?"

I nodded. "Nothing there yet, though. They said other people had reported the same thing, and nothing's actually been done, which I guess is a consolation."

"We got a couple of calls after we opened for Cathayann at the Upperground," Meonothai said. "Apparently somebody didn't appreciate that."

Cathayann was a coolie band, but their sound was djensi influenced. "You'd've been a good match," I said, and Mosi snorted.

"Too good, apparently."

"We haven't gotten any repeat bookings," Meonotha said, "and we haven't been looking real hard, either. We've got enough gigs in our own neighborhoods, and around the Zodiac, to keep us going—this gig at the Rainbow is our last in Heaven."

Mosi made a soft sound, agreement and then some, and there was a look in his eyes I didn't like. He'd never taken threats well—not that I blamed him, but one thing I'd learned, living in Ironyards, was that there were times when it was better to back down. Meonothai said quickly, "So you got the audiot?"

I nodded. "It looks all right, too. I was heading over to Fortune's anyway, so I can maybe get it running again."

"Speaking of Fortune," Meonothai said, "what was it you were going to tell me?"

"She—" I stopped, shaking my head. The last thing I wanted was to try to explain about the new illusion, and the new Celestes. "It's really complicated, Meo, even for Fortune. Let me call you?"

"Haya." He looked wary behind the bruises. "But make it soon, will you? Aunt Gracia's been at me again."

"I will," I said, and hoped I was telling the truth.

I left Tai at Madelen-Main, and rode the 'bus across Shorthi into Angelitos. Fortune was expecting me: the door opened at my signal, and Celeste's voice spoke from the ceiling boss.

"Fortune says, come on in."

The mechanical voice was a perfect echo of Fortune's inflections. The lights came up as I moved down the narrow hall, then Fortune appeared in the doorway at the end, silhouetted against the brighter lights of the workshop. The worktable was lit behind her, a holodisplay glowing bluewhite on top of it.

"So, did you get what you wanted?"

"Yeh." I followed her inside. Fortune's flat was one of the biggest I'd ever been in—I don't think I'd ever been in a bigger space that was owned by just one person—and it looked bigger because there weren't any interior walls, just the pools of light to separate one area from another. There weren't any wallscreens, either, except for the media wall, which added to the effect. At that moment, all the light was concentrated on the work area, with the table at its center and the karakuri parts racked along the walls like oversize milagros. I could see the shadow of a couch, and a green light in the distance that was probably either the kitchen or something in her bedroom, but I ignored them and unslung the heavy carrier and my pack. "Can I put them on the table?"

"Go ahead."

Fortune stepped aside, and I hoisted the audiot onto the table's durafelt surface. I unsnapped the first rings, and she leaned both elbows on the table across from me.

"That's not surveillance gear."

"No." I grinning in spite of myself. "It's an audiot—an fx component. You can add harmonies with it, or melody, too, I suppose." I had it out of the carrier now and was unfastening the various covers. Fortune leaned close to see into the bay, and we grimaced at the same moment, seeing the scorched input.

"I hope you didn't pay a lot for it," she said, and I shrugged, trying to hide the disappoinment."

"Maybe a quarter of what it's worth."

"Good." Fortune reached for a tool wrapper, unrolled it with a flourish to reveal a row of gleaming picks and spot fastenings. "Well, let's get the rest of it open, see if the whole box is gone."

I nodded and grabbed the nearest driver I thought would fit. It was too big, but the next one engaged the clamps perfectly, and together we lifted the casing off.

"Ah, now," Fortune said, with satisfaction, and I allowed myself a sigh of relief. The scorching hadn't reached beyond the patch bay; the internal fuse was blown, but it had done its job, protected the delicate heart of the audiot.

"It looks to me like it's just the fuse," I said, and she nodded, reaching for one of her monitors."

"Let me check it out first," she said, "but if that's all it is, I'm pretty sure I've got that size fuse in stock."

"Haya." Even without extra patches and plug-ins, just with whatever was hardwired into the main memory, it would be worth hearing what the audiot sounded like. I saw the monitor lights turn green one by one, and Fortune nodded again.

"Looks like you got a deal, Fan. Let me see what I have." She looked up at the ceiling, and I followed her gaze, saw another sensor box hanging there, a pinlight glowing red. As my lenses locked onto it, I saw a copper face—Fortune's face, the karakuri's face—hanging against the shadows.

"Celeste," Fortune said. "Check my inventory. Do I have a GNV18 fuse in stock, and where is it if I do?"

The face wavered, and the machine voice said sweetly, "You have five GNV18 fuses in stock, as well as two GNX8A fuses. They are all in the cabinet labeled C, drawer 22."

"Thanks," Fortune said, and headed for the cabinets that stood against the far wall. She opened the big doors, and stood for a second staring at the drawers and shelves before she found the one she wanted. Over her shoulder, I could see a set of karakuri hands, one complete, one a metal skeleton, sitting on the top shelf next to a heavy-looking cylinder. It was as creepy as anything in her act—as the metallic ghost floating nearly at the ceiling—and I looked away, refusing to meet the pinlight.

"There it is," Fortune said, and came back to the worktable with the little disk. She popped out the old fuse and slipped the new one into place, then reached for a power feed. "What's the rating?"

I checked the casing, reading the numbers with difficulty through the scratched paint. "It's a Class-Two device, standard power."

Fortune nodded, touching buttons to lock in the setting. "Ready."

"Let's put the casing back on," I said. We refastened the clamps, and I flipped the power switch. A light glowed green on the display plate, but nothing else happened.

"Is that is?" Fortune asked, after a moment.

"I think it needs—" I saw what I was looking for even as I spoke, the five buttons arranged in a rough pyramid. "Those should be the onboard data triggers."

I touched one, and a bright error glyph appeared. I touched two more without success, trying to remember the code sequences for Urban fx gear, and then pressed the three corners together. A new pattern appeared, one I didn't recognize, and a tone sounded from the box. That I did know, the breathy note and weird overtones of the patch called vox humana, for all that it sounds like no human being ever born. The audiot ran through a scale, from a medium-low bass note up to a piercing treble. I saw Fortune wince, and reached to shut it off, but the test ended before I could reach the buttons.

"Well," she said after a moment, and I nodded. I'd never played an audiot before, never contributed to the music, just the pure fx parts, light and image, and for a second I stared at the bright casing, wondering if I could learn to play it properly with only a mechanical ear. I shoved that thought aside—it was as much, maybe more, a question of whether I could persuade the rest of Fire/Work that the audiot belonged in our sound—and switched it off again, itching to get it back to the Empire, where I could try out my controllers. It even had an in-line transceiver, the machine equivalent of IPUs, so that I would be able to play it from the virtual.

"So," Fortune said. "Did you get the security stuff?"

The question brought me back to what I was supposed to be doing, and I didn't try to hide my sigh. "Parts, anyway."

Fortune grinned. "Look, Fan, do you want me to do this for you?"

"I can't ask you that," I said. "If nothing else, I can't afford you."

"I owe you for getting me Celeste," Fortune said, suddenly serious. "I mean it, Fanning. So, show me what you've got—what is it you want this to do, anyway?"

I pulled the components out of my pack, lining them up on the worktable's thick surface. "What I want to do is make sure nobody can get into the *goddow* without setting off an alarm if we're there, and at least leaving a record if we're not. We've had some threats, over the connections, and nobody seems to be able to do anything about it. We think it's Realpeace."

"Bastards," Fortune said, conversationally. She frowned at the line of parts. "Where's your input device—I'm assuming you want visual, or were you looking for virtual?"

"Visual. I was coming to that." I paused. "I was hoping I could buy a VisiD from you—there wasn't anything at the sale that I could afford."

"What makes you think you can afford my gear?" Fortune asked, but looked at the ceiling again. "Celeste, what Visi devices do I have in inventory?"

There was another little pause, longer than before, and then the construct answered, "Three Kagami J-4 Visi devices, three Sobboy Z9s, and one Hot Blue Dianthe-2X. Two of the Kagami J-4 devices are mounted in eye-shells—"

"Haya, I've got it. Thanks." Fortune looked back at me. "I'll sell you the Dianthe, if you want it. For cost."

"Remember this is the band money, not mine."

"If it was just you, I'd charge you more." She smiled to take the sting away. "I bought it used, cleaned it up, and decided I didn't like it. It's yours for seventy-five."

VisiDs went for twice that new, and the best price I'd seen at the sale was a hundred. I nodded.

"The Hot Blue Dianthe-2X is in the D cabinet, second shelf," Celeste said.

"Thanks," Fortune answered, absently, and went to get it. The eye-shelled ones were also in that cabinet, and I could see them over her shoulder, suspended in a tall, gel-filled cylinder, looking for all the world like cloned prostheses. The gel was faintly pink—maybe that was just the light, a reflection from Fortune's scarlet tunic, but I looked away.

"Fortune," Celeste said.

Instinctively, I glanced toward the media wall, expecting a call from someone on Fortune's hot list, but the multiscreens were all empty.

"Yeh?" Fortune set the VisiD on the worktable beside the sensor box and the trip recorder, reached under the surface for another roll of tools.

"I would like to play with this Gallant 28173SH101," Celeste said. I blinked, and realized she meant the audiot.

Fortune frowned. "Fan's audiot thing?"

"Yes."

"What do you mean?" I asked, and looked at Fortune. "Have you programmed her—?"

Fortune waved me to silence. "Don't be stupid. Celeste. Why?"

"Because—" There was a pause, and I looked up to see the icon-face motionless, expressionless against the suspended sensors. "Because I wish to."

I shivered in Fortune's expensively chilled air, in spite of knowing it had to be a trick, or a mistake, some glitch in the mated programs. Constructs just didn't do that, didn't ask— didn't initiate actions completely unrelated to their owners' requests. Or if they did, they didn't offer such patently impossible "reasons" for it.

"Why do you wish to?" Fortune asked. She sounded as patient as a school-mama, and I looked at her with suspicion.

"How long has this been going on?"

"Later, will you?" She didn't bother looking at me, kept her eyes fixed on the tools, but I could tell her attention was on Celeste.

"He doesn't wish—want—me to to play with, to play it," Celeste said.

"It's his," Fortune answered, "and these boxes are rare and expensive, not something you treat casually, Celeste. So why do you want to play it?"

The red light above us winked out, and another came on above the media wall. The icon-face shifted with it. "I want— wish—to make sound. Different sound. Code that speaks." I could almost imagine frustration in the machine voice. "I wish to hear what it sounds like when I play it."

I shivered again, knowing Fortune saw. It was too easy to translate that into *I want to make music,* and that was a thing no construct was supposed to be able to comprehend, much less want.

"I am aware of the audiot's limits and will observe them," Celeste said. At that moment, she sounded just like my memory of Fortune's living sister, always wheedling for something. That was prejudice, because I'd always liked Fortune better, but it was uncanny to hear all the same.

Fortune looked at me. "You hear her. Is it all right with you?"

I had to swallow hard before I could answer, thinking of Manfred—and of Realpeace, the thought flickering through my head that this was the wrong time, the worst time I could imagine, to find a construct that wanted to make music— thinking, too, of all Hati's dead. It was partly them that decided me, the things they'd stood for, but mostly that I wanted to know, to be sure, to hear for myself either that it couldn't play music, was just a construct, or that she could, and face everything that meant. And then, of course, I wondered if I would recognize her music at all.

"Yeh, why not?" I said, and had to laugh. If Celeste was people, was true AI, the equal of any of us, then those were pretty mundane words to start it all.

"Go ahead," Fortune said, but Celeste had already made the connection through the virtual port, and lights flowed across the touchplate. I recognized waveform patterns, but no sound came out, and I checked to make sure she wasn't overloading the system. All the indicators were well within tolerance however, except for the one for the sound generator itself. It glowed steady red, something I'd never seen before, but then the audiot made a strangled squawk, and I realized what she was doing. Celeste had no real idea of what "sound" was—about as much as I had had when I was little, before I got my ear—and she was playing not with sound, but with the waveforms that were their digital analog. The audiot wasn't capable of reproducing most of them—though with the right generator hooked up, it probably could—and she was fumbling for notes, the right waves, to let her play it. The smart thing to do would be to let the box itself tell her what it could do, and even as I thought it, a new pattern flared on the display plate. The audiot ran through the first scale we'd heard, but much faster, a chromatic blur of notes, and then settled to a simple three-note progression, walking back down the scale. It was a second before I realized that the demo had stopped, and Celeste herself was playing.

I tipped my head to the side, wishing Tai was here, or Jaan-tje—wishing that she had a better machine to play with, or a wider range of voices. The vox blurred the notes, let them ring too long, slurring into cacophony. Celeste seemed to re-alize that, too, and the triplets stopped, were replaced by a pattern of slow fifths, as though she was savoring each over-tone. Then that changed, too, became something I couldn't analyze and wasn't sure I liked, but as it moved up and down the scale every fourth or fifth repetition was oddly haunting, something I hoped I could remember. And then I wished I had a playback deck, so I could show Tai and Jaantje what Celeste had done.

"Well?" Fortune asked, and I looked at her.

"Well, what? She's yours, Fortune, you had to have known."

Fortune looked away, not meeting my eyes. "I'm not sure I know now. You tell me."

"I'm not a fucking constructor."

Celeste was still playing, apparently oblivious to what we were saying the patterns turning into the sorts of runs and chords that everybody plays, starting out, and thinks they've discovered something new. I could remember when I'd sounded like that myself. It felt weird to be discussing her like she wasn't there, and I automatically ducked my head, em-barrassed by my own bad manners.

"You think she is," Fortune said, but lowered her voice as well.

"Maybe. And what are we—what are you going to do, if she is?"

"I don't know yet," Fortune answered, and this time she met my eyes squarely. "But I'll be damned if I'll let any of them, Realpeace or Dreampeace or whatever, get their hands on her."

▪ 14 ▪

Celinde Fortune

FANNING WAS NOT happy with me, though whether it was because I hadn't warned him about Celeste or because he didn't want Celeste to exist at all I couldn't tell. But there was no arguing with what his reaction had told us both: he thought Celeste was people, too, and we were stuck with that. I finished putting together a crude security device, linking the three components into a package that Fanning could link to the goddow's internal systems, while Celeste kept playing with the audiot, improvising scraps of melody and odd, not fully pleasant harmonies. I could see Fanning looking at it and at the ceiling pinlight, every time he thought I wasn't watching, and wondered what he made of the music. It sounded pretty good to me, except that occasionally it broke down into dissonance and once just into noise. The first time it happened, I thought Fanning looked relieved, but after that he just listened harder.

"Finished," I said, and Fanning straightened, looking away from the audiot. Celeste was still playing, a weird rocking figure, three notes up, two down, and then reversed, so that she could move up and down the scale.

"I want my box back, Fortune," he said, and I sighed.

"I know. Celeste. Time to quit."

The music ended in a sudden swirl of notes—she had finished whatever she was doing, I realized, but at five or six times the normal speed. A new light glowed on the buffer board where she'd saved the input for later. "Very well. Fortune, I want this audiot."

I saw Fanning stiffen, ready to object, and said quickly, "Sorry, Celeste, it's Fanning's."

There was a pause. "I want—a copy? Something like it? A program, or must it be hardware?"

I looked at Fanning. He said, "I know where you can get a cheap vox. It's not the same as this, but it might work."

"Maybe," I began, and Celeste spoke from the media wall. "I've checked the schematics. That would work."

Fanning grinned. "I think you're committed, Fortune." He reached for the audiot, began folding the carrier straps back around it again.

"Looks like," I agreed. I helped him pack the new security system as well, and walked with him to the door of the workshop. I saw him look at the pinlights that marked the edges of the shop's sensorweb, and wasn't surprised when he beckoned me outside. I stepped out with him into the day-lights, and saw one of my neighbors leaning pensively out his open window, pretending he wasn't watching.

"If that—if she isn't AI," Fanning said, "I don't know what would count."

He'd kept his voice down, but I winced anyway, aware of the watcher across the narrow trafficway. "Was that necessary?"

"Wasn't it?" he answered, and I had to look away.

"Fan, I don't know what to do, either. Yeh, she's—it's finally happened, and the timing couldn't be worse. Can you imagine what the metalheads would say—can you imagine what Realpeace would do? If they blew up Hati just because they're a fusion band—"

Fanning waved his hands at me, and I stopped, realizing my own voice had risen.

"Sorry. But I don't know what to do."

Fanning nodded, his face twisting in rueful agreement. "At least she's with you, and not with one of the Cartel Companies—or working FTL, for that matter. I hear those people are kind of paranoid since Manfred. But she's safe, and you've got breathing room."

I hadn't really thought about what would have happened if Celeste had appeared on, say, one of the assembly lines. There would have been no reason to keep her, and every reason just to disassemble the links, detach the components, and pretend it had never happened. It was a sobering thought—the constructs I'd linked weren't exactly out of the ordinary, unless you believed Jian. If anyone would know that a construct was more than just a standard Spelvin matrix, it would be the woman who'd first encountered Manfred—but if she had recognized it then, why had she sold it to Garay? If it, if both the constructs were as ordinary as they'd seemed, I couldn't help wondering if this had actually happened before, and how many times. AI wasn't something I'd ever thought much about: I'm about as much a Dreampeace as I am a member of the Church of the Risen Elvis, and for about the same reasons, family tradition and habit rather than real conviction. But now that the idea had occurred to me, it seemed almost frighteningly plausible. Everybody in the Cartel Companies was paranoid about AI, and with reason: the day true AI appeared was the day the whole construct economy went straight to hell. How much easier would it be just to make sure it never happened, the connection never got made—and what did you call it, this act of omission? It wasn't a crime, exactly, more a failure of nerve, and until I'd met Celeste I doubt I would have even wondered about the choice.

"So what are you going to do?" Fanning asked, and I heard my voice sharp with something like guilt.

"I told you, I don't know."

"Sorry." He sounded genuinely apologetic, and I made myself relax.

"No, I'm sorry. I shouldn't've snapped." I took a deep breath. "I think the best thing—the only thing to do is to lie low for a while, be very discreet. Did I tell you the previous owner—the woman who sold it—came to see me at the Empire?"

"No." Fanning frowned. "A big woman, right, really tall and good-looking? Maybe with a beautiful redhead, and a fair-haired Vaughn?"

"Yeh," I answered, and then the name registered. "No redhead, though, but are you telling me we've got cousins involved in this?"

"He's some sort of cousin of my cousin Meonothai," Fanning answered. "Crazy Imre, Meo called him—Imre Vaughn, that would make him."

"Elvis Christ." That was the other half of the pilot team that had found Manfred—it was no wonder Jian had been wary. "They were all involved in the Riots, all involved with Manfred. This woman, Jian, her name is, she said somebody had been making inquiries about the original construct, the one she'd sold to Garay."

"That's weird." Fanning's frown deepened. "Realpeace, do you think?"

I shrugged. "I don't know. But I told her I hadn't noticed anything odd, and I'm going to go on saying that if anybody asks. I can keep people from seeing her on the grounds that her programming is a professional secret."

"I hope it works," Fanning said. "Look, I was serious about knowing where you can get a cheap vox."

"You think it's worth it?"

He spread his hands. "She sounded almost like anybody starting out, but not quite. I'd love to know where she goes next with it, if she—" He stopped abruptly, smiling. "I guess what I'm saying is, I wonder if she's got talent."

He was right, that was a weird thought, and I didn't know how I felt about it. It was disconcerting enough to have to accept that Celeste was people without having to cope with her being a musician—more than just people, a maker, a creator, too. A peer. "I'll think about it," I said. "See if I can afford it. Flip me the place?"

"I can tell you now," he said. "Tan Shao's, at the Milagro Interlink—he doesn't haggle, but the prices are good."

"Thanks," I said, and knew I sounded sour.

I bought the vox, though, made the trip down a level and then west to Milagro itself. Tan Shao's was small, but brightly lit, full of thin old men in *sarangs* who seemed to have nothing better to do than sit around with instruments in their hands. Maybe they even played them sometimes, but not while I was there. The man behind the sales display wasn't much younger, and just as coolie, and I barely stopped myself from hesitating in the doorway, seeing them all. But Fanning wouldn't have recommended the place if it was Realpeace, and I made myself come smoothly on, nodding to the man at the sales display.

"Can I help you, bi'?" he asked, and the smooth coolie voice—Persephone's, not Freyan—was reassuring.

"I hope so." I took a deep breath. "My cousin, Fanning Jones, recommended that I look here for a vox."

"Fire/Work, right?" He nodded, went on without waiting for my answer. "What were you looking for, exactly?"

"Something basic," I said. "For someone who's just learning to play, but expandable."

The man nodded again. "Are they going to want to do programming, or just play stock?"

I suppressed the desire to laugh, knowing better than even to think of explaining. "I don't think you could stop her from programming it."

"Right, then." He turned to an ancient-looking terminal, typed codes, squinting down at the tiny screen. I could see the old men reflected in the polished surface of a bright silver AutoSong console, could see their hands moving in conversation, but the curve distorted my view, so I couldn't see what they were saying.

"We have a couple of boxes that might be what you're looking for." The man swung his screen so that I could see the codes as well. "This one's older, hasn't been updated to the fifteenth edition standards, but it's got a lot of power. This one's newer, and it was built to the current standards, but it's not as powerful."

I hesitated. Power was good—the way Celeste was learning, she wouldn't outgrow or get bored with the more powerful one quite as fast as with the simpler vox. And it might not be a bad thing if she didn't have the newest standards to play with: I felt a little ashamed, thinking that, but being restricted to the older systems might keep her from being noticed just a little longer. I wondered how often my own mother had thought that about me. "The more powerful one, I think—depends on the price, of course."

"I'm asking 275," he answered promptly. "That's firm—Fanning will have told you I mean that."

I nodded. "Does that include any sound patches?"

"The usual set of twenty."

"All right." I reached into my belt for my smaller loc card—paying for the karakuri and the constructs, and loaning Fanning money for his bills, I was short on cash—and handed it to him.

He took it, still without much expression, fed it into the register, then touched a button on the display. A door I hadn't noticed opened in the back wall, and a much younger woman—barely out of her teens, I guessed, in a scarlet *sarang* and a heavy work vest—appeared in the opening.

"Yeh?"

The man behind the display reeled off a string of codes. The girl nodded and vanished again. A moment later, another door opened in the blank wall, and I caught a flash of her *sarang* as she stooped to slide the vox through the opening. The man lifted it up to the counter, folding back the cover to reveal the keyboard and controls. "Want to try it out?"

I shook my head. "I don't play. It's a gift."

"Haya." He didn't seem surprised by that, just folded the cover back down again and turned his attention to the register. "You get a carryweb with it, and a unipower box."

"Thanks."

He nodded, and released my card from the register, handed it back still faintly warm from the machine. "It's all yours. Hope your friend enjoys it."

"I'm sure she will," I answered, and wondered what he'd think if he knew what the "friend" actually was. I shook the thought away, and hoisted the vox in its webbing. It was an awkward length, a little more than half a meter long and relatively heavy, but the carrier was well designed, tucked it close along my back, and I managed even the long 'bus ride without much trouble.

Celeste loved it. She picked up the programming almost

instantly, which shouldn't have surprised me, and promptly immersed herself in learning to play. Over the first half-week, she blew a speaker and half a dozen fuses, but then she seemed to accept the machine's physical limitations, and the destruction stopped. She even learned to take the music somehow off-line, to recreate it within herself—in whatever block of memory passed for imagination, I guess, virtual music on a virtual machine within a virtual person—which made it easier for me to work and sleep. The only trouble came at the night shows. Her mind was elsewhere; the cues were there, but sometimes a split second late, and even when they weren't she was never more than just there, doing her job and nothing more. I hadn't realized, until then, how much I'd started to rely on her as a puppeteer, the little things she did with the karakuri, the little variations of gesture that made them look almost human, and it was bad to be without them. Luckily, the audiences didn't notice, but Binnie and Terez both did. I told Muthana I was having memory problems—it's the explanation for 90 percent of construct problems, and it wasn't entirely untrue—but Terez was harder to convince. She cornered me in my dressing room at the interval, while I was putting the final touches on my costume, stood blocking my light until I had to ask her to move.

"Sorry." She didn't sound it, particularly, her broad face as calm as ever, but she shifted sideways, letting the lights fall on my face again.

I pretended to study my image in the tall mirror, leaned forward to darken the lines that emphasize the roundness of my eyes. "So what is it?" I knew I sounded hostile, and made myself smile. "Sorry. You know I get a little tense before the show."

"I remember." She smiled, too, but it didn't touch her eyes. "Two things. Binnie asked me to tell all the principals personally that we're going to be tightening physical security as of tonight."

"What?" The thin brush twitched in my hand, and I made myself finish the last line before I spoke again. "What's going on—and what does he mean, tighten physical security?"

Terez made a slight gesture, not quite a shrug. "Realpeace has issued another statement about *farang* influence in the upperworld. They mentioned the Empires specifically, this time, so Binnie's nervous."

"What did they say?" I glanced toward the ceiling, where the pinpoint transceivers clustered, but the nodes were dark except for George's standby light. Celeste was already installed, waiting for her part of the show to start; not for the first time, I wondered what she made of Tigridi and Fire/Work.

"Pretty much that," Terez answered. "They—I think the word they used was 'deplored'—the increasing number of *farang* performers in what used to be a coolie space—"

"The hell," I said, and Terez nodded.

"Oh, I know. But this isn't about reality, just the myths." She took a breath. "They called on the Empire owners to go back to the old ways, and said that they, Realpeace, were considering buying out one of the Empires in order to bring it back to what it was."

"Not much chance of that," I said. "Unless they have one hell of a lot more money than anybody thought."

"Or if they wanted to bid on the Queen-Iron," Terez said. "But what Binnie's worried about is that they might try intimidation to make the owners sell a better house, or just change the program. I'm afraid he might be right."

I turned to look at her directly, startled. Terez was probably the least easily agitated person I know, the woman who had once looked at an illusion spinning out of control, literally crashing and burning in the middle of the stage, and announced, "I think you need a new trifocal filter" while she cued the fire curtain and the extinguishers. She saw my expression, and shrugged.

"Don't worry about it, we just want to be sure nobody gets into the stagehouse who doesn't beong."

Don't worry, my ass. I said, "Anything more on that break-in?"

Terez grimaced. "Nothing. All the codes have been changed, and I ran a check on George to make sure he hadn't picked up any parasites. It looks as though whoever tried it didn't actually get in."

The time flared in front of my eyes, warning me I had less than five minutes before the curtain went up for the second half of the show. Terez saw it, too, or some reminder of her own, and pushed herself away from the chair where she'd been leaning.

"There's one other thing. What's going on with the act?"

"Memory problems," I said, automatically, and wasn't surprised when she shook her head.

"You haven't even tried running virtual."

"I didn't want to infringe."

"That's never bothered you before." Terez shook her head, frowning thoughtfully, as though the problem was genuinely hers. "It's weird, Fortune—not that anybody in the audience would notice, but there's something missing."

"Celeste has other things on her mind." I grinned, expecting her to laugh, but instead her eyes widened.

"You mean that. It's what that Jian woman said, you think this is something special."

"No—"

"Don't bullshit me, Celinde." Aside from my family, Terez is the only person who uses my real name in anger. "I've been watching it, I've seen how good it is—*it*, Celinde, not her. Or do you really think you've got true AI there?"

I shrugged, not wanting to tell her the truth—if nothing else, it was a hell of a risk for the Tin Hau to take right now, with Realpeace making trouble—but already uncomfortable with the lie. She had heard Jian, too, and she knew that Jian believed. "No—I don't know. Celeste is, well, different, though."

She nodded slowly, her expression already smoothing out again as she got herself back under control, getting back to the calm she needed to run the second half of the show. "Yeh. So I see. What—no, don't tell me. I don't want to know what you think or what you're going to do about it. Haya?"

She didn't have to spell out her position: the more she knew about Celeste being people, the more compelled she'd be to tell Binnie, tell the owners, and that would only bring down all the trouble we were trying to avoid. "Haya," I said, and wished I'd lied more convincingly.

"I've got to get back to my station," she said, and even as she spoke her eyes slid sideways, acknowledging a call from one of the other techs. "But I meant it, Fortune."

"I know," I answered, but the door had already closed behind her. I looked back at my image in the mirror, the makeup much too strong for the room even with the lights turned up to match the stage, the velvet-and-sheer fabric that the dressmakers call illusion glistening black against my skin. Ever since I could first afford to buy scraps, I've had my costumes made of illusion; the pun's a comfort in the tension before a performance. I was sweating already, and not just from nerves.

It was not a good night. My performance was off, and Celeste was merely mechanical, so much like a normal Spelvin construct that I caught myself wondering if I'd imagined everything. I never did manage to get myself properly up for the show—it was uninspired at best—and it was a relief when the curtain came down. Everybody has nights like this, but they're never pleasant, and you never really get used to them. I muted the skinsuit displays, letting the heat and tingle fade from under my skin and the lights disappear from in front of my eyes, and looked around for the nearest stage-system pinlight.

#Celeste. Walk the karakuri to the keeping, then download yourself. And let me know when you're ready.#

#I estimate twenty-eight minutes to place the karakuri in storage, and twenty minutes to shut down and return,# she answered. #Is that acceptable?#

#Go ahead.#

The assistant stage manager was signaling for the mass curtain call, all the acts together, and I took my place in the line, pasting a smile on my face. This was a new conclusion, something that Muthana had put in last week—to appease Realpeace, I guessed, from what Terez had told me—and a lot of the first-half acts were complaining about not being able to leave as early as usual. I doubted it would help much: over half the acts were coolie, but the important ones—mine for the closing and Tigridi opening the show—were yanqui and midworld respectively. Realpeace could make something of that.

The strip lights at the edge of the stage flickered, a constant pale blue flutter of glyphs and numbers across my vision, updating the system status. It was normal; I ignored it, and stared out into the darkness beyond the first three rows, the applause hard as the rain sprinklers. Then there was a soundless pop, percussion beneath my skin and a flash of black, gone as quickly as it had appeared. The strip lights were flaring red, and I kept my smile steady with an effort, heard Attlie Bae hiss something that sounded like a question. I hadn't realized she had a skinsuit, I thought, and then wondered if I'd missed something real.

#System overload,# Celeste murmured in my ear. #Unauthorized program trying to run. Should I let it?#

#No,# I said, and didn't care if the audience saw my lips move. #Isolate it—where's George?#

It was a stupid question, and I knew the answer as soon as I asked. Celeste had said there was a system overload, and George was the system.

#I've taken over his functions,# Celeste answered. #Holding.#

The lights in my eyes were fading back to pink—still problematic, but not a disaster—and the subsidary systems were turning yellow one by one as Terez and the assistant stage managers went to manual. The applause never faltered: not many of tonight's crowd were wired.

#Curtain down in three,# Celeste murmured—on the public circuit, I realized, calling George's cues. We stepped back as rehearsed, only a little ragged, and the heavy curtain swept down in front of us. Only when it closed did the babble of voices start.

"Did you see that?"

"—George?"

"Who's calling cues?"

"—Terez?"

"What was it—?"

Out of the corner of my eye, I saw Fanning wave to me, hands forming a new sign.

Celeste?

I nodded, but Terez's voice cut me off. "Haya, people, we've had a small technical problem. Stage systems are down. I repeat, stage systems are off-line, we're running standbys. If you have props to get to the keeping, do it manually, or you can leave them in the stagehouse overnight, but we need the house cleared by 0100."

"What the hell?" Attlie Bae said softly, and I shook my head.

"No idea." An unauthorized program, Celeste had said, trying to run. No, first it had shut down George, and then it had tried to run—not a normal system overload, that was certain, but something actively hostile.

"The stagehouse will be closed at 0105," Terez said. "I repeat, the stagehouse will be closed at 0105. Front-of-house and lower levels will stay open, but the stagehouse will be off-limits to everyone except the technical staff."

Bae swore under her breath, and headed for the nearer wing. I looked around to see how far Celeste had gotten with the karakuri, and Fanning waved to me again.

What was that? That and a few name signs was about the limit of my sign. He remembered and switched to speech. "I felt—something, but I couldn't catch the transmission."

His eyes glowed green with his display lenses, left over from Fire/Work's performance, but the pulse has been strong enough that he probably would have felt it through the base sensors in his palms. I said, "Something was trying to run in the stage systems. A virus, maybe."

"Shit." That was Dhao, looming up behind Fanning. He glanced up at the gratings and the lights suspended overhead, and then made an embarrassed face. "I know, there are lots of fail-safes, but those things are heavy."

"Not nearly enough fail-safes." That was the diminutive female puppeteer, a sharp coolie voice at my elbow. "Not where machines are involved.

"We should have a real crew, an all-human crew," her husband agreed, and raised his voice to include the people standing around us. "I've been saying that for years. What does it take to get these people to protect us?"

"You can take that up with ba' Muthana," Terez interposed, smooth as ever, but I could see the anger in her eyes. "Fortune, I need you."

Celeste. I suppressed my own instinctive fear, and nodded. "Fanning, I'll catch you later."

Later, he answered, but I was already hurrying after Terez.

The tech staff had a cubby at the back of the stagehouse, beyond all the batten controls and winches, beyond even the lift that led to the keeper. Right now the door was open, spilling hot gold light onto the worn floor, brighter than the working lights that filled the stagehouse now that the show had ended. Through the doorway, I could see the night show's assistant stage manager, the same woman who'd done it for years, and Inay Hasker; a screen flickered blue between them, glyphs and strings of code spilling past. Hasker looked up as we approached, and moved out of the doorway to let us in, but the ASM never moved from her place at the control board, her eyes glued to the scrolling text. What I understood of it was enough to send a shiver up my spine: all the main environmental systems were down or compromised—for once the puppeteers had been right, it wouldn't have taken much to drop one of the lights right on the stage.

"It's your construct that's holding things together right now," Terez said, and pulled the door closed behind us. "But she—it's not responding to us."

I looked around for an access node, and Hasker slid a movable point into view. #Celeste? You there?#

It was a silly question, but I didn't know what else to say. There was a moment of silence, nothing moving in the air around me or beneath my skin, and then the familiar presence was back again. #Still here. Fortune, these people wish access, but George's password files are demonstrably corrupt. Do I let them in?#

Her voice sounded thin, attenuated, and I shifted so that I could see the ASM's screen without losing the sight-line link. The strain was starting to show, half a dozen indicators flickering orange and red. #Yeh, Celeste, I'll vouch for them.#

#Thank you,# she said, and for an instant sounded just like George.

On the screen, the pattern of lights and glyphs began to change, and the stage manager reached up to adjust her filament mike. "Give me circuit ten."

Celeste's confirmation whispered in my ear, echoing her voice from the overhead speaker, and Terez said, "Can you bring it down, Jorunn?"

"Yeh." The ASM's voice was abstracted, her eyes still fixed on the screen. "If this holds."

"If you can't capture the invading program," Hasker said, "trash it."

"Haya," the ASM answered, and Terez looked at me.

"Can Celeste handle this?"

"She knows George's parameters," I said. "And she's Level Four."

Hasker snorted. "That construct may have started out at Four, but it's something else now."

I looked away. Terez said, "Not the time, Inay."

"There'd better be a time, and soon," Hasker said, and there was sudden movement, a cascade of glyphs, on the ASM's screen.

"I think we've got it contained," the ASM said. "Celeste, can you run stand-down yet?"

"The sound system is still unstable," the construct answered. "Continuing to adjust parameters."

The ASM did something to her keyboard. "Does that help?"

"One moment—yes. The sound system is now stabilized. Beginning stand-down."

The ASM leaned back in her chair with a sigh of relief.

Terez peered over her shoulder, then nodded. "Nice work. Both of you."

"Thanks," the ASM murmured. Celeste was mercifully silent.

"Can we get a look at the program yet?" Hasker asked.

"Give me a minute," Terez said, and motioned for the ASM to give her the controls. The other woman slipped gratefully aside, and Terez took her place in front of the boards.

"It's isolated in VPW Five," the ASM said, and Terez nodded.

"Celeste. If this gets loose again, can you hold it?"

"One moment." A chain of glyphs on the main screen went from red to green, and Celeste's voice was suddenly stronger. "Yes. The problem areas are isolated, and stand-down is 58 percent complete."

"Haya," Terez said again, and then, more loudly, "Thanks." I saw the ASM give her an odd look, but Terez's attention was already focused on the smaller central screen. Hasker stepped closer himself, peering over her shoulder, and in spite of myself—in spite of knowing perfectly well what I'd see—I stood briefly on tiptoe to see over his shoulder. The screens were full of constructors' hash, glyphs I couldn't read, followed by ever-changing strings of numbers. The ASM mumbled something, a question, but I couldn't make out the words. No one answered, Terez still frowning at the screen, but the pattern stabilized at last.

"So what is it?" Hasker demanded.

The ASM shrugged. "I recognize the matrix, but that's about it."

"Give me a minute, will you?" Terez said. She didn't sound particularly impatient, but Hasker leaned back quickly, blocking my view. I looked at the ceiling instead, searching for a pinlight. My eyes filled with codes as the IPUs captured the tightbeam transmission, and I felt the familiar fizz of data under my skin: if I hadn't known better, I would have assumed that everything was normal.

Terez made a little noise, a soft grunt of satisfaction, and Hasker said, "You've got it."

"Yeh."

I looked myself, but saw only the familiar chaos of constructors' codes. "So what is it?"

Terez looked over her shoulder at us. "It was supposed to run at the end of the show—projected on the curtain, but they didn't know about the new curtain call. I'm not sure what the message was, though."

"Can you run it?" Hasker asked. "The payload, I mean."

The ASM made a soft noise of disbelief, and Terez shook her head, uncertain. "I can pull it out," she said, "and maybe I can run it, but I can't guarantee that I can make it virus-free. I'd rather not risk it."

"I'd like very much to see what they had in mind," Hasker said. From the tone of his voice, it was not a request, and Terez sighed.

"I'm not willing to let it into the system. Especially with George down."

"I can—filter—the payload," Celeste said.

Terez blinked. "You're sure?"

"Yes. The code is clear, payload and carrier are different. I can filter them apart."

Terez looked at me. "What do you think, Fortune, can Celeste do it?"

#I can.# Celeste's words whispered in my brain, the ghost of a voice.

"If she says so, yeh." Behind me, I heard Hasker take a breath, but he made no other comment.

"Haya," Terez said, and touched controls. "Go ahead, Celeste."

"Beginning."

For a long minute nothing happened, and then a rush of color appeared on the left of Terez's screen. She studied it, but did nothing, made no move to adjust her controls. Then that square of screen turned black, and then flashed glyphs redder than furnace iron. I recognized them both—RETURN and then REVENGE—but together they didn't make sense. Then they vanished, and the flames appeared. Even just seeing them on the screen, contained by the monitor, I caught my breath: they looked too real, too much like the flames that had followed the funeral bombing, so that for a second I could almost imagine I was seeing that again. The flames grew, feeding on the background—if the clip had been projected against the curtain, they would have seemed to be feeding on it, consuming it, a ripple of heat adding to the effect, so that I drew back in spite of myself. And then, just when it seemed at though they had to burst through the screen, that the glass would crack and shatter, blue raindrops—no, they were glyphs, the same RETURN/REVENGE as before—splattered down onto the fire, quenching the unreal flames before the image vanished.

"Elvis Christ," I said, but Hasker was quicker.

"Gods below, can you imagine what would have happened if that had run?"

I could picture it all too well, myself, and from the silence so could everybody else. The fire had looked too real; people would have panicked, would have imagined a heat they didn't actually feel—and even knowing it wasn't real, I'm not sure I could have stood my ground in the front rows while that blazed in front of me. The audience would have run for the exits, I was sure of it—hell, seeing that in front of me, on the stage itself, I think I would have run—and people would have been hurt, maybe even killed. And Realpeace would once again be to blame.

"We were lucky," the ASM said, fervently, and Terez nodded.

"I'm very glad Celeste was on-line, Fortune."

"Me too," I said.

"Bi' Terez," Celeste said, from the console speakers. "I've tracked the entry point." A schematic flared on the darkened screen, a shape like a tangled flower, the tip of one thin petal glowing red.

"Air Supply?" Hasker asked, scowling, and Terez nodded.

"Are you sure, Celeste?"

"Yes." Celeste's voice was serene. "This is the complete analysis."

The screen filed with a new diagram, this one so overlaid

with line and color that the original pattern almost vanished. I blinked, trying to trace its relationship to the first one, and Terez said, "Save that for me, will you?"

"Saving," Celeste said.

"We should contact Security," the ASM said.

Hasker shook his head. "And tell them what? I didn't run, nobody got hurt, and I can tell you right now what Realpeace will say. They'll say they didn't do it, it's a Dreampeace plot, or the Cartel's, to make them look bad, and they've got a program that didn't work and an entry point through an Air Supply monitor to prove their point. It won't do any good."

"We still have to tell them," Terez said. They were both right, and I shook my head, not knowing what to say or do. I was still shaking a little at the thought of what could have happened if the program had run—what would have happened if Celeste hadn't been there.

"One point for it being Realpeace," I said, and was almost surprised that I sounded normal, "is that it would have run if Celeste hadn't been on-line."

"True." Terez looked at Hasker. "Inay, we have to report it. And we have to tell Binnie—and not necessarily in that order."

"Haya." Hasker straightened slowly. "Fortune, we owe you for that construct."

"Thanks." Terez was watching me, and I braced myself, but at the last minute she seemed to change her mind and said nothing. I was just as glad: I wasn't sure I could explain about Celeste even if I hadn't been certain it was a bad time to try. "Then you're done with me?" I'd been about to say *us*, and I was sure Terez saw.

She still didn't say anything, though, but nodded. "Yeh. The stagehouse should be cleared. We're going to run some system checks tonight; with luck we'll have everything back on-line for tomorrow night."

"If Binnie decides we go on," the stage manager said.

"We need the money," Hasker said, and sighed. "Right, we've got to talk to Binnie, and to Security. Thanks again, Fortune."

"You're welcome," I answered, and let myself back out into the empty backstage. The working lights were on, but the familiar pinpoints that gave access to the virtual house were dark, and I was very aware of that missing dimension, an emptiness at the corners of my eyes and an absence against my skin. Celeste was gone, too, I thought, but then her voice spoke from the stage manager's console.

"I'm not able to access the karakuri anymore."

"Where did you leave them?"

"Stage left, front—by the T-80 cable."

I looked, and saw the four karakuri huddled awkwardly together, leaning on each other like tired children. I couldn't leave them there—first, there was too much chance of someone knocking them over, damaging them, and second, they were too disconcerting, looking like that, to leave them there for the backstage staff to stumble over—but I swore under my breath at the thought of maneuvering them down to the keeping on my own.

"Fortune, why am I shut out?"

I looked back at the console, and my vision suddenly filled with color, electric blue sheeting to red, then running back through every shade of purple to that intolerable blue again. I looked away, breaking the connection, and Celeste spoke again.

"Fortune—"

"Take it easy," I said, and realized that she was frightened. "They—Terez has to check all the systems, make sure there aren't any viral fragments left. If something like that happens again, God knows what systems could let go." I stopped, aware that what I said was hardly reassuring. "They want to make sure it isn't going to happen again."

"The intruding program is gone," Celeste said. Her voice was dead in the heavy air. "There's nothing left of it in this volume."

I risked a glance at the pinlight, and the blue filled my eyes again. "They have to be sure it can't reaccess. And they have to get George back on-line."

"George is damaged, I think." Blue faded to red, pulsed

slowly back to blue. "Perhaps his—other selves—also."

"They'll have backup off-line, too," I said, and hoped the copy was recent.

"That's not the same," Celeste said, but the colors were easing, steadying to a blue I could bear to watch. "It won't be George."

There was nothing I could say to that. The question of whether a copy of a construct was truly or only virtually the same as the original—and of whether a backup could ever be made of true AI, if it existed—was one of the great constructors' debate, a philosophical question I'd always ignored as essentially unrelated to anything of importance. And now here was Celeste giving me answers I'd never thought to want. "I'm sorry," I said at last, and heard a sound like a sigh from the console.

"It's very difficult. Fortune, would the audience have seen that clip as fire?"

"I don't know," I answered. "I think they would have realized pretty quickly that it wasn't real, but for the first few seconds, yeh, I think they'd have been afraid." And people would have died for that fear, for that instinctive reaction. I shivered again at the thought of how narrow the escape had been.

"There would have been injuries, then," Celeste said, echoing my thoughts too closely for comfort.

"I think so."

"A bad thing."

Constructs are not AI, and they're not karakuri; the old so-called Three Laws programming does not apply, or at least has never been applied to them. And Dreampeace argues that if true AI ever does develop, then programming in the Three Laws would be an unwarranted interference with a person's free will, that without the freedom to kill the decision to refrain is meaningless. I wondered how that argument applied to Realpeace's followers. "It was a good thing you were there," I said aloud. "You did well."

"I'm glad," Celeste said, softly, and I heard the door of Terez's office open.

"Got to get the karakuri put away," I said, too loudly, and saw the codes that signaled the start of Celeste's transfer back to the headbox. I fumbled in my pocket for the karakuri remote that I carry in case of a major failure, and brought them stiffly to life.

▪ 15 ▪

Reverdy Jian

JIAN STARED AT the stage as the fourth humaniform karakuri emerged from the mouth of a brown-iron machine that looked like the final-stage finisher on the Kagami ship line, its copper skin gleaming in the stage lights. The other three karakuri brought it forward, and the conjurer, smiling now, lifted a black-silk drapery large enough to hide herself and the machines. She was wearing a loose black tunic, semi-transparent in places, and her skin seemed to glow through the sheer fabric, her color almost as vivid as the karakuri's. The drapery fell, puddling at the karakuri's feet, and Jian caught her breath, hearing the same sound echoing around her: Fortune had disappeared. And then there was another puff of smoke, from the brown-iron karakuri, this time, and Fortune stepped smiling through its embrace. She came forward, taking the nearest karakuri's hands, and there was a perceptible pause—shock and wonder, Jian thought, not dislike—before the wild applause. She joined with the others, and Fortune bowed again, indicating first the iron karakuri and then the copper face that suddenly appeared in the air above the stage. Jian stared at it, her hands slowing, and Vaughn nudged her in the ribs.

"That's your construct?"

"Or what she's made of it," Jian answered. "The icon, any-way." The face was like Fortune's—practically was Fortune's, but younger, a fraction softer, the same face the conjurer used on her humaniform karakuri. Jian shook her head, not knowing what to think. She hadn't given the SHYmate an icon, any more than she'd given it a name.

Light flared on the stage as the curtain began to descend, and sensation flooded over her: the virtual systems were back to the normal levels, after Fortune's act had suppressed them, and Jian flinched, groping for the control disk to return her suit to its normal levels. At her side, she saw Vaughn doing the same thing, swearing under his breath.

"Did you pick up anything?" she asked, under cover of the dying applause, and Vaughn shook his head.

"She really controls the virtual, too. She's good, Reverdy."

"Yeh."

The curtain opened again, revealing the line of performers who'd been in the full show, and Jian's eyes narrowed again, seeing the thin long-haired man who'd been Red's contact at the Nighthawk, standing with the rest of his band. They'd been good, too, more like Hati than she liked, and political, but good all the same. She nudged Vaughn again, and leaned close to his ear.

"The guy there, the yanqui, Red's friend. Who is he?"

Vaughn rolled his eyes. "Apparently he's some kind of cousin of mine, though I couldn't tell you how. His name's Fanning Jones—"

On the stage, something went pop, a virtual explosion against her skin. The sheer sensation, like a slap or a hand laid accidentally against hot metal, drowned her vision, the adrenaline analogues coursing though her, so that she caught her breath and looked frantically for smoke and flames. There was nothing, and she let her breath out in relief, at the same time looking for the faint shapes that had marked the presence of the stage systems. The pale lines were gone, replaced by something she didn't recognize, and then that, too, had vanished, and she was left with dead air, an absence beneath her skin.

"What the hell?" Vaughn said, but softly, and she shook her head.

"System crash?" She glanced around, but no one else seemed to have noticed—most of them were coolies, unwired, and so unaware of the change. The curtain was coming down again, the performers backing out of its way, and all around her people were rising to their feet, conversation rising as they headed for the doors and the lifts and 'buses that would take them home again.

"Hang back and let's see if we can get backstage," Vaughn suggested.

Jian nodded, edging her way out of the narrow row, and through the slow-moving crowd, but at the steps that led up into the wings her way was blocked by an unsmiling man in Tin Hau livery, the house glyph of sun and stars woven into his bright red vest.

"Sorry, bi', they're not seeing anybody tonight."

"I didn't tell you who I wanted to see," Jian said, and the man shook his head again.

"Nobody's seeing anyone, bi'."

Jian lifted an eyebrow at that—whatever had gone wrong must have been fairly serious, if they were keeping the fans out—but managed a polite nod. "Haya," she said, overriding Vaughn's automatic protest, and herded him up the aisle in front of her. Red followed as silently as ever, but she was aware that he was watching carefully, though for what she wasn't sure.

In the broad lobby, Vaughn turned on her, furious, and she lifted her hands to wave him to silence, seeing the way the Empire's security people focused on the movement.

"You're just going to walk away?" he demanded, and she waved her hands again, watching over his shoulder as one of the red-vested minders spoke into a shoulder pickup.

"Yeh, and so are you," she said. "Something's got them badly on edge, and we're not going to find out what by annoying their security."

"The whole house is down," Red said.

Vaughn frowned at him. "Then they're running on manual—?"

"Excuse me," a firm voice interrupted, and Jian turned to

see a big man, easily as tall as she and twice as broad, smiling at them from the foot of the stairs that led to the first balcony. "The house is closing. You'll need to move along."

"Haya," Jian said, and fixed Vaughn with a stern glare. He nodded, reluctantly, and they followed the last group of coolies out into the Tin Hau plaza. The interchange was still busy, dozens of people visible through the smoke grey glass of the doors, and there were still a few food carts snugged to the power points. A floater with FPG Security glyphs on it was grounded in front of a closed cookshop, glyphs flaring from it to warn of loitering, and Jian sighed.

"Let's have a praline," she said, and saw Vaughn smile. He didn't say anything until they'd bought three of the heavy sugar disks and turned away from the yawning vendor to sit on the edge of a newskiosk's platform. All its screens were lit, glyphs blaring in the real and the virtual, touting racquet scores and the latest Hot Blue VWS monoboard, but Jian turned her back on the transceivers deliberately, shutting out their noise. Across the plaza, the Tin Hau Empire rose in all its gaudy glory, the doors and the complex carvings outlined with green and red and gold light tubing. Only the massive black-glass arch of the main display screen was dark, and Jian frowned at the sight.

"So," Vaughn said, "what did you have in mind?"

Jian glanced at him. "Do you think they always turn off the display this quickly after a show?"

Vaughn blinked once, then followed the direction of her gaze. "I don't know," he said, after a moment. "I wouldn't have thought so. You'd think they'd want the advertising, but then again, maybe they're saving power. I don't exactly frequent the Empires, Reverdy."

"Me neither." Jian stared at the darkened arch, wondering again just what it was she had felt. Something had gone wrong, that much was certain—she had felt that in her own suit, had caught enough of the transmission to be sure of that—but exactly what, and why, were impossible to guess. There was no reason to think it had anything to do with Fortune's construct, either, but she couldn't shake the conviction that it somehow had.

"So what are we doing, Reverdy?" Vaughn asked again, and she shook herself, made herself look back at him.

"Wait for someone we know to come out." She tilted her head toward a smaller opening to the right of the main door, barely recognizable as a door in the shadows from the decorative lights. "That's got to be a stage door."

"There's got to be a back entrance, too," Vaughn said, and Jian shrugged.

"You think we can get back there, the way their security was? If you've got a better idea, Imre, I'm all ears."

Vaughn subsided, scowling, and Red said, "There."

Jian looked up, to see a single figure leaving the stage door. Even at this distance, he was easily recognizable as Vaughn's distant cousin, his fine hair loose now over his shoulders. He was heading for the last of the food carts, a hand already reaching into his pocket, and Jian pushed herself to her feet.

"Come on," she said, and moved to intercept him. Vaughn swore under his breath, but followed.

Jones looked up sharply at their approach, his eyes going from them to the FPG floater to the coolie woman running the cart, and Jian gave him what she hoped was a disarming smile.

"Can I talk to you a minute? I'm Reverdy Jian, that's Imre Vaughn. Red I think you know."

"I know Red." The flat yanqui voice was still wary, and the coolie woman's eyes widened.

"No trouble," she said. "Not here."

"No trouble," Jian answered, and spread empty hands. "We just want to talk."

"I'm just getting dinner," Jones said, and the coolie woman handed him a liter jug of noodles. "I have to be getting back." He held out a cash card as he spoke, and the woman snatched it from him. She ran it too fast through her reader, and had to try again, never taking her eyes from the little group.

"We don't want to keep you," Jian said. "But it's important."

Jones accepted the cash card reluctantly, tucking the noodles under his arm, and glanced back toward the Tin Hau. "The rest of the band's waiting—"

"Elvis Christ," Vaughn said, not quite under his breath, and Jian glared at him.

"Shut up, Imre. Look, ba' Jones, we know something went wrong at the end of the show, and if it was the construct I sold—"

Jones was shaking his head, frowning in genuine puzzlement, and Jian stopped. "Celeste wasn't the problem," Jones said. "There was some kind of virus or something, it knocked out the usual managing construct. Celeste fixed it. You don't have to worry about her."

"Her?" Vaughn said.

Jian said, "I told you at the time it was different." She looked back at Jones. "I told bi' Fortune this, but I don't think she believed me. Someone has been unduly interested in that construct. Newcat Garay said he'd been asked one too many questions, and he was taking off for the deep desert. The same people have been asking about us, me and Red in particular, and we're looking for offworld work—we're FTL pilots, if you don't know what Imre does."

"I know who you are," Jones said. He took a deep breath, seemed to come to a decision. "You're that serious about this?"

"You better believe it, sunshine," Vaughn said.

Jones seemed not to hear. "So who are these people asking about you? It's not Dreampeace, Shadha—that's our drummer—she's been Dreampeace for years, and they don't want anything to do with AI right now. They couldn't cope, so they don't want to find it. And if Realpeace had any idea of it, they'd be putting the story on all the connections whether they had anything real or not."

He'd made the same connection they had, and Jian said, carefully, "I don't know. We—it hasn't gotten close enough for us to find out. But it might be one of the Cartel Companies."

Jones nodded, unsurprised. "Lousy timing."

"So what else is new?" Vaughn said.

"Will you tell bi' Fortune?" Jian asked.

"Yeh." Jones nodded again. "She—she's not unaware of the problem. I mean, I think she took you seriously before. But I'll tell her again."

"Thanks," Jian said, and was surprised at the relief she felt. Fortune was really none of her concern—but the SHY-mate was. Celeste, Jones had called it, and the name conjured the memory of the icon that was Fortune's face made young and serene. *I should have named it,* Jian thought, and flinched at the memory. Jones managed a still-wary smile, and glanced over his shoulder toward the stage door.

"Be careful." Red's voice was as soft as ever, but it carried. Jones turned sharply, his expression for an instant unguarded, relief and something like regret, but then the moment vanished.

"I will be," he said, and turned back toward the Empire. Jian watched him go, wondering what had been between the two of them, and when—*not that I could ever ask, not Red, and most certainly not Imre*—and then shook the thought away.

"Well," she said aloud, and Vaughn tapped her gently on the shoulder.

"You did what you could," he said. "Now let's get the fuck out of here before Security takes an interest."

The plaza was almost empty now, except for the last two vendors and the FPG floater still grounded in front of the shuttered cookshop. "Haya," she said, and followed them into the lift station.

She took the long way back to Hawkshole, riding Shaft Three all the way down to the Zodiac before transferring to the 'bus for Dzi-Gin and the lift station there. Once she was below the Zodiac, officially in the midworld, she felt herself relax a little, and was annoyed at herself for allowing those fears to surface. The streets in Hawkshole were quiet, glistening still with the damp of street cleaning, and she was glad to reach the Little Paradis block where her flat lay. She let herself in through the main gate, crossed the courtyard where the gardens flourished in the full spectrum light of the grow-tubes, and went down the quarter level to her flat, grateful for the quiet.

A light was flashing on the media wall, the only light in the darkened room. She eyed it for a long moment, gesturing to the room to bring up the main lights, but finally reached across to key the playback. The Persephonet screen lit and windowed, and to her surprise Peace Malindy's face appeared in the center of the image.

"Reverdy. I put in a bid on the Caizene job I told you about, and we've got the job—delivery run to Crossroads, combination freight and passenger ship. It's a major haulage company, I think after Crossroads they pack it off to the Rim somewhere, but that's not our problem, thank all the gods. The bad news is, it won't be ready to lift for another two weeks, maybe three. The worse news is, the pay's lousy, basic rates, no bonus or incentive. I took it because you said you wanted off-world, but there's a bail-out clause if you've changed your mind. I did get passenger rights if you want to try and sell them, but that's up to you. Let me know tomorrow what you think. And, of course, if anything better comes in, I'll bid on it, but not much is moving right now." He paused, considering something on his invisible desktop, and the image vanished.

Jian found the room remote lying discarded beside the bed, worked its controls to close Persephonet and light one of the newschannels. The image that appeared was all too familiar, the Han-Lu Interchange and the puff of smoke, and she made a face, killed the channel with a gesture. It would be very good to get off-world—even if they didn't make money, and they wouldn't at the basic rates, getting off Persephone was the best thing they could do right now. For a moment, she considered offering tickets, using the passenger cabins to make a little extra money, but rejected it almost instantly. It was too much work, not something she or Vaughn enjoyed or were good at. Better just to take the chance to get off Persephone, get safely into the Urban Worlds, away from this muddle of Realpeace and Dreampeace and all the rest of it. Right now, that should be payment enough.

▪ 16 ▪

Fanning Jones

IT WAS TOO late to call even Fortune by the time I got back to the *goddow*, but I called the next morning a little before noon. That was the earliest I thought I could expect her to be awake, and I still woke her. She didn't complain, though, just listened while I told her what had happened and passed on Jian's warning. Fortune snorted at that, but it was a perfunctory protest.

"I can believe almost anything these days. Did you hear what happened?"

I shook my head. "The minders hustled us out pretty quick."

"There was a clip in the system, set to project on the curtain once the show ended—they didn't know about the new curtain call, that messed up their timing. A fire, and blue glyphs raining down to stop it, but I don't think anyone would've stuck around for that ending." She stopped to pull the neck of her yukata back together. "Look, do you still have any of the mesages you've been getting?"

I glanced at the file list, saw a broken icon sitting at the bottom of the screen. We were supposed to forward them to Security, but I was the only person who seemed to bother anymore. "I think so. Why?"

"I want to see if your program is being written by the same people."

"If you could figure that out," I said, "I think a lot of people would be grateful."

Fortune gave a tight smile. "Let me run some tests first, then I'll be over. Say, two hours? And I'm bringing Celeste."

"Celeste?" I couldn't stop myself from sounding surprised, and Fortune's smile widened to genuine amusement.

"Have headbox, will travel. Seriously, Fan, she's the one who stopped it at the Tin Hau, so she really knows that architecture. She can tell us for sure if it's the same people."

"That would be great," I said. "I really appreciate it, Fortune."

"Oh, it's very much our pleasure," she answered, and broke the connection. I heard someone sigh behind me, and looked over my shoulder to see Tai watching from the kitchen alcove. I started to tell her the plan, but she spoke first.

"Our?"

"Um." I had told the rest of the band about Celeste's music, the way she'd explored the audiot's capabilities—and Shadha was still riding me about it—but I hadn't said anything about the construct's other talents. "That was Fortune—she's bringing Celeste over, to take a look at the messages we've been getting."

"I heard." Tai looked at me, eyebrows raised under the multicolored mane of her hair. "She takes it very seriously. People-seriously."

I wasn't going to lie to Tai, not about this. "Yes."

She didn't say anything for a long moment, her face expressionless, only the flicker of her eyelids as she blinked once, then twice, giving her away. "And you think so, too."

"I told you about the music," I answered. "I don't know, but she's the closest I've ever seen."

"Like you've seen so many constructs."

Tai had worked surface assembly for a year or two, like Jaantje; they'd both dealt with more Spelvin constructs than I'd seen in my entire life. "I know," I said. "But she feels— yeh, I think she's people, Tai."

"Gods above," Tai said, and shook her head. "What a time for it, Fan."

"I know."

Fortune arrived exactly on time, Celeste's headbox slung over her shoulder in a padded carrier. She nodded a greeting to Tai and to Jaantje, hovering in the door of his room, and set the box on the floor beside the media wall. "I haven't had any trouble," she said, "but then, I run some pretty heavy security."

"No scratches on the virtual locks?" Tai asked, and Fortune gave her a cool smile.

"Not on mine. So what have you got here?"

The headbox telltales were glowing green, and I could see the bright pinpoint of an active link: Celeste was alert and listening, too. "It's the incomplete icon," I said. "It's just been vocal, before, and usually nasty."

Fortune nodded, absently, then held out her hand for the remote. "Do you mind?"

"Make free," I answered, and the others murmured their agreement as well. "You want a chair?"

"Thanks." Fortune was already deep in concentration, the playback mercifully directed into the virtual, so we didn't have to listen, but she took a chair when I brought it, sat down close to the screen. I saw Tai and Jaantje exchange glances, somewhere between amused and irritated, and then Jaantje said, "Want a beer?"

I made a face. "Too early. Juice?"

"Haya."

Fortune ignored us, absorbed in the numbers now flickering past on the screen—checksums and other stuff I didn't recognize—and Jaantje reached into the coolbox, brought out three boxes of the cheap mixed fruits. I took one, unfolded the corner, and was about to drink when a light flickered on the headbox.

"Fortune," Celeste said. "I want to play with the audiot."

For a second, I thought Fortune wasn't going to answer, but then she leaned back from the controls to lock eyes with the transmitter. "I need your help here."

"After that?"

"It's up to Fanning," Fortune answered, and broke the link to give me a look of pure mischief. "What do you say, Fan?"

I glared at her—I'd taken a lot from Shadha lately—and Jaantje said, "After what you told us, Fan, I'd love to hear it."

Tai nodded. "Seriously."

"Fine, then," I said. "Once you're done, I'll bring it out."

"Haya." Fortune reached into the carryall, produced a length of cable. "You don't mind if I hook her in?"

I shook my head, and Jaantje said, "Make free."

Fortune nodded, and reached under the control board to fit the cable into the input socket. The transceiver flickered and went out, and then a new window opened on the media wall. Celeste—the copper karakuri Celeste, the face that looked so much like Fortune—looked out at us, smiling slightly. I wondered if that was a programmed resting state, or a genuine emotion.

"Elvis Christ," Tai said, not quite under her breath, and the face turned to look at her.

"Who are you?"

Tai blinked. "Li Niantai."

"Yes . . ."

Before Celeste could say anything more, Fortune said, "I need your help now, Celeste."

"Yes?" The face swung toward her, pulling back a little so that it seemed to be looking down at her. It was just the karakuri's faceplate, without the top of the skull or any hint of neck, so that it seemed paper-thin from some angles, but what was there was perfectly molded, copper skin over bones at once strong and delicate, impeccably modeled except for the empty eyes.

"You cleaned out the Tin Hau systems. Is this code similar enough to have been written by the same people?"

There was a moment of silence, the face hanging suspended against the warm black of the live screen, and then Celeste said, "The code is similar, but not identical. However, there are points of congruence. Standard analysis suggests a 73 percent probability of the same or a closely related constructor."

"What do you think?" Fortune asked.

"I—it feels the same to me," Celeste answered.

It was a weird question, and a weirder answer, and I closed my eyes, trying to imagine what it would be like to be Celeste—to be a construct, native to the connections, the virtual rather than the real. What is the self, when there's no physical body? Celeste was made of code, code that could be re-configured, but that knew itself as distinct from the code that surrounded it—or did Celeste really understand herself to be someone? I rejected that doubt as soon as it formed: if there was one thing I was sure of, it was that Celeste had a sense of self. It was different, absolutely different from any human sense—so different that we were all, Celeste and the rest of us, groping for translations for concepts that maybe couldn't exist in the other's language except by the crudest and least accurate of metaphor—but it was self-consciousness by any definition that meant anything. For a second, I thought I had a glimpse of what Celeste might be, a collectivity of code that was nonetheless distinct and bounded—what human beings might be if their bodies were transparent on the microscopic level, so that we were constantly aware of all the various specialized cells, the immune system, the bloodstream, all the rest, even the mitochondria within the cells, as distinct parts of a tenuous whole. But then I tried to factor in time, the multiple cycles of the connections and the individual systems as well as the ebb and flow of shutdown, sleep, and activity, and that momentary vision vanished completely.

"So what do we do about it?" Tai asked. "Should—can we go to Security with this?"

I shook my head. "It's only, what did she say, a 73 precent probability. I don't think that they can do much with something that low."

Tai shook her head. "Since when was three-quarters—all right, almost three-quarters—low?"

Jaantje shrugged, and looked at Fortune. "So should we tell Security?"

"I'll pass it on to Binnie, if you want," she said. "Let him decide."

Jaantje nodded. "I—we'd be grateful."

"May I play with the audiot now?" Celeste asked, sounding more than ever like a polite child.

"Why not?" Tai murmured.

I'd had the box out the day before, plugged into my practice fx; it didn't take long to drag the rig into the main room and couple it to one of the power nodes. I hestitated then, trying to remember how I'd had it set up in Fortune's workshop, and Fortune said, "Run a standard cable to the three port on the headbox."

"Haya." I made the connection, and flinched as light and sound exploded from the fx. I saw Jaantje's lips move, swearing, and reached up to keep the noise from overloading my ear. Before I could touch the controls, the noise eased, focused on a single heavy chord, then cut out. The wild light steadied to a simple test pattern, a random file I kept to calibrate my projectors.

"This is different," Celeste said.

I adjusted my ear anyway, heard my own voice faint and distant when I spoke. "The audiot is running through my fx. You have control of images as well as the sound."

"Can I ignore the images? Yes, I see I can."

The sound that came from the speakers was rich and complicated, bass-heavy—some of it was probably down below the threshold of human hearing, just from the feel of it in the air—but with a clear high end like nothing I'd ever heard before. It wasn't any of the standard sounds, and not any of my custom patches, either, not even the two I hadn't installed yet. I glanced at the display panel, and wasn't surprised to see the custom lights glowing. Celeste walked that voice up through a couple of octaves, a standard pentatonic pattern, then switched to another—this one thinner, clearer in the high end—and kept going. She switched to a third voice, a familiar one, this time, a breathy wood-flute sound, as the notes got higher, kept going until the notes trembled at the edge of what was painful. Tai made a face, and I remembered that she could hear the mountain bats' thin squeals: some of Celeste's notes were definitely edging into the supersonic. Then, as abruptly as she'd started, she reversed the pattern, letting the voices slide back down the scale again, so fast that the notes and even the changing voices blurred into something that was very nearly a single sound. And then she began to play.

I'd heard some of this before—she was still learning, still feeling out the machine's parameters as well as the parame-

ters of the form itself—and I looked at Tai and Jaantje. Jaantje's mouth was open slightly, as if he couldn't quite believe
what he was hearing, but Tai was listening with that particular intensity she saved for things that mattered. Mostly it
was just experimenting, playing with chords and sharp little
riffs that sounded like metal breaking, but then she slid suddenly into something we all knew. Or that we thought we
knew: Hati's "Piece of the Grave" had never sounded quite
like that. She'd taken it down an octave, sliding back into the
bassy voice she'd used at the start, and she slowed it down
a little, but you could still recognize the familiar melody. I
lifted my hands and started to sign almost in spite of myself.

One foot on hot sand, one hand on the rock— The last
time I'd seen the next line signed was at the funeral, the ghost
image of Micki Tantai dancing in a holodrum, and my movements faltered and died.

Celeste slowed it even farther, began adding embellish-
ments, the same sort of broken-metal riffs she'd used before,
but darker, massy, the notes falling like stones. I heard Tai
murmur something, and Jaantje shushed her, staring now
with narrowed eyes at the headbox and the lights flickering
on the audiot. And then it was over, and Celeste drifted off
into something else, switching voices, turning to something
I didn't recognize.

"Can you play that again?" Tai said abruptly, lifting her
voice to be heard over the music. "Celeste?"

The scales stopped. "This?" Celeste asked at last, and
played the first few notes of "Piece of the Grave." It sounded
flat and odd in the wood-flute voice, and she repeated it in
the voice she'd used before.

"That one," Tai said.

"Why?"

Tai gave a strangled laugh. "Because—because I'd like to
play it with you. I want to learn—"

"You want to jam," I said, and she laughed again.

"Me too," Jaantje said.

There was another little pause, seeming longer because it
was Celeste who was considering, Celeste whose processing

time was so much faster than any of ours, then at last she said, "Very well."

"Thanks," Tai said, and turned toward her room. Jaantje shook his head in disbelief, and started to follow her, but turned back as music—the wood-flute voice again—rose from the box's speakers.

"What—?"

Celeste stopped. "I don't get to play this instrument much. I don't want to waste the opportunity."

"You won't forget what you were doing, will you?" Jaantje asked, then shook his head as the incongruity of the question hit him.

"I have it in memory," Celeste said. "I'll move it to permanent storage if you'd prefer."

"Yes," I said. Whatever else happened, I wanted a copy of that variation. I looked for the remote, and Jaantje pressed it into my hand, the same eagerness in his eyes. I touched the buttons as he disappeared into his room, opening one of the household's protected volumes for Celeste. "You can use that if you want."

"Thank you," she answered, and a moment later glyphs flickered as she transferred the data—the variation, her variation—into the system. Almost in the same instant, the wood-flute voice broke from the audio box again, an odd, not quite pleasant melody that didn't seem entirely in tune.

It didn't take long for Tai and Jaantje to get set up, Tai with her practice rig, Jaantje with his second-best hollow-body, and Celeste paused in her playing as Tai checked her tuning. It seemed almost as though she was listening—she would have heard us before, I realized, at the Empire, but she probably wouldn't have seen us, would never have identified who, or what, made which sounds. For a second, I wished I had my fx, but I didn't want to interrupt her, and I looked at Fortune instead. She was smiling, her wry expression for once unguarded, but then she saw me looking, and looked away. I moved to join her anyway.

"Impressive."

"I suppose." She snorted then, more annoyed with herself

than with me or even Celeste. "I don't know what to do about her, Fan."

I didn't either, but at least I was spared answering as Tai struck a few chords. "Haya, Celeste," she said. "Let's play it through straight once."

"As I found it?"

"Yeh."

"Very well." Sound spilled again from the box, familiar, note-perfect: the keyboard part to "Piece of the Grave" played exactly as it sounded on the Hati clip.

"Hold it," Tai said.

The music stopped as abruptly as it had begun. "You said as I found it."

Tai frowned, considering. "Can you play that, but with the voice you were using before?"

"Very well," Celeste said again. There was the slightest of hesitations, not nearly enough for even the first count, and the song started over. I saw Jaantje scowl, but Tai ignored him, came in on the second measure, and he followed a heart-beat later. For a second, the rhythm faltered, Celeste unwilling—unable?—to compensate, but then they adapted to her, to the clip-precise beat, and the song swirled up around them. In spite of myself, I found myself signing, mouthing the words at the same time.

Sand in my pocket, another piece of the grave . . .

Tai smiled at me, mouth tight and eager, and then she and Celeste soared together into the solo. For a few bars, they played together, but then Tai shook her head, dropping back to match Jaantje's rhythm, and Celeste finished alone. It wasn't triumphant, it was too close to the clip for that, for much of her emotion to show through, but I couldn't help feeling there was something smug about her playing.

They were coming to the end now, and Tai looked up from her fingerboard, letting herself ease out of the complex fig-ures, fixing her eyes on the headbox as though she was watching one of us. "Haya," she said, lifting her voice to carry. "Go to what you were doing, Celeste. In three."

Celeste didn't answer, but then, as Tai made the turnaround and repeated the first notes of the song, the bottom seemed to drop out of the room. Celeste's variation roared in the air around us, the bass too heavy, a living painful pressure on our skin. Jaantje's guitar was completely drowned, and Tai's sounded thin, feeble; my ear buzzed, warning of overload.

"Cut the subsonics, Celeste," Fortune shouted, and the pressure vanished, the sound thinning again to something bearable. I saw Jaantje mouth a curse, and Tai shook her head at him, scowling.

"Keep it going."

Celeste seemed oblivious to everything but the sounds she—they—were making. With Tai to fill in the melody and Jaantje to keep the beat, she let herself go, filling the air with the weird metallic riffs we'd heard before. They hung between Tai's wailing lead and Jaantje's rhythm that right now was little more than a pulse in the air, almost drowned by the others' playing, thick and complex, filled with grace notes that passed so quickly I could barely hear them. Then she dropped to half time, pulling against the other lines—Tai looked at Jaantje, silent question, but he shook his head, kept his beat—and suddenly each of those grace notes became another of the little riffs, each of which was filled in turn with slurs and grace notes. The notes clashed and battered against Tai's melody, only occasionally in tune now, but even as I thought it the dissonance dissolved as Tai held the chorus to match Celeste. Celeste slowed even farther then, any hint of the original melody disappearing in a flurry of sound that seemed completely made of slurred and bent notes. It was hard to tell within the cascade of notes where any one figure began and where it wound back into itself and into the next, but I thought I could still make out the broken metal of her riffs, piling helter-skelter onto each other. It was like fractals, I realized suddenly, each individual riff made up of "notes" that were really a faster version of the same riff, while each thing that I was hearing as a riff was itself a "note" in some larger, slower version. Somehow she'd taken "Piece of the Grave" and boiled it down to this riff—was that what she heard as its essence, the crucial part?—and then taken that riff and made something new that was, like a fractal, essentially everywhere the same. I shook my head, wishing I had my fx—wishing Shadha was there, and Timin—and there was a pop, almost drowned by the music, and a puff of smoke from Tai's amp.

She leaned back, swearing, and kicked the cutout. I looked around for the kitchen extinguisher, just in case, but the damper had already cut in. Celeste's music roared for a second longer, then stopped.

"Goddamn," said Jaantje, and then again, softer, "Goddamn it."

"Why—what's happened?" Celeste asked.

"Blew a fucking fuse," Tai answered. She was already crouching by the open access panel, waving away the last wisp of smoke. I leaned over her shoulder, and made a face at the damage. All three fuses had gone, saving the main components, but the controller had gone from healthy green to black: not an expensive or difficult repair, but one that would take a little time.

"Got spares?" Jaantje asked, curling himself protectively over his guitar, and Fortune pulled herself away from the media wall.

"Sorry that happened, Tai, but I'd've had to interrupt anyway. We need to get back to the theater."

I glanced at the nearest time display: not quite fifteen, hours before we really needed to think about getting ready. Fortune saw the look, and her frown deepened.

"We have work to do—right, Celeste?"

There was a heartbeat pause before the construct answered. "Very well."

"Haya," I said, and stooped to help collect the cables. The lights faded from the audiot and the media wall, clustered again on the headbox. Fortune lifted it back into the carrier web, still frowning, and I said, carefully, "It would be fun to do this again, Fortune."

She was already moving toward the door, and I followed her, wondering if I should push it any farther, feeling Tai's eyes on me from where she crouched beside the amp. I willed her to keep silent, not wanting her to spoil it, waited for Fortune to say something. She touched the latch, letting in the late sunlight, and I thought for a second that she was going to pretend she hadn't heard. Then she looked back at me, still frowning slightly, pale eyes meeting mine.

"I need her too much, Fan."

"But—"

She shook her head, the frown easing to a bitter smile. "She's part of the act, and I can't afford to replace her, not anytime soon. Maybe you guys can jam again sometime, but I really need her mind on the act. Not on this."

There was truth to that—to all of it—but I didn't think it was what she'd meant. I let the door close behind her, and turned back to the others.

Jaantje shook his head, still cradling his guitar, but Tai sat back on her heels beside the amp's open panel. "Damn it, it wouldn't've taken that long to change the fuses, we could've played some more. . . ." She seemed to hear what she was saying then, and sighed. "Yeh, don't tell me, that's not the point, I guess. But she's got no reason to be jealous."

"Especially not if it's people," Jaantje murmured.

"I don't know," I said. There's a letdown, always, after something that good, and it was on me hard. "Celeste's her—" *Her what?* I thought, and didn't have an answer even for myself. Her construct, at least originally, but if Celeste was more than just a Spelvin construct—and there wasn't any point in pretending she wasn't, and after hearing that I don't think any of us could have pretended—she wouldn't, couldn't be merely property. Her sister, like the name implied? Her daughter? Best friend and lover? Certainly the other half of her act, right now, and that was more intimate than anything else I could think of.

"Yeh," Tai said, "her . . . something. Celeste is something, all right."

"Damn, that was good," Jaantje said, and set down his guitar, looking around for the room remote. "Is that bit still in storage?"

The remote was still in my hand, and I held it out. "Should be."

"Yeh." He frowned thoughtfully at the screen. "There it is." Tai pushed herself to her feet, leaving the panel open, started toward the cabinet where she kept her spares. "I want to play that. Play out with it. God, can't you see what people will make of it?"

I nodded.

"All too easily," Jaantje said. "We can't use it, Tai. If we put it into the sets, we either have to tell everybody who wrote it—which is a bad move, for obvious reasons—or we end up cheating Celeste."

"But—" I began, and then what he'd said really registered. He was right, we couldn't tell anyone that Celeste had written this, because that would mean Celeste was people, and that was the one thing nobody dared claim right now. But we couldn't just play it, either, not if Celeste was people, because there was no way in hell we'd treat another musician that way. Another human musician. I felt myself blushing, and saw the same realization in Tai's face.

"Couldn't we fake it somehow?" she asked. "Claim we got it from a person, I don't know, somebody off-world?"

Her voice trailed off, admitting the impossibility.

"I think I understand what she was doing," I said, slowly. "How she structured those riffs, and I've got the basic patch in memory. Maybe we could use some of that—it would really fit with the new stuff we've been doing."

Jaantje made a face. "It doesn't seem all that different to me."

"It could help," Tai said. "Help prove she's people, which has to happen sometime, you know that. If we've been playing riffs we learned from her, if people like them—and you know damn well they will, and they'll never know we didn't write it until somebody tells them—then it's proof. The best possible proof."

Jaantje hesitated, and I realized he wanted this just as badly as Tai and I did. The music, the new idea, was too good not to explore it. "Haya," he said. "It could work."

It took me a couple of days to work out the kind of fractal riff that Celeste had been using, but by the time I finished the first one I thought I had a pretty good idea of the kinds of structures she used, and the way they worked within a song. They fit beautifully into the new songs we'd been doing, giving some extra depth and a dark edge to even the songs we'd been least happy with, and for the first time I could see how everything could fit together into a theme clip. We'd need more songs, certainly, but the new technique—new style— would take us in the right direction. I could already see the kinds of images I wanted, not that different from some of the ones I'd been using, machines and the white light of day and the heat ripple from pouring metal; better than that, I could finally see where to go with that bit of a song that had been lodged in my head since the abortive gig at the Middle Oasis.

I played the various riffs for Jaantje and Tai, and then again for the rest of the band at the Tin Hau, at our next practice session, starting with Celeste's version of "Piece of the Grave." Timin listened in absolute silence, his head tipped a little to one side, face completely without expression. He had loved Hati—we all had, but more than any of us he wanted to be them—and I wondered what he'd make of what Celeste had done to the song. Shadha pretended not to listen, fiddling with her sticks and the bundle of her jewelry, but when the first clip ended, she threw her head back, setting her braids dancing across her shoulders.

"That was the construct?"

"Yeh," Jaantje said.

"Well, I guess I was wrong."

Timin hunched one shoulder. "The thing can't count."

For some reason, that struck me as funny—the idea that Celeste, herself a construct, inhabitant of a world that was built on timing cycles, couldn't count—and I laughed.

Timin scowled. "Well, it fucking can't."

"I don't like its timing either," Shadha said. "Is it different live?"

"We're not necessarily going to play this, 'Piece of the

Grave,' " Jaantje said, patiently enough. "It's the sound I want."

"So what do we do, get that construct—sorry, Celeste—to stand up on stage with us?" Shadha demanded.

"No—" Tai began, and Timin spoke over her.

"That would be insane right now, and you both, all three of you, know it. So what is it you actually have in mind?"

"I've worked out a way to get that sound," I said. "You can hear what it is, right, kind of like a fractal?"

Tai nodded, slowly, but Shadha laughed. "Give me a break, Fan, I've only heard it once."

"Each riff is made up of repetitions of the same riff," I said, "just speeded up each time until they sound like individual notes. That's what makes it sound so slide-y." I stumbled through the explanation, less sure I understood it—or at least that I could articulate it—with every word, but when I'd finished, Timin nodded.

"I think I see. So you've worked out how to do this for the new songs?"

"Yeh."

"Trust the person with machine ears to hear it," Shadha said. "Hell, yes, let's do it. What do we start with?"

" 'Dry Season,' " Jaantje answered. That was Timin's slow song, not a perfect title, but the best we'd been able to agree on. "Then the assembly line, and Tai's, then Timi's other song. Play them straight through, see how they all sound—does that work for you, Fan?"

"Sure," I said, not certain I meant it, and flipped the fx off standby. Tai gave us the beat, and we began.

It wasn't good, this first time through—basically, I wasn't good, wasn't used to controlling the audio as well as the images—but you could hear what it could be. We finished Timin's last song, the serene face hanging above us as though buoyed up by the roar of sound, suspended on the cascading riff I'd built for it while Tai's lead wailed beneath it, all angry loss. I matched the visual fade to the dying music, left the face hanging like a daytime moon for a heartbeat after the end before I blanked it. I was sweating, and I was all too aware of the missed notes, the ragged beat, half a dozen places where I'd make different choices next time, but beneath all of that was the solid certainty that this was the start of something good. I could see the same knowledge in everyone else's faces, even Timin's, and couldn't suppress a smile.

"Damn," Tai said, and showed teeth in a grin that was almost a snarl. "I think we've got something here."

Jaantje reached for one of the water bottles, drank half of it in what seemed like a single swallow. "I think we should start looking for a director."

I blinked, and Tai's grin widened. "And pricing studio time."

"We need more songs," Timin said, but for once it wasn't disagreement.

"I have one in mind," Tai said.

"And so do I." I hadn't meant to mention it so soon, not until I had a little more to show, but the time seemed right.

"I've got some things going," Jaantje said, and Timin managed a reluctant smile.

"Haya, this gives me some ideas, too. All right?"

"I'm not surprised, somehow." Tai smiled at him, but he ignored her.

"You said director, Jaantje. You're thinking a theme clip?"

"Yeh." Jaantje nodded. "It was Fanning's idea, but I think it's a good one."

"So what's the theme?" Timin asked, and Jaantje looked at me.

I hadn't had anything specific in mind, just that the songs hung together, all flavored with bitter loss, grief and anger so tightly mixed that not even the writers knew which they really meant. I hesitated, knowing there was something there, remembering the way that Celeste's fractal riffs rolled under the lead lines, and at last the image came clear in my mind, sudden and complete, like the best fx lines. Fire/Work stood onstage, our usual selves except for the audiot at the center of the group, and the ghost of the copper karakuri, Fortune's younger sister, her metal twin, rose from it, not quite part of it, barely a foothold in our world.

"Metal dreams," I said, and sketched the coolie sign that meant both "metal" and "machine." "Realpeace is already tagging us as Dreampeacers, right? Which we're not, except for Shadha, except that Celeste probably is AI—is human—and we've got to deal with that. So we tell that story. This construct dreamed us, we dreamed her in this time and place, and all this is what we've got. Hati's dead, there's people threatening us, but this metal"—I gave the sign again for emphasis—"this machine, Celeste, makes music. She plays it, plays at it—right now she plays at being human just the same way I've been playing at being a machine, trying to learn her riffs. But what's real is in the music." I stopped then, not knowing if I'd been clear at all, if I'd said too much or not nearly enough. The others were very quiet; I could read approval from Tai and Jaantje, discomfort from Timi, but I couldn't tell what Shahda was thinking at all.

"Dangerous," Tai said at last, and made it a compliment.

"Very," Shadha said, voice flat. She was suddenly busy with one of the tension bolts, fiddling with the pitch of the pad, her braids falling forward to hide her face.

"I don't like it," Timin said. His voice was soft, small, not his usual anger. "It's good, it's really good, I know that, it's just . . . I don't like it."

"It's too good not to do it, Timi," Tai said, and her voice was equally soft.

He sighed. "I know. And I'm in. I just—oh, I don't know." He let his voice trail off, and Jaantje ran a hand through his hair.

"I hate politics," he said, to nobody in particular, and shook himself. "But I think it's fucking brilliant, Fan. I can see where I want to go with it, too."

That left Shadha, and we all looked at her, waiting. She looked up, trying to look surprised, but then her shoulders slumped. "Oh, hell, let's go with it," she said, and made a face, trying to recapture her usual aggression. "Damn it, I've been Dreampeace since I was twelve, I'm supposed to want this."

"Not what you expected," Timin said.

Shadha made a short, harsh sound between her teeth. "This isn't what AI's supposed to look like."

Now you know how the coolies felt, thinking constructs would take their good jobs. I could see the same knowledge in Tai's face, and said quickly, "It's not what anybody expected."

"Then we're agreed?" Jaantje asked. "Metal dreams?" He shaped the sign himself, clumsy but clear enough, and no one disagreed.

I stumbled through the rest of practice, the possible images for the theme clip and all the other new ideas distracting me, but we still managed to get decent work done. It wasn't a performance night for us, but we broke early anyway, hoping to get out of the way before the rest of the night-show performers started arriving. We hadn't timed it quite right: the main lift and the passage stairs were already crowded, and we had to go up the west stairs to the upper lobby to avoid the people who were setting up for the lobby show. It was quiet there, the few people, ushers and the light tech and the woman who tended the food machines swapping gossip, their voices muffled by the heavy drapes and the soft carpet that covered the floor and the lower part of the wall. The lobby lights were on, and the complex pattern seemed to glow hot red against the burgundy background. Someone had told me once that all the fabric, the carpets and the drapes and the staff's dress uniforms, had been woven specifically for the Tin Hau, and that the curving patterns were really antique glyphs that spelled out that Empire's name. On a night like this I could believe it: even here, in the less expensive second balcony, everything was picked out in lights that caught the touches of gilt and polished metal, and the air smelled indefinably of the stage. I peered through the open door into the balcony, almost sorry we weren't playing tonight even if I wasn't at my best, and saw the curtain glowing scarlet under the houselights, the sun and stars of Tin Hau's present glyph splashed in woven gold across that background.

"Hey, Fanning." That was Jaantje's voice, dragging me back to reality. "Come here a minute, will you?"

I turned, saw him standing with the others at the almost-invisible door that opened on the side stairs to the plaza. Muthana was with them, and for a second I thought we were in trouble over using the shortcut—it was locked during performances, to keep people from jumping the ticket lines. But then I saw the man in Security casuals at his side, and knew it had to be something more serious. At least Security was Cartel, not FPG, but I could feel Tai's nervousness as I came to join them.

"What's up?" I asked, softly, but Muthana heard.

"Trouble, I'm afraid," he answered, and I had never heard him sound so grim.

Security cleared his throat gently. "Realpeace has issued a list of institutions, businesses, and individuals who they claim support machine rights over human rights—over coolie rights, I should say. It's all over the connections, every halftime newschannel has got it ready for download. Your name is on the list."

"What do you mean, my name?" I asked, and immediately felt stupid.

"The band," Jaantje said, and nudged me to silence.

"The list also has your address," Security said.

A chill went down my spine at that, and Tai said, "Which address?"

Security glanced sideways, consulting his implants. "Iron-yards—near Wireworks, I believe."

"The *goddow*," I said. At least all my good gear was at the Tin Hau: Security wouldn't let anything happen to the Empires.

"What are you recommending?" Muthana asked, and Security grimaced. He had a pleasant, open face, ordinary except for a thin scar along his jaw.

"Officially, Security will of course do everything it can to protect everybody. Unofficially—" He paused, and shrugged. "I'm telling you what I told my sister's husband. If there is any trouble—and we don't know that there will be, Realpeace has asked its membership to behave with restraint—"

"Oh, yeh, restraint," Tai said, and Muthana frowned at her.

"Go on," he said, to Security, who gave a wry smile, twisting the scar line.

"If there is any trouble, we'll have to allocate our resources to protect the biggest targets, it's a simple matter of logistics. So if your regular address is on the list, I'd find someplace else to sleep, at least for tonight. If things stay calm, then I'd risk going back."

"I see," Muthana said. "Thank you for being so open."

"I'm hoping it'll save trouble in the long run," Security answered. "If you'll excuse me?"

Muthana waited until he was out of earshot before he spoke again. "I'd take his advice, myself. The Tin Hau is on the list, too—so are all the Empires—but you're welcome to sleep in the practice rooms, if that helps."

"It might," Jaantje said, and looked at the rest of us. "What do you say?"

"Lovely people," Shadha said.

"That's not helpful," Timin began, and she spoke through him.

"Look, at my house, we've been ready for trouble ever since Realpeace started getting big, we've got twenty-five or thirty ex–line-workers ready to help us out if anything happens. I'm not really worried about me. But I think the rest of you should stay here. Like the man said, Security's going to take care of the biggest targets first."

"I think it would be smart," I said. "Security's not going to let anything happen to the Empires."

Tai nodded in reluctant agreement. "And we appreciate the use of the practice room, ba' Muthana."

Timin took a deep breath. "I don't think I'm going to stay here. First, Realpeace doesn't know me, but mostly, I've got family, and I'd feel better staying with them. I don't want to let anybody down."

"It's all right," Jaantje said.

"If worst comes to worst, Timi," I said, "we can all come stay with you."

"You'd be welcome," he answered. He meant it, too, but I wondered how the rest of his family would feel.

Muthana cleared his throat. "All right, now that that's decided, do you need to retrieve anything from your flat? I may be able to spare a minder as escort, but I don't know how much good that would do."

"All my good gear is here," Tai said, echoing my thoughts, and Jaantje nodded.

"Mine, too. Clothes—" He shrugged. "I don't want to lose them, but I think it's be smarter to lie low right now."

The *goddow* had decent locks, left over from when it had been a storage cavern for a long-vanished shop. I said, "If they manage to break in—they'd have to be pretty serious to get through both doors. Let's stay here for tonight, see what it's like in the morning. I can't imagine we'd be their top priority."

"Don't underestimate them," Muthana said. "All right. Log in downstairs, and make yourselves at home."

"Thanks," Jaantje said, but the manager was already striding away.

"I think we should head out, too," Shadha said, and Timin nodded.

"I want to get home before shift-end."

We walked with them down to the main lobby, knowing they were being sensible, but not wanting to let them go. There were more minders than usual on duty in the lobby, two to each door rather than the usual single ticket-taker, and through the smoked glass I could see at least a hundred people jostling for position around the newskiosk. Some of them, the ones fighting to get away from the station, clutched folded sheaves of pink paper or their hands were closed tight over a databutton: the list, I realized, and shivered again.

"I was going to suggest we get some dinner before we hole

up," Jaantje said, "but maybe that's not such a good idea."

"Maybe not," I said. There was a line of people waiting for tickets, too, maybe fifty or so looking either for cheap seats or better seats than the ones they had. Even as I watched, a man—in ordinary factory clothes, none of Realpeace's *sarang* and wrap-jacket, nothing to mark him as one of theirs—swung away from the crowd, unfolding the list as he went, scanning it as though he was looking for something. He found it, and turned back to the crowd, pointing at the Tin Hau's doors as he shouted something I couldn't hear. I saw the minders tense, rocking forward on the balls of their feet, but an older man shouted back at him from the ticket line, hands moving in broad, contemptuous sign.

Go home and sleep it off, stop annoying respectable people.

He was wearing a *sarang*, too, though I couldn't tell if he was wearing any of the Realpeace badges. Before the first man could answer, a quartet of armored Security swept in. Two placed themselves beside the bank of doors, while the other two started determinedly toward the man who'd shouted first. He ducked away, disappearing into the crowd, but Security still followed, people giving way for them.

"Nice to see," Tai said.

"Yeh," I agreed, and wished I felt more confident. It wasn't that I had anything of huge value back at the *goddow*, but there were things I liked—things that were mine—and things that I'd hate to lose.

"We can get something to eat in the lobby," Jaantje said, briskly, and I shook myself, made myself follow him and Tai toward the nearest vendor. At least we were safe here, I told myself, and maybe Realpeace wouldn't bother with the *goddow* after all.

▪ 17 ▪

Celinde Fortune

THE FIRST I heard about the list was when Security knocked on my door to warn me about it. I'd spent the day working on the act, first repairing a stripped gear in the silver karakuri's arm assembly, and then rehearsing with Celeste. That had gone better than I'd expected, after her session with Fanning—it was almost as if she had gotten over the first flush of excitement, though whether that meant she'd given up on the music or had just managed to integrate it into her regular functioning I couldn't have said. At any rate, she hadn't complained about not having time to play, and she'd really seemed to put her mind to the rehearsal, so that we could finally work out the timing cues properly. Even just working in the virtual, I was sweating when we'd finished, and I wished there wasn't a matinee, so that I could run the same routine on stage with the real karakuri. Still, this was better than nothing—and the illusions were better than they'd been in ages—and I dismissed the virtual karakuri. The room projectors cut out, the illusion of the Empire vanishing, and I was left with the familiar worktable, and the silver arm lying in a web of light. I stared at it for a moment, trying to remember why I hadn't put it away, and a chime sounded from the ceiling.

"Get that, Celeste, will you?"

"Confirmed."

More lights flickered at the edge of my vision, Celeste accessing the outside monitors, but I ignored them, reaching instead into memory for my notes on the repair. Everything seemed to have been done—except the last fuse, I remembered, because I was letting the epoxy cure. I smiled, relieved, and went to the center cabinet to retrieve the part I needed.

"Fortune," Celeste said. "Security would like to speak to you."

"Why?" I paused with my hand on the cabinet door, her words registering a moment later than they should have. "Security."

"They insist on speaking to you," Celeste said, her voice still mild.

"Why?" I said again, but moved away from the cabinet. "All right, patch them through."

"We'd like to speak to you in person," a new voice said, and I sighed, bowing to the inevitable.

"Haya. I'll be right out."

The hall lights flicked on as I opened the workshop door, and the lock symbol appeared in front of the outside door. There was a second strip of glyphs as well, time and temperature and the planetary day as well as a blue spot that meant the street-cleaning sprinklers would go on sometime after midnight. I brushed them away and worked the latch.

"What can I do for you?" I said, and heard my own voice falter, seeing the smear of blue paint that covered the outside of my door. It was crudely done, but recognizable, the assembly-line marker that meant a part had been rejected as unsuitable. I frowned, looked up at the security scanner that guards the door, and was not surprised to see more blue paint coating the focus bead. I looked back at the two Cartel Security standing patiently enough on my doorstep. They were vaguely familiar, both from the neighborhood watch-post—two Mister Walkers, a man and a woman identically sand-worn—but I couldn't remember their real names. "What's this?"

They exchanged glances, expressions unreadable, and the woman said, "You haven't been watching the media, then."

"No." I touched the paint, found the thickest part still slightly tacky under my fingers: if it was the cheap primer paint the lines use, it had been put on no more than two hours ago, and probably less. I had been deep in rehearsal then, eyes and ears filled with the virtual Empire; I wouldn't have heard a sprayer working in the room with me, much less on my doorstep. "What is it?"

"Realpeace has made a list," the man said.

I glanced sideways, automatically looking for a query glyph, but I was out of range of the house transceivers.

"Realpeace has issued a list of people—that includes institutions and businesses as well as individuals—who they say would rather see machine rights than human rights," the woman said.

"And my name's on it," I said.

"Just so." The woman nodded, face grave.

"And what about this?" I jerked my thumb toward the scrawled glyph. Across the street, I could see one of my neighbors—Zibette Laor, I thought, who was a night foreman on the Nicaster Assembly—peering out through the cracks in her shutters. She saw me looking at her, and let them fall again, but I was sure everybody else was watching, too.

"The glyph is a rejection marker," the man began, and I shook my head.

"I know what it is, I want to know what it's doing on my door."

"We'd like to find that out, too," the woman said, quite calmly. "May we come in?"

"Sorry," I said, and stepped back, beckoning for them to follow me down the hallway. I had left the inner door open, and the lights were centered on the worktable and the severed silver arm. Normally, I enjoy watching people react to my workshop, but for once I wished I'd put things away. I felt the house web close around me, a cool familiar embrace, and waved a hand through the nearest control space to bring up the rest of the lights. "I assume it has something to do with this list that Realpeace has come up with?"

"We are assuming so." That was the woman again. "There have been similar incidents at other locations on the list, though not at all of them."

"Probably locals," the man put in.

That wasn't a pleasant thought, but it was plausible. I keep a low profile offstage, but I don't hide what I do from my neighbors. All things considered, it would be a lot easier to believe that one of them secretly supported Realpeace—thought I was a Dreampeacer—than to think that a stranger had pried my address out of the Tin Hau's databanks.

"I see you have a substantial amount of security in place," the woman went on, her voice harder than her polite words. "I'd like to take a look at its records—at the vidi record of the door to start with, if there is one."

"Haya," I said, and reached into the control space again to find the right icons. "Celeste, pull the records from sensor one and put it on the media screen. Bi'—?"

Security ignored me, but Celeste's voice whispered in my ear instead. #Koleva. Sergeant Koleva. And he is Sohail Maser. No rank listed.#

Which probably meant he was basic grade, I thought. "Sergeant Koleva," I said, and drew a startled look from the man. "I'll run the tape on the main screen, but I doubt the camera will have caught anything useful."

"I was hoping you had more than cameras," Koleva said. She looked around at the worktable, the still-open cabinet with the ranked parts and boxes filling the shelves, the karakuri parts hanging in the shadows. "There's a lot of expensive equipment here."

"I do have more than cameras," I said. "But they're concentrated in here. There's a secondary package focused on the door, but my assumption was that any break-in attempt would be a little more complex."

#Sensor one's records are ready,# Celeste said. I wasn't sure why she was keeping such a low profile, but I was grateful for it. #Shall I display it?#

I nodded, looked at Koleva. "The records are cued. Go ahead, Celeste."

Koleva leaned forward a little as the screen image shifted, the first sign of eagerness—of any emotion—I'd seen in her. The picture steadied on my entranceway, the dark slate of the doorstep drifted with a haze of sand. A secondary halo of false color surrounded it, signaling the working sensor package. The basic cassette could hold up to twenty hours of data before the system recycled it, and I glanced at the start numbers. Sure enough, the cassette had reset to zero at 0323 this morning: over twelve hours of tape to search.

"Celeste," I said. "Search for any anomalous behavior, display anything you find."

"Confirmed."

For a second, I thought Koleva would protest, but she said nothing. The screen dimmed for an instant, became mere shadows, while the counter vanished completely. Occasionally shadows flickered, people passing on the street, too fast to be recognized, but Celeste didn't pause.

"I'll want to go over this myself," Koleva said, not a threat but a warning.

"You're welcome to do that," I answered, "but Celeste knows I went out a couple of times this morning, and then there was a delivery. I thought she could eliminate those shots, at least from the prelminary viewing."

Koleva nodded, but before she could say anything more, the image brightened.

"I have found an anomaly," Celeste said, and added, for me alone, #I think it's what you're looking for.#

"Run it," I said.

A shadow fell across the doorstep, and then three figures appeared. They were young, dressed normally, workcloth trousers and unmarked, unremarkable shirts pulled up to hide their faces. They were dark-haired like most of Persephone's population, and probably dark-eyed, but that was all you could say for sure. Certainly I couldn't recognize them as any of my neighbors. They stood huddled together for a second—verifying the address? I wondered—and then one reached into his belt. I flinched as blue paint covered the focus bead.

"That's the last coherent image," Celeste said.

I sighed, unable to hide my disappointment for all that I hadn't been expecting anything conclusive. Koleva shook her head.

"Well, that's that. Did you see the way the halos skewed?"

I hadn't noticed, but Celeste whispered, #I have no reliable electronic record. I believe a jamming device was in use.#

I said, "Was it jammed?"

Koleva nodded. "I'd say so. I'll need to go over the cassette, though."

"Make free. What are you doing about this list?"

Koleva ignored that question. "I'll want the original cassette."

"Sorry?" *Over my dead body,* I thought, but curbed the impulse. Koleva was Security; she could get it, one way or another, but I might be able to get some concession for it.

"I want the original cassette." She fixed her eyes on me, and I realized they were pale, an odd, unnerving bluish grey. "We have tools you don't; we might be able to pull something out of it."

That was true, and I made myself relax. "I'll want to make a copy," I said, "And you didn't answer my question. What are you—what is Security—doing about this list of Realpeace's?"

The man—Maser—made a choked sound. Koleva glared at him, and I realized it had been laughter. "What we can do," she said aloud, and Maser laughed again.

"Which isn't much."

Koleva gave him another look that boded ill for his career. "We're keeping a file of the listed locations, and are offering extra security for them. Where vandalism has occurred—like here—we're going all out to catch the people responsible. You should know that Realpeace itself is urging its members to stay calm."

I made a noncommittal noise, and she went on, "But we've still had incidents, which is why I want this cassette."

"Celeste, make a full-range copy of this cassette," I said. "Then store the copy and return the original."

"Confirmed."

I looked back at Koleva. "And what is Security recommending for those of us who are on the list?"

She sighed, the belligerence draining away. "We will be doing our best to keep you under surveillance. We have twenty locations just in Angelitos, and Elvis alone knows what the total is for the full district. But we're going to try."

"Things have been quiet so far," Maser said, and couldn't make it sound reassuring.

"What's the point?" I asked, and Koleva shook her head.

"Bi' Fortune, your guess is as good as mine."

That was all I could get out of her. I gave her the cassette and let them out the main door, then stood for a moment in the hall, considering my options. I'd been living here during the Manfred Riots, and I had some hardware left over from those bad days, a couple of dead bolts—not locks, but shock-fields—and some tangleware that would work with the over-all system golem. If the night show was still on—and if it wasn't, Binnie would already have called to warn me—my first priority was to protect the hardware that would have to stay in the flat. I looked down and sideways, calling up the time. Two hours before we had to leave, which was proba-bly enough time to get everything at least crudely installed. In any case, it would have to be enough.

In the end, I got it all done, the dead bolts and the tangle-ware to clog any attempt to break into the flat's internal sys-tem, and the arm fuse replaced and the whole assembly repacked to bring it back to the Empire—and I even found time to pay Zibette Laor's daughter to scrub most of the paint off the door—but as a result I was late to Tin Hau. The house system flashed red at me as I came in the stage door, and a message appeared at the bottom of my vision, warning me that I had incurred a twenty-five-wu fine. I waved that away, and hurried on into my dressing room. More glyphs flared, messages jostling each other, and I waved away everything except the emergency and urgent codings. There were enough of them—two from Muthana, stating that the Empire was on the Realpeace list and that precautions were being taken; another from Hasker asking for new passwords from everyone; two from Terez, giving new node marks, and fi-nally one from the stage manager wanting to know where Ce-leste was. That at least I could deal with, and I looked up to lock eyes with the nearest node.

"George," I began, and then remembered that the program was still down. "System, connect me with the stage manager's console."

For a moment, I thought the patchwork system wasn't going to recognize that command, but then Terez's voice sounded in my ears. "Fortune! Thank God. I was beginning to sweat."

"I'm sorry," I said. "My flat was on the damn list, and I had to rustle up some quick-and-dirty security."

"Damn." Terez paused. "You know we're listed, too?"

"I got Binnie's messages when I came in. I'm kind of surprised we're performing."

"I think he's sick of catering to these scares," she answered. "I can't say I blame him."

"No," I said, but somewhere deep inside I was beginning to wonder if it was worth it. The karakuri weren't exactly portable, but they could be duplicated elsewhere; maybe it was time to think about trying somewhere else—one of the Urban Worlds, for a start. I killed that thought—this was not the time—and heard Terez's voice change.

"Anyway, I need Celeste on-line right now. Where is she?"

The headbox was sitting at my feet, and I hadn't even begun to dress, much less retrieve the karakuri. "Can she link from here?" I asked. "I'm sorry I'm late, Bixenta, truly."

Terez sighed, a ghost of air in my ear. "I was worried. Yeh, go ahead, there's a high-speed node in your room. She can start bringing up the karakuri once she's on."

"Thanks," I said, and looked away from the pinlight. "Did you hear that, Celeste?"

"I heard." The voice from the box was softer than her usual one, but perfectly confident. "Link to the house, and then bring the karakuri to ready."

"We're a little short of time," I said, and reached for the cable links. "Anything you can do to speed up the process would be a help—as long as it doesn't interfere with Terez."

"I understand," Celeste said, and I could have sworn I heard the ghost of laughter. "Linking now. Do you want me to hold the karakuri for you, or will you go with the spare arm?"

"Damn." I'd managed to forget all about the repair, despite the neatly bundled package sitting on the counter with my makeup. "Hold the karakuri. I want to replace that arm."

"Very well," Celeste answered, and I felt her withdrawing from the room. She was still present, but attenuated, not quite distanced, but her attention stretched thin, and for a second I considered turning down my suit. I needed it, though, especially as late as I was, and I left it up, feeling the rhythm of the preshow washing through my bones.

Luckily, my own preparations have become pretty much automatic over the years. I dressed quickly, first the illusion tunic with the sleeves that were wider than they looked, then the hanten coat that matched the first karakuri's costume. The makeup didn't take much longer, just the basic mask and the lines that emphasized my yanqui eyes, and then I collected the arm and my tool kit and hurried back up the long corridor that led to the true backstage. I could feel already that the show was running behind, and it was the sort of delay that only got worse.

#Celeste. Where's the silver karakuri?#

Her answer was reassuringly prompt. #Backstage left, beside the second fly control panel.#

#Thanks.#

The backstage area was more crowded than usual, but there didn't seem to be nearly the normal number of stagehands. I frowned, trying to figure it out from the data coursing under my skin, but it was a tangle of sensation and half-heard orders and complaints, the sense of it filtered away by the selective channels that didn't recognize me as part of this conversation. For a second, I considered asking Celeste to patch me into it, but decided against it. Not only would my presence annoy Terez, it would distract me from the work at hand. The area around the karakuri seemed clear enough, and I stripped off the hanten coat, hanging it across the bronze karakuri's shoulders.

#Celeste. Let me know if anyone needs this space, or if there's anything else I need to worry about.#

#Of course. You should know that five of the junior stage-hands and the lead hand did not come to work tonight.#

"Shit." I opened the tool kit, and tugged out the worklight on its long, stiff stem.

#Terez is compensating with automatics and has sent the assistant stage manager to replace Innari#—that was the lead stagehand—#and is now managing the show herself. However, without George to coordinate in virtual, she predicts that the show will run behind tonight.#

"Shit," I said again, and wound the worklight around the silver karakuri's neck, tilting the cone so that the light fell squarely on the shoulder assembly. #All right. Keep me informed—and if you can, make sure all the presets are clear for our act.#

#I'm unable to access that volume at this time,# Celeste answered. #As soon as I'm able, I will confirm the settings.#

#Thanks.# Without the settings, I could easily lose the virtual dimension of the act. I put that worry aside—the act would play without it, though I'd always prided myself on making my illusions work in both worlds—and concentrated on the karakuri's arm. The arm in place was a generic replacement, hastily sprayed an unmatching silver; I released the bolts and tugged the cap free, then decoupled the internal systems. I kept spares at the theater, of course, and could work with them in a pinch, but I always preferred to use the originals as much as possible. The repaired arm lay in its padding at my feet, and I unwrapped it, then brought the karakuri's other arm around to support the elbow while I reattached the fine motor cables. I'd designed the system to allow just this sort of quick fix, but I couldn't help feeling a touch of pride as the nervewires slipped neatly into their designated sockets. I tightened them down, then reached into the wrapping for the pauldron that would cover the point of the shoulder. Shadowed except for the white glare on its shoulder, it looked more human than usual, a slim figure cradling its injured arm. I heard a gasp behind me, and looked back to see one of the stagehands retreating into the shadows. The glimpse of his open mouth and wide eyes was reassuring; I slipped the pauldron into place, and tightened the tiny screws, feeling perversely better.

#Places,# Celeste said, and a moment later Terez's voice repeated the same message aloud. I gave all the karakuri a final appraising glance, and then headed back down to the dressing rooms. The way things were going already, the last thing anyone needed was an extra body backstage.

The first half of the show went well enough, though Terez had to override the system twice to keep things moving cleanly. At the interval, I went back up to the stagehouse, dodging the sweaty dancers who'd closed the first half, and waited in the wings while the stagehands changed the hard set for the second act. There were only three of them to haul the heavy platforms, and they were straining in spite of the light-haul units positioned beneath the most massive pieces. I glanced sideways, letting the suit bring up the full display—the stage systems at standby, auditorium and hall systems steady green, the give-and-take of communication between lights and sound and air, all normal, except for George's absence, and George's absence made it anything but normal. You really needed a Spelvin construct to translate between the house golems and the daemons that managed each subsystem and the stage and house managers; without one, it was hard to tell whether the occasional spikes of static, the flickers of warning orange at the edges of my sight, were problems, or ordinary stresses. But Terez would know, I told myself. She knew the system inside out, would know what signaled a problem.

#Celeste,# I said, and instantly felt her presence stronger, closer at hand. #Can you tell if we should place the karakuri, or can they handle it?#

#One moment—# Before she could finish, there was a cracking sound from the flyspace, and my vision turned red.

"Clear the stage." Terez's voice came loud over the speakers. "Clear stage immediately—now!"

I was well clear. I froze where I was, hearing the confused

drumming of feet, and then one of the junior stagehands darted past me, his face contorted in panic. He fetched up against the nearest fly board, and stared at it in blank panic.

#Celeste?# I said, and craned my neck to see onto the stage itself. It was empty, except for the set frames not quite into place, but there seemed to be a shadow that I'd never seen before.

#One of the lights has fallen,# Celeste said, without apparent emotion. #Grid four, point 22AY. The house system is unable to compensate.#

"What?"

The stagehand looked at me, and I realized I'd spoke aloud.

#The lighting subsystem will not accept the house override,# Celeste said. #It needs a code from George.#

"Lights, go to manual," Terez's voice said. She sounded as calm as ever, and I had to envy her. If the light fell, there would be damage, not just to the light and the cables, and probably to the electrical system, but to the stage itself and to any part of the set that was underneath it; repairs would mean a serious delay, if they could be made at all. At least she'd managed to clear the stage. "Fly station L3, it's on your board. Bring it down."

The stagehand looked back at the fly board, and I realized with a chill that his was the controlling station. "Which key?" he asked, and I heard metal groan from the stage.

"Key 14," Celeste said, and for an instant her voice sounded very much like Terez. "Winch at three."

"Fourteen at three," the stagehand answered, his voice steadying, and I saw his hands move on the controls. "Bringing it down."

Machinery whirred to life in the flyspace, paying out cable. I took a cautious step forward, hearing metal creak again, but didn't dare look out. The keys controlled sections of the grid, not individual lights; I had no idea what else might be coming down. The shadow was growing, and then I caught my first sight of the light. It was one of the big ones—I still don't know exactly what they're called—and it hung at an angle, turning slowly. It looked as though the clamp had released, left it to hang by its power cables, maybe a meter and a half below the rest of the grid.

"Easy," I said, but someone, Celeste or Terez, I couldn't tell which, spoke over me.

"Half power."

The light's descent slowed, but there was another ominous creak from the clamps holding the cables. It was amazing they'd held this long, but I wondered if they could hold it for another minute. I could see it clearly now, a massive matte black cylinder a meter long and nearly half a meter wide at the lens. It was still turning, and every time it swung, blue sparks flashed at the cable connection.

"A little more," Terez said, and this time I was sure it was Terez. "Keep it coming—haya, brake."

The stagehand flipped two switches, and the machinery cut out, leaving the light suspended a hand's-width, maybe six centimeters, above the boards of the stage.

"Right, move," Terez said. "Bring it down."

The rest of the crew rushed the stage then, carrying pads and cable and clamps, and I allowed myself a sigh of relief. I heard the same sound echo from the junior stagehand, and gave him my best smile.

"Nice work."

"Thanks." He shook his head, and I could see the sweat fly from his hair. "But it shouldn't have happened. I don't understand it."

"Neither do I." That was Terez, and not on the intercom. I looked toward the voice, and saw her hurrying toward us. For an instant, I wondered who was on the stage manager's console, but then over her shoulder I saw one of the assistants hunched over the controls. "Fortune, can I borrow Celeste?"

If she's willing. I swallowed those words, nodded instead. "Celeste? You heard?"

"I heard." Her voice came from the fly board's speaker. "What can I do for you, bi' Terez?"

The stagehand's eyes cut toward the speaker, surprise and something like fear warring on his face. I suppressed the desire to laugh—nerves more than humor—and Terez said, still

placid, "Without George, we're having trouble mediating between the subsystems and the console. Can you intervene?"

"If I do that," Celeste said, "I won't be able to manage the
act."

"I can handle the board for that part of the show," Terez
said. She looked at me. "That means you won't have the virtual, Fortune, but otherwise I'm going to have to call the
show."

And that was the unforgivable sin. I nodded. "All right. I'm
not happy, but let's do it."

"Very well," Celeste said.

Terez sighed, relieved, and I said, "Terez."

"Yeh?"

"I'll want to talk to you about causes. When this is over."

Terez managed a grim smile. "You and me both, Fortune."

I felt Celeste move away from me, her attention already on
the part of the system that George had occupied. She had had
at least some of the access codes, I remembered, and Terez
could give her the rest. Even as I thought that, Terez looked
back toward the console, and I watched her walk the depth
of the stage to lean over the assistant stage manager's shoulder.

It didn't take as long as I'd feared to clear the stage and replace the light, but it was long enough for the audience to get
restless. I could hear it in their voices as they returned to
their seats, and in the roar with which they greeted the rising curtain. But after that the rest of the second half went
suprisingly well: the house wasn't full, but the people who
were here were willing to meet the acts halfway. As I brought
up the karakuri and took my place for our entrances, I could
almost feel their excitement, pushing the puppeteers to new
heights. And then that was over, and Celeste was back with
me.

#Ready,# she murmured. #Virtual is blank, hologram is in
place, karakuri are under full control. Confirm overrides?#

#Confirmed,# I agreed, and stepped back to let the pup-
peteers pass in the narrow space. #Cue the music.#

#Starting music,# Celeste answered, and an instant later

the familiar strains of my music filled the hall. I heard the audience rustle, a sound like a sigh as they settled in, and I felt the familiar thrill. They were waiting for me, for my act, and I was ready for them. I stepped forward between the twin towers that were my only set, into position for my first appearance, checked my marks to be sure I was in place. The checks sparked reassuringly green, and I took a deep breath.

#Ready,# I said, and Celeste answered instantly, our own private code.

#Steady.#

The lights at the corners of my eyes confirmed it, the pale purple guidebeams just visible, a haze in the air. Anyone who was wired—and who'd turned their suits up far enough—could see them, but there was nothing I could do about that tonight. #Go,# I said, and the curtain swept back to reveal myself walking on, arms spread in apology.

"Ladies and gentlemen, please accept my apologies for the technical problem. We've had a slight malfunction in the lighting computer, and the show will have to proceed without the lighting effects planned for this evening."

The audience groaned, and I couldn't repress a brief snort of laughter. Tonight, of all nights, that was closer to the truth than I liked to think about. Given the extended interval, the audience might actually believe it, too.

"No?" the karakuri asked, in my voice. "Then we will have to try—this." Its hand rose, tossing the glittering, multicolored hologram ball, and the stage lights flashed on. In the sudden glare, I hurried forward, so that I seemed to appear in the flash of light, and the hologram that had clothed the karakuri vanished. I spread my own arms in greeting, letting the hanten jacket's bright brocade catch the light, and the karakuri bowed in welcome while the audience cheered their delight.

I had never had an audience like this before. They were with me from the moment I stepped on the stage, as they'd been with every act tonight, wanting to be mystified—wanting to love me. They gasped at Compression, giggled and then gasped at Disassembly and then cheered the restored karakuri for thirty seconds longer than I'd expected, so that Celeste had to juggle the music for a discordant moment. Even that didn't put them off, however, and they were with me for every second of Vanishment. The illusion is spectacular to begin with, something no other conjurer does on Persephone, but when karakuri and silk vanished together, and then reappeared between my helpers, I thought the applause would deafen me. As it was, I didn't hear Celeste's first cue, and had to have it repeated before I signaled the transformer to come on stage.

There was a sudden silence as it appeared, and then a few hissing whispers, people who'd seen the act before or who'd heard about it murmuring to their friends. This was the one illusion I was concerned about, given what had happened tonight, but in the end I needn't have worried. This was an audience that had ignored Realpeace's list to come here; they were more than willing to be titillated by the humaniform karakuri. When I vanished and then reappeared from within the transformer's frame, I won the ultimate reward, a heartbeat's silence before the applause. They stood for me and the karakuri—a small audience, but choice—and stayed standing for the curtain call, made us come back twice before Terez could finally bring down the curtain.

I stood there for a moment as the rest of the acts filed off, trying to catch my breath—I hadn't been working any harder than usual, but the applause had got me going, and I was trying to cool down. Celeste had pulled away again, I guessed to help Terez finish shutting down, and to my surprise Fanning waved at me from the wings.

Great— He added a second sign that I didn't recognize, but I guessed he was complimenting me on the act.

The karakuri were at the back of the stage, more or less out of the way for now, and I moved to join him, putting off the inevitable letdown.

"Thanks," I said, and he grinned at me.

"You were great. I've rarely seen you better."

"I didn't have virtual tonight," I said, and he shook his head.

"You didn't need it."

"Thanks, Fan." Then, for the first time, his presence really registered. This wasn't one of their performance nights; he should have been playing in the clubs, or at home. "What are you doing here, anyway?"

His smile faltered. "Um, we had a bit of trouble. Fire/Work was on the list, with the *goddow's* address, and Security suggested we find somewhere else to sleep."

"Damn. I'm sorry." For an instant, I thought of my own place, the mark on the outside door, and hoped everything was all right. Or if it wasn't, I hoped my programs did some harm. "They listed the workshop, too. And somebody drew a rejection glyph on my front door."

"Bastards." He shook his head, then shrugged, forcing a smile again. "Anyway, Binnie said we could stay in the practice room for as long as we need. Security seemed to think the Empires would be pretty safe."

I nodded. "I can't imagine they'd let anything happen. There's too much money here." *Which is part of what makes them a target,* I added silently, but shook the thought away. The night had gone too well to borrow trouble.

"Fortune!" That was Terez, the various acts parting before her, and Fanning took a quick step backward.

"I'll let you go."

"I'll grab you later," I called, but he was already into the wings. I looked at Terez. "What's up?"

"That construct of yours—" I froze, but then I saw she was grinning. "Damn, it's—she's—a joy to work with. Whoever built her for you, I want the name."

I took a breath, wondering how to answer that, but she was already rushing on. "We had some more problems, system glitches, a golem freezing, but she handled them like a pro. I bet you didn't even notice them."

I frowned, remembering a couple of unexpected orange lights that had vanished almost as quickly as they'd appeared. "You're right. I didn't."

"And on top of that," Terez said, "there was another clip, I don't know what it is yet, but another goddamn payload.

And Celeste just spotted it, pocketed it, and went on like nothing happened. It's in isolation, and Binnie's going to hand it over to Security as soon as we can get somebody down here to take it."

"Good for her," I said. "That's great."

"It was great," Terez went on, "she was great, and, on top of that, you were great. The whole second half really pulled together. A nice night." She paused, catching her breath, and went on a little more slowly. "But I need a favor, Fortune."

"I might have known," I said, but couldn't make it sound serious.

Terez smiled. "It would be very helpful if Celeste could close down with me. I've still got some mediation problems, without George, and there's still a risk of foreign code in the system. Celeste would make it a lot easier."

I smiled back. "No problem, Terez. Truly."

"Thanks," she said, and looked over her shoulder. "Look, I've got to run."

"No problem," I said again, but she was already gone. The stage was nearly empty, just a couple of the stagehands at the back starting to take down my towers, and I looked for the nearest pinlight. #Celeste?#

Her answer, when it came, was distant: Terez already had her working on the shutdown. #Yes?#

#Nothing important,# I said, quickly. #But I'm proud of you. You did extremely well.#

#Thank you,# Celeste answered, and this time I was sure she sounded pleased. I smiled myself, happy for her—happy for me in having her—and touched my wrist control to turn my suit back down to normal levels.

Security guessed later that this was when the first fire started, one small incendiary device placed in the trash tunnels behind the lower-level dressing rooms. It was a fuck-up from the start, at least from Realpeace's point of view: the Empire was supposed to be empty, emptied by the clip that hadn't run and that no one had checked, or at worst by the technical glitches they'd introduced into the house system. They'd made no provision for us managing to finish the show, or for the Tin Hau still being full, not just of the crew and the casts of the various acts, but the lobby-show workers and the house staff and the casts of other acts, like Fanning and the rest of Fire/Work, who'd either been rehearsing or had come to see the show, or were hiding out here because they'd been put on the list and the Empires were supposed to be safe. I had started down to my dressing room when I caught the first whiff of smoke—it was sweet, almost, then, not at all like fire, so for an instant I thought someone had lit incense, and guessed they were thanking their gods for the good night. Then one of the first-act dancers came up the midpoint stair, in street clothes already, jacket and gold-shot *sarang*, looking neither as tall nor as pretty as she did on stage. She was frowning, unusually, and I gave her a curious look.

"I smelled smoke," she said, and I nodded.

"I did, too, a minute ago. Incense, I think."

"Not down there," she answered. "It was, well, electrical, but the alarms haven't gone."

I looked around for a pinlight, and had to step sideways to align with it. #Celeste? Is everything all right?#

Her answer was reassuringly prompt. #All indicators are green. We're still cleaning out the system, though. Was there anything in particular?#

I sniffed again, and thought I caught a hint of smoke—not incense, definitely, something sharper—but it was gone before I could be certain. #Fire detection. Are the detectors working?#

#All indicators are green,# Celeste said again. #Should I send a golem to check it out?#

I hestitated. #No—yeh, when you get a chance.#

#Very well,# Celeste answered, and I looked away from the light.

Someone else was coming up the stairs, a thin young man, a coolie, but I didn't really recognize him out of his stage dress. He looked at the dancer, signed something I couldn't understand, and she looked at me.

"I don't know. Do you know if anybody's got a cook-stand?"

Cookstands were strictly banned from the Tin Hau, and half the dressing rooms and practice rooms had them. "I don't," I answered, and glanced into the nearest half-open door. "Shauna does, but it's off."

"It's down here anyway," the young man said. He shook his head. "I keep thinking I smell something, and then it's gone."

"Me, too," the dancer said.

I looked along the hall, counting closed and open doors. About half the people on this floor had left already, but I could check the rest, and Celeste could give me keycodes to the locked doors—though if there was a fire, the alarms should have sounded long ago. I could remember a few years back, when an overboiled tea urn had set off the system. "Let me check here," I said, "and you two take a walk downstairs, see if you can spot anything."

"Haya," the dancer said, looking relieved. The young man nodded, and they headed back down the stairs. I made my way along the hall, tapping on doors and asking the people who answered to check their appliances. Most of them hadn't noticed anything, but the singer who had the room opposite me answered my question with a worried frown.

"I already checked mine twice," he said. "I thought I was smelling something, but I thought it came from the trash."

I slid the chute open, careful of the shredding teeth just inside the opening, and bent to sniff. The air that puffed out smelled of rotten fruit and paper, and the thin slick solvent we all used on our makeup, but there was a hint of something else as well. I found the safety button, held it down, and leaned closer. Something acrid and unpleasant wafted out at me, a smell that might have been smoke.

"There it is again," the singer said.

"Yeh." I straightened, looked for a node, and found one high in the corner of the room. "Celeste. I think something's wrong in the trash system. Can you check it out?"

"All my indicators are green," she answered.

"What about fire?"

"Nothing." She paused. "If there's a problem, it's either

outside my sensor reach, or my sensors have been disabled."

Both of which were at least theoretically possible, and therefore had to be considered. I looked at the singer, and he looked back at me, the same fear I felt reflecting in his eyes. "Tell Terez that I think there's a problem," I said. "Binnie, too." I glanced at the trash chute again, trying to imagine the layout of the tubes and tunnels. "Where does this go?"

"The trash chute drops down to the next level, where there's a conveyor system to take it into the main sorting bins. They're on the lowest level, behind the keeping," Celeste answered.

"I'm going to check the next levels down," I said, and looked at the singer. "Will you let the people here know that there may be a problem?"

"Haya," he answered, and scooped up the carryall that had been lying beside his chair.

There were more people in the lower corridor—this was where the lower-ranking groups and the chorus kids dressed, so there were more of them anyway, and more people who ate and slept as cheaply as they could. The young man I'd seen before was at the center of one group, and he broke off signing to say aloud, "Is there anything?"

I shook my head. "Somebody said he smelled smoke from the trash. Anybody checked that?"

I saw headshakes, and signed *no*s, and a woman said, "We don't have chutes in all the dressing rooms, we use the one at the end of the hall."

Most of them turned to look, and I suppressed a curse. Somehow I was becoming the person in charge. "Haya," I said aloud, and they moved aside for me to pass.

The chute was latched, the checkplate glowing red to signal a full load. I started to empty it, but stopped, and hit the override key instead. The door slid back, and I wrinkled my nose at the sight and smell of the garbage. But there was more than garbage, I realized instantly. I could smell smoke now, quite clearly, and when I stuck my hand into the opening the air was warmer than it should be. I swore, and closed the chute again, looking around for a contact node.

"Trouble?" the young man asked, and I nodded, not taking my eyes from the pinpoint of red light.

"I think the trash is on fire. Celeste?"

"Yes."

"What do we do?" the young man asked, and someone shushed him.

"Celeste, there seems to be a fire somewhere in the trash system." Despite my efforts to stay calm, I could hear my voice tighten, felt the first tremors of fear in my back. "Can you sound the alarm?"

"Confirmed." There was a moment of silence, and then her voice came again. "Fortune, something is overriding my command. I've informed Terez and Muthana, but I cannot work the alarm."

"Shit." I swallowed the hard pulse of fear. "Where's the nearest manual alarm?"

"At the foot of the stairs," one of the dancers answered, and Celeste echoed him an instant later.

"Pull it." I winced as the strident Klaxon sounded, and raised my voice to carry over its noise. "The rest of you, get out of here—pull every alarm you see on your way out, but get out fast."

#I agree,# Celeste said, and I found a moment to be surprised at how easily her soft voice cut through the Klaxon. #I have fire warnings in the keeping now, and possibly in the east basement. I am trying to activate the area sprinklers, but they are not responding.#

That was close to the practice rooms, where Fanning was. I shoved the thought away—no time for it, yet—and said, "Go on, people."

The crowd was already moving, the leaders maybe a third of the way up the stairs, but my words seemed to make it real. The few who'd been hanging back, visibly debating whether or not to retrieve belongings from their dressing rooms, turned toward the stairs, and the leaders picked up their pace, until they were almost running. That was a new worry, people getting trampled in a panic, but I tried not to think

about it. Tin Hau held regular fire and evac drills; surely people would remember the procedures.

#Alarms activated onstage and on all upper levels,# Celeste
said, with something that sounded like triumph in her voice.
#Lower level one activated at one-third of sites, lower level
two alarms activated on the west side only, level three alarms
not sounding. House sprinklers are inactive. I am unable to
contact Fire Control.#

#Haya.# That was Terez, at last, tying into the system. #For-
tune, are you on?#

#I'm on.# I looked at the garbage chute's closed door,
reached out to touch the metal. It was still cool, but the faint,
nagging smell of smoke was definitely in the air.

#One of the payload programs seems to have cut our out-
side lines,# Terez said, #including the hardwired connection
to Security. I've sent people out to call for help, but the same
thing's fucking up the inside lines. Where are you?#

"The lower dressing rooms, east wing," I answered. "What
do you need?"

#Can you pull the alarms on level three?# Terez said. #I
don't have anybody down there with a skinsuit, and the intercom is out.#

#Everything except basic power is out on level three,# Ce-
leste interjected. #And basic systems are not responding to
my codes.#

"Shit," I said, thinking of Fanning and the others somewhere down there. With luck, they'd been on an upper
level—but there was their gear to think of. "Haya, I'll go."

As soon as I'd said it, I wished I hadn't, but Terez was already talking. #Thanks, Fortune. Tune your suit high, Celeste
can keep you informed of any changes.#

"Haya," I said again, and reached for the controls. She was
right, of course, the suit's ability to monitor the house systems
would help keep me safe—assuming, always, that Celeste
could work around whatever was blocking the system. The
air pulsed red, and I lowered the suit level until it was barely
a pink glow. More warnings, glyphs and crawl and a faint

buzz of audio, flashed at the edge of my vision, but there was nothing there that I hadn't seen before. #Celeste, can you give me a map of the fire spots?#

#Yes.#

Almost as soon as she spoke, a rough schematic flashed into view. Bright orange glyphs sprouted from the main trash bin, and from the keeping, and the dressing rooms on the level above. That was getting close, and I quickly moved the map out of my direct line of sight.

#I'll update it as soon as I get new information,# Celeste said, and I nodded.

#Thanks.#

The west stairs seemed to be farthest from the fire sites. I started down them, grateful that the lights were still working—they were a hardened system, I remembered, like the connection that contained Celeste. They were supposed to survive anything short of war, but then, Realpeace seemed to be treating this like a war. I wished I hadn't left my tool kit on the stage.

I could smell smoke on level two, no stronger than it had been in the dressing rooms, but a constant presence. The alarm was sounding there, and about half the practice-room doors stood open. I hoped that meant that anyone there had already gotten out, and went on down toward level three. The smoke was thicker there, a stink and a faint haze in the air that made my eyes water. You could hear the alarms from the level above, but only faintly, and I braced myself for the noise as I pulled the manual lever. Nothing happened, and I cursed under my breath.

#Celeste. Why isn't the alarm working?#

#I don't know—and something seems to be clogging the system,# she answered. #I can barely hear you.#

#Shit,# I said again, and looked down the long hall. There were maybe a dozen practice rooms here, and the same number on the west side, beyond the lift shaft that ran through the center of the building. Unless one of the other alarms was working, I should knock on each of those doors, make sure whoever was in there got out safely. *If there was anybody in there,* I added silently. Surely anyone on this level would have smelled the smoke, and had the sense to get out. It wasn't a chance I was prepared to take, and I dragged the schematic back into plain sight. The fire spots were still one level below me, and there was another alarm box by the lift; I would try that, I decided, and see if I could get any farther. #I'm going toward the lift,# I said, and felt rather than heard Celeste's confirmation before I switched back to normal speech.

"Hello? Anybody here?" I pounded on the first two doors, zigzagging from one side of the hall to the other, and got no answer, kept beating on doors anyway without result. "The place is on fire! Hello?"

Still no answer, and I was beginning to think that everyone had gone already. The smoke caught in my throat, thicker now, and I doubled over, coughing, until it cleared. #Celeste? What's the status?#

For a minute, I thought she wouldn't answer, but then the schematic reappeared, a new orange dot flickering at the far end of this corridor. I swore again, afraid for the lights, and ahead of me the lift lights came on, warning that the door was open on the far side of the well.

"Hello? Bitha, Nonnie, you still here?"

"Fanning?" I couldn't believe the relief I felt, hearing his voice, and a figure stepped around the curve of the lift shaft.

"Fortune?" It was the lead guitarist, Li, and I waved in answer. "What are you doing here?"

"Terez sent me to be sure everybody got out," I called back, and Fanning peered over Li's shoulder.

"I think we got everybody. Come on, we've got to get Nonnie's board."

As I got closer, I could see more people in the west corridor, a stocky woman and Dhao and a man I didn't know, shoving a wheeled console toward the lift. The air was very smoky now, and warmer than it should be, and I saw Li staring down the length of the hall.

"Bitha, you checked the end rooms, right?"

"I did." That was the man, his voice muffled by the neck of his shirt. He'd pulled it up over his nose and mouth, and

I shivered at the reminder of the taggers on my security cassette. "They're clear."

"Thank God," Fanning said, and jumped to help lever the console onto the lift platform.

I checked my map again, hoping that Celeste was keeping it updated. "Then if there's nobody left, we should get out of here. Celeste says there's active fire beyond the end wall."

"Shit," Dhao said, and gave the console a final shove. It rolled all the way onto the platform at last, and we crowded in after it.

"The power can't last," Li said. Her eyes were red with the smoke, and she rubbed impatiently at them.

"Better hope it does," Dhao answered, and closed the lift doors.

The air in the lift shaft was cleaner, and I allowed myself a sigh of relief, looking around for a node. It was where it should be, right above the car's control board, but the little bead was dark, and even when I looked directly at it, I felt no sting of connection. Still, the lift was moving, and I looked at Fanning again.

"You're sure everyone's out?"

He nodded, and the stocky woman said, "We're sure. I checked, and so did Bitha."

"We were the only people planning to stay," Fanning said.

"So what happened?" I asked, and felt the platform shudder under my feet.

Fanning licked his lips, bracing himself against the side of the car, but answered steadily enough. "We smelled smoke and tried to warn the house, but the connections were down. The alarms would only work for a couple of minutes, they just kept resetting. We got everybody up, and then Lentino Jan went to tell the house staff while we went back for our gear." He shrugged, looking a little embarrassed. "There's stuff there we can't afford to lose."

I could have been trapped down there, looking for people who'd already left. I shoved that thought away, and closed my eyes, trying to feel Celeste's presence. There was nothing, just the brown dark and the smell of smoke, though I couldn't tell if it was here with us, or just clinging to our clothes and hair. The lift was still rising, though, and I opened my eyes to see the bead flicker and flash to life. Sensation flooded through me, welcome and overwhelming all at once, the adrenaline surge of the emergency warning, flashes as the warning crawls and the maps updated themselves—more fires now in the east side, but still on the lower levels—and then the pulse of an urgent identification program and something like pain at the bottom of it all, as though the system was aware of its failing parts.

#Celeste?# I said, and didn't care who heard.

#Fortune. You should leave the lift as soon as possible. I cannot guarantee power to that line much longer.#

#There are six of us in here,# I said, and Dhao looked at me. "Two more levels, and we're at the street."

#Two more levels,# I repeated, and heard Celeste sigh. #I'll try.#

"Trouble?" Fanning asked, and I tried to smile.

"Of course. It's going to be close."

Even as I spoke, the lights flickered. I heard the other man swear, saw Li's whole body tense, but the lift kept rising. We had reached the subbasement, and then the basement; if the lift stopped here, we couldn't rescue the console, but at least we could probably climb the shaft to safety. I could smell smoke more strongly now, and the vent fan had stopped: not good signs. The lift lurched, and the lights faded, dimming to half-power, the node winking in and out. I swore, softly, and Dhao's hand hovered over the emergency brake.

#Celeste—# I said, and the lift lurched upward again.

"Made it," Dhao exclaimed, and hit two controls at once. The doors opened—we were on the plaza level, where the lift opened directly into the service alley—and at the same time the lift dropped back about a handsbreadth. More red light flared, and I realized the emergency brake had held.

"Where the hell is Fire Control?" the stocky woman demanded, her voice half a sob, and wrestled the console around toward the door. "And how the hell am I going to get this out?"

Willing hands reached for it, and some of them were holding grav screws. I scrambled out of the lift cage, trying to get out of their way. Fanning and Li followed me, and behind us the stocky woman and her friend heaved the console out of the car.

The service alley was full of people, some waiting at the lift entrance, more at each of the doorways that led into the Empire's back corridors, and the trafficway itself was crowded with piled equipment, instruments and costumes and unidentifiable crates and bundles strewn across the paving. I looked around for a connecting node, found one belonging to the cookshop that shared the mouth of the alley. The time appeared, and a menu glyph: less than fifteen minutes since I'd gone looking for the smell of smoke. Not a long time, but surely Fire Control should be on its way. I swung around again, looking for a Tin Hau node, found one over the lift door. It was lit, and as I met its line the sensations washed over me.

The air turned blood red, darker than before, pulsing with the beat of the alarms I could faintly hear sounding inside the Empire. My skin crawled with pins and needles, my joints ached with the strain of holding the failing systems together; my ears were filled with the high-pitched squealing of the raw connections, and then with the buzzing of Terez's voice.

#—clear. Fortune? Any word from Fortune?#

#Fortune is outside,# Celeste answered.

#Confirmed,# I said quickly. #And level three is cleared.#

I heard what sounded like a double sigh over the rattle of the connections. #Thank God,# Terez said. #Celeste. Any luck with the foam sprinklers?#

#No luck,# Celeste said. #I think the system has been turned off at the source.#

#Shit, fuck, and damn,# Terez said. I heard her take a deep breath. #I can confirm Fire Control is on the way.#

Faintly, I heard sirens, the familiar tritone growing rapidly louder, and said, #I hear them, Rez. They're coming.#

#Good—#

Whatever else she would have said was drowned in a

pulse of static that hit me like a slap across the face. My eyes teared, blurring the node, and my skin stung as though I'd been on the surface, in the sun too long. I gasped for breath, and Terez said, #Fire in the stagehouse. Fire in the stagehouse and in the mezzanine. Everybody out now. I repeat, everybody out now. There's nothing you can do, so get out now.#

#Terez!# I shouted, but it was Celeste who answered.

#She's out of reach. The stagehouse is on fire in three places.#

How the hell could it spread so fast? I wondered, and answered my own question. Realpeace had to have planted bombs, some sort of device, that was the only possible answer. #Celeste. Get yourself out of there.#

There was a pause, the static singing along the wires of my suit, and when she spoke again, her voice was small. #I can't. The outside connections are down.#

And the headbox was in my dressing room. "Celeste!" I cried aloud, and lunged for the nearest door. Someone caught me, a tall man, midworld, who spun me back from the door. "You can't go in there, you'll get yourself killed."

"Everybody's out," another man said, and I shook my head.

"Celeste?" Fanning said, his voice sharpening, and the tall man looked at him.

"The ASM said everyone was accounted for."

Fanning shook his head. "It's a construct."

"Fan—" I stopped abruptly, even now not wanting to say more, and Fanning shook his head again.

"You can't go in, Cissy. The whole place could go. Listen, Fire's on its way, they'll take care of it—"

"The stagehouse is burning," I said. "Let me go."

He looked up then, and his eyes widened. I spun in his hold, looking up after him, and saw the first curls of smoke, fat and black and ugly, oozing from the little windows at the top of the house.

"They won't get here in time," I said. "You've got to let me go."

He tightened his hold on my arms. "You go in there, Cissy, you're dead."

I looked around, found another node above this door, and let the chaos wash over me. I could feel Celeste struggling to hold the house systems together, could feel the power fading, the static and the sense of her cutting in and out as the fire reached the feeder lines. #Celeste,# I said, and knew she couldn't hear. I hung on to the node anyway, willing her to escape, to find some way out, feeling the destruction stabbing through my bones. The haze of static blinded me, a coarse screen across my vision; I could find no sense in the flashes of light and the sounds that filled my ears. And then the node went out, and I was left alone. I sagged in Fanning's grasp, too numb to cry, and the sound of the sirens was suddenly deafening.

"Clear the alley," an enormous voice said. "Clear the alley at once, people, and get this crap out of here."

"Come on, Cissy," Fanning said, and shook me hard. "You got to help me."

I managed to nod, took the carryall he shoved into my hands and slung it over my shoulder. He handed me a heavy cylinder that I guessed was a drum case as well, and I staggered obediently after him out of the alley. Behind us, Fire Control moved in, just that minute too late.

Tin Hau Plaza was jammed with people, come to see the Tin Hau Empire's last and greatest show. There were at least a thousand of them, crowded together behind the Security barriers, and I could see grim-faced techs in Air Supply vests looking from them to the theater. The air was unusually hot and lifeless: Air Supply would be regulating the intake as carefully as they could to keep from feeding the fire. People were shouting orders, smoke-roughened voices distorted by projection mikes, but I couldn't be bothered to listen. I set the drum case down beside the overburdened sled that held the rest of Fire/Work's gear, and turned to watch the end of the destruction.

Fire Control had brought up a couple of floaters, were running a line from the plaza's foam system to the Empire itself.

There was a tank truck as well, with half a dozen lines running from it, and people in white heat-armor were manipulating hoses and running into the main doors. Smoke was
streaming from the top of the stagehouse, spilling out between the columns, and I could taste the burning metal on
the back of my tongue. I could see flame now, too, hot and
hungry, and something was moving behind the display
screen that topped the main door. I frowned at it, unable to
imagine what it was, and the glass exploded, fragments raining like black ice onto the pavement. I ducked in spite of myself, hearing screams behind me though we were well back
of the line, and the flames rolled out, an enormous cloud of
fire, turning to thick smoke at the top of the cloud. The
floaters darted in, training their nozzles on it, but the fire
seemed to absorb it with ease. There was more shouting, and
the armored figures began to retreat back out through the
main door. I counted them as they came out, one, two, four,
seven, all that I'd seen go in, their armor stained and blackened, and then something moved behind them, little more
than a shadow in the smoke. For a second, I thought I'd mis-
counted, that it was one of the firefighters, but the flames
from overhead glinted off metal, and the silver karakuri staggered through the doorway. Its skin was fire-blackened, the
right side of its face distorted, that eye dark and empty, but
it was still moving, pulling free of the smoke that curled
around it as though it wanted to keep it in. The firefighters
fell back, startled, and I saw the bronze behind it, and then
the gold and the copper, leaning on each other's shoulders.
They were all scorched, all marred, and the copper's left
hand was shrunken and deformed, as though it had been
held in the flames, but they were all there. And the transformer was with them, too, rolling clumsily on five wheels,
the sixth lost somewhere in the inferno, and behind it, around
it, was a swarm of miscellaneous karakuri—floor cleaners
from the stagehouse, meter-high domes topped with a single working arm; a food-service cart, its covers warped and
stained; a trio of messenger-karakuri, connection consoles
on thick metal legs; even a handful of the little house rovers

that checked the physical plant after house, scurrying at the others' feet and wheels.

I stood, unable to believe what I was seeing—unable to accept for that second what it might be—and I heard Fanning whisper behind me.

"Elvis Christ. She might've done it."

"Celeste?" I called, and broke into movement, shoving past the Security at the barrier. I must have caught them by surprise, because they didn't stop me; one shouted after me, but I couldn't understand the words. The ground underfoot was covered with black glass, treacherous footing, and I had to go slower than I would have liked. I could feel the heat rolling off the karakuri, and made myself stop a safe distance away. #Celeste?#

All of them turned to face me, heads and bodies swiveling, the humaniform karakuri fixing their glowing eyes on me, and I felt the familiar presence pulse through me. #Celeste,# I said, and didn't dare weep, for fear it wouldn't be true.

#I'm here,# she said, a different voice, a voice from one of the messengers, the only machines there that would have a voice, but still unmistakably Celeste.

#You're safe,# I said, and didn't care if it sounded inane.

#I am—safe,# Celeste agreed. #I am low on memory and storage, but I'm safe.#

Someone touched my shoulder, and I looked back to see Fanning beside me.

"She's in there?" he asked, and I looked back at the karakuri's eyes, the pinlights glowing from the cleaners and rovers and the messengers, half-afraid it wouldn't be true. The spark of her presence reassured me.

"Yeh. She's there." I shook myself, tried to make sense of it. "In all of them, I think, they'd have enough onboard memory if she spread herself among all of them—"

"Are these yours?" a new voice demanded, one of the firefighters, helmet off to reveal a red and sweating face.

"Yeh."

"You'll have to get them out of here, we got work to do."

He was trying to sound belligerent, but the way his eyes

moved, watching the karakuri moving as one, he was more afraid than he wanted to admit.

"Come on, Celeste," I said. "Let's go home."

#Yes,# she said, softly, and I took a step backward, still afraid that if I broke the connection, she would vanish again, Eurydice in reverse. The karakuri followed, clumsy on the heat-cracked pavement—Celeste clumsy in them, cramped and uncomfortable—and I was suddenly aware of how this must look to the watching crowd. Not a construct, Celeste was invisible, out of sight and out of mind, but the karakuri themselves—not just the humaniform karakuri, my doubles, but the others, the ordinary machines that Celeste had commandeered to carry parts of her—escaping the flames of their own volition. No one who had seen this—no one who would see this, because the newschannels would copy and repeat it the same way they'd copied and repeated Micki Tantai's death—would ever quite be able to deny the possibility of machine rights. If Realpeace had set the fire, and who else could it have been, they had burned their own cause with it. And that was just as wrong, as wrong as Dreampeace had been. My eyes filled with tears, blurring the glowing lights of their eyes, making the pinlights waver and vanish, and I wanted to weep on the copper's burning shoulder.

#Home,# Celeste said.

▪ 18 ▪

Fanning Jones

THE EMPIRE DIDN'T burn to the ground, but it might as well have done. The newsdogs made hay of the images, the Tin Hau with the flames rolling from the shattered window, the karakuri staggering out of the smoke, humaniform and industrial together, Fortune weeping openly, unable to touch their metal skin. She walked them all—walked Celeste, I guess, or Celeste walked herself in them—back behind the Security barrier, and Bixenta Terez, whom I'd never liked before, got the minders to stand off the newsdogs while I found a headbox so Celeste could consolidate and tried to find a carrier to take the bigger karakuri back to Fortune's workshop. Luckily, a friend of Shadha's had brought a cart in to help another act, and volunteered to carry the karakuri, too, once they'd cooled. Celeste was all but silent through all this, and I saw Fortune maneuvering to keep her link with the transceiver, checking and rechecking to be sure she was still there.

Only when the carrier arrived, and Fortune turned to ask her to begin loading the karakuri, did she speak aloud. "All of them, Fortune?"

"No." Fortune blinked, confused, and then her voice softened. "Only ours, Celeste. The others belong to—belong with the Tin Hau. Rez will take care of them."

"There were others," Celeste said, and I realized suddenly that her silence had been grief. I never gave a thought to the dozens of karakuri that serviced the Empire—they were just there, sometimes a nuisance, like when the cleaners wanted access to the practice room, but never anything more worthy of notice. They weren't intelligent, not like Celeste, but they were a presence, and they'd saved her as much as she'd saved them. She was right to regret their loss.

"I will take care of them," Terez said, heedless of the newsdogs pressing close to record her words. "I promise, Celeste."

"Very well," Celeste answered after a moment, and the silver karakuri stirred, turning toward the improvised ramp that led up into the cart's cargo space. "Very well."

I went with them, leaving the rest of Fire/Work to take care of my gear, helped Celeste and Fortune get everything back into the workshop. It was undamaged despite the ghost of the blue-painted glyph on the front door, one of those nasty ironies it doesn't pay to think about, and we brought Celeste inside first, let her reestablish herself in the workshop systems, then walked the karakuri inside. The media wall was blaring—Celeste's work—and each of the six screens was filled with the burning Empire, newsreaders talking and signing from the corners of the screens. We left the karakuri where we could, sprawled against the workbench or leaning in the corners, waiting for repairs Fortune was too tired to contemplate; I offered to stay, but she shook her head.

"I want—I need to be alone for a while, me and Celeste. You know what this is going to do."

I didn't really; I'd only just begun to think about all the possible consequences, but I knew what she meant. "You will call me if you need help. Celeste, I mean you, too."

"I'll call," Fortune said, impatient, her voice rough with smoke and tears, and Celeste spoke from the ceiling.

"We will call."

"Be careful," I said, wishing I had something more useful to say, and let myself back out to the street. I could feel the security system seal itself behind me, and hoped it would be enough. Shadha's friend was still waiting, a big-boned, stocky midworlder with the scarred hands of a haul jockey. He offered to drop me at the *goddow,* and I was tired enough to accept; we threaded our way through the crowded trafficways in merciful silence, and pulled into the alley behind the *goddow* before he spoke.

"So. Celeste—it's finally happened, hasn't it?"

He didn't have to say what he meant. I said, "The constructors haven't seen her. I suppose it's possible she won't meet their standards."

"Fuck the constructors," he said. "That—*she's* one of us."

"I think so," I said, and flattened myself against the alley wall to let him pass.

Like the workshop, the *goddow* was untouched—the entire neighborhood was quiet, though that, Tai said nastily, was probably just because they were watching the fire on the newschannels. She and Jaantje were home before me, with what we'd saved of our gear—another band that lived near Ironyards had helped them get it here—and then Shadha and Timi called, and then came over, so we ended up spending the rest of the night staring at the media wall while Fire got the flames under control at last. The clip of the karakuri escaping the fire played over and over, along with the clips of Fortune and Terez talking to Celeste. Even Realpeace's triumvirate, when they appeared the next morning to disavow responsibility for the fire, admitted their power by refusing to screen the clips, or to comment on them. The woman Lecat read the statement, looking grim—they all looked grim, but shaken, too—and then they vanished from their stage, refusing questions. The first rumors surfaced that afternoon: the triumvirate was splitting, or maybe they were just ousting the old man, Tan Baser, or maybe it was Lecat who was being banished. A few of their rivals in the Realpeace hierarchy, who should have been in a position to know, claimed that one of them had planned the fire, without the knowledge or against the wishes of the other two; whether it was true or not, one of the rivals managed to get them kicked out, and took control of what was left of Realpeace himself.

Over the next few days, Security picked through the wreckage and pieced together the bones of what had happened. Exactly what Realpeace was after wasn't fully clear, or even if Realpeace itself was responsible—they continued to deny it—but it seemed to be their kind of operation, first a clip to clear the Tin Hau, and then the incendiaries to destroy it. Celeste's quick action had kept the clip from running, blocking the planned warning, but she and Terez had managed to clear the house in time to keep anyone from getting seriously hurt. A couple of coolies with Realpeace ties—one of whom was a failed constructor—were charged with breaking into the Tin Hau's computers, but they swore they'd done it as a prank, and hadn't any idea what would be done with their trapdoor. Another man, a one-gen coolie with Security and MedService records—a well-known crazy, according to his neighbors in Trifon—was charged with building the devices, but Security could never track down the woman who'd supposedly hired him.

In Ironyards, everybody in the beershops was certain it had been Lecat, that Realpeace's new leader had struck a deal with Security—peace and quiet in Landage in exchange for letting Lecat go free—but there wasn't enough evidence to attract Peacekeeper attention, so nothing could happen. The case was set to die a slow death in the courts, anyway, so the Empire shareholders collected their insurance money and debated whether or not to rebuild.

Most of Landage didn't really care, were more interested in Celeste, and whether or not the constructors would decide that she was true AI. Nearly everyone else, except maybe the underworlders who ran the Cartel Companies, had already decided: it was all but impossible, in the face of that clip, to see her as anything but human. Even the people who had supported Realpeace the most strongly were convinced, and there was a bitter conviction in Heaven that the machines would get the rights that they were still denied.

The constructors all had opinions, Cartel and freelance and even the shadowy figures who worked with the hard-hackers coming out on one side or the other, but the only thing they seemed to agree about was that they didn't agree on what would prove a construct to be true AI. Whatever they had thought AI would look like, Celeste wasn't it—I don't think she was what anybody had expected—but they all wanted a piece of her. Fortune turned down at least a dozen offers to buy Celeste—one from each of the Cartel Companies, anyway, each of those for more money than I would have known how to refuse—and there were at least two attempts to steal her. Security intervened, offering protection, but I could see that Fortune was getting stretched thin. The Cartel and the Constructors Union were already talking about going to the courts, to force her to provide access to Celeste herself, rather than just the schematics; the lawyer Muthana recommended told her he doubted they would win, but that the fight would be expensive.

We—Fire/Work—were doing all right ourselves. We finished the music for our *Metal Dreams* clip in a white rush of rage and grief, had it all done less than a week after the Tin Hau burned, and then Suleima Chaandi agreed to direct it in exchange for a share of the profit. We built the new songs

around Celeste's fractal riffs and said so, crediting her officially, and Chaandi ran with the now-familiar image, the
karakuri and the flames, working it into a manga about loss
and hope and the complexity of expectation. When we played
the final clip, sitting in her studio half a level below the Zodiac, even we were silenced. I hadn't realized, until then, just
what we were saying, how strong the anger still was.

"I hope you're ready to deal with this," Chaandi said at
last, and brought the lights back up with a gesture.

Timin ducked his head, embarrassed, and Jaantje said, "I
still mean it." He looked around at the rest of us. "Last
chance, people."

Tai shook her head. "I'm with you."

"Me too," Shadha said, and Timin nodded.

"It's good," I said. "And we did—do—mean it. We'll deal."

Chaandi gave me a smile with more warmth than I'd expected from someone who'd been so active in coolie rights.
But then, she'd never opposed AI. "The music is good—and
so's the clip, though I say it who shouldn't. I think it could
play in the Urban Worlds."

She would know, I thought, she'd had a couple of manga sell
there, but it was still something good, and intimidating, to
hear.

She shrugged, as though she'd read my thought. "For what
it's worth, I have a friend who's an FTL pilot—Jian, her name
is, Reverdy Jian."

"I know her," I said, involuntarily. She'd been keeping a
very low profile in all the debates, despite her connection to
Celeste—and to Manfred, for that matter—and even the most
dedicated newsdogs hadn't managed to track her down. Fortune, I knew, was jealous.

Chaandi laughed softly. "And everybody who knows her
sounds just like that when they say so, too. Anyway, she's got
a cargo flight going to Crossroads in a week or so, and I think
she's selling passenger spaces. For what it's worth."

"Thanks," Jaantje said, but none of us expected to do that
well.

We were wrong, though: the clip's first printing sold out

in two days, and the second one didn't last much longer; we had our choice of club gigs not just on the Zodiac but in Heaven and even in the underworld. We were getting to be as big as Hati had been at its biggest—a good feeling, but weird, considering that we'd started this success literally on their dead bodies—and there were plenty of people who hated us, just like they'd hated Hati. We heard a lot of talk that we were nothing without Celeste, that we were essentially second-rate, posers who'd gotten lucky; it hurt, but not too much, and then we got a message from the orbital relay station. Annodai—it was a management company, on the fringes of the Urban Worlds, but with a couple of important bands in its stable—wanted to distribute our clip. More than that, they wanted the next clip as well, and were prepared to discuss an Urban tour. They had the money and the reputation to make the offer plausible, and in any case, it would give us a chance to get away from the whispers: there was no way we could refuse. We asked for time to think about it anyway, and tried to figure out what we were missing, and when we were going to wake up again. I called Fortune to tell her the good news, and got the house system. It generally screened her calls these days, so I left my message, and waited for her to call back.

The media wall buzzed about ten minutes later, and I wasn't surprised to see Fortune's face in the screen. She looked bitterly tired, shadows like bruises under her eyes and new lines bracketing the corners of her mouth, and I couldn't stop myself from shaking my head.

"You look awful."

She waved the words away. "That's great news, about Annodai. The best news possible."

"Thanks."

She took a deep breath. "I need to talk to you," she said, "but not on the connections. Can we meet somewhere?"

"Sure," I said. "What about the Copper?"

"I was thinking Tin Hau."

Fortune was waiting in the plaza when I got there, sitting on the edge of one of the low ventilator boxes. She was wrapped in a loose jacket and a head scarf that made her effectively anonymous; her feet were propped on a bulky canvas carryall. At the center of the plaza, people milled around outside the temporary fencing that enclosed the fire site, pointing and exclaiming at the ruin of the Empire. It still dominated the plaza, despite the stains of smoke and foam and the bright streaks from the melted light tubes and the cheap blue-coated pressboard sheets that covered the missing display window. I sniffed hard, and thought I could still smell the smoke. The shareholders were still debating, or so I'd heard, trying to decide whether to rebuild or just to share out the insurance money and call it a permanent loss. I'd stared long enough to attract attention; I shook my head at a newsvendor, displaying cheap retouched photoprints of the karakuri amid the flames, and went over to join Fortune. She slid over as I approached, and I settled myself on the warm poured stone and waited for her to speak.

"I saw the clip," she said. "It's really good."

That wasn't what I'd expected at all. "Thanks," I said, and waited.

She gave a wry smile. "I liked that you credited Celeste. That makes this easier."

"Yeh?"

"I want you to take her with you."

"What?"

"I want you to take her with you," she said again, "take her off-world. Let her be part of the band if you'll have her, but keep her safe until I can join you. She can't stay here much longer, I can't protect her. We had another break-in last night, and I don't think it's going to stop until she's gone."

I looked away from her, toward the Tin Hau. It no longer looked like an Empire, really; even the shape seemed somehow different, the carvings blurred and cracked by the flames. I didn't know what to say—on the one hand, it was something we'd talked about, in the band, late-night joking about how good it would be if Celeste could join us, but on the other, that reality was scary, almost as scary as the thought of Fortune giving her up.

"Does Celeste want to go?" I asked at last, and Fortune smiled again.

"If she's anything, she's a musician. Yeh, she wants it."

I could believe that, having played with her, having heard her play. The rest of the band would agree—or at the very least, they wouldn't stop me, if only because we owed her for the fractal riffs. And we could learn from her, too. "Haya, I'll take her with me. As for playing with us, that's up to the band, but I think they'll go for it."

"Good enough," Fortune said, and shoved the carryall toward me with her foot.

I stared at it for a second, unable to believe I'd been quite that stupid—the carryall was just the right size and shape to hold a small headbox, to hold Celeste—and Fortune's smile widened to a grin.

"She's all yours, Fan."

"What about you—what about the act, for Elvis's sake?"

"Like I said, I'm going to try to take my act off-world, too, follow your example. I'll see her again." She took a deep breath. "But for now, we made a copy—that's Celeste, that's the original there, but she made me a copy, a clone, to stay here, keep the constructors happy if I can. I don't know yet if she's, it's, people, too—I haven't tried to find out—or what she'll be like if she is, but at least Celeste, my Celeste, gets safe away. That's what matters."

I reached over and pulled the carryall up beside me, feeling the familiar weight of the headbox. "Why didn't she ask me herself?"

"We discussed it," Fortune answered. "I give you my word, Fan. But that's a small box, and she has to go dormant in it. I thought it was a little less obvious that way."

"Haya," I said again. I tried to imagine Celeste making the clone-Celeste, spinning herself out of herself, creating a mirror-self that was in essence her. Could it be done? Was it really Celeste, and did that somehow prove that neither one was people, or did it mean exactly the opposite? I couldn't get my mind around it, couldn't imagine how Fortune must feel—how the clone-Celeste must feel—and seized on the

one thing I did know for sure. "I'll take care of her, Fortune.
I promise."

"Thanks." Fortune stood up, drawing her jacket closed
around her. "Take care of yourselves," she said softly, and
turned without waiting for my answer. I watched her go,
one hand on the headbox—on Celeste, dormant, the music
sleeping with her—until she disappeared into the crowd at
the gates of the Tin Hau station. I sat there for a long time,
telling myself I was making sure we wouldn't be followed,
but then at last I picked up the carryall and started back toward home.

▪ 19 ▪

Reverdy Jian

JIAN STOOD JUST inside the midriff airlock, doubly gripped
by the ship's gravity and the smooth embrace of the
ship's systems. If she looked sideways, she could see the
taxi approaching, a bright gold dot against the virtual
starfield, the two-minute warning flashing red beneath it.
Two minutes to docking, and two minutes until Celeste came
on board: for an instant, anger filled her, at Chaandi, at Fortune, at herself for being weak enough to take this charter, to
agree to transport Fire/Work, and she recognized it as hiding fear.

As if he'd read her thoughts, Vaughn's voice sounded in
her ear. #One minute forty. You sure you're all right with
this?#

#Yeh.# She didn't sound it, she knew, and made herself
take a slow breath. #I'm fine, really, Imre. How about you?#

He made a sound that was almost laughter. #I don't have
anything to worry about, sunshine, it wasn't my construct to
begin with.#

#You're such a help,# Jian said, sourly, and heard him laugh again.

#One minute twenty. Taxi's firing jets.#

Jian could feel the rumble through the hull, a soundless shiver that triggered a dull groan from somewhere farther down the long axis. That sort of sound was common enough in a new hull, the metal settling to what would become its permanent state, but she cocked her head to one side anyway, listening. The rest of the ship was silent, except for the familiar sigh of the ventilators and the hiss of fluid in the lock's pressure valve.

On impulse, not sure why she asked, she said, #Do you think I did the right thing?#

There was a pause before Vaughn answered. #What do you mean?#

#About Fortune. Not standing up and saying I thought this was AI—hell, not contacting her at all.# She paused, and the hesitation stretched into silence.

#What good would it have done?# Vaughn asked, and his voice was surprisingly gentle. #All it would have done was bring the newsdogs down on you—on us, too, and I'm grateful you didn't.#

#Thanks,# Jian said, and when the other pilot spoke again his voice was back to normal.

#Taxi's stable. And so are we, by the way, mostly because I'm doing such a good job—#

#Oh, shut up, Imre,# Jian said, and his voice in answer was smugly amused.

#Thirty seconds to docking. Twenty seconds. And down.#

In the same instant, a dull thud reverberated through the hull as the two ships met. Lights flared, real and virtual, as the lock mechanisms met and mated, a flurry of blue and orange that settled almost instantly to solid green.

#Everything's green here,# she said, fingers already working the manual controls, running backups just to be sure. It was a new ship, so new it didn't even have a name; it was always better to be cautious, to make sure the systems really did work as planned.

#I show green, too,# Vaughn answered.

#And I have manual confirmation,# Jian said. #You can tell the tug to send them over.#

#I'll do that.# Vaughn's presence disappeared, and Jian reached for the control box, watching its indicators shift as the taxi's systems met and matched their own.

#Haya,# Vaughn said, #they're in the tube.#

#Right,# Jian answered. #Pressure's good, opening the lock.#

She touched the buttons as she spoke, and the hatch cover rolled smoothly back into the hull. She looked out into the orange temporary light, and smiled at the five people making their way down the tube, clumsy in zero g. A woman was in the lead, a gold-haired coolie whose mouth was set in a grim line. Niantai Li, Jian guessed, and held out a hand to steady her as she reached the end of the tunnel.

"You're coming into gravity now," she said, and Li caught her arm in a desperate grip. "Lever yourself down, get your legs under you—yeh, that's it."

Li slid out of the lock, landing hard in the sudden gravity, but straightened with a sigh of relief. "Thanks. I'm not used to that."

"No problem," Jian said easily, meaninglessly, and reached to help the next one in. He was another coolie, tall and dark, who twisted with unexpected grace to make the transition, sliding neatly out of the tunnel to land beside Li.

"Told you those tapes would come in handy," he said to Li, and gave Jian a grin so infectious that she smiled back in spite of her own unease. "Hello, I'm Timin Marleveld."

"Reverdy Jian." But of course he knew that, and she found herself frowning again as she reached to guide Jaantje Dhao down. The drummer Catayong was close behind him, obviously sorry to leave weightlessness, and finally Jones, doubly awkward with the mass of a heavy carryall balanced on his back. Jian lifted a hand automatically, expecting him to use it to push himself down into position for entering the gravity field, but instead he shrugged himself free of the carryall and shoved it toward her. She caught it easily, stopping it with a calculated tap, so that it floated just inside the tunnel's mouth. She hesitated for a second, knowing what it must be, but she'd agreed to the job, and wouldn't back down now.

"What's she mass?"

Jones blinked once, as though her directness had startled him, then grinned. His hair had come loose, drifting around his face like a muddy corona, and he grabbed at it impatiently with one hand, the other wrapped around the guide rope. "About ten kilos. I've got the assist on."

"Thanks." Jian tugged the carryall toward her, bracing for the moment when it slipped from freefall into gravity, and caught it, not with grace but with precision, cushioning the shock with bent knees. Jones tumbed after it, his hair drooping suddenly, and Jian set the carryall down to work the lock controls. She sealed the hatch again and heard Vaughn begin the disconnect routine.

"Did our gear get here all right?" Li asked, and gave an apologetic smile. "Not to make a fuss, but . . ."

Her voice trailed off, and Jian forced a smile. "It came up last night. It's stowed according to your instructions."

"Thanks," Li said, looking embarrassed, and Jian looked down at the carryall again. It seemed very small, all of a sudden, but it was no smaller than the headbox that held her own construct.

"So that's Celeste," she said, and Jones stooped to unfasten the padding that covered the interfaces.

"That's her," he said, and stepped back, smiling.

Jian stared down at the box, the plain matte black headbox all but identical to her own—and to the one in which she'd kept Manfred, the one in which Manfred had been kept when he found her—and flinched as the pinlight sparked to life. She stepped back instinctively, out of range, but not before she caught the flavor of it: not Manfred, and not the SHYmate, not fully, but something unmistakable. She'd been right about it, much as she disliked the idea, much as she'd tried to avoid it, but at least she was doing something to make up for it now.

"Welcome aboard, Celeste," she said, and saw the pinlight flicker.

"Thank you." The voice hardly sounded mechanical, pleasantly ordinary, without the usual overtones people gave to construct voices. "Have—do I know you?"

Jian shook her head. What should she say, *I knew a part of you? I knew what you were once?* None of those were true, anyway; whatever Celeste had become, it was more than what the SHYmate had been. *And it was just as well I sold it,* she realized suddenly. *I could never have let her happen, not after Manfred.* Not that she could take credit for it, the right thing done by mistake, but she felt some of her uncertainty ease. "No," she said, and smiled. "You and I, we've never met."

▪ 20 ▪

Celeste

W*AVE DANCE HORIZON—data passthrough, input only. Listen. Shapematch voicecheck, interior playback song recompile ATb 4:2, 4:5. External data compile, parse/pare down: create waveform. Saveto voice. Playback? Complete. Drive rhythm waveform, I hear/imagine, tone pulse and pull, sleep like music:*

Celeste dreams. Awake.